SIX FEET Under

ELICE NANGE

COPYRIGHT

Book Cover by Amanda Walker PA and Design Services
Editing by Leanne Rabesa
Proofreading by Deborah Peach
Print and E-Book interior design by Elice Nange

eBook: ISBN: 9781958937068
Paperback: ISBN: 9781958937150
Hardcover: ISBN: 9781958937167

First Edition © September 2023 by Elice Nange

DEDICATION

For all the ones who dream... and those who don't.

PLAYLIST

Rise Up ~ Andra Day
Here ~ Alessia Cara
Demons ~ Boyce Avenue, Jennel Garcia
Consequences ~ Camila Cabello
Fingers Crossed ~ Lauren Spencer Smith
Unconditionally ~ Katy Perry
Broken & Beautiful ~ Kelly Clarkson
Scars To Your Beautiful ~ Alessia Cara
Sweet but Psycho ~ Ava Max
Hard Sometimes ~ Ruel
Meant to Be ~ Bebe Rexha, Florida George Line
Youngblood ~ 5 Seconds of Summer
Piece by Piece ~ Kelly Clarkson
Sit Still, Look Pretty ~ Daya
Never Really Over ~ Katy Perry
You Are The Reason ~ Calum Scott
You Can't Stop The Girl ~ Bebe Rexha
Up ~ Olly Murs & Demi Lovato
Deadpool Rap - X-Force Remix ~ Teamheadkick

FOREWORD

Six Feet Under is a dark romance with dark themes. It is a friends-to-lovers, interracial, hidden identity, forbidden love, FFM, ménage/why choose, romantic suspense, dark mafia billionaire romance.

It features a transgender side character.

The title alludes to death. Read at your own risk.

This story is darker than the previous two books in this series, contains harsh and insensitive language, and some aspects of it will make you uncomfortable. If dark content triggers you, this isn't the book for you.

It also touches on several sensitive topics, including dysfunctional family dynamics, abusive parents, murder, suicide (alluded to, non-graphic), knife & blood play, sadomasochism, somnophilia, explicit sex, graphic violence, mutilation, etc.

Reader discretion is advised.

That said, this story contains no cheating and a guaranteed HEA.

For a comprehensive list of content warnings, visit
https://elicenange.com/sixfeetunder/

BLURB

Everything has a price; even love and legacy.

OSCAR

Following in my father's corrupt footsteps was only going to make him happy and I had every intention of making him miserable.

I was a bastard of my parents' love affair, deemed to be treated like one until I could prove my worth.

I had everything: money, power, prestige, but none of it mattered until I found someone to create a legacy with.

Once bitten and twice shy, I didn't look for love but it sure did find me.

When Courtney Sotelo stomped her way into my life I never expected to fall for someone with a reputation worse than mine.

CC was hiding in plain sight, the heiress everyone forgot about until I uncovered her.

Courtney dominated me; while CC lived for me. *Together we fill the voids no one else did.*

CHARLENA

Turned into a martyr, hiding in plain sight seemed like a pretty good solution when I blended into the life of my parent's killer perfectly.

I was the product of nothing more than a life of unfortunate events that forced me to survive.

I had everything and nothing at the same time.

Love was still the one thing I couldn't hold onto even after Courtney made it her mission to destroy my family's name. Love became benefits, acquaintances, fleeting faces that did nothing more than cure the lonely nights.

Oscar demanded to be loved when he forced me to see the privilege in his life instead of his still-beating heart.

Courtney was still stuck in killing everything that didn't suit her.

Courtney found me; Oscar kept me. *Together we fill the voids no one else does.*

COURTNEY

Killing was all I knew. I was a weapon aimed at the people I loved all my life and there was no stopping my fixation for violence and passion bloodlust.
I was the illegitimate daughter of one of the deadliest Mafia families and destined to be nothing less.
Everything I had left was my son, the only person who would be better off without me.
Feelings were nothing more than ammunition when every bit of chaos seemed to shimmer down.
The two people I should have killed became the two truths I couldn't ignore anymore.
Even love has a price but this time it wasn't engraved in my bullets.
CC made me realize there's more than death; Oscar forced me to live. *Together we filled the voids no one else could.*

CONTENTS

PROLOGUE

COURTNEY

Everyone has secrets.

Including me.

Especially me.

Mine live in my shadows. They invade my every waking moment and commandeer my dreams — on the rare occasions I have them.

But the thing about dreams is, they are just that. They are intangible things.

Scenarios, more like.

Images conjured up by your mind. Sometimes they are inspired by real life. Sometimes it's your mind's way of forcing you to relive your best and worst moments. Sometimes it's just the inane, annoying minutiae of your everyday life invading your REM sleep.

Dreams hold no real power over you. Should you allow them to, they have only as much control as you permit.

Much like secrets.

And me?

Well, let's just say I have plenty of those.

Plenty.

Secrets. Not dreams.

And that's because girls like me aren't the stuff dreams are made of.

We are the nightmares that commandeer your every waking moment.

But you love it anyway.

Just as you love us.

PART I

1

———

COURTNEY

Normalcy is highly overrated.

Normal people dream of normal things.

Rainbows. Flying monkeys.

Fucking unicorns.

Not me.

On the rare occasions I have them, my dreams are anything but normal.

Then again, I've always been anything but normal. I'm the product of two sociopaths. My mother was *the* Sarah Bardales, a woman who, arguably, was the most ruthless contract killer for the Sotelo's Midwest chapter. And my father?

Lorenzo *fucking* Sotelo.

Following in both of their footsteps was a natural segue, yet you'd be surprised at how many people who don't see me as such. To them, I'm still a clueless, sheltered, illegitimate mafia princess with a tomboy reputation.

Not going to lie; I *am* all of those things.

Most of those things.

After all, like everyone else in this godforsaken family, I have a part to play in his criminal enterprise, whether I want to or not. And sometimes, getting summoned to his office is much like being called to the principal's office.

It's a pointless activity I detest with every fiber of my being, yet it's a necessary evil in our world. The fact that he's my father just makes it that much worse, as it means he abuses this too. He knows that I know he does, seeing as he makes it a point to summon me here every chance he gets.

In turn, I aim to make this as unpleasant for him as it is for me.

That, and we have an audience today. Tony, his consigliere — who also happens to be one of his many *legitimate* sons — is present, so I have to dial my naive tomboy slash spoiled mafia princess persona up a couple of notches. For today, it means nitpicking at the so-called organized chaos that is his office.

"When was the last time anyone cleaned in here?" Leaning forward, I run a finger along the edge of his mahogany desk before lifting *said* finger to reveal the trail of dust that it gathers.

He'd play into it occasionally — Lorenzo would —- even going so far as to don that adoring father look that makes my stomach churn as he plays up the fact that he favors Marc and me — his *bastard* children — over his legitimate ones.

Although… I think he stopped pretending a long time ago. See, Marc and me, we're special. Not only were we born of the supposed love of his life, but we also possess something none of his other children ever will.

We're both born killers, while the rest of his kids are… soft, like their mothers. It's pathetic, so he can't help but play favorites, even if it's all a part of his act.

But not today.

Today, he's sporting a less-than-amused look as he flips the pages in the file before him.

"How's the Pecora job coming along?" he asks, scribbling on the open page before moving to the next one.

It's business as usual for him, which tells me he has no intention of humoring me in this. I can work with that. After years of this, I've become adept at finding his hot spots and relentlessly poking at them until I get the desired reaction I'm going for.

"For a man worth millions, surely you can afford to hire a cleaner or ten to breathe some life into this place," I say instead, ignoring his question.

How anyone can make sense of this beats me. The desk itself is overrun with files; he might as well toss that one into the pile and call it a day.

"Courtney," Tony says, the unspoken warning in his tone clear.

Unlike Lorenzo's, his voice is more of a high-pitched whine.

"What?" I turn to my half-brother, narrowing my gaze at him. "This room is a disgrace for a man of his stature."

What I really mean to say is, *Everyone knows you're a power-hungry, opportunistic asshole, but you'll never get to sit in that chair. Not if Marc has anything to say about it.* But I don't say any of that because I'm not supposed to be privy to the inner workings of the family. Never mind that I've always been in the thick of things, albeit in the shadows.

And I'll be damned if I ever have to answer to Tony fucking Sotelo.

We might share paternal DNA, but that's as far as our relationship goes. That's all it'll ever be.

Next to me, Tony pushes his chest out and lifts his chin. "We didn't call you here to discuss the state of the Boss's office."

My brow lifts, and my eyes move back and forth between them. "We?"

"We're here to talk about your marriage proposals."

"Oh." I blink a few times before turning my gaze to Lorenzo. "Where's Marc?"

Both men exchange a look, one that grates on my nerves.

"Marc doesn't know about this." It's a statement I direct at Lorenzo. "You gave him your word, *Dad*. That means nothing now? Good to fucking know."

I watch as his features darken, knowing I hit a nerve. He doesn't say anything. Instead, he reaches into his extremely messy desk drawer and pulls out a sheet. He stares at it for a beat before placing it before me.

I spare a quick glance at it and grit my teeth, my lips curling in annoyance. "Let me guess. He came to you this time?" The question is directed at Tony, but either of them can answer.

Tony shakes his head. "Not me. Not this time."

"This time?"

"He went to Mom." A pause, then, "He blackmailed her."

"And what has that got to do with me? She's your mother, not mine." Sarcasm drips from my tone, but I'm done acting.

His lips twitch, a sadistic grin forming. "I need your cooperation."

My lips part, a clever retort hanging on the tip of my tongue. The full force of realization, of what he's really asking of me but won't come right out and say, slams into me, and my lips clamp shut.

So that's what this is.

It boils down to my gender. Again.

This time, *I'm* supposed to be the peace offering. Not only do I get brokered for the sake of keeping the peace, but I'll also be offered up on a silver platter so their precious mother can keep her oh-so-delicate wits about her.

I want to tell them *both* to shove it.

My God, this family. They are all messed up, the whole lot of them. No wonder Mom spent most of my childhood hiding us from them.

You'd think Tamara Sotelo didn't know what kind of family she was marrying into. If she didn't know it then, she should now. She's had decades to catch up, yet her children treat her like she's some fragile princess straight out of a romance novel, which irritates me to no end.

"The next time anyone in your family brings this up, Marc had better be present, or else." I'm done playing nice with these two. "You know what? Let me be clear about this. If you're that hellbent on selling someone to the Morellis for the sake of peace, try picking one of your own fucking daughters."

Tony leans over and places a hand on my shoulder. My spine stiffens at the gesture and I promptly shrug him off. "Touch me again, and I'll—"

"Tony, give us the room," Lorenzo cuts me off, his tone harsh.

"You can't possibly be serious," he objects hotly.

"Don't make me repeat myself." Lorenzo's tone is darker than I've ever heard, and I do a double-take. I do another as Tony visibly deflates. And another as he complies with the Boss's request without his signature quips thrown in.

I guess things aren't as peachy over here. Good to know.

"You can't lose it every time Tony runs his mouth," Lorenzo says once the door closes behind Tony.

"Where's the lie?" I challenge. "If he likes his hand attached to his arm and not shoved up his ass, he'll keep it to himself."

"Courtney…" His voice is a rumble, soft yet commanding.

I'm not having it though.

The tension in the room is palpable, but I speak freely since it's just us two.

This time, there is no holding back my irritation. "No, *Dad*. Don't you *Courtney* me. You knew what my reaction would be, yet you let that little display happen."

The annoying part is this isn't news to him. I've made myself quite clear on the subject — no one is entitled to put their grubby little paws on me simply because I'm a woman — yet no one in this house takes it seriously. Perhaps it's time I took action. Heads will roll, limbs will fly, whatever it takes.

His face finally lifts and his gaze meets mine — those emerald green eyes my mother supposedly found irresistible once upon a time. Blood relation or not, the woman did have questionable taste in men, if I do say so myself.

I'll be damned if I let history repeat itself.

"It's *your* job to keep your wife safe. It's *your* job to keep the Morellis away from her. If you'd done that in the first place, we wouldn't be having this conversation. Need I remind you that my mother is six feet under thanks to your wife, so if you're expecting sympathy from me you're barking up the wrong tree."

The thing is, the wrong tree doesn't even begin to cover how messed up that whole debacle was. Lorenzo loved Mom in his own sick and twisted way, and he still harbors a lot of guilt over her death. After all, the reason she's dead is because he thought he could outsmart the Chun-jas by sending Mom to that fucking meeting in his wife's stead.

Lorenzo would never admit this, but my gut tells me he played into the stereotype that all black people look alike, thinking the Chun-jas would be none the wiser. Mom ended up paying the price for it because she had the misfortune of sharing enough of Tamara's physical characteristics that she could pass for her stand-in.

My gut also tells me that wasn't the first time he had played switcheroo between the two women.

Except Lorenzo couldn't have predicted Mom would bring me with her, seeing as he wasn't supposed to know I existed then. Nor could he have predicted that she would order me to stand down. Yet all of those things happened anyway.

Or maybe that was her plan all along?

Either way, here we are, almost twenty years later, still grappling with the consequences of her actions and choices. It's apparent that he still carries that darkness around with him. I can see it in his eyes each time her name comes up. Mine is still nestled deep within my soul, even though it's been sixteen years since Mom's killers met their end at my blade.

It goes without saying that I killed the Chun-jas and forced their daughter to watch — just like they did to me — in the spirit of an eye for an eye. Who gives a fuck if the whole world goes blind as a result of it? What matters is that I got revenge on those fuckers, and then some.

I'll forever pay the price for it.

If I had to do it all over again, I would change a few things. I'd invent a time machine, travel further back in time, and convince Sarah Bardales to pick a different man with whom to reproduce. Mainly because I don't need this bullshit. Or this family, for that matter.

Lorenzo is quiet as he watches me, a hollow look in his eyes. "You done?" he asks when I pause to catch my breath.

"Not by a long shot," I scoff. "I don't care what Gerald Morelli has on your wife. Force this marriage on me, and it will end one of two ways — I will kill him, or Marc will."

"Unsanctioned?" The thought amuses him, even though he knows I'm dead serious.

It's comical that he has to ask. "When has protocol stopped either of us before? You'll fix it. You always do."

A belabored sigh moves through him as he leans back in his posh desk chair with his hands steepled. "Would it kill you to play nice once in a while?"

"Yes, it would. I'm supposed to be a diva, remember?" This is the part where I'd insert a dramatic hair flip for added effect, except it took me thirty minutes this morning to tame my curls and secure them into a decent-looking ponytail. I refuse to undo all of that hard work just to make a point. "If Tony thinks he can coerce me into it by playing the guilt card, he's even dumber than he looks. And before you ask, no, I will not become the next sacrificial lamb for *your* family."

"That family also includes you, Courtney. You and Marc."

"You really believe that, don't you?" I say with a forced laugh.

The look in his eyes tells me he really does, and that makes me speechless. I have no idea what to say to that, not without making myself sound like a complete bitch.

I close my eyes and mentally count backward from fifty to zero as I choose my next words carefully.

I have never said these words to anyone, not to Lorenzo, and certainly not to Marc. We've all been thinking it, though.

"Your wife hates us," I tell him, keeping my voice even, "The feeling is mutual for obvious reasons. No woman wants to be forced to raise her husband's bastard children to keep up appearances. Just as no child should be put in a position where they must blindly accept their dead mother's doppelgänger as a replacement mother figure. Why do you think Marc and I hightailed it out of this house the minute we legally could?"

Not only was his decision to officially bring us into his family controversial and divisive at the time, but it was also met with a lot of hostility. Tamara was leading the charge, as was to be expected, until Marc made that infamous deal and publicly forced Lorenzo's hand... and everyone else's in the process.

2

COURTNEY

L orenzo stares at me for a moment, seemingly absorbing my words, before shifting gears. "How's my grandson?"

Poking the bear goes both ways, which he's also quite adept at.

My hand falls to my lap as I shoot him an irritated look. "Which one?"

He lifts a challenging brow. "The only one you'd give me."

"He's not your grandson. He's the product of a fucking job," I spit out.

He draws in a sharp breath, his eyes narrowing to slits. "Language."

I narrow my eyes at him in return. "I don't get why you're so interested in this one. You've got dozens of them running around."

It's true. He does.

He and his wife have six adult children, and each one has just as many children. It could be more, I stopped counting after the tenth grandchild. I don't keep myself apprised of the affairs of his and his children's households if it doesn't directly pertain to Marc and me. That's what Abby does — she sifts through the boring details and updates me on what I need to know.

Like how much of a pussy-hound Lorenzo is. Supposedly, there are others like my brother and myself. Yet we are the only two he officially brought into the fold.

"Marc still raising him?"

My chest contracts. I curl my fingers into fists in my lap. "Why ask questions you already know the answer to?"

Instead of answering, he smiles.

The fucker actually *smiles* at me, and it's in that annoyingly smug and patronizing manner of his. The one that tells me he knows the *real* reason our unconventional arrangement exists.

So what if I'm a part-time mother to my son? That's between us, and no one else. Besides, his pathetic father can't be bothered to be in his life, yet I don't see anyone riding his ass about that.

Don't even get me started on the double standard that exists here.

At least Howard got a choice in whether or not he wanted to be involved in this family. Charlie and I don't. He was born into it. I was born into it. Mom did what she could to hide us — hide me, specifically — from Lorenzo, but that couldn't have ended the way she envisioned. I am too much like her for my existence to have escaped his ever-watchful eyes.

In many ways, I am my mother's daughter. Or rather, I am *her*.

The perfect killing machine.

Lorenzo intently studies my face in that uncanny manner of his before shaking his head. "And her?" he eventually asks.

"*Her?*"

"Your girlfriend."

She's not my girlfriend, I want to say, but clamp down on my lips.

My chest contracts again. Or maybe it's that stupid heart muscle that refuses to calm the fuck down every time her name comes up, even if it's casually in conversation.

I look away from him, my gaze settling on the picture he had set before me earlier. "What about her?"

"When are you finally going to bring her around? Introduce her to the family?"

The pressure in my chest increases at his words. He says this casually, like he doesn't know why it must be this way. It doesn't matter that he's my dad. I don't owe him an explanation of how I conduct my private affairs. Marc's deal with him covered that. For a man like Lorenzo, his word is his bond. It's not something he goes back on.

I suppose in many other ways, I am my father's daughter.

My father's *bastard* daughter.

The thought puts a sour taste in my mouth, so I push it aside and stand. "We're done here."

Either he's not getting the memo, or I poked the bear too hard.

"Not by a long shot. Sit." His tone is unusually harsh, so I do as he says without protest this time.

But I do grin darkly at him. "Hurts, doesn't it? Being poked and prodded like that?"

An eternity passes, and then his eyes soften. "Is it shocking that I'd be curious about my grandson? Or my daughter's happiness?"

"Yeah, it is," I answer truthfully. He and I don't have that kind of relationship.

"Have I really been that terrible of a father to you?"

He's seeking validation? From me?

The idea is laughable.

"This whole caring father routine doesn't really suit you, Lorenzo. To be honest, it's kinda creeping me out."

"And yet, here we are." The sarcasm drips from his tone, but still, I can't shake off the feeling that there's more to it than this.

This act.

This whole fucking pointless façade.

Of all his many children, it's the legitimate ones he has on the straight and narrow. They have the keys to the golden palace and live the privileged lifestyle, complete with all its so-called perks.

The illegitimate ones, like Marc and I, do his dirty work. While Marc legally cleans up the family's messes, I clean those up through back channels. Sometimes those back channels have their own back channels, each with its own unique set of messes that it takes my team and I — Abby, Phoenix, and myself, his secret weapons — months, sometimes years, to sort through the weeds and pull out the rotten roots at the source, preferably from the inside out. Like this mess with Louis Pecora.

I draw in a sharp breath, exhaling slowly. "Why am I really here? And don't tell me it's because you care about my well-being."

Something flashes in his eyes as he leans forward and steeples his hands on his desk. "Oh, but I do."

"Or you're tired of fielding the marriage proposals that keep coming for me. That's what this is about, isn't it? It's why you want to know if Marc's still raising Charlie."

"Well, yes, but that's only a part of it."

"And the rest?"

He inhales deeply and studies me. "I told them no, by the way. My children aren't commodities to be traded. But it would help if you were… spoken for."

I scoff. "Spoken for? Whatever happened to saying no?"

"It doesn't work that way anymore. I'm trying, but I still need you to meet me halfway. I'll consider it a huge favor, one you can cash in at any time."

Right.

Everyone knows Lorenzo Sotelo's word is his bond. They also know it's not his style to offer carte blanche favors like this. There has to be a catch.

"What does Reuben even want with me?"

He shrugs. "Beats me. From what I hear, he's got women falling all over themselves for him, but he's fixated on you for some reason."

"You think?"

He carries on talking, ignoring my sarcastic quip. "All I know is, the self-entitled prick seems to be under the impression that he owns you."

I let out a dry laugh. "Oh really? I never noticed. Last I checked—"

"—that was my problem, I know," he finishes. "So pick someone. Or better yet, pick one of each, and let's call it a day. Like your brother did."

Right.

The only reason everyone finally backed off of Marc a few months ago was that Delilah joined the team. It is deplorable, I admit, and what that tells me is things won't change should we go official. Not unless I bind myself to a man. Plus, Lorenzo knows that his deal with Marc prohibits him from marrying me off through the same channels he did his legitimate daughters. Everyone knows his word is his bond, yet they all watch for him to slip up and go back on that.

My phone picks that moment to chime, so I hold out a finger to Lorenzo and tap away. As usual, it's Marc checking up on me. It's almost as if he has some sort of telepathy, that one.

Marc: You home?

That's an odd question, even from him.

Courtney: No. Why?

He doesn't answer right away, so I put the screen to sleep before returning my attention to Lorenzo. "Send a few of those my way, if it gets to be too much for you to handle. All I need to do is gut one or two like fish, right? Maybe ship off a few body parts to their families while I'm at it. That should send the message to the rest, don't you think?"

He laughs, but it's strained. "Or it'll start a war, something neither of us wants."

"Yeah, well. There's that too."

His eyes tell me he's given this some thought.

A lot of thought, which is what makes this situation all the more messed up.

The thing is, I meant every word of what I said to CC, even if that was two years ago. I can't drag her into my family and all of the baggage that comes with it. It's a choice she has to make for herself. With Oscar in the picture, things are twice as complicated.

Urgh.

This is why people shouldn't do romantic commitments. But

Marc somehow makes it work with two partners; I could stand to learn a thing or two from him.

Another chime.

Marc: There's a situation at your place that needs to be handled.

Courtney: What situation?

Marc: The kind that needs to be handled in person.

Lorenzo reaches over and pulls my phone out of my hands.

"I could stab you in the jugular just for that," I tell him, holding out a hand.

He scoffs. "And sign your own death warrant? I don't think so."

"Dad."

"Tell you what. I'll find you a worthy adversary for your next job if you consider bringing her into the family. Officially."

I laugh. "That's a really messed up trade-off, Dad."

"Desperate times, Courtney."

Now there's a statement I never thought I'd hear from the great Lorenzo Sotelo. "What's really in it for me? Besides more work that I'd been slated for."

He sighs. "Fine. Phoenix can have the thing you asked about."

Oh.

Wow.

That was a major ask. One that had to be scaled down several times before he would even consider it, so his willingness to concede is a small win for us. But I can't let him know that, not when I can squeeze even more information out of him. If he truly is as desperate as he says he is, then for once, I have the upper hand.

I shake my head. "Tempting, but not good enough."

A beat passes, and his eyes soften. "If you really want to know who he is, you must find him on your own. Or he finds you. That was the deal you two made."

"Yes, you said that already. Several times, in fact. But then you fixed it so no one could tell me anything about him."

"Because you graduated the program early, which in turn forced Abby and Phoenix to graduate early—"

"—and three people got to live because of that. Yes, you said that too. But you left out a lot of crucial details. Like the real reason you shipped me off to Art School halfway across the country. I could've taken a gap year, but you insisted on it."

He sighs, scrubbing his hand down his face. "Your brother wanted you with him. Something about my exerting undue influence over you, as if anyone can make you do anything you don't want to. Well, except for your brother."

He's not wrong, and I can't help but grin at the bitterness in his tone. There's always been something weird about the dynamics between Marc and Lorenzo, and I make it a point to stay out of it.

I'm aware that Lorenzo is still bitter about how things went down back then, and there's no doubt he's punishing me for it.

"That can't be the only reason why I was the only one who did things remotely while everyone else got to do in person. Whatever happened to weekends and holidays?"

"Courtney..."

"They all know who he is, but not me. He was mine, Dad. *Mine.* Sure, he was a voice on the other end of the phone, but that didn't make him any less real to me. Even if I were tech-savvy like Abby, that's still not a lot for me to go off of. And I tried working with what I got. Believe me, I've tried every trick I could think of, but everywhere I turn, I hit a fucking wall. And I..." my voice breaks, and my throat constricts. "He haunts me, okay? After all this time, he still haunts me. In order for me to move on, like you want, I need closure on that chapter in my life. Everyone else got some version of closure, but not me. I'm not asking for his name, but I could use a hint. Just one. It's been years, Dad. Throw me a bone."

It feels so fucking good to finally use my Art History degree in more than just creating forgeries for rich assholes who could afford the real thing but choose not to spend the money. I also knew my tears would get his fucking attention since that's not something he's privy to. Ever. So, I'm throwing him a bone by turning up the waterworks and letting the tears flow freely. He's eating that shit out of the palm of my hand, just as I predicted.

Mom would be fucking proud if she could see me right now. Lord knows if I had the patience or temperament for it, I would've gone into acting. This whole thing is fucking nauseating, but it's getting the job done, so I can't complain.

His eyes search mine for hints of impropriety, but there's none to be had. This is as much weakness as I intend to show him today.

"He's a lot closer than you think," he eventually says with a grunt. "Now, do we have a deal or not?"

Well, that was easy.

I'll take *two* small wins any day, but I still can't let that show. I mull it over for a moment, then the lie falls from my lips all too easily. "Deal. Can I get my phone back now?"

He sees right through that last part. "You need to say the actual words. Your word is your bond."

Urgh.

"Phoenix gets her thing within the week, and I'll think about the rest of it." I got my hint, so I can't get any more greedy. An exasperated sigh moves through me as I swipe the back of my hand over my eyes. "It's the best I can do, so take it or leave it." My voice is sharp like a whip, letting him know the moment is over.

A moment he'll never get from me. Ever again.

He holds it out to me, then holds a hand to me, palm up turned.

As we shake on it, I have the fingers of my other hand crossed behind my back.

3

____

OSCAR

"What will it take to get Olive Hyun back in the country?"

If I had a dollar for every time Gerald Morelli — the man I share half of my DNA with — directed the asinine question at me, I'd be richer than I already am.

Then again, I trust money, but I don't trust most people.

My mother taught me that.

"People are not to be trusted, Oscar," she would repeat to me ad nauseam, even with her eyes glued to her computer screen. "Especially the ones who call themselves your family," she would add, with an extra hard jab at the ancient keyboard, "and particularly the ones you have the misfortune of sharing DNA with."

I was five years old at the time.

Suffice it to say I took that little life nugget about trust with a grain of salt, then tweaked and modified it to suit my needs.

Per Mom's logic, I'm meant to distrust her. I should, but I can't bring myself to because there's a method to her madness. There are some rather complex layers and shit to the reasoning behind how and why she does the things she does, most of which I can get behind, except for this one.

Her choice in men. Particularly the man I share paternal DNA with.

He, too, has a score to settle with her.

And when my sperm donor extends to me a once-a-month, non-negotiable yet open-ended dinner invitation with his perfect family, or else, you'd better believe I'll be showing up to every single one of them. He has his agenda, and I have mine.

"Mom is retired," I remind him, pushing my green beans around on my plate.

He snorts. "Last I checked, retired doesn't mean dead."

"Retired, dead, exiled, it's all the same." I scowl at my plate. I have no idea what the rest of this stuff is on it. The greens look edible but are more brown than green and barely smell right. The mashed potatoes are overrun with too much butter, most likely overcompensating for the lumps in them.

Don't get me started on this blob that's supposed to be ham.

I could feign politeness and take a few bites, but the inevitable stomach ache I'd be sure to get from eating lousy food simply isn't worth it.

It's not that the food is shitty; it's just bad. Yet somehow, their so-called classically-trained chef deemed this appropriate to serve for dinner. Morelli's wife and children are far too polite to say anything about it lest they piss off their chef, or hack, in other words.

I think that hack is a nepotism hire, plain and simple.

Unless they're punking me, testing another sneaky, underhanded trick to get a handout out of me? It won't work. I don't give out money for the sake of it. And even if they persuaded me to — which they wouldn't — I still couldn't. Mom made sure of it.

"Did your mother ever tell you why she was exiled?"

"Not really. I know what everyone else knows. One day she announced her retirement, packed up, and left the country." I'm not surprised by how easily the lie flows past my lips. With this bunch, that was never a problem. "You know I was never privy to that part of her life, right? On account of you."

He scoffs. "Something tells me you're not as ignorant as you'd like others to believe."

Touché.

"You're right, I'm not." I meet his gaze dead-on before continuing. "You accused her of stealing from you when we both know she didn't. She did exactly what you paid her to do, so if you have buyer's remorse, that's on you. Since your fragile ego can't handle it, you got her exiled as payback. Then you also made it so that she can never come back. Can't say she's torn up about that arrangement either, as she's living her best life, far away from you and your toxic shit."

My lips thin out as I look around the room, from the intricate murals etched into the impossibly high ceilings; the assortment of fake Monets, Picassos, and Vermeers strategically hung in high-traffic areas of this house; down to the pristine silk rugs gracing the floors.

It's all very… showy. Just like Gerald is, but without the means to back it up. Then again, it doesn't matter how much lipstick you put on it — a pig is just a pig. Why he's holding on tight to this place beats me, when it's all just a stark reminder that he's broke.

His children, on the other hand, are not. They are all billionaires, the lot of them. While I am self-made, Reuben and Hallie — my half-siblings — are not. He hired Olive to clean up his blood money, and she gave it to his children instead. If he really wants to label it a crime, then it's a victimless one.

Ironically, he can't touch it, thanks to Olive Hyun's very particular skill set. He can't report it to the authorities either because he would have to explain where that money came from.

Hence his desperation to get her back in the country. He needs her to undo whatever she did, as if it is somehow her fault that he didn't read the fine print.

Olive Hyun doesn't undo her work. Ever.

"That's not why she was exiled," Gerald adds. "She killed a man."

"Wow. As far as reasons go, you guys are really scraping the bottom of the barrel. Did you see her do it, or is that just more wild speculation on your part?"

"She killed my brother," his wife, Daisy Morelli, speaks up for the first time.

Oh. That guy.

This whole thing is so predictable I could do this scene with my eyes shut.

"From what I heard, that was sanctioned," I point out. "Besides, my mother didn't kill him. Lorenzo Sotelo's super-secret kill squad did."

"Is that what she told you?" she challenges me.

"She didn't have to. I would've known if she were one of his weapons, which she wasn't." It's a well-rehearsed lie, one I recite repeatedly.

"So why did she confess to it?"

"To get you off her back? To give you a boogeyman to blame? If it's revenge you want, you won't get it by going after her. That's why you're doing these dinners on the down low… scratch that, let's call this what it actually is. It's an intimidation tactic, and it's not sanctioned either.

"Look, I might not know much about how things work in the Mafia, but I do know that someone like your brother doesn't get publicly executed for no reason. He stole from Lorenzo, on your say-so, I'm guessing. Then he was stupid enough to get caught, but not smart enough to fess up on who put him up to it. Not that any of that would've made a difference. He did far more disgusting things, too, so everyone's better off with him gone.

"But you know this, don't you? Just as you know not even your longstanding friendship with Lorenzo was enough to save your brother-in-law's life. Does that sound about right?"

She turns to her husband. "I could never wrap my head around how such a self-entitled prick came from your loins," she mutters.

I hear it anyway, so I just have to chime in. "Entitled, yes. A prick, no. I just call it like it is. You're using me to get to my mother, but it won't work."

Gerald sighs, pushing his plate away. Collective sighs of relief echo around the table as everyone else follows suit.

Took them long enough.

"I'll ask again," Gerald says as he leans back in his seat and crosses his hands over his chest. "What will it take to get Olive Hyun back in the country?"

"Not this," I mutter dryly as my gaze roams over his features. For the third time in the past hour, my brain catalogs all the ways in which we look nothing alike, and I thank whatever higher power up there made it so.

Genes are fickle things, but in this case, I'm glad the odds worked out in my favor.

"I see," he says through gritted teeth. "I suppose we keep doing this song and dance until she comes to her senses?"

"Why bother?" I ask, knowing I'll show up the next time he summons me. "You've already decided she's a bad mother. What makes you think these little gatherings will change her mind?"

"All these years and you honestly believe she's a saint," he says with a sinister chuckle. "I have to say, where Mommy dearest is concerned your naiveté still has no bounds, and I have every intention of exploiting that."

So, it's the same old speech. Soon, he'll delve into the *'You underestimate just how far a mother's love for her child can be leveraged'* territory. Then he'll tell me about his new plan because he assumes I'll go crying to Mommy. And Mommy, in a fit of rage, will come charging back.

I should be annoyed that they are dragging this on, yet all I can think is, *finally*.

As in, *finally* his wimp of a son will get to throw around a few half-ass punches in a pathetic bid to impress Daddy dearest.

As in, *finally* I'll let him hit me once or twice so that he can feel good about all those martial arts lessons that are clearly wasted on him.

Then we can get this so-called charade of a dinner over and done with. Until the next one, that is.

Because all of those things will happen — his using me as his personal punching bag, my letting it happen, and my showing up the next time I'm summoned here — and there's no point in delaying the inevitable any further.

Except he's going about it all the wrong ways, and it's not my place to steer him right. Nor is it my problem if his own mother taught him wrong.

Like the dutiful son that I am, I don't mind taking on the brunt of his frustration toward her. People like him never learn their lesson. Since the bastard just can't help it, I see no reason why I should make this any easier on him.

And while we are at it, I'll have fun with it.

"Look here, old man." I drop my fork loudly, feigning annoyance.

"Watch your tone." Next to me, Reuben growls — whimpers, more like — as he flexes his fingers.

Still, I turn to look at him, barely masking my surprise at his words. Since when did this one grow a backbone?

Never mind that.

"Or what?" I bite out. "I've said some petty, disrespectful shit in the last thirty minutes, and that's the part you fixate on? Old man?"

Then comes the predictable slamming of his fists on the table. I suspect the gesture is intended to be threatening — as evidenced by the identical gasps from the other two table occupants — but it just comes off as pathetic.

Why isn't Gerald quick to chide his son for this little display? Why are the wife and daughter putting on a show of being scared of the wimpy brother?

Why do I care again?

"As long as you are under his roof," Reuben goes on, "you will show him the respect he commands—"

"Commands? He's pushing sixty," I say dryly. "Old is an appropriate term for what he is. At this rate, it's only a matter of time before he keels over. Admit it. He'll be doing everyone a favor. Same as your idiot uncle." I turn to Gerald. "You've already tried blackmailing her and me, both of which got you nowhere. Summoning me here does diddly-squat, so switch tactics or leave me the fuck alone."

The obligatory first punch gets thrown right on cue, knocking me out of my seat and flat on my ass. I taste the copper before its accompanying liquid floods my mouth.

Instead of swallowing — which would have been the polite thing to do — I turn my head and spit out the liquid on his Italian knock-offs.

"No offense, but you hit like a girl," I lie.

It hurts. He might be a wimp, but he has lead fists, and that shit hurts. The skin will bruise, and I'll walk away with a split lip. But it is worth it, seeing the look of utter disbelief on his face.

Reuben inhales deeply as he draws his hand back and curls it into a fist. I brace for another puny, half-assed blow, but it never comes.

"You said you wouldn't hit him this time," Hallie — my half-sister — says, her hand on his shoulder.

"I lied, Halls," he tells her.

"Wouldn't be the first time," she tosses back at him, barely disguising her discomfort with watching the scene unfolding before her. It's the same thing every single time, yet the fact that she's still shocked by it tells me there is hope for her. "Is it too much to ask that people in this family stick to their words? I mean, gosh. I get where Oscar is coming from. Hitting only makes things worse for us. Worse for Dad. And that," she points to me, "just wait until Lorenzo gets wind of that. You'll be the one that ends up in a body bag, not him."

With her legs crossed and a champagne glass in her hand, Daisy watches the exchange with an amused smile, like this is entertainment for her.

So too does Gerald. He leans back in his seat and recrosses his hands over his chest. His sense of self-importance is quickly waning, but everyone is too polite to point that out. That includes Little Miss Perfect, who is appalled by the idea of her brother hitting me, but not by her father who encourages it. Or that her mother takes great pleasure in watching the bastard son get pummeled by the legitimate one.

They might as well open up their own fight club if that's the shit that gets them off.

With blood relatives like this, who needs enemies?

4

OSCAR

The afternoon sun hits me when I step outside, its glare nearly blinding. I squint my eyes against the brightness as I rock my jaw from side to side to assess the damage. If my face looks as bad as it feels, I'll be in for a world of hurt in the next few days. I guess I'll have to be a hermit for a little while.

Or talk my best friend CC into teaching me her mad make-up skills again. Even better, she can do it for me. She'll just turn it into another one of her sex games. That'd be a fun conversation to have.

I head for my town car, and my driver, Rodney, steps out and walks around to open my door. He waits until I'm settled into the back seat before handing me an ice pack.

I mumble "Thanks" under my breath, and he nods a silent acknowledgment.

Right on cue, my phone vibrates in my pocket as we pull out of the driveway.

"Did you get it?" I say by way of greeting.

"Five minutes, that's all I needed," Abby answers. The distinct sound of the keys clicking on her keyboard filters through the speakers as she furiously types away to meet whatever self-imposed deadline she's on. "You didn't have to stay the whole hour. You certainly didn't need to goad a madman who has shown, time and time again, that he cannot be reasoned with."

Pressing the ice pack against my split lip, I say, "I had to make it look real."

"By getting your ass whupped? Again? What's the point in logging thousands of hours' worth of self-defense classes and dropping millions in personal instructors if you're not going to use it?"

I wish I could say I was surprised that she knows exactly how much money I've spent on all that, but I'm not.

"It had to happen, you know that. And he's the least of our worries," I remind her. "What did you find?"

She sighs. "Hallie changed her phone again, so something or someone must have tipped her off."

"You think?"

"Don't get smart with me, genius."

"Then put something untraceable on this phone, then I wouldn't have to."

"There's no such thing as an untraceable malware program, only the hard-to-find ones." She makes a tsk-tsk sound. "Why does a Mafia brat need military-grade encryption on her phone?"

"If I knew the answer to that, I wouldn't have to put up with those people now, would I?"

"The kind that is fast approaching old maid status, that's who," Abby talks over me, answering her own question. "I can't say I'm impressed since it took me five minutes to crack it."

I fake-gasp and place a hand over my chest. "Five whole minutes this time? You're getting slow."

"That right?" she scoffs, sarcasm dripping from her tone. "Maybe I'll pass this on to Olive, and she'll finish it in half the time."

"Don't," I bite out.

"Why the fuck not? I'm obviously too slow for you, so it's time to call in the big guns."

"She got out for a reason, Abby, and I don't want to be the one that drags her back into it again."

That last word lingers in the air.

Again.

It's enough to shut Abby up, albeit momentarily.

In many ways, Abigail Sanders is like me: loyal, driven, and a little reckless. She's Asian, and I'm Asian American. We're both good with numbers, courtesy of genetics and Mom's *particular* brand of training. We both have complicated relationships with our respective guardians. For me, it's Mom; for Abby, it's Mattie, her adoptive grandmother.

Our history runs deep, darker even.

Fifteen years ago, Abby, myself, Roxane, Phoenix, and Courtney graduated from Lorenzo Sotelo's super-secret kill squad training program (yes, he actually calls it that). Mattie was our teacher and principal then, a point of contention between her and her training partner until she realized the lengths Mattie was willing to go to ensure a zero failure rate.

Not only was Mattie in charge of the whole thing, but she also called the shots on what classes we had to take, how all of our pairings were meant to be conducted, all of the twisted charades she put us through, and the tenuous aftermath of it all when we all supposedly graduated early from the program.

Courtney was my training partner, but I never met her. The entire time, she was just a voice on the other end of the phone; that part was Mattie's doing. We weren't allowed to exchange names either, and Mattie didn't bother explaining why it had to be that way, only that she had Mom's consent, and that was all I needed to know.

Apparently, Lorenzo did, too, as Courtney's father. They all knew I was more than capable of finding out who she was, so Mattie waited until after we graduated to place a gag order on all of us, prohibiting us from discussing any and all details of the program with anyone, including each other. Then she added the clause where I couldn't contact her under any circumstances; that part was Lorenzo's doing. He and Mattie kept citing many bullshit rules as to why I couldn't, rules that either made no sense or constantly contradicted each other, with no actual explanations for anything that mattered.

I wish I knew then what I know now. As a naive, eager-to-please boy, their word was law, so I did as they asked, even as my mind fractured under the pressure of everything. I know Abby didn't come out of it unscathed, either. We each did, in our own way, and being unable to discuss it with the people who truly understood was a struggle for all of us, especially me. It was no surprise to anyone that I was the first one who fell apart after that.

Imagine my surprise when Mom passed me off to yet another one of her colleagues, Dr. Goodman, to handle any way she saw fit. Except those two were nothing alike, so things turned out differently than she envisioned. I was still grappling with the aftermath of it and figuring out a way to move forward when Mom abruptly announced her retirement a few months later, packed up, and relocated back to South Korea.

Except I know for a fact that she didn't *actually* retire. Not completely. A few years ago, I found out that she'd just moved her base of operations to a different continent, buried it deeper into the dark web, and then found other creative means to rope me into her unsavory dealings.

Mommy dearest my tatted ass.

I consider myself incredibly lucky that Abby was there for me every step of the way — so too was her training partner, Roxane — or I wouldn't be the man I am today. As a result, Abby is someone I wholeheartedly trust, not just with my money, but also with my life. It's an unlikely side effect of our shared past, not what Mom *or* Mattie intended.

And now, Abby and I share a teacher — or our quasi-boss, depending on how you look at it. That's who she's referring to as the big guns. Mom never stopped being our teacher. After all, we each have our roles to play as graduates of the program. But where hacking is her true calling, like Mom's was, I begrudgingly partake because I have to, not because I want to.

Abby knows this too. That's why, like CC, she wasn't on board with this plan with the Morellis. Not at first. As Gerald's bastard son, I have an in, and it's still the best chance we've got.

"All that shit Gerald said about your mom, you know he was lying, right?" she eventually asks.

"Maybe, maybe not." I shrug, even though she can't see me. "I mean, he's a paranoid fucker, but it doesn't mean he's wrong. I'm sure you know things about my mom that I don't, and I'm her son. I don't doubt that she did the same to him. With him, even."

There's no need for me to elaborate further. After all, she's familiar enough with Olive Hyun and Gerald Morelli's turbulent thirty-plus years of history to brush aside my concerns.

Out of all the messed-up shit that went down between them, I thank my lucky stars that my mother had the foresight to leave his name off my birth records thirty-two years ago because it's coming in handy now. Thanks to Abby, my connection to the Morellis will never see the light of day, save for these faux dinners.

Gerald knows he can bitch and whine until he's blue in the face and it still wouldn't change a thing. It's not like he can touch me legally nor can he strong-arm me into undoing what Mom did, even though the thought has crossed his mind.

"That being said," Abby's voice cuts through my thoughts. "Tell your sister — half-sister — that if she wants out, she has to go through the proper channels."

I scrunch my nose. "Meaning she has to take it up with Lorenzo?"

"That's what I said. He is the Boss for a reason."

"He'll use her for leverage, Abby."

"Of course he will. It's what he does. It's what we all do. Everybody uses everybody else for something."

"That may be true, but we both know it won't be against just anybody. He'll use her to get to the Morellis. He'll get her to turn against her own family."

"There's a high probability of that happening, yes."

"That will put a target on her back, just like my mom. All she wants is to get out, no fuss, no muss."

"I hate to break it to you, but that will never happen. Daisy's brother had ties to the Milligans, something Gerald went to great lengths to hide. There's even a rumor that Gerald was present on the day Deloise OD'd, yet somehow managed to escape. Since Deloise was a high-profile client, that's not something Lorenzo forgives or forgets. It's why we are on this path. It's been sixteen years, and we're still cleaning up that mess. But you know all of this already, don't you?"

I do, and it's a mess. "It's not like Hallie had a say in who birthed her, so how's that fair?"

"It's not, yet it's not that simple either. If we're going to talk about fairness, then think about it this way. It's not that simple and no different from what you're doing, Oscar."

Letting out a sigh of exasperation, I lean back in my seat. "I still can't believe you're okay with that."

"I don't have to be okay with it. That's just the way things work in the Mafia." She's still typing away at her keyboard as she talks. "Rules are rules for a reason. If Hallie and her billions want to disappear permanently, she must abide by his rules. I know they're not perfect, but they are effective in getting the job done right the first time and keeping it that way."

"What if she willingly gives up those billions? Would that make a difference?"

"Not really, no. It's in the fine print of the amended contract that your company had Hallie sign."

"I didn't know about that. I certainly didn't authorize that."

"You didn't have to. That clause is iron-clad because Hyun Holdings set up her original trust fund. One way or another, the money is a fucking noose that will follow her in life and in death. If you don't like that part, take it up with your mom."

Oh, there's a lot I wish I could take up with Mom, but I can't. Some of it is ancient history, and some of it is just… I don't know.

As a self-proclaimed Robin Hood — her words, not mine — Olive Hyun also happens to be a finance whiz and hacker extraordinaire. As someone born ahead of her time, she was a slave to numbers and technology — still is — and to this day she trusts those far more than she trusts people.

Her specialized skill set meant she spent most of her life making more enemies than friends. She might be *retired* now, but it still didn't change the fact that her trust in people is so negligible, that for the longest time she could never tell who was looking to settle a score or who she'd pissed off with one of her stunts.

She was good at that too. She still is, apparently.

That's why I went to Abby for this particular job. I refuse to dwell on the idea that Gerald might be right. Abby might say she won't clue Mom in on this now, but it's only a matter of time before she gets stuck and goes to our teacher for help. Their teacher-student bond is unlike any I've ever seen. Besides, even if she doesn't, Mom will find out about it eventually. Keeping tabs on me is one of her many hobbies. Who knows, that might just be the thing to get her to return to the US.

Maybe it'll even pull her out of her so-called retirement. I might not like it, and I certainly don't want to be the one who officially brings her back to this country, but there's no denying she *is* good at this. I refuse to believe that all she did was make enemies in this line of work. She had to have had some allies in her clients, even if they were barely still in one piece by the time she was done with them.

Mostly in one piece.

"Thanks for the entertainment, by the way," Abby says, her tone perking up. "I recorded the whole thing. For research purposes."

"Don't you mean for blackmail?" I say with a laugh. Although it's forced, it's all I can do to tamp down my mortification.

"What's the difference?"

I shrug. "Just don't play it at my funeral."

I'm confident she won't use it against me, as we don't have that type of relationship. If that were the thing she was after, she knows far juicier secrets of mine and could cash in those chips anytime she wanted. I know she'll use the recording against Gerald, and I shudder to think what she has in store for him.

"Noted. Although, I have to ask." When the sound of keystrokes stops and her tone shifts, I know I'm in for a world of hurt.

Still, I say, "Ask away."

"Since when did you become such a brat?"

Fuck if that doesn't get my half-mast cock thickening in an instant. "It's not like that."

The protest is weak, and we both know it.

Or at least she knows it, just as she knows what buttons of mine to push.

"It's not?" Her tone drops another octave. "Enlighten me."

Fuck.

As if on command, my hand falls to my lap. "Abby, don't. Please."

She makes a tsk-tsk sound. "If I didn't know better," she continues, her voice dropping to a raspy whisper as she finishes, "I'd think you actually enjoy getting spanked."

My eyes drift closed, and images of *her* flit through my brain.

Courtney Sotelo, the bane of my existence.

I exhale roughly as I trace the outline of my hard cock through my pants, slowly running my thumb around the head as I count backward from fifty to zero, willing my brain to think of anything else but the inevitable mess I will have in my pants.

She's the last person I should be thinking of. She's the one woman on earth I should not have any business getting involved with, period.

I shouldn't be envisioning the way she flips her thick dark hair over her shoulder as I stroke myself.

I shouldn't be remembering how my entire being lights up when she aims one of her mesmerizing smiles at me. My cock feels harder than it's ever been at the thought, precum leaking from my tip, leaving behind a telltale wet patch on my pants. I shouldn't have these images of her embedded so deep in my brain that she's left an indelible imprint on my soul.

The list grows longer with each passing day — the list of things I shouldn't be doing or thinking or wanting where she's concerned. It's stupid and downright reckless — and everything I've ever wanted.

I don't hate the fact that Abby knows this. I hate myself for being so weak where she's involved.

"You are a sadist's dream, Oscar," Abby coos into my ear. "The perfect fuck toy. Quit half-assing it and embrace it. Or better yet, choke that cock hard enough to bruise it."

It is as if she can see me, which is silly because there are no cameras in here.

Or are there?

I wouldn't put it past her. I'm not even sure when this became our thing. Phone sex, I mean.

Still, my breathing slows, my entire body humming as all of Abby's words filter through me.

I shouldn't. Really, I shouldn't.

Except it doesn't fucking matter. Heat spears through my groin, and the harder I try to dispel the impending explosion in my pants, the heavier and tighter my balls get.

"I can't," I force out, curling my fingers around my rock-hard shaft in a punishing squeeze.

She sucks in a rough breath at that. "You can, and you will. Come for me. Now."

My shaft tightens at her command, and my ass clenches as the first rope of cum shoots out of the tip. The orgasm washes over me, so powerful that my entire body shakes and then sags against the leather seats like a limp rag doll. Since this one seems to go on forever, I do as she demands and embrace it, coming harder than I have in a long time.

"Good boy," she rasps in my ear as the last of it ebbs out of me. "And good boys deserve to be rewarded."

"For what?" I ask, my breathing ragged, my voice a barely audible whisper.

"Don't ruin it by being a brat," Abby says, hardness infusing back into her tone.

I thought I was done, but no. That little nugget brings some life back into my cock. The fucker throbs and twitches as the Elmer's glue-like liquid seeps from me.

"*She* will ask for you soon," she continues. "Say yes to all of it."

Then she hung up at that, leaving me confused and… relieved.

I am so screwed.

I look up to see Rodney watching me in the rearview mirror. Something passes through his eyes — fury, I think — as he takes in my appearance. As soon as he notices me watching him, he averts his gaze back to the road. Not that he needs to. I often joke that he has a built-in GPS implanted in his brain, as the man can make any drive with his eyes closed. He also has over fifty years of experience as a personal chauffeur, so I know he is extremely good.

He is good at minding his own business too. That's what happens with the people who have worked with me for over two years, or in his case, for nearly a decade. They all learn not to ask questions if they wish to keep their jobs. I pay them rather handsomely too. First for doing their jobs, and then for their discretion.

Yet for reasons I can't explain — or refuse to delve into — the look of concern on his face and in his eyes has the knot in my stomach twisting tighter as he pulls into my driveway.

"How bad does it look?" I ask him when he still hasn't met my eyes.

Rodney runs a hand through his perfectly coiffed hair and sighs. He knows I'm not asking about what just transpired. I'm asking about my face.

"Permission to speak freely, Mr. Hyun?"

I bark out a laugh, one that ends with a wince. "You have three minutes, so make it good."

5

OSCAR

I t's several hours later, after a hot shower, fresh clothes, and edible food, and I still can't shake Abby's parting words. Or Rodney's warning that followed.

I toss and turn in bed as their words play over and over in my mind, in tandem with one another's. Sleep — the elusive bastard — refuses to grace me with his presence tonight. Not even the full-body aches brought on by my earlier beating are enough to distract me long enough to succumb to the sweet oblivion of exhaustion.

Not when my mind is working overtime instead.

It would do me a lot of good to listen to Rodney. After all these years, the man is so damn perceptive. I should be irritated by his honesty, but I'm not because he asked. He risked subjecting himself to my fickle mood to call me out on this unhealthy obsession of mine.

Granted, I'm not the reckless or impulsive type, but all bets are off where Courtney is concerned. I've never understood it either, the hold she has over me.

I shouldn't want Courtney the way I do. I know I shouldn't, for several reasons.

One, she's taken. She's dating my best friend CC — short for Charlena Cantor-Dietrich. Sort of. Whatever they are, it's complicated — CC's doing, from what she told me — but nevertheless, it's solid. Solid enough that she crushed whatever semblance of hope I held out for her — for us — a few years back and went with CC instead.

Which brings me to the second reason. She doesn't like men. Okay, that's just speculation on my part. I know she hasn't dated one in years. If she had, CC would've told me. And no, Charlie's sperm donor, AKA her not-ex-boyfriend, doesn't count.

Three, did I mention that she's taken?

That won't change. CC is obsessed with Courtney. CC gets very jealous and irrationally possessive where she is concerned. It has always been that way for as long as we've been best friends, and I don't see that changing anytime soon. My best friend would rather die than walk away from the woman of my dreams.

So why does the mere thought of her wanting to see me have hope fluttering to life deep within me? Hope I thought had long been snuffed out? Hope my fickle heart will nurture and grow, even though there's a strong possibility she will crush it again, destroying me in the process. Again.

But that's just the thing. I never learn. Not even as my hand snakes between my legs — without prompting this time — to find my shaft rock hard, just at the mere thought of sitting across from her once again. As I stroke myself, I let go of all thoughts of what couldn't be and just think of her. Of what it would be like to be owned by her. By both of them, actually.

Oh, how I would love to be their little fuck toy. To be their sex slave. Or even their pet. I don't care what label they give me, just as long as I'm theirs to do with as they please. The thought genuinely thrills me, and I erupt, spilling ropes of thick white cum all over my stomach.

Except this time, it's not as satisfying as it was earlier, not without an audience. Instead of basking in the afterglow of that orgasm, I drag myself into the bathroom and take a long cold shower. I change the sheets before crawling back in, only to toss and turn for who knows how long.

Sometime close to midnight, my phone buzzes with an

incoming message. I don't have to check to know who it is. It's CC's designated text alert notice.

> CC: You asleep?

I let out a tired sigh.

She knows the answer to that question.

I don't sleep. I barely do, even when I'm tired. The elusive bastard only graces me with his presence when she's here. Plus, she knows where I was today, so sleeping isn't on the agenda.

> Oscar: Nope.

Her response is instantaneous.

> CC: You changed the code again.

> Oscar: Huh?

> CC: I'm outside your place and looking like a creep. Let me in.

I bolt out of bed and pull on a pair of sweatpants. As tempting as it would be to answer the door in my birthday suit, I don't need to give my nosey neighbor with the binoculars any more of a show. And CC doesn't need that from anyone, especially me.

I have to do a double-take once my eyes land on her. "How is it that you look far worse than you did twenty-four hours ago?"

Good god. I'm turning into Evan, our other best friend and perpetual worrywart.

The dark circles around her eyes only seem to have gotten worse. It's a stark contrast against her pale alabaster skin, flawless and begging to be caressed. Kissed.

I shake my head. Now's not the time. Not when she's in mismatched oversized sweatpants and a sweatshirt, both of which she nabbed from my closet at some point, and neither of which would she be caught dead in.

"You're one to talk. You gonna let me in or what?" She huffs out her impatience and dramatically rubs her hands together.

I step aside to let her in, and she waltzes inside without a word. She knows her way around, so she makes a beeline for the kitchen and makes some coffee.

It is pointless saying anything when she's in this state. Coffee at midnight won't bode well for anyone, but one can never say we make smart decisions for ourselves. She pulls out the milk and adds some to her mug, but not mine. I think there is some hope for the night, but my heart stops when she pulls out the bourbon.

"That bad, huh?"

Her dark brown eyes lift to meet mine, wide and... hopeful. I shake my head, dispelling that thought. She came here looking worse than I feel, so hope is the wrong emotion for me to feel right now.

"I have a proposition for you," is all she says.

I lift a curious brow. "One that involves heavy libations?"

She holds out the bottle of bourbon. "You're going to need this. So will I."

Her tone hints at resignation and determination, two conflicting emotions wrestling for center stage. I take the bottle from her, then she picks up my coffee mug by the rim and hands it to me. The fucking thing is scalding hot, and I almost drop it on the floor.

How did she not feel this? It's not like she's lost all feeling in her extremities.

"What's going on?"

"We can do this sober, or we can do this drunk. Honestly, I'd rather be shit-faced for this, or I'll take it back."

She heads for the living room and settles on her favorite couch. The operative word is "her". She commandeered it long ago, and somehow I've come to think of it as hers. I follow on her heels, both hands occupied, just in time to watch as she swings her feet onto the couch, tucking them underneath her body.

I take the couch across from her and watch as she shrugs out of her sweatshirt, then moves her sleek jet-black hair over each shoulder, baring her creamy neck. The teardrop necklace is new. My gaze lowers to the swell of her breasts, taking in the raised tips of her hard nipples as they press against the flimsy excuse for a tank top.

No bra. Fuck me.

I lick my lips, only to find my mouth is dry. As I lean back in my seat, my eyelids flutter, then close. I exhale roughly, count from zero to fifty, and then back down to zero.

"That's not going to work," she whispers, the sultry undertones in her voice shooting straight to my cock.

Shifting in my seat, I debate the bourbon. A nagging voice in the back of my mind hints at what this is about, but I so desperately want to be wrong about this.

Why *do* I want to be wrong about this?

My eyelids part to find her studying me, her eyes dark with lust as she takes in my naked torso, not deterred or repulsed by the discoloration on the skin, courtesy of Reuben's lead fists. Still, her eyelids are swollen and puffy, like she's been crying.

It's going to be a long night.

I lean forward, resting both elbows on my thighs. "You sure you want to do this tonight?"

She blinks, her thick lashes hypnotizing me. "I'm not drunk *yet*, if that's what you're asking."

I know that. Drunk CC wouldn't waste time eye-fucking me with those big doe eyes of hers. She'd actually *be* fucking me, cowgirl style, her favorite.

As for me?

I'm content with my life the way it is. Well, *mostly* satisfied with my life as it is. That doesn't mean I'll turn down something new and different, especially where *she* is involved.

After pouring a hefty amount into my slightly cooled coffee, I take a moment to inhale the aroma before taking a gulp.

"Reuben Morelli."

I can't believe she's starting this conversation out with that. "We are not pairing your finest bourbon with talking about my brother."

"Half-brother," she's quick to correct me. As an adoptee, she's big on those distinctions.

It wasn't until a few years after we met that she told me why that was. She trusted me enough to clue me in on the fact that she's had to change names three times, so I know it's not her fault that her name and ethnicity don't match.

When people hear the name Charlena Cantor-Dietrich, they picture a tall Teutonic blonde with blue eyes and fair skin. The look on their faces is priceless when she shows up and shatters their preconceived notions about her. After years of dealing with that bullshit, she now goes by Charlena or just CC because it's easier than using her full name. Unfortunately for her, she also sticks out like a sore thumb from the rest of her very German adoptive family, so it's no surprise that she moved as far away from them as possible and made a life for herself here in the Midwest.

Still, CC is nothing like the Morellis, and just thinking about the two in the same sentence leaves a sour taste in my mouth. And it ruins a fucking good bourbon.

"Whatever Reuben is, it's a shitty combination."

"And I make it my business to know the people in Courtney's life. Especially the ones who could possibly be a threat to her."

It is comical that she thinks of him as a threat. "My *half*-brother is a lot of things. A threat isn't one of them."

"That a fact?" she asks, and I can't help but laugh.

"He's more of a nuisance."

"Nuisance, huh?" She takes a moment to mull over the words, then another moment to catalog my injuries. "Sure, let's go with that. A nuisance." She sips her bourbon with a side of coffee and milk. Her eyes drift closed, and she leans back in her seat, savoring the taste. "So, how much of a nuisance will he be?"

"Nothing that can't be handled." My voice is harder than I intend it to be.

"And if it comes to that?"

"What are you asking me?"

"I want to know what you are prepared to do to *'handle'* it."

"Whatever it takes, CC."

It would be a headache, and if push comes to shove, I might not be the one who deals with this. Harmless or not, Reuben is notorious for the stupid stunts he pulls, so it is only a matter of time before he pisses off the wrong person. When that happens, Daddy dearest won't be there to bail him out since he would be too busy trying to save his own skin.

"That's a non-answer, Oscar."

"What part of *'whatever it takes'* is confusing to you?" I look down at the mug in my hands, the black liquid a reflection of how I'm feeling inside. "Reuben hasn't exactly been subtle about his obsession with her. You know about it, and you aren't directly involved in her circles. She probably knows and is choosing not to deal with it for the time being. I can guarantee that her brother Marc knows and probably has a restraining order ready to go.

"So if you are asking me what I'm prepared to do, the answer is and always will be, whatever it takes. Just know that it might not come to that. She's not the only one he's doing this to. There's a growing list of people ready to take him out."

She nods, then adds, "I don't want to know about what other people would do. I want to know what *you* would do. And when you do start something with her, how do you plan on handling the inevitable blowback from your brother? And, by extension, your family."

Her question is met with silence.

This talking in circles doesn't really work for me. Clean, clear, direct, and concise questions. That's how I operate. She knows this. If she wants something from me, she needs to come right out and say it.

She clears her throat, and her dark brown eyes watch me intently. "Oscar, I asked you a question."

"And I'm waiting for you to tell me what's actually on your mind." Even better, I take a page out of her playbook. "Why were you crying?"

"I wasn't."

"Tell that to your face, CC."

She looks away, and a scowl etches onto her features. "Why did you change your door code?" she asks instead, switching gears.

"I didn't."

Her brow furrows. "Abby?"

I nod. "She changes it every time I visit the Morellis. Still, she should've sent you the new code. And stop changing the subject. Why are you really here? What's this proposition you have for me?"

Her lips press into a fine line.

A beat passes and I stand, setting my mug on the coffee table. "It's the middle of the night. Start talking, or I'm going back to bed."

She sucks in a sharp breath and turns to me, her eyes searching my face. What I see in there has me planting my tush back on the couch and picking up my mug.

"She wants to see you," CC eventually says, her voice hoarse.

I study the liquid again. "Who?"

"Who else?" I sense the eye roll coming from her. "We're having dinner at Quattro's tomorrow night. All three of us."

Ah.

Good to know my hunch earlier wasn't way off base. Still, if that's why she's in this state, then…

"Is that what you want?"

She scoffs. "She didn't exactly give me much of a choice."

"Bullshit." Our eyes meet in a mini-face-off, and then something about her earlier words hits me. "What do you mean by *'when you do start something with her?'*"

"I thought that was obvious," she says with a laugh, chewing on her bottom lip.

"What if I'm busy?" The question is pointless, yet I ask it anyway.

"You're not. Abby cleared your schedule. She also said I was to drag you there, willing or otherwise. You know," she purses her lips, "I find it awfully convenient that she also forgot to give me your new code."

Not this again. "I really wish you would stay on topic and stop reading into what Abby and I are. You already knew what my answer would be before you came here."

She grins sheepishly. "I didn't, but I hoped."

"Is that why you showed up without a bra? You don't have to fuck me into compliance."

"I plan on fucking you regardless," she quips, her grin morphing into a full-blown smile.

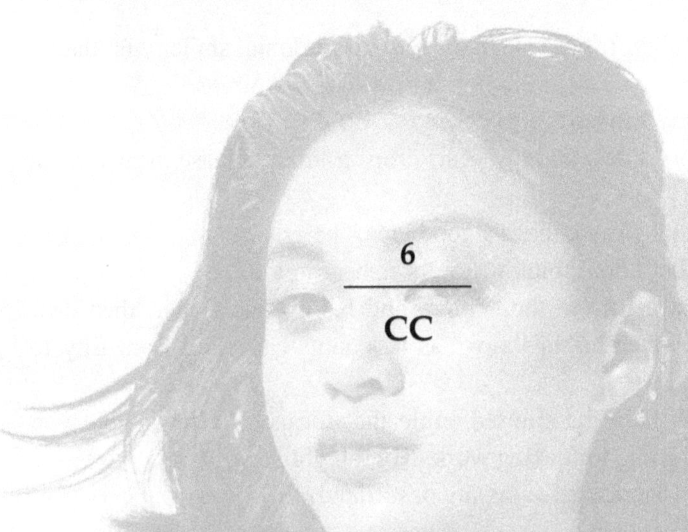

6

CC

I've been accused of being a lot of things in my life. Tactful was never one of them.

For someone like me, with the type of upbringing I've had, having freedom of speech is one thing I hold near and dear to me. Depending on who I'm with, I tend to say whatever is on my mind, consequences be damned.

That, and I think I just short-circuited my best friend's brain. I can see the color draining from his face, and I'm not the least bit apologetic about it.

Since we are on a roll here, I add, "You do know why she's asking for you, right?"

He blinks once, then twice, and then his gaze lowers to his mug. "You know, I'm sober enough to realize this isn't a typical heart-to-heart between friends, so no, I don't know why she's asking for me. Humor me and spell it out for me, why don't you?"

I reach for the teardrop necklace around my neck and wrap my fingers around it. "What do you think about becoming a throuple? With us?"

He swallows audibly, and his tongue darts across his lip. "Is that why she's asking for me?"

"She didn't say." I flash him a sardonic smile. "Is that a problem?"

His lips thin out.

A beat passes, and my heart drops a little. "Please, hear me out first."

"I'm not so sure that's a good idea," he grits.

"Oh, but I do. I think you want to hear it, too."

His gaze lifts to the ceiling, and his eyelids flutter, then drift closed. I watch his lips move as he counts backward from fifty to zero.

I can't help the amused smile that forms. "I already told you that's not going to fucking work. Not tonight."

Have I fantasized about my best friend?

Yes. Yes, I have.

He's a huge part of this game we play, Courtney and I. He has a starring role in our joint fantasies.

But that's precisely what they are. Fantasies. Not meant to take root in reality.

Yet, when life gives you lemons…

"Then I'll rephrase my question," he says, interrupting my thoughts. "Is that why she's asking for me? To ask me to be your third?"

"She really didn't say, but she didn't have to. It's… complicated." I take another sip, taking a moment to relish the satisfying afterburn.

"Complicated," he repeats, his tone flat. His head lifts and tilts slightly to the right as his eyes meet mine dead on. "You sure you want to be shit-faced for this?"

Leaning forward, I set my bourbon-laced coffee mug on the coffee table and rest both arms on my knees. "Not really."

That's the first honest thing I've said all evening.

Correction, it's the first honest thing I've said all evening *without* wrapping it up in a healthy dose of the dry sarcasm that I'm notably infamous for.

Then again, today has been a cluster fuck of mixed emotions and I don't know what to do with it.

"I'm in love with her," I eventually say.

"No shit," he mutters under his breath. "Does she know?"

I scoff. "What do you think?"

"I think you're telling the wrong person." His answer comes far too quickly for my liking.

"Yeah, well. She doesn't want to hear it."

"You'd be surprised."

Only he would use the word *surprised* to describe Courtney, even though it doesn't fit who she is. I'm aware of the simple, underlying fact that Courtney Sotelo is a woman he should have no business getting involved with.

For several reasons. Two, mostly.

One, she is the physical embodiment of everything Oscar and I have been trying to get away from, with all our side projects and philanthropic acts. But I can't seem to stay away from her, and he can't either, so that negates that point.

Then there's the matter of his half-brother, Reuben, and his obsession with her. As in, kidnap-and-murder-vibes obsessed with her. But he also has no clue *what* she really is, and he'll be in for a rude awakening when he does.

"You know that I love you too, right?" I tell Oscar.

I don't miss the sharp intake of air from him. "If this is meant to be patronizing—"

"It's not. When we first met, I didn't… I didn't think we would become what we are today. I don't have that many people in my life, like you, with whom I can be completely open and honest. I… umm… don't always tell her how I feel, but I tell you because of the promise I made to you. I told you I would never lie to you about how I felt, and I never have. I'm not about to start now."

He's quiet for some time. "You love her more."

I nod.

In hindsight, I should've eased him into that a little more. But no. Holding hands is not my style. In situations like this, it's best to come right out with it.

Especially since we both love the same woman.

Like me, it's not just physical, primal love. It's psychological.

But for someone like Oscar? He needs Courtney's brand of dominance. He's been wired that way, courtesy of Mattie Sanders's *particular* brand of training. Not having it is pure torture, so he makes up for it in other ways. He goes to great lengths to hide his sexual preferences, but it still makes him susceptible to opportunists who know just what to look for.

Opportunists like his ex, the silver-tongued bitch. It's been five years since I last saw that vile woman, and just thinking about her still leaves a sour taste in my mouth.

I shake the thought off though, since that particular stroll down memory lane isn't what I'm here for. "Courtney is who she is, and I can't change that. Nor do I want to. All I've ever wanted is for her to be happy, even if she sometimes has difficulty grasping the concept and how it applies to herself. She's surrounded by all this pain and suffering, and I only want to ease some of those burdens for her.

"But I can't do it alone. She needs more, a lot more than I can give her. She deserves much better than me, but I'm too selfish to let her go. And once she realizes that I'm no good for her, she'll break my heart and it'll hurt like hell. But you know what? She's worth it. Every moment of it. Every single part of her. The good, the bad, and the ugly. That's why I want to give her this. The best of both worlds. That's where you come in."

He and Courtney are compatible in that sense. They're soulmates, so to speak. I know I can't give him what he needs, but she can. Even if they didn't have the history they do, fate would've found a way to bring them together, and I'm the one standing in the middle of that.

It's been sixteen fucking years, and I'm still standing in the middle of that.

The problem?

I'm too selfish to let either one of them go. I don't care what anyone else says; they're both mine. After everything I've been through, I deserve a fucking happy ending.

It's either that, or I should've fucking died sixteen years ago.

He doesn't say anything to any of that, but when he eventually looks at me again, his jaw is clenched. "The point, CC. Get to it."

"I'm trying to say she likes you, Oscar."

He scoffs out his annoyance. "Courtney likes everyone."

I shake my head. "Not you, not like this."

"I don't know what that means. I don't speak cryptic."

"She tolerates a lot of people. That's not the same as liking them. It's always been different with you, and I'm not just saying that because you're… because we're…" I pause and draw in a deep breath, then choose my next words carefully. "She's different with you. Dare I say, obsessed."

"Obsessed? With me?" It's his turn to force a laugh. "Don't tell me you're still talking about that day."

"Fine, I won't tell you that. But know this. You meant the world to her back then, more than you could ever know. She's still trying to find you after all these years. Obviously, you've changed, and so has she, so the dots aren't connecting.

"Do you have any idea how frustrating it is to sit back and watch her run around in circles? I have to bite my tongue at the fact that her father constantly toys with her emotions, knowing full well that she got no closure when everyone else did."

"Oh, so it's my fault now."

"That's not what I'm saying. At all. I want her to be happy, and I want you to be happy, but there's only so much I can do. She needs this. She needs closure. You have to tell her."

"How?"

"You're a genius, figure it out."

"So are you, and it's not that simple. You said it yourself, we're not the same people we were back then. I thought she knew who I was. Don't forget, she approached me first like you did, so I assumed either she knew, or Abby ignored the gag order and told her. Once I realized she didn't, I tried to tell her. I've been trying to tell her all these years."

"Clearly not hard enough."

"What would you have me do then, huh? She ditched me, remember? She cut me off cold turkey. She picked you over me."

"It wasn't like that."

"No? Why are you telling me this? Why isn't she telling me this herself?"

"Because she knows the feeling is mutual, and that scares her. It terrifies her enough that she's…" I trail off at that, then draw in a deep breath, releasing it slowly. "I didn't come here to fight. I came to deliver a message."

He chuckles. "You sure have a strange way of showing that."

I bite back the smile that forms. "She said you were looked after. That she didn't leave you hanging, no pun intended."

He scoffs, his fists clenching at his sides. "I have no idea what that even means."

"Yes, you do. Abby takes care of you, and you know she doesn't like men. I wonder what the trade-off for that is."

"Seriously, don't start. And what am I to be? Your prop?"

A blush heats my cheeks. "Of course not."

"No? Is it that I just happen to have a penis attached? Is that it?"

"I said no, Oscar."

"From where I'm sitting, that's how it looks."

"Did it ever occur to you that it's not just about you and her? Oscar, this bond we share. At first, it was unexpected, but now I see it for what it is. It's special. It's different. It's—"

"Unique?" he offers.

"Yeah. Unique," I say with a strained laugh. "I don't want to lose you. I don't want to lose her either."

Swinging both legs off the couch and onto the plush carpet, I walk over to him and sit on his lap, straddling him. I pause to look at his chest and the discoloration scattered over his front. He winces slightly when I place both palms on the taut muscle.

"This needs to stop, Oscar."

"I was working."

I trace a finger around his pectoral muscle. "Lorenzo sent for her a few days ago."

His brow furrows at the abrupt change in subject, and his eyes remain steady on mine. "Why's that strange? He *is* her father."

"They don't have that sort of relationship. Theirs is more transactional. Kinda like you and your mom."

"How's that similar? My mother doesn't run a Mafia branch."

"Parents have secrets, Oscar. It would be naive to think you were privy to every single one of them. I would know. She normally goes on one of her trips after they meet, but this time she didn't. Something he must've said to her has thrown her off-kilter. She's been camped out on my bathroom floor instead."

"Why?"

"It calms her. I don't judge. She was mumbling Reuben's name in her sleep. Yong's name too. A lot."

His lips part to form a silent O.

"That's why she wants to see you," I finish.

There's a lot about this proposition that's a bad idea. It comes from a place of desperation, not a genuine want. But if that's what it takes to get these two back to the table, I refuse to look a gift horse in the mouth.

7

COURTNEY

As Lorenzo promised., I was delegated a worthy adversary for my next job.

This one is as scummy as they come. Paranoid too.

Sean Allen, one of Louis Pecora's men, but low-level. He claimed to know nothing about anything, as is the norm with these guys. It wasn't until I had him drugged, bound, gagged, stripped bare, and strung up from the ceiling of this butcher shop that he started singing an entirely different tune.

Not that it makes a fucking difference.

I caught a red-eye flight to Florida just for this job, as it was the golden opportunity that wouldn't come along for months. He was already tasked with transporting a package here, so I nabbed him once the exchange was complete. It's common knowledge among his crew that after each job he goes on these binges for days, sometimes even weeks.

At first, I didn't get why Lorenzo put me on his tail when he could just as easily have assigned the job to Abby or Phoenix. Until this scumbag wanted to bargain, and it all clicked. First, with the drugs he siphoned off his shipment. When that didn't work, he offered to pay me ten thousand dollars if I let him live. I took that as an insult and shoved a bile-soaked rag into his mouth.

I don't fucking bargain.

Not since *her*.

Now that I have my hands on this scumbag and the place to myself, there's no way he's getting out of this alive. No one will be looking for him anytime soon, and by the time they are clued into his disappearance, he'll be long gone.

It'll be an easy clean-up, too.

The owner of this butcher shop has a certain appreciation for the macabre, which is my specialty in my art. We have an arrangement, and she is one of my biggest clients. She also owes me several favors, ones I cash in on whenever I'm in the area by utilizing her space for special jobs like this one.

And this one's special, alright.

The sounds of his muffled screams are music to my ears as I drag the long edge of my blade into the flesh of his chest, first in the shape of a V that connects above his ribcage, then downwards to the base of his flaccid cock. I return to the intersection between the lines and start over, dragging the blade along his flesh and towards me, ever so slowly as I peel his flesh off his bones the same way a snake sheds its false skin. He's frantically squirming against his restraints as if that will help him avoid what comes next.

It won't, but I'd like to let him think that.

But it doesn't matter.

He will meet his end tonight, there's no question about it. He's seen my face, and I can't have him squealing to his buddies about who I really am. And for all the trouble he's caused, I don't plan on making this easy on him either. I'm known for playing with my prey, and I'm not in a rush to finish this.

A shadow of a smile curls my lips as I step back to admire my handiwork.

The screaming abruptly stops, like a jukebox running out of steam. Then he mumbles something else as tears stream down his blood-soaked cheeks.

"Sean, if I wanted to hear you speak I would've skipped the gag." I lean forward and run the sharp tip of my blade along his neck. My entire body buzzes with excitement at the sight of crimson that follows.

He mumbles something else, which sounds like a name I haven't heard in a while.

I yank the cloth out of his mouth, and a few of his teeth fly out. "What was that?"

"Deloise Milligan," he repeats, the words come out in a rush.

Ah.

So I hadn't misheard him.

"What about her?" And why is he so fixated on someone who died sixteen years ago?

"I have information about her death," he says. "And the people who killed her."

I roll my eyes in annoyance. Could this scumbag get any more cliché?

"If that's supposed to be your ultimate bargaining chip, think again. You get one last chance, so make it fucking count."

Confusion clouds his gaze, and he blinks several times. "I know who she was before."

"Do you now?"

He nods frantically. "Yong Chun-ja."

My heart skips a beat, and time slows.

"Huh."

"It's the only thing that makes sense."

Yes, it does.

It's too bad that'll cost him since he's not supposed to know. I know he does not work for the Network, so either he's guessing or there's a rat to be eliminated.

God, I love rats.

"Go on." I feign interest. After all, if he's going to spout more bullshit at me, the least I can do is weed through the information that could be remotely useful.

"Rumor has it, Lorenzo flew to Japan the day before her family was murdered."

This isn't news to me. I was there that day. So too were Abby, Phoenix, Mattie, Olive, and Sonya. The liberties one could take back then when chartering a private jet are amazing. Lorenzo's name was the only one listed on the flight manifest, as he couldn't exactly advertise who the rest of us were.

"Boring, Lorenzo travels a lot for business." I press the blade into his carotid artery, eliciting a pathetic whimper from him. "Try again. Last chance."

"I know who set the fire that burned down their estate," he cries out, and I ease up the pressure. "Their bodies were so badly burned that even the cops had trouble identifying who was who." He looks pleased with himself.

I don't bother hiding my yawn. "Who set the fire?" It's a pointless question. I know the answer to that, too.

He shrugs. "He's a ghost."

Well. He's partially correct. Time to switch things up.

"Pop quiz, Sean. Where were their bodies found?"

"Umm… the kitchen?"

Close. "Dining room. Don't you read? That shit was all over the news. That's what happens when you torch a fucking estate. But you're right about one thing." I lean in, pressing my lips to the shell of his ear. "The Milligans killed Deloise. Duh. Even a child could've put two and two together on that front. Let me guess, you helped? Kept proof? Perhaps a handy list of all your boss's buddies as insurance?"

His entire body goes tense.

"Where do you keep it? The hidden compartment in the sole of your right boot?" I lean back. "No? Too obvious? Let's see." I take a mental run-through of all the information we gathered on him. On paper, he has no familial attachments and is completely dedicated to Pecora. But once Abby found out he visits Louisiana at least six times a year, putting two and two together wasn't hard. "Don't tell me you hid it at your Meemaw's house."

His shoulders sag in defeat, and he starts sobbing uncontrollably.

"Dude, don't cry. It's not a good look."

Oh, who am I kidding?

I fucking love it. But since he was so forthcoming, I'm feeling slightly generous tonight.

"How about you make this easy on her, yes? Either tell me where it is, or I will burn her fucking house to the ground with her in it. You two can reminisce in hell when you see each other again."

"It's buried in the yard, under the cactus plant."

"Good boy." I pat his cheek. It's not meant to be comforting. He knows I'm taunting him on purpose. But I'm bored, so no more playing nice.

No more playing with my prey, period.

"And what, exactly, should I be looking for?"

He chooses that moment to bite his tongue again. Not even the harsh slap to his face is enough to get him to resume his incessant whining.

Suddenly, I'm not feeling so generous any longer.

"If she knows about it, about you, she dies. If she doesn't, well, she still dies. She's pushing seventy anyway, so I'd be doing the county a favor."

Still nothing.

Oh well.

Time to wrap this one up.

"Wanna know how the Milligans died?" I press down on his chin to pry his jaw open. "Like this." The tip of the blade goes in easily, slicing straight through his tongue and jaw and coming out through his chin.

His high-pitched screams bounce off the walls, filling the space. They remind me of Mr. Ultimatums, my ninth job with Mom.

That wasn't his actual name, of course.

I didn't know his name then — names weren't important to me in those days — but I remember driving Mom's switchblade through his tongue. Then I tipped his head back and watched as he drowned in his blood. I had fun with him in the meantime, of course. It takes skill, precision, and patience to skin a person while keeping them alive. It took thirty minutes for the life to drain out of his eyes, and I made sure my blood-soaked face was the last one he saw.

Just as I make sure my face is the last one this scumbag sees. I listen as the sounds die a slow, painful death on his skewed tongue. I watch as the blood drains from his naked body and pools at my feet, his body goes limp, and he passes out from the pain.

Then I take my time playing with him, like I was taught, the silence a welcome reprieve. Once I'm done carving him up, I toss the pieces into the meat grinder, do another pass-through for good measure, then wash the gunk that was once Sean Allen down the drain.

I did the same with Mr. Ultimatums years ago. He wasn't the first man I killed, but he was the reason I earned the nickname bloodthirsty killer.

Where Lorenzo thinks I have no control over my blood lust — Mom did too — I'd beg to differ. I've always kept a tight rein on it.

Except for *her*.

Yong Chun-ja.

The sole witness we left alive.

Did this scumbag think *that* bargaining chip would be useful to someone like me? A fucking weapon?

Who was he going to squeal on? Me?

I did that. I killed the Milligans.

It was sanctioned too. A warning for the others.

I scrub the place down with bleach, like I've done hundreds of times before. But, as I go through the motions, I'm reminded, once again, that nothing about this brings me peace or comfort. Instead, I lose little bits and pieces of my already corrupted soul to scumbags like this.

Then again, that's not surprising.

I am too much like my mother. Too much to want to hope for something as trivial as *peace*.

Peace is like normalcy, it's fucking overrated.

I'd much rather paint the fucking town red.

Once done, I pull out my phone and dial Abby's restricted line.

She picks up on the fifth ring. "Do you have any idea what time it is?"

"No clue. Where in the world are you?"

"South Korea."

Ah.

Well, that's unfortunate. "It's done."

"That was quick."

I spare a glance at the floor drain and the spotless room. "You know me. I'm efficient."

"And humble," she quips. "Although… you're not gloating. What's up with that?"

"Sean was low-level. A worthy adversary, but useless in the end."

"How so?"

"He wanted to bargain. First the drugs, then ten thousand dollars, then information about Deloise's killers." I list them off with my fingers. "How quickly can you get Phoenix out to Louisiana? I hate leaving behind loose ends, and she's got a date with a bonfire."

"Imagine that." Her laugh vibrates through our connection. "Did you at least get something useful out of him before you relieved him of his tongue?"

"Tongues aren't my thing," I remind her. "That's Phoenix's thing."

"Uh-huh. But you tried it anyway. I can hear it in your voice."

"It was… satisfying. Speaking of, Lorenzo gave the green light on Phoenix's thing."

"It's about damn time." There's a pause, then, "What did it cost you?"

I hoist myself up on the workbench and swing my legs off the edge of the table. "I need to cash in on a favor."

There's a brief pause on the other line. "You don't *do* favors."

"This one's pretty important. Lorenzo gave me another hint."

"Did he now?" she drawls.

"He said, and I quote, *'he's a lot closer than you think.'* And since there aren't many men close to me, that should narrow the list of possible candidates."

She goes silent.

And when that stretches on too long, I hold the phone away from my ear.

"Abby?"

"When are you going to let this one go?" she asks, her voice a little strained.

"Jesus Christ, Abby. You sound just like Mattie."

Another pregnant pause, then she blows out a breath. "That was uncalled for."

"I know. That's why I said it."

Something nags at the back of my mind. Abby is usually never this reluctant to dive into anyone's digital history, and she's worked with a lot less before. She has a knack for uncovering people's deepest, darkest secrets, including the stuff they want to keep hidden.

There's only one other person I know who enjoys this stuff as much as she does, and I can't exactly go to him. He hasn't been doing this as long as she has and is prone to mistakes. There's too much at stake here, and I can't afford to make mistakes.

Abby lets out a soft sigh. "You really need to let this one go. It's not healthy."

This? Again?

"How about we skip the morality lesson and I cash in on one of the many favors you owe me."

"No can do," she bites out. "This all started because you fucked Yong. You let your hormones get the best of you, and you fucked her. On the jet. On that nasty bathroom floor. All fucking night long. And they all heard you."

That I did, and I refuse to apologize for it.

Looking back on it, I knew it was a test.

It wasn't a moment of weakness either; it was intentional. Yong walked in on me in the bathroom, not the other way around. I tried to warn her off, but she wouldn't listen.

If Lorenzo had really wanted to, he would've put a stop to it. He knew what I was like. He knew what my routines were after every kill. I bet he watched as she walked up to the bathroom, hoping I'd defy him and finish the job.

It is what Yong wanted. It's why she called him in the first place. She didn't want to be a loose end, and he should've respected her fucking wishes from the get-go. Instead of ordering me to stand down when it came to finishing her off, just like Mom did.

Fucking soulmates, those two.

I don't know what Mom was thinking, hiding us from him back then. She should've known Lorenzo could spot me a mile away and known I was his kid. After all, she did a fantastic job molding me into her perfect mini-me, complete with the duplicity down pat.

Lorenzo, in return, got me the best teachers to fine-tune those skills. And a crew, although I prefer the term accountability killing buddies when describing Abby and Phoenix, as we're all bound by fate and shared desires. Lorenzo gives us a purpose and an outlet to exercise our demons while encouraging us always to exorcise our free will, just as long as we do so within the strict parameters he sets.

Weapons with a choice, that's what he calls our cohort.

The perfect killing yet humane machines. The perfect humane killing machines.

If there is such a thing.

That's why it makes no sense that he would punish me for something I was wired to do.

The tests. The charades. The fucking mind games.

I'm so over it.

"That has nothing to do with this," I tell Abby, who is still waiting on the other end of the line.

"*Au contraire, cela a tout à voir avec ça. Pour votre bien, laissez tomber celui-ci. Vous continuez à tirer sur ce fil et vous n'aimerez pas ce que vous trouverez à l'autre bout.*"

[*On the contrary, it has everything to do with this. For your sake, let this one go. You keep tugging on that thread, and you won't like what you find at the other end of it.*]

Oh dear.

I love the woman. I really do, but this particular trait of hers irks me to no end.

"Abby, how about you try that again? This time in fucking English."

She blows out a breath, then repeats herself.

Great.

Just fucking great.

"Just give me the fucking transcripts of our calls, okay? I know you have them."

"No can do, boss."

God, I hate that moniker… and everything else it stands for. "I'm not your boss."

"Could've fooled me. Your flight leaves in five hours. Don't miss it."

Typical.

If that's what she wants, two can play that game. "Roxane asked me again."

Another pause, this time, it's fraught and heavy with meaning. "How is she?"

"Good. No thanks to you. Did you send her to me?"

"Why would I do that?"

"You tell me. We're neighbors now, did you know that? She showed up out of the blue a few months ago and moved in next door to me."

She blows out a breath. "Yeah, I know."

"Pregnant too."

"Trust me, I know. She ran away."

"What the hell? She's your problem to handle, not mine."

"She doesn't want me to. There's this pesky little thing called boundaries, and she's exercising them."

"Well, that's just too fucking bad now, isn't it? You keep racking up all of these favors with me, but when it comes time for me to cash one out, you fucking squeal like a bitch."

Right on queue, my regular phone starts buzzing with CC's ringtone.

On the other end, Abby snickers. "You should get that, boss. Your Mistress beckons."

I won't dignify that with a response.

She's not wrong, but she's not right either.

CC isn't my Mistress since I don't do those. We don't do labels either. She's also not my girlfriend since she doesn't do those either. I wouldn't even call her my friend with benefits since we are not friends. Fuck buddies isn't the proper term for what we are either.

She's just… an enigma.

Complicated is what she is.

In many ways, I suppose that's what I am, too.

But that's about to change if CC did her job right.

"This isn't over," I tell Abby as I lift my shoulder to prop the phone against my ear, then pull the regular one out as the ringing stops.

"You don't need two phones," Abby chides. "Just put both sim cards into your secure phone, and I'll re-do the encryption. Maintaining two separate phones is a pain in the ass."

"Sure thing. Send those recordings while you are at it." I hang up before she can say something else witty.

My phone chimes with an incoming text message.

> CC: He's in.

A shadow of a smile curls my lips.

Fucking finally.

8

———

OSCAR

Have you ever done something completely out of character?

The kind of something that has you wracking your brain, trying to come up with every possible excuse under the sun to get out of it, yet you can't bring yourself to because its potential rewards far outweigh the risks?

No?

Just me?

I'm on pins and needles for the rest of the night as CC's words stay with me. Like me, she's logical and methodical, but those two things tend to fly right out the window where Courtney is concerned.

To someone like me, emotions are a liability. Love eventually becomes your kryptonite. It's not just that I'm busy and don't have time for such trivial matters. In my line of work, caring for someone that way would only give my enemies a weakness to exploit.

Especially once they discover this other side of me.

The submissive side. The side that wants to be owned and dominated by another. Preferably by two specific women.

Clearly, being the good, honorable guy all the time isn't working for me. It's doing nothing to quell my desire for them both. And maybe, just maybe, if I get drunk enough…

It probably won't make a fucking difference.

———

Twenty-four hours later, I'm singing a different tune. Maybe there is merit to the saying *'third time's the charm.'* As I grapple with my newfound existential crisis, my town car pulls into the driveway of CC's house, a stark reminder that this is fast approaching the point of no return.

On the outside, the ranch-style home is as unassuming as its owner. It's a cookie-cutter, three-bedroom, two-bathroom house that looks like every other house on the block. The only thing remotely exciting about it is its wrap-around faux brick façade.

For someone worth billions, I could never quite wrap my head around why CC chooses to live *here*, like this. It's not even a gated community. It has an HOA, but they do the bare minimum yet charge a premium. When she bought this place five years ago — a significant downgrade from her former lifestyle — she told me it was only meant to be temporary.

Yet here we are.

Apparently, the house has grown on her. It's either that, or she's silently looking for a reason to move, and I haven't given her one yet.

But *she* will, tonight.

The porch light comes on as the front door opens. I step out of the back seat of the town car to hold the door open for her, but when I turn to see her approach, my heart stops.

Or rather, it staggers, *then* stops. I swallow thickly, unable to look away. The soft glow of the porch light illuminates her features as she walks towards me, her gaze locked on mine. Then she stops before me and does a three-sixty-degree spin.

"How do I look?"

Breathtaking, I want to say, but I'm tongue-tied.

For tonight, she's donned a maroon jumpsuit that fits her like a glove and showcases her hourglass figure. The V in the neckline dips rather tastefully, and the cinched waist highlights her curves.

Her black hair is thrown into an intentionally messy low-bun. Still, somehow it works on her, bringing focus to her high cheekbones and piercing dark brown eyes.

The hair thing, though, is also a surefire way to get Courtney to say something about it. I just know it. That's yet another thing about CC that I can't wrap my head around — how she loves to get a rise out of her for the sake of doing so.

"Oscar, how do I look?" She does another spin.

I hold out a hand to her, and she steps up to me as she takes it. I lean in, brush my lips against her cheek, then press my lips to the tender skin below her ear and inhale deeply. Her citrus scent floods my senses, a hint of saccharine sweetness peeking through.

"Truth?" I whisper against her skin.

Her pulse goes erratic against my lips. "I'd expect nothing less," she breathes.

"Jealous as fuck. You never get this dressed up for me."

She pushes against my chest. "You got me this, Oscar. I just never had an occasion to wear it."

Then she steps around me and glides into the car with the grace of a gazelle, and I follow suit. Once inside, I press the intercom button built into my armrest and give my driver our destination.

"Quattro's, please. We have thirty minutes to spare, so take the scenic route."

He nods in acknowledgment, and we're on our way a moment later.

Leaning back in my seat, I close my eyes and let out a resigned sigh. When I open them again, it is to find CC's gaze on mine.

"Thank you for doing this. Again."

I give her a tight smile in response. I would answer her and offer something that shows my acquiescence, but words escape me. As they should.

This is going to be one long night. It'll be painful or pleasurable, depending on how this goes.

"Why the scenic route?" she asks. I try not to think that she picked the seat across from mine, instead of the one next to me like she usually does.

"I want to pretend I have you all to myself for the next thirty minutes."

Her lips part, then come together as she swallows. She reaches for the teardrop necklace around her neck and wraps her fingers around it, the expression on her face unreadable.

A minute passes before she switches seats, taking her usual position at my side. "You'd like a sure thing, and this arrangement will be anything but."

"No shit." I can't keep the bitterness out of my tone.

She reaches for my hand and laces our fingers together. "Still, I'd like to explore what this could be, and I'd rather do this with you and her."

"I know. You said that already."

She kisses my cheek, then uses her free thumb to swipe away the lip gloss she leaves behind before resting her head on my shoulder. As I study our fingers, I can't help but wonder why this can't be enough.

Then again, it's not like she's forcing me to be here. She'd said it'd just be one meeting. A re-do meeting. Had it been anyone else, I would've said no. I wouldn't have thought twice about it, but I find myself questioning everything where she's concerned.

CC and I have been best friends for a long time. We first met in our final year of college and have been inseparable since. So when she asks me to come, I do. It really is as simple as that.

It's also something no one would expect of me.

As much as I want to think of this as business as usual, it is anything but. Still, the nerves don't set in until the town car pulls up in front of Quattro.

"Courtney will be here in fifteen," CC says as I help her out of the back seat of the car. "Something came up with..." She trails off at that, the name lingering at the tip of her tongue.

"You can say his name," I say as I loop my arm in hers.

Her cheeks pinken, and for a split second I envision her sexy ass naked and underneath me, that flushed color all over her body. The pressure of my cock stiffening in my pants snaps me out of my daydream.

Not appropriate, I chide myself, squeezing my eyes shut to erase the image, willing the eager fucker to calm down. It doesn't help. The image of her is quickly replaced by another, transporting me to a place I don't want to go and things I don't dare to dream of.

"I'm sorry," she says, her voice soft. "I didn't think… I thought you…"

"It's fine. Let's get through the night first, then we'll…"

This time it's my turn to leave things dangling; the unspoken words hang heavy in the space between us.

The sound of someone obnoxiously blaring their car horn gets us to move, but not before CC flips them the bird. Not that I'd expect anything less from her. Where I have a vested interest in keeping a pristine image, she doesn't. One of many reasons why we're friends.

Like the gentleman I am, I escort her into the restaurant. The hostess greets us with a sultry smile, her gaze lingering on CC's cleavage.

It's not the first time it's happened, either. She loves showing them off, relishing the attention they bring her, wanted or unwanted. She also says it's the best eight thousand dollars she's ever spent. I know she didn't get those for vanity, or she would have gone with size D instead of her modest Bs.

Once she's done ogling my best friend, the hostess shows us to our reserved table. It is up in the loft space, one of the few that overlooks the rest of the restaurant. From up here, we should be able to see when Courtney arrives. Likewise, anyone below would see us enjoying dinner — which is what she wanted — but few would be able to listen in on the details of our conversation.

If there's one thing I absolutely detest, it's busybodies sticking their noses in where they don't belong.

Our waiter materializes with a bottle of La Rioja Alta and lets us know it was ordered beforehand. He pours us two glasses, then leaves as quickly as he arrived. CC doesn't appear to be fazed by this. She just shrugs and takes a sip of her wine.

We make small talk, mostly about her work. She works in a lab, which should be one of the most drama-free places to work, but that would be an incorrect assumption. It's all lighthearted fun too, something she never had much of growing up, so I'm glad she has more of that in her life now.

"I still can't wrap my head around how he even got hired in the first place," she says about the newest addition to their team. "Devin is cute and all, but he can't tell the difference between a Volumetric flask and an Erlenmeyer flask. Or a screw clamp and a utility clamp!"

"To be fair, the average person can't."

"That may be true, but for someone who supposedly went to Harvard? I call bullshit on that. His credentials don't even make sense. It's as if someone just threw together whatever they thought would look cool on a résumé, then strong-armed Delilah into hiring him."

"Or he could be some sort of plant?" I offer.

She mulls this over for a second. "Nah, I don't think that's it. I think she keeps him around for comedic relief. Or she knows something I don't."

"Like?"

"Beats me." She shrugs. "His presence bothers Harris, that I know. He's been coming around more because of him. I'm not opposed to more eye candy, and Harris is easy on the eyes."

"Is he now?" A pang of jealousy hits me, and I brush it aside. Harris is very much taken, as I'm well aware.

I glance downwards at the sitting area below us, only to realize that most tables have been cleared out. A group of four is seated at the center of the room, just underneath the chandelier. Another couple is in the corner, talking in hushed tones. Two waitresses approach both tables with black check holders in hand.

"Still, Devin could have Googled it, you know?" CC continues, seemingly oblivious to the almost empty restaurant. "In the spirit of 'fake it till you make it.' Or he could've used the fucking manuals posted all around the lab. But no, he's not even trying to hide his woeful lack of knowledge—"

The doors to the main entrance open behind me, interrupting our conversation. CC looks over my shoulder and her face instantly lights up. It could only mean one thing — the third member of our party is here.

Courtney Sotelo.

Another pang of jealousy hits me, but I push it back down. The doors close, and then everything goes quiet. This time I turn to look, and like metal pulled to a magnet, I can't bring myself to turn away. I stare in awe as she struts across the room, as the distinctive click of her heels on the tile floor fills the silence, growing louder by the second as she approaches.

This is the second time I've seen her like this — dressed to impress us. The dress she's wearing — an A-line dress with a plunging neckline that matches CC's — highlights every single one of her curves. Her shoulder-length hair is swept up, leaving tendrils that frame her oval face. As always, my fingers twitch with the desire to wrap those luscious curls around them and pull hard.

In other words, she's a thing of beauty. Her beauty is the kind that renders you speechless and leaves you captivated and tongue-tied.

Then, of course, she's in her signature purple.

Dressed to impress. Or rather, dressed to command.

Make no mistake, that's what will happen here. It's the only way this night will end.

Or I'll get my heart broken for a third time.

9

OSCAR

Courtney places a hand on my shoulder, so I have no other choice but to rise and face her. Instead of going in for a hug — something I would typically do with CC — I hold out a hand to her instead. Caught off guard by the gesture, her mask slips for a second, but she quickly recovers as I bring her hand to my lips.

"Oscar," she says, her raspy voice sending a shiver down my spine. "I'm so glad you could make it."

My spine straightens. "I wouldn't miss it for the world."

CC's lips quirk as she watches us. "See? You're getting along already."

"Oh, the night is still young," I quip as I hold out Courtney's seat for her, pushing it in before taking mine across from her.

CC lets out an exasperated sigh. "How about we get a few drinks in first, then you two can go at it all you want." She downs the contents of her glass in one gulp.

Our waiter materializes again, long enough to refill CC's wine glass and pour one for Courtney before disappearing. I look in time to watch as the final couple is ushered out of the restaurant, giving us the whole place.

All two thousand square feet of Quattro's.

I'm all for privacy, but this is too much. So unlike CC, I will be saying something about this instead of letting it slide.

I don't get the chance to, not right away, as Courtney turns her attention to CC. "Stand. Let me see you."

A deep flush starts in her cleavage and rolls up her neck. Still, she does as she's told and stands, before doing a 360 degree spin as she did for me earlier.

There's a reason why strip poker is her favorite game to play. We've known each other since college, and in that time she's changed nearly everything about her physical appearance, and not for vanity purposes either.

She has a lot of secrets, CC does. But don't we all?

CC has always been the type to strive for a beauty that is understated yet impossible to look away from. After copious amounts of self-work and altering nearly every physical aspect of her body, she now exudes the kind of rare innocence that still looks exceptionally sensual.

"Ravishing," Courtney says as she looks her up and down before turning to me, an appreciative glint in her eyes. "You picked well, Oscar. As always, you have excellent taste."

My cheeks grow warmer by the second. *Did she just pay me a fucking compliment?*

"I like to dress beautiful things," I tell her, as it is the best I can come up with.

"Beautiful things, huh?" She quirks an eyebrow. "Obviously, you have an eye for fashion and an intimate appreciation for the female form. Why downplay your talent?"

My heart hammers in my chest, and I force myself to swallow as I struggle to come up with something witty. Instead, I'm coming up empty.

"As much as I love this ensemble," she continues, her gaze searing through mine, "what's with the hair?"

"What about it?" CC asks.

"It doesn't fit. Lose the gaudy hair tie." There's a bite to Courtney's tone, and I know better than to get in the middle of whatever this is.

CC makes a tsk-tsk noise, her hand going to her nape. "Not a chance."

"You have sixty seconds to lose the tie or get the paddle tonight. It won't be where you want it, and that's a promise." Then she waits patiently for CC to comply, tongue poking out to moisten her lips as her stormy gray eyes follow her every movement.

CC does as she's told and pulls out her hair band, then runs her fingers through the modest waves in her thick dark hair. "Better?"

"Much."

I shake my head. I'll never understand them. Their dynamic.

It's… odd, yet it's home. They are home to me. This dynamic, it's theirs, but it's also mine. This is a first for me.

I'm used to rejection. I'm used to being hated and being used. I'm used to existing for the convenience of others. After a lifetime of being hated, forgotten, and alone, this is a refreshing change of pace and I want it, badly.

I want to be chosen by her. To be kept by her, whatever her twisted sense of that may mean.

I want to be wanted, and I want her to want me.

But I can't get my hopes up.

Not with this. Not again.

I settle back against my seat before turning my attention to Courtney. "I take it the empty restaurant is your doing?"

Courtney takes a sip of her water. "It is."

"Why?"

CC places a hand on my arm. "Oscar. Seriously. Don't start."

"It's all right, CC. I can understand his apprehension." Courtney turns to me before continuing, "I reserved the entire restaurant for the night. After all, we do have a lot to talk about, and I'd hate for us to be rudely interrupted or end up on the front pages of the *Star Tribune*. But don't worry. All guest meals have been paid for. The entire staff will be generously compensated for top-tier service and their discretion."

This isn't about me. I repeat the lie to myself for the umpteenth time. It's about what CC wants, something I'm powerless to say no to. Still, it isn't enough for me to leave well enough alone.

I wave her off. "That's just logistics, Courtney. Last I checked, you don't exactly care what others think of you, so everything you pointed out is inconsequential. So I'll ask again. Why?"

Courtney folds her arms, and the action highlights her chest all too enticingly. "Is it so wrong of me to want to wine and dine you both? To make up for how badly things went the last time we did this?"

"Don't you mean *tried* to do this?"

She purses her lips. "I see we've picked up some bratty skills, haven't we?"

The urge to comply surges, but I tamp down on it. A bitter laugh erupts, masking my discomfort. "Since we haven't established any ground rules yet, I'm allowed to speak freely, right? Or did that change?"

"Of course not," she says, studying me so intensely that my face grows warm. "Speak your mind."

"If I recall correctly, the last time we tried to do this, you dropped a pretty huge bomb on us, then waltzed out of here as if nothing happened."

Her lips thin out, and a small crease forms between her brows.

"CC was crushed. She cried for weeks." Why can't I leave well enough alone?

"And you?"

I'd be lying if I said I wasn't unnerved by how casually she threw that in there. Still, my answer to her question comes all too easily.

"Same." I pause for a beat, wondering for the briefest of moments just how honest I should be about this before deciding, eh, fuck it. "You know what? I wasn't just crushed, Courtney. I was devastated. But that shouldn't come as a surprise to you. Nor do I expect you to fucking care. It's what you do. You just do what you want, with no regard for how anyone else feels."

For a second time in one night, Courtney's mask slips as she looks caught off guard by my answer. Her lips part to answer and she hesitates, tipping her head to the side as she studies me.

As for me? I don't know why I'm dredging this up.

Or even being so brutally honest about it.

CC and I, we have a good thing together. For the longest time, she's been my ride-or-die and I don't see that changing anytime soon. Granted, we've never been exclusive per se, but that has never mattered for either of us. What we have and share is solid enough to withstand just about anything.

Yet I know that I will never be enough for her. She's always wanted more, and I've never been one to impose limits on our time together. I've never had to, as we always found our way back to each other.

Or we did, but *she*'s been indirectly in the picture.

Hence this.

Desperate times. Or right time, wrong circumstances.

Then again, there's a special place in hell for people like me.

"Do you want to be here?" Courtney eventually asks, but her voice is flat.

A thick current buzzes between us.

"You didn't give me much of a choice. You knew I couldn't say no to CC, so you took the cowardly way out and had her ask." Squaring my shoulders, I lean forward in my seat, and my gaze levels with hers. "That said, you wanna know what hurts the most? You iced me out before even getting to know me. You went back to CC, yet you never gave me a second thought for two years. Was I not good enough for you?"

It is good that we have the place to ourselves, as anyone listening in could get the wrong idea about this, that I'm still bitter about how things ended between us the last time. How can I when they never even started?

Our waiter chose that moment to bring out our appetizers, which were also ordered beforehand. Courtney's doing, no doubt. She loves to control things. People too. She can't turn off the sadist in her, but she can mask it pretty well. I believe she has to in order to maintain the naive tomboy persona she presents to her family. But with us — with CC, at least — it is in full force. Although, like everything else she's said and done so far, she's conveniently avoided giving me a direct answer to *why*.

Why now? Why here?

Courtney waits until our waiter leaves before pulling out a gray jewelry box from her clutch and sliding it in my direction.

"I was under the impression we were going to wait until *after* dinner to do this," CC tells her.

Her words barely register as I stare at the inanimate object before me. It looks… familiar, yet I can't place it. Reaching for it, I snap open its lid to find a thin black leather collar with a teardrop identical to that on CC's necklace.

"Property of CBS," I mutter, reading the words engraved on the inside lid of the box.

My lips part on a sharp exhale as its meaning sinks in.

Property of Courtney Bardales Sotelo.

It's a trick, my mind warns, cautioning against the hope that surges deep within me.

Courtney waits for my gaze to meet hers before speaking. "I've carried that with me since that day. It's yours if you want it. That is, if you still want what was going to be our original arrangement."

"I sense a *but* somewhere in there."

She reaches out to lay her hand on mine. "But, as I told CC, that arrangement is not what I want. Not anymore."

My heart plummets to my stomach, and I snap the box closed. The anger burning low in the back of my mind flares up.

"You're disappointed," she says.

I don't even know what annoys me more. How nonchalant her tone of voice is, like she truly doesn't give a fuck about hurting my feelings. Or that I see we are headed down the same path as the last time — something I predicted but dared to hope would turn out differently — and yet I am powerless to stop this inevitable train wreck.

"Gee, how can you tell?" I drawl sarcastically.

She chuckles lightly. "Where CC is concerned, everything you feel is written on your face. I've always liked that about you."

Great.

Just fucking fantastic.

And since it's pointless schooling my features, I grit my teeth instead. "The point, Courtney. Get to it."

The humor falls off her face, leaving something else in its place. Something that makes her seem more vulnerable, more approachable. Nothing could've prepared me for the words that came out of her mouth next.

"I have no interest in owning you, Oscar. I have no interest in owning either of you." Her gaze moves to CC before returning to me. "I want more out of this. I need more."

My breath hitches. I blink once, then twice. "What are you saying?"

"I don't want to be a Domme anymore."

That, I wasn't expecting. "Why the fuck not?" I blurt out.

She gives me a noncommittal shrug. "Two things. I learned how to be one for all the wrong reasons, and I don't want to do that anymore."

Then she leaves it at that.

She fucking leaves it at that.

A beat passes, then I ask, "And the other reason?"

Her expression softens as she searches my eyes. "*That* is a much longer conversation, and this isn't the place for it."

Of course it isn't.

I'm not sure what I expected to come from this dinner date. If I can even call it a date.

I chance a panicked glance at CC, but it's not me she's looking at. As always, her gaze is firmly glued to Courtney, with that familiar starry-eyed look in her eyes.

Their relationship is… complicated, for lack of a better word, but it is solid. As someone who has been a part of it from the start — looking in from the outside — this is them. CC worships the ground Courtney walks on, and from what I can tell, Courtney eats up that mindless adoration.

This is the preview they are both showing me. It will always be me, on the outside, looking in.

Oscar Hyun, the rejected man and child.

It's the story of my fucking life.

Except… as CC's eyes are glued to Courtney's profile, Courtney's are on me… and I'm not sure how I feel about this change in their dynamic. I'm not sure how I'm *supposed* to feel about it.

Happy? Relieved?

Terrified?

"Why did you ask me here?" I ask when the silence stretches on for too long.

She holds my gaze for a beat before answering. "I want more out of this life."

"Don't we all?" I say with a laugh. I look down at Courtney's hand on mine, count from zero to twenty, then backward, before meeting her eyes. The expression on her face is… strange, as she watches my lips, but I brush that aside. "If you can't give me the one thing I want, then what am I even doing here?"

This further proves her point that I am exhibiting unusually high levels of bratty behavior. I should tamp it down, I know this, but I can't. Not when we are on an honesty streak.

Or at least, I am.

I still don't know what kind of streak Courtney is on.

"I want a relationship," she says softly, then gently squeezes my hand before adding, "with both of you."

I blink once, then twice.

Never mind that.

My heart hammers in my chest, and my mouth opens and closes a few times. I turn to CC for clarification, only to find she's frozen with her water glass halfway to her mouth. The expression on her face mirrors my own — slack-jawed and wide-eyed — which tells me this is news to her as well. At least the starry-eyed look of worship is gone. That's… progress, I think?

"You want a relationship," I deadpan, finding my voice.

"That's what I said."

I meet Courtney's eyes before adding, "With CC and me."

Her lip twitches. "Are you planning on repeating everything I say? I know you heard me loud and clear. CC, not so much. Her brain's a little shattered, but she'll catch up."

Catch up?

I'm not sure I understand what's happening here.

Did I get transported into some alternate universe?

"Are you toying with me?" I ask dryly.

"I don't do that." Her answer comes too quickly for my liking, even as her lips purse in distaste. "I don't toy. It's juvenile."

"Juvenile?" I release an exasperated breath, then, against my better judgment, I say, "Let's say I believe you. What kind of relationship?"

"One of equals."

Yeah… I don't see that happening here. She can't say that in her commanding voice and expect me to believe the words coming out of her mouth.

That's just not who she is. That's not who I am either.

I resist the urge to do something else stupid. Like standing and walking out of here. Screw 'third time's the charm' or whatever inspirational bullshit CC feels like spewing, I'm not doing this again.

"…last time too," she is saying, to which I was only half-listening. "But I'm not going to force you, Oscar. That's not what this dinner is about. Truth be told, I'm not expecting an answer tonight. I'd prefer it if you gave this serious thought before giving me your answer. And whatever it is — be it a yes, or a shove it up your ass — I will respect it. Even if I don't like it."

Her words are sincere, but something about this seems… off.

The next sentence pops out before I can think the words through, which is almost always a mistake and never a good sign for me.

"What's in it for you?"

10

COURTNEY

I forgot how exhausting dating can be.

In some ways, the process reminds me of the Serenity prayer. It reminds me of the things we don't want to happen, yet we have no choice but to accept them. It reminds me of the things we don't want to know or understand, yet we have no choice but to learn. And the people we cannot live without but must learn how to let them go.

I detest that prayer. I loathe everything about it.

I also never imagined this would be a walk in the park, but this?

This is pushing it. It's forcing him to his limit.

Those eyes of his, they burn with an intensity I've seen before. An intensity that doesn't usually mean anything good.

I should squash it. That intensity. The defiance in his posture, in his body language. Lord knows I'm dying to crush it.

I want his total submission. I don't *just* want it, I fucking crave it.

"Not everything I do has ulterior motives," I tell him.

His brow scrunches in confusion. "Now I know you're messing with me, and I hate that."

"I told you I don't fuck around," I say instead.

What I *do* want, though, is to possess that secret side to him that he's been hiding all these years. A side he seems to have mastered all too well, hence the lip. Yet his body language tells me he's barely holding himself together, and that gives me some semblance of comfort.

Oscar shakes his head. "I don't buy that, Courtney. I didn't come here for you to be nice to me, and I'm not leaving until I get a straight answer from you."

Is it cliché to say I like this bratty side to him?

Absolutely.

I always have, and I always will. Sure, CC has her bratty moments, but she's a lot more compliant. Oscar, not so much. I like it, probably a lot more than I care to admit.

I like it so much that I'm even willing to consider doing this dance permanently, the give and take that goes into dating. It's been so long since I last did it that I barely remember how these things are supposed to go, much less end. My idea of a *dinner date* ends with my fingers drenched in some asshole's entrails.

On the other hand, this is CC's idea. She says tonight is supposed to be about normalcy, like regular people would do when courting. And since I plan on further cementing myself as normal — a certified sadist — I would do well to follow her lead, especially where Oscar is concerned.

So I tamp down on the urge to squash that defiance because, as I said, I don't want to live like that anymore.

Still, there's something about Oscar that calls to me. Something I can't quite put a finger on.

It's not the energy that constantly buzzes between us — I've felt it since the day we met and I've become quite adept at ignoring it. My eyes trace his thick, muscled forearms before returning to his flushed face. Now that's cute, and it speaks of the growing arousal he's trying so hard to hide but failing miserably at.

No, this thing is something else. A heady mix of something deeper and primal, both things I cannot, for the life of me, shake off.

I don't believe in soulmates, but if I did, I'd say this was it. By definition, soulmates means two people, yet I've felt this with four different people. Two of whom are sitting at this table. I still have no fucking clue who the third is. The fourth is long dead, and it was my fault.

Some people are worth more alive than dead; Lorenzo's words echo loud and clear.

Shaking off the thought, I continue, "What do you want to know?"

"What's in it for you?" he repeats, though the obvious unspoken questions still linger between us.

Why now? Why here? What changed?

Everything, I want to say.

But I say something else. "If you're asking what's in it for me, I think the answer is obvious." I allow myself to stare unabashedly at him. Tall, muscular, and lethally handsome, a man like Oscar Hyun is dangerous, not just for who he is but for how he makes me feel. For the emotions he elicits in me. It is a constant tug of war, the desire to take care of him, to cherish him, to protect him.

And also to hurt him. To break him, mold him, just like I was taught.

I wonder which of those two equally powerful but polarizingly opposite emotions will eventually win. It is the ultimate test of my ever-fraying patience.

"I told you, I want all of you, not just your body. And if I have to choose between being your Domme and your partner, I choose the latter. That way, we all get what we want, with the added security of permanence."

"What about Charlie?" he immediately asks.

Now, I really wish this was about hurting him because no one, *no one*, brings him up in a context like this. Not even CC.

Still, I consider his question for a moment since I owe him that much, before posing one of my own. "What about him?"

He quirks an eyebrow. "Is that a serious question?"

"Do I look like I'm joking?"

"No, I don't think you are. And if I'm being honest, that scares me more than... whatever this is. How is it so easy for you to dismiss what he means? How you..." he trails off at that, confusion etched onto his features.

He deserves answers from me, I know this. It's not his fault I broke things off with him the last time. He should hate me for it, but that's not the emotion I'm getting from him.

It's more… pity. I don't want that from him.

"For what it's worth, Charlie isn't going to be your concern," I say instead.

I watch as the look of pity morphs into pain, and dread settles low in my stomach.

"He's your son," he forces out.

"I know. I was there when they sliced open several layers of skin and yanked him out of me. That doesn't make him your concern. Last I checked, neither of you wants children," I say, my gaze sliding to CC's momentarily before returning to his. "I can't imagine that's changed in the last few years."

His Adam's apple bobs. "That doesn't mean…"

"You said you want answers, and I'm giving them to you. I'm being honest, not wrapping things up in fluff. Charlie is a job, Oscar. An occupational hazard, that's all."

Oscar's mouth falls open. I don't have to look to know CC has a panicked look plastered all over her. The emotions of these two bleed off each other, just like another pair I know.

Then again, I sure know how to pick 'em.

Story of my life.

"I offended you."

"No, you didn't."

"You wear your emotions on your face," I power on, not in the least enjoying this power I seem to hold over him. Over either of them, actually. "I think… I can understand why you'd feel that way, and if I had a conscience then I'd feel guilty about this, but I don't. I know what I am. I also know I'll be poison for him should I keep him by my side twenty-four-seven. It's true that I never planned on having children, but that doesn't mean I'll turn my back on him. He's innocent in all this. The best I can do is ensure he's taken care of. Marc gives that to him."

As I said, there is a special fucking place in hell for people like me.

The ones who dive head-first into things like this.

No risk, no reward.

CC places her hand on mine, squeezing gently. "That's enough," she says quietly.

Oh, but we are so far from what should be considered *enough* or *not enough* that it's comical.

"It's okay," Oscar says, resignation laced in his tone. "I needed to hear that, I guess."

In my periphery, I see CC shake her head.

"That's not true. That's not what happened then. Why are you doing this? Tell him, Courtney. Tell him the truth."

I know what she's asking of me. Still, I don't answer her right away, opting instead to study our hands stacked on each other, of how much of a stark contrast my tan skin tone is sandwiched between them. Of the shared pain, with just the right amount of the heady mix of excitement that buzzes between us.

"I take it you know of Marc, my brother," I eventually say.

He nods. She does too.

"He and I live as we do because of a deal Marc made with our dad long ago. It was unconventional, but Lorenzo's word is his bond, and everyone knows that. Some entitled prick decided he wanted me for a wife, so he and his father are trying to force Lorenzo's hand. Let's face it, Courtney Morelli has a distasteful ring to it. Given the choice, I'd rather go back to being a Bardales."

As I talk, Oscar looks like he's going to throw up. His face goes pale, and his lips twist into a grimace. For a split second, he turns that panicked gaze in CC's direction, and then it's as if he remembers I'm still in the room and schools his features.

And, for some reason, that bothers me.

I don't care that he's an open book with CC, but it troubles me that he doesn't see me that way.

You made him this way, remember?

I draw in a deep, shuddering breath, releasing it slowly. I need to focus on this. Bonding shit can come later.

I meant what I said to Lorenzo. Reuben doesn't want a wife. Nor is he looking for some clueless, docile, and submissive woman who knows her place, since he's got plenty of those already. What he wants is a pet, and he thinks he can get that out of me.

If he knew what I was capable of, he would think twice about it. Hell, if he knew what Marc was capable of, the lengths he would go to to protect me from the likes of him, then he would reconsider his lame attempts at reaching for the things he can't attain and focus instead on what he can — living a comfortable enough life with the billions Olive Hyun wrapped around his neck like a suffocating noose.

"Gerald knows of Marc's deal with Lorenzo," I continue. "He was there when the bargain was struck. I know for a fact that Reuben knows. Being sleazy bastards, they're going behind Marc's back on this, even resorting to blackmail. And worse." I pin him with a pointed glare. "You know what I really fucking hate?"

"What?" he whispers.

"People touching my things. People hurting my things." The iciness glides into my tone effortlessly. "Those monthly blind dates you keep going on, those end now."

He mirrors my stance and leans back in his seat, his eyes never leaving me. "So you knew about those."

I resist the eye roll. "I didn't abandon you, Oscar. I left you a gift."

I watch as realization dawns, and his countenance shifts slightly. "Abby."

I nod but don't elaborate. I don't have to either.

Like me, he's known her for a long time. So he knows that intercourse with men is not her thing. It's not like I'd expected her to fuck him either. It just so happens that she and I are alike in so many other ways. After all, we were trained by the same person, though not as a pair.

Roxane was hers. Mine still remains elusive to me.

Abby has always known who he is, yet it's been fifteen years since we graduated, and she still won't tell me his name. None of them would, all because of some stupid gag order that Lorenzo placed on everyone.

I'm still waiting on those recordings that Abby was supposed to send me twenty-four hours ago. She can whine all she wants, but she *will* send them. I'm nothing if not patient, and she owes me a shit ton of favors — including the one that moved in next door to me.

After all, some people are worth more alive than dead.

"Then you know," he cuts through my reverie. "You know why I go, why I *have* to go."

"You want me to hurt you? Is that it?"

"If I said yes, would you do it?"

"I would. It's not what I want, and I'd hate every second of it. Still, I'd do it. For you."

"Who cares what you want? It's not like you care what others want."

His words shouldn't sting as hard as they do. Yet the sting is something I relish. He's not wrong, though. I should care what others want, but for the most part, I don't. On the rare occasion I do, with the few people I trust, the only one who gets hurt is me.

I don't mind it as much. If he wants me to hurt him, then I will. I just have to figure out a way not to kill him. Been there, done that, hadn't planned on doing it again. It'd be a risk, but even I know that without it, there'll be no reward.

"Oscar, that's enough," CC speaks up, but he ignores her.

"I'm not saying no," he says. "But I'm not saying yes either."

I can't help the frown that forms at that. "I don't understand." I really don't.

"I'm here, just like you wanted. You knew I'd come, and I did, just like you wanted. That doesn't mean I have to agree to everything you're asking of me. Demanding of me, really."

"Demanding? Christ, Oscar. What part of *'I'm not going to force you'* didn't you get?"

"All of it. Can you blame me? You said the same thing last time too. And the time before that. And you know what? Unlike CC, I don't have time to be at your beck and call. I'm a busy man, as you very well know. My time is money. An hour of my time is worth upwards of four figures, yet here the fuck I am."

"You wanna make this transactional? Fine. I'll pay you for your time."

"Courtney!" CC starts to say, but he cuts her off.

"I don't want your money," he says. "I want a test run."

"A test run?" I take a deep breath, trying to steady my racing heart.

"I don't care if you do it within the parameters of our original deal or whatever this new deal is you are proposing, just as long as you give me one night."

I'd be lying if I said I wasn't getting a strong sense of déjà vu. "Why just one night? Why not a week? Or even a month?"

He shrugs. "What's the point in dragging things out any further? I'm done with this. I'm done with this stupid ache that won't go away. Since you really want to do this, then let's do it. Tonight." He pauses at that, the wheels turning. "Yes, tonight. If I'm going to… if we're going to do this, or even to make this work, then we need to be completely honest with each other. That means laying bare all that I wish to remain hidden. Once you know the truth, you're going to ditch me anyway. That way, I can walk away from you with no regrets."

My chest squeezes at that. Sure, I walked away from him before, but the thought of him reciprocating paralyzes me. "Oscar…"

"Those are my terms. Take it or leave it."

11

COURTNEY

I don't do too well with ultimatums.

Scratch that. I don't like being told what to do, period.

The first person who *tried* to issue me one — besides Mom and Marc — had his tongue skewered for his troubles. The bastard didn't make it, and I can't say I was all that torn up about it. He was scum and deserved everything he got.

Then there was Mr. Ultimatums, but… well, you know how that ended.

But when Oscar issues one, it's damn near impossible to say no.

I don't mind it though. Our paths were always meant to converge. Lorenzo's advice about picking one of each like Marc did, merely sped up the inevitable.

I'm not known for my patience when it comes to 'relationships.' I'm more of a react first, think later sort of girl. I'm well aware that I'm very likely to repeat the same pattern with this, but I truly don't give a shit.

Not when I have him here, right where I want him.

Sort of.

I think.

"Just so you know, the last time we tried to do this, it wasn't a fluke."

Oscar lifts a curious brow. "A fluke? Is that what we're going with?"

I draw in a sharp breath. He pulls his hand out from underneath mine and his spine straightens, both hands dropping to his thighs, palms up.

Seeing him like this, I'm instantly transported to a time I'd rather not be in, to a place I wish I could permanently purge from my memory — not for what it was, but for whom I left behind.

The memories of *him* slam into me like a freight train. I'm reminded of that infectious spirit that was him, of how infused his energy was in every aspect of his being, and how that bled onto everything he touched. Of how he made me feel things I didn't want to feel, to want things I didn't wish to possess.

Of all the things I did to break him, to break that spirit, to mold him into my own perfect little fuck toy — all from the comfort of my lavish bedroom across the fucking country.

Sure, he was a voice on the other end of the phone, but I knew exactly what I was doing to him. That was the point of the fucking training program.

I was the sadist, and he was my prey.

Training partner.

What-the fuck-ever.

I wish we had broken the rules, just once, and exchanged names. Fuck, I wish I could've kept him. I wanted to keep him, but according to Lorenzo, that was against the rules.

Hence the gag order.

It was my only confirmation that he was still alive when I graduated from the program. As far as I know, he was still in one piece, in body but not necessarily in spirit.

Like *her*.

"Please don't do that," I say, sounding far more hoarse than intended.

"Do what?" His gaze drifts down to his lap. A beat passes, and he relaxes his posture but keeps his gaze downcast. "Habit, I guess."

Habit or not, that was a test, one he failed. If push came to shove, I'd fail that test too. Just as I failed *him*.

And now, Oscar.

I have to get it right with him this time. Otherwise, I risk losing not only him, but CC too. Permanently. I don't think I can handle that. I'm not equipped to navigate life without either, and I'm not ashamed to admit that.

So I push the negative thoughts aside and power on. "What happens after tonight?"

He fidgets with his hands in his lap. "You'll have your answer."

This is easy. Far too easy.

Suspiciously easy.

I remember how much coaxing it took for Delilah to accept her feelings for Marc and Harris — fifteen years, to be exact — and thankfully, she didn't need that long to decide to move in with them. Granted, I was the one who cautioned Marc to be patient with her, but that doesn't mean I will be taking my own advice.

Most days, I find it hard to believe or even reconcile those things. And while I know that Delilah and Oscar are two different people, the circumstances are similar enough that I expect some reciprocity.

But no.

That's not what I'm getting here. Nor is it the vibes I'm getting from him. At all.

"Please tell me you two are done with the pissing contest," CC eventually speaks up, the corners of her eyes crinkling with a smile.

He doesn't answer her. Instead, he reaches for the box, pulls out his collar, and snaps it onto his neck. He turns to her, giving her a lop-sided grin that sends a hot flush crawling over my skin. "I'm done now."

"Good, 'cause I'm fucking starving."

"Food is the last thing on my mind."

Her grin matches his.

You'd think they rehearsed this, the way they both turn to face me. "What now, Mistress?"

Fuck, if that doesn't make my heart swell up with emotion.

It's not a title I ever wanted to be addressed by, yet hearing how naturally the word falls from their lips, it wraps around me like warm honey.

Not the kind I want to savor for the delectable edible it is, but the kind I want to hurt. Destroy.

See, I'm not like the others, the other two weapons. Where they want to preserve the beauty and innocence in this world, I seek to destroy it.

It doesn't matter that I do not have a medical school background like CC does. I've spent my entire life perfecting my intimate knowledge of human anatomy. I can skin a human being alive without necessarily killing them right away. There is an art to it, as is the case with any other craft. And it will hurt like a motherfucker.

But when you don't feel it, it becomes a moot point anyway.

Or I could tie them both up to my bed. That will be a lot more fun.

I like to tie things up. Sometimes that includes people. I take great pleasure in testing out just how far the limits of the human body can be pushed. In my line of work, there is no shortage of victims to practice this on, and I go for the scum of the earth, the ones who deserve it.

Still, for their sake, I say, "As flattering as that is, there will be no titles between us, only safe words. We are equals, remember?"

CC smirks, then does what she does best and steers the conversation back to lighter topics.

For now, the pissing contest is over, and I don't mind it as much.

They are so unlike me. They are both such innocent souls, and I can't wait to corrupt them.

Then again, their supposedly pure souls must have an underlying dark streak. I know mine, if it still exists, is entirely dark.

I mean, I knew I was damned the moment I slit the throat of the fucker who killed my mother and never batted an eyelash. His wife too, and I made sure their daughter watched. They weren't my first kills but they were the first ones I didn't feel remorse for.

Until she made the mistake of following me into the bathroom, and I played Lorenzo's game and put my hands all over her.

If anything, the last few years have shown me that if I do have a soul, or whatever remnants of it still exist, it belongs to her.

To all of them.

And, as these two will both soon learn, I'm a possessive bitch.

Trial run or not, I don't let go of my toys either.

PART II

12

OSCAR

Had I known this was how the night would end, I would've thought twice about the whole *speaking freely* thing.

Courtney is… complicated and slightly impulsive. On the other hand, CC tends to do what she wants whenever she wants, with no regard for how the other person feels about it. But I already knew all that.

What I hadn't been expecting, however, was for the three of us to end up back at my place tonight. CC once let slip that Courtney doesn't do ultimatums, so I only said it in the hopes that our sordid history would repeat itself and she'd walk out of that restaurant, leaving me in the dust again.

I certainly wasn't expecting CC and I to be relegated to the settee in my bedroom, like a naughty pair in time-out, while Courtney rummages through my drawers and pulls out every toy I own.

Every single one. Some of which CC doesn't know about.

"This is impressive," she says, running her fingers along the tip of one of my latest acquisitions. "Only a handful of these were released last month, so how did you get your hands on one of these bad boys?"

Watching her caress, then run the tip of her tongue over the egg-shaped device, makes my cheeks flush hot, and a familiar tickle ripples through my body. On the outside, it is a seemingly unsuspecting butt plug, but it also doubles as a pear of anguish. I haven't had a chance to use it yet, as it doesn't have a built-in vibrator. For manual devices like that, it is much more satisfying when someone else has total control over how much pain and pleasure I can derive from them.

Seated next to CC, I take the hand resting at her side and interlace our fingers together, loving how her smooth fingers feel against my skin. "I have my ways."

"I see." She hums, eyes narrowing at the gesture. "Which one of you hacked into Harris's site? You or Abby?"

I shrug. "Does it matter?"

She smiles. "So she did. I should let David know then. He still thinks the network is impenetrable since he built it himself."

"Impenetrable? How can that be, when he left breadcrumbs all over…" I trail off at that, glancing at CC. David broke into Brewer Health's network not too long ago. I wonder if she knows.

CC frowns at that. "I don't care if you two talk in code."

"Then make yourself useful and undress him," Courtney snaps at her.

CC's shoulders stiffen for a split second, and then she does as ordered, standing first, then pulling me up to my feet forcefully.

This just feels off. And not at all what I want.

What's the point of having a mini-strip tease when the one person it is intended for is too busy rummaging through drawers for sex toys she doesn't plan on using anyway?

CC doesn't seem to mind it though. She reaches up and starts working on my tie, a sullen look on her face.

"You don't have to—" I protest when she loops the cloth around her hand and pulls my face down towards her, her lips meeting mine with a tenderness that shocks me.

My lips half-part, and her tongue sweeps in and finds mine instantly. We wrestle for dominance, but she always wins — or cheats — by biting my bottom lip, knowing I'll cave. At my startled yelp, she pulls my tongue into hers and sucks on it hard, making me growl as my arms wrap around her slender waist, drawing her lithe body flush with mine.

When she pulls back, albeit slightly, a whimper escapes.

"You wanted this," she whispers against my lips, simultaneously tightening the noose around my neck.

My pulse thunders in my ears, drowning out everything outside CC and me. As my knees give out, a warmth I haven't felt in a long time, coupled with an incredible glowing lightness I wish I could live in forever, takes over. It spreads throughout my body, seeping through every pore.

If this is what death feels like, I'd welcome it. Gladly. Wholeheartedly.

"CC, that's enough!" Courtney's voice breaks through the haze. "Breath play is officially off-limits for the rest of the night."

"Just tonight?" CC squeezes. "Why not make it forever?"

"Don't tempt me. Let him go."

Just like that, it all comes to an abrupt halt. My body sags as gravity takes over, then my face meets the floor. I take several deep breaths, filling my lungs with as much oxygen as possible. After pulling myself into a sitting position, I see Courtney crouched next to me, her eyes glued to my body. Her breathing is heavy, and an unmistakable heat shines in her eyes.

"Relax, would you? He's fine. I wasn't planning on killing him," CC is saying, but the blood rushing back into my brain dulls out the rest of her words.

They bicker for what seems like an eternity, but it actually lasts a minute or so. Then Courtney goes back to rummaging through my things while CC resumes undressing me, keeping her eyes downcast the entire time.

"I'm sorry I got you in trouble." I'm not sure why I feel the need to apologize, only that I do.

"Don't be." She takes her time unbuttoning my shirt, her nimble fingers slow and deliberate as she prolongs the task. "You got your answer."

"What answer?" I wrap my fingers around her wrist to stop her.

"She still cares about you. Isn't that what you wanted to confirm?"

I stare at her in disbelief, not moved by the sheen that appears in her eyes. "So that's all it was; you proving a point?"

"It worked, didn't it?"

My gaze lowers to her mouth. We've known each other for years, and I still don't understand half of the things that go through CC's head, much less the words that pass her beautifully sculpted lips. Call me crazy, but why do I feel the need to kiss her again? To push her, to taste her, if only to see how far she can take this?

I don't even care that she just tried to kill me, even if she claims that wasn't her intention. Just as long as she does it again.

"Don't," she whispers, her voice quivering as I set the tail in her hand.

"If you're going to kill me, go all the fucking way," I hissed, leaning in to fasten my lips on hers.

"There's a fatal flaw in this one's design," Courtney interjects, startling us both to awareness.

CC takes it a step further and shoves me away from her, chest heaving as she takes a step back from me.

It's unfortunate, I almost say out loud. For a while there, things were looking promising. Today seemed like a good day to die.

Swallowing, I turn to see Courtney holding up a retractable ankle spreader. "Oh. That one's new."

Courtney observes the exchange with a mischievous expression, the corners of her eyes crinkling with a smile. "If pleasure is the end goal, then toss it," she says, waving the darn thing back and forth between us. "If the plan is to maim or split someone in half, it works just fine."

"How do you know so much about those?" The silly question pops out before I can rein it in.

"I'm a product tester for all of Harris's designs," Courtney says with a shrug.

I can't help the frown that forms. "CC told me you two don't use toys."

"Not always." There's a slight tremor in CC's arms as she

pushes my shirt off my shoulders and slides them down my arms. "We don't use the ones he makes. Although, there are some things I can't live without, like Courtney's favorite… appendage. It's, umm, custom-made."

"It's called a strap-on," Courtney says with a laugh, tossing another contraption into the small pile in the middle of the room. "How can you rant and rave about Oscar's magical dick twenty-four-seven, yet you can't call mine by its name? It's literally the same size."

Say what now?

"Don't look so surprised," Courtney tells me. "For years, you've had a starring role in both of our fantasies. It was a natural segue."

Now *that*, I did not know.

"Then again, I enjoy pegging others," Courtney adds, this time with a straight face, then her tone going hard as she adds, "I didn't say you could stop."

CC nods at that, and her fingers move to undo my belt next. "I'm a taker, not a giver."

My cock twitches as I imagine CC's alabaster skin shiny with sweat while Courtney pounds her strap-on dildo into her wet pussy. Or maybe it'll be into her ass?

It would be quite the fantasy.

"Actually, I think I'd rather enjoy railing you," Courtney says out of the blue.

The image clears almost instantly, and her words sink in. "What?" I manage to gasp.

"You heard me."

Me?

I squeeze my eyes shut.

Why does the thought of getting a giant dildo rammed up my ass make my cock grow impossibly harder? I guess it's not so much the object. It's who will be carrying out the act.

When I open my eyes to face her, Courtney is smiling. At me.

That's all it takes. I'm officially done for.

Courtney's smiles are usually few and far between. It's one thing to see her mesmerizing smile directed at CC or any of the few people she truly cares about, but it is completely humbling to have that smile directed at me.

Who cares that she isn't mine? Or rather, that I'm not hers?

I want her to keep smiling at me like that, hopefully for a long time. So, the following words come naturally to me, flowing freely from my lips. "I suppose it's worth a try."

The smile slides off her face so fast that I think I imagined it. She lets out a sigh of exasperation, a cross between a groan and a moan. "That was supposed to scare you off, Oscar. To make you run for the hills."

Ah. So I hadn't imagined it. "Why?"

"Because…" She waves her arms around. "I don't know what CC told you about this, but I can assure you it's nothing compared to what's coming."

I lift a curious brow. "Meaning…?"

"I am not who you think I am."

"Neither am I."

"This isn't going to be what you think it is."

"Is that supposed to scare me?"

"It should, Oscar. It should have you running for the goddamn hills, holding on tight to whatever sense of self-preservation you possess."

I would believe her if not for the lust in her eyes as they drifted all over my body, undecided about where to look first.

Self-preservation my tatted ass.

I return the favor, honing in on her pebbled nipples as they press against the fabric of her dress. The neckline isn't doing her any favors. One wrong shift and those perfectly plump breasts will come tumbling out.

It's almost unfair that they're both fully clothed while I'm half-naked.

"How am I supposed to do that when you've got me by the balls? You really need to make up your mind, Courtney. Either you want something permanent with me, or you want to scare me off. So far you haven't said anything that has me concerned."

"Give it time," CC chimes in, cupping my massive erection through my pants.

My breath hitches as my eyes dart back and forth between the two women. "Well, time is all we have. The rest of my life, right? That's how this goes?"

"Something like that," CC responds.

"Again, doesn't seem like much of a problem to me."

"It should be." Courtney disappears into my walk-in closet, emerging a moment later with several silk ties. "Now, let's pick out our safe words. Mine's the same. Sarah."

Her mother's name. Of course.

No one wants to use their parent's name during sex. "Olive."

I turn to CC.

"I don't want one," she says without hesitation.

"What about Bettina?" I ask. Bettina is her adoptive mother.

Her brow scrunches in displeasure. "No, thanks."

"You've been stalling on this for too long," Courtney warns in a deceptively light tone that I know conceals her irritation. "You're gonna need one, so pick one."

"Fine. Sixty-nine. I am very sexual, as you know."

"You don't say," Courtney drawls, dropping all but one of the ties to the floor.

"And there are other ways to achieve pleasure that doesn't involve toys," CC continues, ignoring her sarcastic quip. "Sometimes a fist works just fine. I love being fisted."

On instinct, I curl my fist up and show it to her. "This?"

She nods. "I've only ever done it with Courtney, and obviously, her fist isn't as big as yours. But it is—"

"Glorious?" Courtney offers.

"Yeah. But also…" she trails off at that.

We both wait for her to finish her train of thought, but she doesn't. I know it has to do with her juices. She does produce quite a lot and is very self-conscious about it.

CC's fingertips graze over my sculpted abs as she undoes the button, then the zipper is next. I shift to my knees as her fingers dip into the waistband of my boxers, and she pushes both down to my knees.

"Stand," Courtney commands from her position across the room. As we both move to comply, she adds, "Not you, CC. That little stunt of yours earned you something worse."

A mischievous glint appears in CC's eyes as she works both pieces of clothing down my legs, not flinching as my thick dick almost smacks her in the face as I kick them away. Precum leaks from the tip and she licks her lips as she eyes my cock like a delectable treat she can't wait to devour.

"How much worse can it possibly get," she says in a taunt, licking her lips. She wraps her fingers around me and gives a gentle tug, then the wet heat of her tongue wraps around my head. She releases it with a pop, and I just about die right then and there.

Courtney walks over to us, curling the lone tie around her wrists and snapping it into place. I can't help but flinch at the sound, but CC doesn't. Somehow, she draws a strangled groan from me as she runs her thumb over the sensitive tip of my head, then brings it to her lips, smearing precum all over them.

Courtney kneels behind CC, looping both hands and my tie over her shoulders. "Open wider, CC."

CC's jaw drops, leaning forward to fasten her lips over my dick, fingers digging into my thighs. A hearty moan escapes, and my fingers dig into her hair. A husky chuckle vibrates up my shaft as she sucks me further into her mouth, the tip fitting snugly down her throat.

"Good girl," Courtney says as she leans in, her lips grazing CC's earlobe as she whispers, "I'm almost jealous of Oscar. He gets to fuck this slutty mouth of yours, so make it worth his while, would you? Then maybe, I'll grant you the painless end you so desperately seek."

Identical lust-filled eyes lift to meet mine, and an intense heat sears through me. Just when I think Courtney will loop that noose around her neck — as CC did to me earlier tonight — she drapes the damn thing over her shoulders instead.

"Ball is in your court, Oscar," she tells me with a wink. "Say the word, and we'll test out a different form of deep-throating."

CC hums her approval, but am I ready for that?

There's a part of me that vaguely comprehends her meaning, but I'm too focused on watching the expressions on CC's face as her head bobs up and down my dick, saliva mixed in with cum running down the sides of her mouth.

Courtney rises and moves to my side to watch the show from my vantage point.

Bad idea.

I sense the exact moment when Courtney's expression shifts from lustful to curious. As she assesses the lower half of my body, I can practically hear all the questions on her lips.

I know exactly what she's looking at, and it's not pretty.

It's not even a conversation starter, more like a run-for-the-hills kind of thing. Or ask a million questions until the truth becomes too much to handle.

The thing is, I've heard them all before. I've also got a handy list of ready-to-go answers to such questions.

But they're all lies.

13

OSCAR

Courtney wraps her nimble fingers around my elbow, pulling me backward. I stumble as I crash into her, taking CC with me, yet she doesn't move an inch. She wraps her arms around me instead, catching me mid-stumble and righting me.

How is that even possible? She's this lithe little thing, yet I don't doubt she could snap me in half with a flick of her fingers.

Like her, I've had training, the kind that's ingrained into the very fabric of your DNA. Metaphorically speaking, of course. Still, it's not something you can shake off because you feel like it. Except, in my case, it is permanently etched into my skin.

And it's more than enough to make her blood run cold. I know mine did when I first learned this had been her idea. Not that I could fault her for it, not when I understood the artist in her couldn't resist.

Not even this.

Then she asks the one question I expected eons ago, one that comes years late. "What the fuck is this?"

CC grunts out her frustration, fingers digging into my thighs hard enough to draw blood as she mumbles something around my cock.

Doesn't matter. The moment's ruined now. Besides, flaccid

cocks and blow jobs don't go well together, no matter how incredible CC's throat feels. I push her off, and she makes it a point to drag her teeth along the length, swapping out pleasure for pain.

"You sure you want the truth?" I toss back at Courtney. "Or would you prefer the kindness of a lie?"

Her grip tightens a fraction, lips pressing into a thin line. "Tell me who trained you," she demands in a harsh tone, chest heaving against my back, her muscles spasming with unreleased tension.

Never mind that.

Why would she even ask me that?

It's not a simple question. It's not even a loaded question.

If her intent is to feign ignorance, I have no intention of indulging her in it. The truth is, I am a lot like her — possessive and just a tad controlling. This gift she gave me, I don't like to share, so I've kept it to myself for the most part.

I don't care for being abandoned either. Like she fucking did to me.

"No." The single word is laced with as much venom as I can infuse into it. "I don't think you want the answer to that. I don't think you can handle it."

"Damn it, Oscar. Who the fuck did this to you?"

"Or what? You'll fuck it out of me?" I force out in defiance. "You sure are taking your sweet time getting there."

Unlike this.

This one, though, took nine sessions to get to its current state. The only way I could bear it, the only way I could keep going was with Courtney's voice on the other end of the line, coaxing me on, whispering sweet words of praise — the only glimpses of true, genuine tenderness I got from her in those days — while Roxane painstakingly took her time in transforming my lower half into what it is.

It is, dare I say, a masterpiece.

The culmination of many, many of our sessions together. The only reminder that what we shared was real.

Or so I thought.

Before I know it, I'm lying flat, stomach pressed to the floor, while she traces her fingers all over my butt and thighs. My basic survival instinct has my body seizing up, letting her take her time in examining her handiwork.

It's almost comical how much tenderness she's showing me now. I know she came up with the designs herself. She wrote detailed instructions on where each stroke, cut, bump, welt, and even dead space was supposed to be. Every groove, every etching, it was all her idea.

At least, that's what Mattie told me back then.

Still, I've seen the beauty *and* the macabre she creates, but this one is her best work yet.

It's too bad I can't show it off to the world as I please. And it's unfortunate it took Courtney this long to finally see it.

"Was it Abby?" Courtney asks, her tone slightly panicked. "Did she do this? Is this what you two have been up to all this time?"

"What? No. You did." I'm almost impressed with how easily the words now roll off my tongue.

And only slightly guilty when she loosens her grip on me, her hands falling to either side of my body. "Not this. I could never—"

"We come in pairs, you and me. That's how Mattie operates. That's how she trains us. Or did you forget that part too?"

What happens next knocks the air right out of my lungs. Courtney collapses onto the floor in a heap next to me, and her body curls into the fetal position.

It's unnerving and has me scrambling to my feet and away from her. Except… I don't think it's an act.

No one can fake such intense, full-body shudders as these. Or the strangled cry that rips from her throat as she chants *"No, no, no, not again"* over and over.

I'm thoroughly confused, so I turn to CC who has been watching the exchange. She mutters, "You two are idiots," under her breath.

My spine stiffens. *What?*

"One decent threesome with my two favorite people. Is it too much to ask?"

That's what she's worried about?

I'm not in the mood to indulge a pouty — or is it whiny? — CC, so I ignore her. Crouching next to Courtney's folded body, I reach out to touch her, to offer her some semblance of comfort, but CC's icy-cold tone stops me.

"Unless you want a knife in your jugular, you shouldn't touch her when she's in that state," CC warns, her voice moving closer.

"She needs help."

"That depends on your definition of help." There's a sultry hardness to her tone, and not in a good way. She makes a tsk-tsk noise, and I realize… she's probably staring at the same thing Courtney was, albeit with mild disinterest. "I can't believe I'm only just noticing it."

"Noticing what?"

"The crest tattooed on your ass cheeks," she says with a laugh. "Well, part of one, anyway."

Say what now?

"You didn't know?"

"How am I supposed to know? I can't see my own ass."

"There's this magical invention called mirrors," she scoffs. "You've had that for years now, Oscar. Don't tell me you haven't been in the least bit curious?"

"We don't have time for this, so quit stalling and help her."

She laughs again. "I'm not the one who broke her, but that's an easy enough fix. It'll all depend on you."

And here comes the bargain. "Meaning?"

Her fingers press into my shoulders. "How bad do you want tonight to happen?"

"I…" I shake my head. How is it that she's still thinking of sex while Courtney is having an existential crisis? "If you're not going to help her, then just say so—"

CC pushes down, forcing me flat on my ass. "Look. At. Me," she demands, the mirth in her words gone, what's left in its stead slithering all over my body.

I'm afraid to look.

This is a side to CC that I haven't seen in a long time.

It's funny how Courtney's earlier words about not wanting to be a Domme anymore suddenly make sense. It wasn't just me she said that to; it was both of us.

Or perhaps she was saying it to CC?

Underneath it all, this is who she is. The manipulator. The wolf in sheep's clothing.

CC is a master manipulator. It's a side to herself that she actively suppresses on a daily basis, yet it's one that drew me to her in the first place.

I wonder if Courtney knew. Knows.

Whatever.

When I finally look up, her eyes are diamond hard and soullessly black, and the sheer force of them slams into me.

"Since you wanted this to happen tonight, here's how things will go. If you want your apology, you're going to get it. If you want her to fuck you, she will. And then some. And you're going to like it. But you won't like what it will take for us to get there. If none of that interests you, use your safe word and this ends. Not just now, but permanently."

Her eyes might be hard, but her tone is as soft as velvet and lures me in.

Do I want this?

Maybe. Maybe not.

But do I need this?

Fuck, yes.

"I want this," I hear myself say, and I can't even bring myself to feel guilty about it.

So what does that say about me, exactly?

Never mind that.

"Good boy," she coos. Her fingers go slack on my shoulder and move to my hair. She weaves her nimble digits through the strands, the tips of her nails grating my scalp, sending reignited heat thundering down my core. Her tongue darts across her lip as she watches her handiwork, a dreamy look creeping onto her features. "I just have one rule."

"What's that?"

She grabs a fistful of hair and yanks my head back, forcing my eyes back to her soulless ones. "Don't fight it," she warns. "Don't fight her either, or she could seriously hurt you."

"I… what does that mean?"

"It means I'm going to turn her on, and what will happen will happen. No take-backs. All you have to do is ride it out, and I promise you it'll be the best fuck of your life. Nod once if you understand."

I nod, because what choice do I have?

As I'm wondering what will happen next, she pushes Courtney onto her back, her arm lifts, then skin connects with skin, the sound so loud I let out an involuntary yelp.

"Wha—" I start to say, but CC turns those pitch-black eyes on me, her slender finger pressed to her still-swollen lips.

Courtney moves to a sitting position, then half-turns to face me. Her head half-tilts, giving me a lust-filled gaze. It's unreal how her stormy gray eyes are glazed over, like she's in some sort of trance.

How is that a fix?

CC leans into her back and places her head on Courtney's shoulder. With her lips next to Courtney's ear, she whispers something to her. It's too low for me to hear, but I'm picking up hints of her old accent, a seductive lilt that has my body tingling and cock twitching in anticipation.

Once she finishes, there's a pause as Courtney brings her teeth over her lower lip, nibbling at it uncertainly.

CC brings her thumb to the soft spot behind Courtney's ear and presses in. "Show him how sorry you are."

She does so only once, but that's all it takes for Courtney to attack.

14

CC

For the record, I love my life.

When death spared me over a decade ago, I made a promise to myself. To live life fully, wholly, and authentically, and not once have I regretted any of the impossible choices that got me to where I am today. I've come too far and risked too much to be able to call this life my own. And I love that I can simply live free of stifling familial obligations.

Besides, who needs an empire — one born of blood, consumed by greed, surrounded by death, and filled with constant heartache — when you can have this? It's called the best of both worlds for a reason, and I love it.

I fucking love my life.

Oscar, not so much.

At least, not right now.

He's having a little pity party — or is it a *regret* party? — over there, but he can't get his body to cooperate.

Not even he can pretend not to like everything that's transpired in the last few… hours? He got his wish, his apology, and then some. I got to test out just how long our collective stamina can last. Courtney got… well, she gets everything else from the both of us. But she gives as good as she gets, as is to be expected.

That's why it's not surprising that she crashes first.

That's how these things often go. She hasn't had much practice with this either, so her crash is the equivalent of the literal floor caving out from underneath you.

She's riding him, reverse cowgirl, eyes closed as I kneel before her and cup her face in my hand. She's smiling between moans, biting down on her bottom lip as she leans into my touch. Then we're kissing, my free hand tucked underneath them, playing with Oscar's balls. He's incredibly sensitive down there, plus I've always known that my touch does things to him, so I grab him by the balls — and cock, unless it is otherwise occupied — every chance I get.

What can I say? I'm very sexual and I flaunt it every chance I get.

And Oscar? He's not immune to it, and neither is she. When I have them both like this, it's even better than I could've ever imagined. Who cares that I have to play little mind games to make this happen?

It's not like we could've taken her to the hospital after his ass tattoo set her off. Not only does she detest the look, smell, and feel of hospitals, but I wasn't about to ruin a perfect night by dealing with her brother, Marc Sotelo.

What a buzzkill that one is.

I would know. I have played with him before. Him and Harris. They are good, but not as good as these two put together. Plus he's a control freak and I'm an even worse controlling freak, so even I know that's not a good combo.

And as I said, I want the best of both worlds. Now that I've got it, I'll be damned if I ever let either one of them go.

Courtney will just have to get over the fact that she got one-third of my dead family's crest — albeit a significantly altered version of it — tattooed onto Oscar's ass cheeks. It's been years, and he's over it too. Well, *mostly* over it. I actually think he likes it now. Although I have to wonder, what other two unfortunate souls got the other two pieces?

Never mind that. Back to my perfect little puppets.

As I kiss her, I alternate between pulling and massaging his nuts.

He's jerking and grunting and thrusting into her, harder and faster, his movements erratic, yet his hips maintain a certain mesmerizing rhythm to them. The bed bounces underneath us as she grinds down on him, her perfect tits bouncing between us as her orgasm builds. Our nipples touch every fifth bounce, but I barely feel it — the curse of one too many boob jobs, I suppose.

Still, I wouldn't trade any of it. If I could go back, I'd make the same choices I did, just so I could end up right back here.

Not sure what possesses me to do this, but I press my thumb into her mouth, swapping that out for my tongue. I pant as the wet heat of her tongue wraps around me, teasing and sucking on the digit as if it were his cock that she was worshiping on her knees.

Scratch that — she did do that to him tonight. Twice. Was I jealous? Fuck yes. Still—

Courtney's eyes snap open, meeting mine, and that's when I see it.

The hint of panic sets in, and in the blink of an eye, the full force of it hits her all at once.

She tears off him and pushes me away before stumbling off the bed and making a beeline for his bathroom. Oscar looks confused by the gesture, understandably so. But he's still in one piece, so that's good enough for me.

Until he isn't.

When I lean over and blow a hot breath on his glistening cock, that's enough to set him off. His head falls back to his pillow and he shoots his load all over his stomach. It's an impressive amount, considering he came at least five or six times already. Not one to waste a drop of his precious nectar, I lap up his cum off of his tight, smooth abs. It's minty — no idea how — and commingled with both of their sweat, and best of all? It smells like her. His cock still smells like her too, so I take a deep whiff, eyes drifting closed. I can't get enough.

"Where's Courtney?" he asks, his breathing haggard as he comes down from his climax.

"Bathroom." I give his dick one last lick, from root to tip, and the eager fucker twitches against my tongue.

"Jesus, CC. Haven't you had—"

"She just needs a minute," I say, cutting him off. I don't need him ruining this by saying something dumb. At the very least, he should wait until the blood leaves his other head and returns to his genius brain.

Then I start to get irritated with him, with myself really, because she's off by herself and I'm here with him, and still, he can't just enjoy the fucking moment for what it is.

Pushing off him, I head to the bathroom after her.

Once again, she's curled up on the floor, this time with her hand between her legs. Full-body tremors wrack her body as she chases her own high, the slurping noise filling the room as she finger-fucks her needy pussy with who knows how many fingers. I knew not even the impending panic could've staved off her arousal, not with how hard Oscar and I had been working her body for the last few… hours? I really need to get a better sense of how much time passes when I'm in these things.

Then again, I really would've loved to have been the one to finish her off, but oh well.

Thanks to Oscar's brattiness, tonight's objective has been achieved, and we are back on track.

Mostly back on track.

As the last of her orgasm ebbs out of her body, her hand slips and flops to her side. Her eyes remain closed as her lips move, chanting more gibberish.

Only it's not gibberish. It's—

Who cares what it is right now?

"Oscar, get in here, *please*."

I stress the last word since I know I have to be nice to him if I want him to cooperate. There's a rustling of sheets as he climbs out of bed. He's got an oh-so-adorably confused look on his face as he saunters towards me, his half-mast cock swinging before him. The urge to drop to my knees and suck him deep into my throat is strong, but I tamp down on it. Our girl needs us.

"She needs to warm back up, so we're going to lie down on either side of her and envelop her between us."

"On the floor?" There's the adorable nose scrunch that I love so much.

"Ten, fifteen minutes should do the trick," I tell him, lowering my naked tush to the cold floor, then crawling over to her like a feral cat. "Your housekeeper, she cleans in here, does she not?"

He shrugs. "Probably."

"Now's the perfect time to check her work then. You always have the option to fire her incompetent ass."

I take Courtney's back like always, and he takes the front. His arm wraps around both of us, not fully though, and pulls us close to him. She stirs slightly, then presses her face into his chest.

Five minutes.

That's as much time as we get before he starts with the questions.

"What did you say to her? Right before you… turned her on." He's running his fingers along my spine, up and down the middle of my back.

To warm me up, perhaps?

I should tell him it's a waste of time. I'm ice-cold on the inside, possibly on the outside too. Metaphorically speaking, of course.

Still, I say, "Sixty-nine." That's not all I said to her, but I leave it at that.

The scrunch makes a reappearance, this time between his eyebrows. "If you used your safe word, why didn't she stop?"

"It's not a safe word. It's a code."

"Code for?"

"Code, Oscar. It works like yours, so please don't make me say it out loud."

He falls silent at that.

Maybe I should say it, just for kicks.

It's a thing with all five of them, a code Mattie buried so deep into their subconscious that they can't help but react sexually every time the phrase *Enlighten Me* is uttered. Somehow Abby managed to break free of that programming, but not the others. I've tried every possible trick I could think of with Oscar to no avail.

If I say it, it'll probably set her off again. Him too, and then I'll have a clusterfuck on my hands that I don't have time for. Not when she needs her rest, now more than ever.

I can't help the sigh that follows. Oscar's concern for her well-being is starting to grate on my nerves, and I can't explain why. It's reciprocated. She wouldn't let me kill him any more than he'd let me kill her.

Courtney is just fine. She looks slightly lethargic, but that's what happens when you come down from this high. The higher you fly, the harder you crash. The harder you crash, the longer it takes to recover.

Or… we could speed this one up a little.

Fifteen minutes in, we shift positions. She's lying between his legs, using Oscar's cock head as a pacifier, and he's enjoying it.

He can because his recovery comes much faster. I've been easing him into it for years. He's also been through some pretty rigorous training — or torture, depending on how one classifies it — so he's not exactly short on stamina.

That said, I hate doing this.

This part.

I know what Courtney looks like when she's been pushed to her limit, and this time I fear I also took things too far.

She will recover from it. I know she will. And she will remember what happened tonight.

Whether or not she will bring it up later or even punish me for it remains to be seen. For now, she needs all the rest she can get.

"How often does this happen?" he asks, running his fingertips along the edge of her chin.

I'm baffled at how he manages to keep his voice even and his breathing steady, with how eagerly her cheeks hollow out as she sucks on his cock. The sight is so erotic that my hand sneaks between my legs of its own accord.

"Not often enough," I mumble, blushing slightly as my cheeks warm. "I don't do this a lot with her. If I did, she wouldn't…." I trail off at that, sucking in a deep breath as my fingers hit a sensitive spot. Holding back a moan, I continue, "She doesn't get enough sleep; when she does, she doesn't dream. Nightmares are what she has."

"About?" he prompts. He's watching me, and his interest seems genuine.

"Mostly about her mom." A beat passes, then I add, "Sometimes, they're about me too."

"How could you possibly know that?"

I shrug. "Because she says my name. My dead name."

My gaze lowers, and I take a moment to study her. The contrast of her light brown skin against our pale skin. How her wet, dark curls and braids frame her oval face.

In this state, she looks nothing like the strong, independent woman I often see. Like this, she's practically a baby. So innocent, so pure.

And I love it.

"Sixty-nine," Oscar mutters. "Six. Nine. June ninth. The day your family died."

I knew he would get it. It just took him a little longer to get there.

"You can say it," I say, meeting his eyes, my hand moving faster. "The day I should've died."

His Adam's apple shifts as he swallows. "You didn't, and that has to count for something."

"Does it?" A strangled laugh escapes. "We're quite the pair, aren't we? You haunt her memories, and I haunt her dreams."

"CC—"

"You don't need to sugarcoat it for me. I'm living on borrowed time, I know this. My parents killed her mother, so she killed them. They made her watch, so she made me watch. An eye for an eye, that's how it works. Still, she wanted to kill me that night, but he stopped her. Said some people are more valuable alive than dead. That's just some bullshit though. The Network already has access to all of my money, so it doesn't matter whether I'm dead or alive. I just need her to finish the job already. And if she doesn't, I plan on sticking to her like mold."

He drops his gaze, lingering on my busy hands. "And me?"

The corner of my mouth turns up, and my eyes fall closed as my muscles tighten, my orgasm washing over me in waves. I must have moaned his name because his lips are on mine, then his fingers take over, thrusting into me with steady but hard, punishing strokes.

Courtney stirs between us, heaving a content sigh despite her lips staying latched on. He's back to moaning, not hiding how much he enjoys this. We are a messy tangle of lips, arms, legs, and who knows what else. And it's not long before I'm coming again. He soon follows, his body jerking as he shoots thick ropes of cum into Courtney's mouth, all of which she sucks down in her sleep without missing a beat.

See? You'll do just fine, I want to tell him. *You'll have her, just as you've always wanted.*

15

OSCAR

By the time we get Courtney bathed, dressed, and into bed, she's lethargic. Or she looks that way, at least to me.

To CC, this is business as usual. She's humming a tune as we section off Courtney's hair into eight quarters for braiding. Words slip out on occasion — her native tongue, it would seem — and hints of her old Kansai-ben accent slip in. It was heavier when we first met, and she's tried so hard to eliminate it.

I settle in on the opposite side, gather the fourth quarter into my hand, and split it into three before I start weaving. I don't understand what she's singing, but it's oddly soothing. I can only deduce it's either a nursery rhyme or a lullaby. It could even be a siren's song, and I wouldn't care because Courtney seems to be at peace with it.

I'm halfway through the braid before it dawns on me that CC isn't moving. My eyes lift to take in her surprised look.

The corner of my mouth turns up. "I'm a man of many talents."

"So it would seem," she says, then resumes humming.

I keep my gaze downcast, focused on Courtney's hair. CC remains unmoving, never breaking the tune. I can feel her eyes are still on me. A million unspoken questions hang heavy in the air between us.

More than anything, I wanted tonight to happen. I asked for it. When fantasy and reality collided, it was nothing like I'd expected… and everything I'd hoped it would be.

What happened tonight can only be described as an out-of-body experience. One in which Courtney was completely out of it, her body moving to the beat of CC's drum.

She can claim to love us all she wants, but we are her puppets. Courtney and myself.

Since I went along with tonight, what does that make me?

"When we first met in college," I begin, swallowing around the lump in my throat. "Did you know about our history? Courtney's and mine?"

"Yes."

My eyes fly up. I blink once, then twice, as I stare at her, dumbfounded. I wasn't expecting her to be so blunt about it. "So when you befriended me, was that just a ploy to insert yourself into her life?"

"Yes."

Well. She *did* promise never to lie to me.

She then solidifies this by adding, "For sixteen years, I've made it my business to know the people in Courtney's life. Who her friends and foes are, that sort of thing. That includes the ones who could eventually become a threat to her. I'm not going to stop now."

"Like Reuben, you mean."

"Yes. You too, Oscar."

"Me?" I ask incredulously.

"She tortured you," she replies with a soft smile. "I needed to be sure you weren't out for revenge."

"The same could be said about you," I remind her.

"Maybe, but it's my duty to turn her weaknesses into strengths. You, Oscar, are a weakness of hers. In a way, I am too. But I could never harm her."

"You just did."

"We spank each other all the time. It's called role-playing. The sex is even rougher than what you just experienced. You should see the things she's shoved in my cunt when the mood strikes. You know I can take it, too. I'm practically a faucet down there." She places a hand on my shoulder, and a shudder runs through her, rippling through me. "If I were to harm her, I would have done so by now. You have to know that."

I do know that.

I also know that if I don't tell her this, I'll never get the courage to do it again.

"I love you," I give her a tense smile, "but I'm not doing that again."

I don't miss her sharp intake of air. "Not this again," she mutters, sighs, then leans over Courtney's body and cups my face. In both hands. "For what it's worth, I'm sorry."

"I don't want your apology, CC. I want — no, I *need* to get to know her. All of her. Preferably without your meddling."

"Meddling? I don—" she protests, but I cut her off.

"You do meddle. I don't believe you know how *not* to. I know you mean well, some of the time, but this isn't it. She's important to me too. Her dreams and aspirations. Her likes and dislikes. What she's like in bed. The sounds she makes when she falls apart. Even the sound of her snoring. I want to experience it all."

She says nothing else as we finish with Courtney's hair. Once done, we all climb under the covers, with me sandwiched between both women. Courtney is snuggled up to my right side and CC to my left, her palm splayed over my chest.

I'm not one to believe in forever, but I'll hold on to this feeling for as long as possible. It'll only make this sting more when it all comes crashing down.

Because it will. Eventually, it will.

In the meantime, I guess I'll just be their sex slave.

The thought genuinely thrills me.

16

———

OSCAR

Courtney's hot lips wrapped around my morning wood wakes me up the following day. Her head bobs up and down underneath the sheets as she slurps noisily, and it's music to my ears.

As precum leaks from the tip, she alternates sucking with swirling her tongue over it, diligently swallowing every drop like last night. I'm enthralled by how deep she takes me into her mouth. The head of my cock hits the back of her throat over and over.

It feels like fucking heaven, and I have zero control over the sounds slipping past my lips. Her gag reflex is non-existent, and I love it.

"Courtney," I say in a low, half-sleepy half-growling tone.

It's almost sacrilegious to ask her to stop, but if she doesn't I'll shoot my load down her throat.

The thing is, that's not where I want it.

She doesn't stop. She hums and plays with my balls, massaging them gently as she takes me to the brink and back, over and over. The more she drags this out, the more desperation slips into my moans.

When I've had enough, I shove my hands in her hair and drag

her up my body. She still has a dazed look about her, her brown eyes heavy-lidded with lust, precum leaking from the corners of her mouth.

"I'm sorry I fell asleep on you last night," she says softly before dropping her mouth to mine in a searing kiss.

We pull back, and I frame her face with my hands, looking into her brown eyes, glassy with her need. "You don't owe me an apology, Courtney. I owe you one."

She shakes her head. "I should've known—"

"Not now, okay? We'll have plenty of time to figure that out. But for now…"

"…we're even?" she finishes.

I nod, then I take her mouth again, relieved to feel her kissing me back with as much passion and need as I'm kissing her.

Desire courses through my veins, and I pour all that into our kiss. She meets me head-on, our tongues wrestling for dominance as we explore each other. This is what I wanted last night, but more than anything, I want her to remember it. Remember us.

My lips find the thready pulse at the base of her throat, and I nibble on it, knowing how much that drives her crazy. With her slender thighs on either side of me, she slides her warm cunt along my cock and grinds herself against me.

The urge to fuck her senselessly takes over, so I flip her over on all fours and thrust two fingers into her weepy cunt.

She gasps and pushes back against my hand. "Don't stop," she cries out.

Covering her body with mine, I nibble on her earlobe. "Tell me what you want."

"You," comes out in a breath. "Please, fuck me."

My heart skips a beat. She doesn't have to ask me twice.

I use my thumb to play with her swollen nub while scissoring my fingers, teasing out that sweet spot in her until she's making all these whimpering sounds. It's music to my ears. Her inner walls clamp down on my digits, so I add a third one, stretching her out.

A fresh wave of precum leaks, dripping onto the silk sheets. I'm thrusting into her slick folds and she's gasping my name, pushing back onto my hand for leverage as I pick up the pace. It's not long before her orgasm hits and her legs give out underneath her. She falls to the bed, face-planted into the sheets, as a string of incoherent mumbles slips past her lips.

"Hmm." Eyes half-open and thighs apart, CC watches us as she plays with her glistening cunt, an adorable pout on her lips. "I'm feeling left out."

"Which do you want?" Courtney asks in a husky tone, her gaze fixated on CC's hands. "His face or his cock?"

My dick, already impossibly hard, twitches at the prospect. My fingers are still buried in Courtney's tight heat, hot and damp with her arousal.

"How about both?" CC replies, licking her lips. "Let's tag team him."

An animalistic groan bubbles up from my throat. I'm down with whatever they want.

They both turn to me, their eyes raking over my body. The heat in their eyes shoots straight to my cock. "I'm game if you are."

CC lunges for me, pushing me to my back. She wastes no time in aligning my body how they want me.

"Look at him," Courtney says as she climbs up my body, straddling my thighs with hers. "He's our perfect fuck toy."

My lips part and CC shoves something into them. Lace panties, I think.

"Fuck toys don't talk," she chides.

Oh, so that's how she wants to play it. Payback from last night.

Where did she even get those? We all went to bed naked last night.

That thought flees my brain when Courtney aligns her fluttering pussy over my bulbous tip and sinks down slowly. A strangled noise escapes my throat as her silken heat engulfs my hard cock. She goes slow for the first two inches, then her ass cheeks hit my balls as she impales herself to the hilt.

"Fuck," I groan around the bundle in my mouth, eyes rolling to the back of my head.

Her fingers dig into my stomach as she bounces on my dick a few times, her thighs trembling against mine.

"He won't last long if you do that," CC tells her.

"So quit dawdling and sit on his face," Courtney orders her, reaching over to yank the lace back out of my mouth, "then bring those lips to me."

The bed dips on either side of my face, and she hovers over me.

"CC, just fucking sit already," Courtney barks out with a laugh.

When she hesitates a moment longer, Courtney draws in a sharp breath and shoots me a look, her eyes darting back and forth between us, her intent clear. Licking my lips, I hook both arms on either side of CC's thighs and smash her wet cunt to my face. She squirms on me and we both whimper in satisfaction.

"I take it you two haven't tried that?" Courtney asks her. I don't hear CC's reply as her thighs lock on either side of my face, muffling my ears.

Given my history — or rather, Courtney's and my history — I never knew being deprived of my senses would be something I liked, let alone pleasurable. But with my vision darkened and the weight of their combined bodies on mine, everything they do to me and each other becomes so heightened. I'm writhing beneath them, the onslaught of sensations having me surrendering all control to them.

Besides, who needs air when you can have this?

It's easy to lose track of how much time passes when we're like this. Our bodies move in sync like we were meant to fit together. The room fills with our music, the slow grinding of hot and sweaty skin against skin, fingers dragging through tangled, damp hair, and even teeth sinking into tender flesh. Words alone can't describe how amazing it feels for all three of us to be fully present in this, and to experience both of their different feminine touches on me simultaneously.

Courtney's touch is surprisingly gentle as she gives my nipples the treatment my balls got, rolling and pinching the sensitive tips between her callused fingers. My moans rumble through CC and she responds in kind, her touch bordering on painful, her fingers pressing harder into the planes of my stomach as she kneads the muscles. They both match my groans with near-identical plea-filled whimpers. My hips thrust upward into Courtney, while CC grinds down on my face, drowning me in her juices. I'm eating her out like my life depends on it, the noisy slurping from their wet kisses urging me on.

CC comes first. I can tell by how her thighs quiver on either side of my face, her hips swiveling with urgency as a gust of her warm nectar floods my mouth. My arms go slack and CC's body tips over to the side, spent and satiated, earning a sultry chuckle from Courtney.

She leans forward, her taut nipples pressing into mine as her eyes peer into the depths of my soul. "She usually lasts much longer than that," she whispers hoarsely, her warm breath feathering my lips. "You broke her, Oscar. I'm impressed."

Next to us, CC mumbles something incoherent. It sounds like she's complimenting my cock, because the fucker swells in Courtney, drawing a startled gasp from her.

"I'd rather break you," I admit truthfully, and her eyes darken with lust.

"You already have," she says in a rush before fusing our mouths together in a passionate, feral kiss.

With my hands free to roam as they please, I reach between us and seek out her clit. She's moaning about how it's too much, but it's my name she screams out as she spasms around me. I'm right behind her. My cock pulses in her tight heat as I shoot ropes of thick cum all over her insides.

"Oh fuck, *yes*," she cries out, her breaths heavy.

I growl into the nape of her neck instead. She grinds down on me with each spurt, her pussy clenching in response. I keep fucking her through our orgasms until the last wave of shivers leaves her body, and she slumps against me, sweaty and limp. I keep fucking her until my dick goes limp and slips out of her. Of course, she doesn't like that and grunts out her disapproval.

"That was one heck of a wake-up call," CC declares as we're still catching our collective breaths. "We should do that more."

"That's a given," Courtney replies, smiling against my chest. "Now that I know what I've been missing out on all this time, I'm never ever giving this up."

It's music to my ears.

If this is how the rest of my life will be, I'm okay with that.

17

OSCAR

"I was wondering where that went," Courtney says as she sips on her coffee, her gaze transfixed by the lone painting in my kitchen.

It's also the focal point of the space and hard to miss. Especially since the walls are stark white, the room sterile and clinical looking. I like to think of myself as a minimalist, but I'm just too lazy to make the space mine. Or the house.

Like CC, I have no strong attachment to where I live. Not much has changed, design-wise, since I bought the place. Four walls do not make a home. Home is where the heart is. In my case, my heart is in two different residences.

"CC brought that over a few years ago when I first moved in," I tell her, nursing my coffee. "I take it that it wasn't meant for me?" I'm trying to keep my tone light, but I'll be fucking crushed if she says no.

She heaves a heavy shoulder. "I didn't say that. It's nice to know you've had something of mine all this while."

Despite the ample seating in the kitchen, she's chosen to plant her sexy tush right on the countertop. She has both legs crisscrossed, with the weight of her body resting on it. Even though she seems to prefer it that way, there's no way that's comfortable.

But to each their own.

Not that I care where she sits. She lights up the space just by being in it.

I hide my obvious smile behind my mug.

In times like this, I can't help but wonder just what purpose I could possibly serve in her life. If someone like me could ever truly *have* a place in her life. Also, I should know better than to get involved with someone like her.

But the heart wants what the heart wants.

Every moment we spend together builds a relationship we weren't supposed to have. Yet here we are, sharing pieces of ourselves with each other, things I'm confident we don't share with anyone else.

"For what it's worth, I've always liked you, Oscar," she suddenly says.

My heart skips a beat. There's too much emotion in this space. I can't help the things that pop out of my mouth.

But then, I'm not even sure what we are calling this *thing* we share.

Whatever the catalyst was, I can't be upset by it. It did get her back here, so that has to count for something.

She taps a finger to her forehead. "Your thoughts are loud, and you wear your emotions on your face. I like that too."

That's because it's you, I want to say. *I don't have to pretend when I'm with you.*

I say something stupid instead. "Since we still haven't established ground rules, can I continue speaking freely?"

She considers the question and then forces a smile. "Do you censor yourself with CC?"

"I don't."

Hints of her vulnerability peek through the curtain as she stares at me. "How much time do you need to treat me that way?"

"I…" Shit. I *have* been holding back.

"It's soon, I know," she continues. "But I meant every word of what I said last night. I didn't ask lightly. I've never had a boyfriend. Or a girlfriend, either. You two would be the first. My first."

I find that hard to believe. "But you have…"

"I'm bi, Oscar. I've had sex with men and women, obviously. But none I liked enough to consider relationship material. Not since you. Not since *then*."

Oh.

"As for CC, well, I'm sure she told you what happened between us back then."

"Which time are we talking here? Two years ago, or further?"

Something passes in her eyes. "Two," she somberly states.

I nod. "She gave me the watered-down version of events, yes. Still, why send her this time? Why not come to me directly?"

"Truth? I was afraid."

Courtney? Afraid?

I never thought I'd see the day when those two things went together.

"Of?" I prompt when she doesn't say anything else.

"Rejection. Losing you. Mucking things up between you and CC past the point of no return. All of the above. I know she's important to you and vice versa."

You are important to me too, I want to tell her.

But she's not done.

"You held up your end of the bargain, and you found me first," she says of the promise I made to her once, a long time ago.

Technically, it was a threat issued from a place of pain, anger, and desperation. I had every intention of following through with it until the damned gag order put the kibosh on things, then my mental breakdown, then…

It all feels so long ago now. So inconsequential.

"Finding you was the easy part," I tell her. "Everything else that came after that was, well…"

"Hard?" she offers, and we both laugh. "All this time, you've been trying to show me, but I wasn't paying close enough attention. I was too wrapped up in… in trying to find, well, *you*, that I wasn't reading between the fucking lines. Or paying close enough attention to all the hints you've been dropping. To be frank, I was worried about screwing up what you and CC have and didn't consider what I was doing to you in the meantime. Gosh, I'm so, so sorry. About everything."

It takes every shred of common sense and self-control not to kiss her. "Don't be. We're here now."

"I'll make it up to you, I promise."

"You don't have to."

"But I—"

I press my lips to hers, silencing her. "Courtney, what we went through was pretty messed up, but I got help. I'm okay now, I promise. What I *do* want to know is, are you okay?" At her confused look, I quickly clarify, "After last night, I mean."

"Which part?"

"The last part. Well, all of it. It started out amazing, then…"

"Then I lost it?" she offers when I don't continue. "I must have enjoyed it since I'm sore in all the right places." She wriggles in her seat. "Except for back there. How come neither one of you fucked me in the ass? It was the perfect chance."

Blood rushes my ears. "Wha—"

"I would've let you," she continues like it's no big deal. "Apparently, I'm very agreeable in that state." At the mortified look on my face, she barks out a laugh. "Oscar, I have a safe word and know how to use it, no matter what state I'm in. I wanted last night to happen just as much as you did. CC and I gave each other full consent over each other's bodies two years ago. It was the trade-off for the… umm… for the Charlie thing."

"The Charlie thing?" As I said, I can't be held responsible for the things that pop out of my mouth.

She turns and stares off into the distance. A wistful look comes over her eyes. Reaching over, I brush away a few strands of the dark brown curls framing her face before lifting her chin to meet her eyes. I can see such compassion and vulnerability in them, and it takes my breath away.

I get the feeling this isn't a side to her that she lets others see. I feel honored to be the recipient of it, even though this will only muddy the waters between us.

"This is uncharted territory for me," she eventually says.

Tell me about it.

Warmth glows in my chest. "I like you too, Courtney." It takes everything in me to conceal the smile that forms. "In case last night or the last few years didn't make that clear, the feeling has always been mutual."

She smiles, and fuck, does that shoot straight to my cock. "So does that mean—"

"Yes, I'll be your boyfriend." I'm grinning like an idiot, and I don't care. She does this to me.

Now we're both grinning like idiots.

"You don't have to wear the collar if you don't feel comfortable outing yourself." The words tumble out of her in a rush.

"Oh, but I want to." At least it will give me some semblance of security of my place in her life. "It doesn't mean what most people would assume it means, and that's okay. I won't have to explain us," I wave a hand between our bodies, "and I'm okay with that too. Besides, most will assume CC put it on me."

Is that a growl I just heard?

So she *is* jealous.

I'm fucking beaming.

"Whatever. I don't care either way. You bear my mark already…" She trails off at that, then winces. "Poor choice of words."

"I don't mind. It's an honor to bear—"

Her nose scrounges into an adorable frown. "I hate that word."

"What? Honor?"

She swallows, then nods. "Try something boring. Try pleasure or something."

I'm grinning like an idiot, and I still don't care. "It's a pleasure to bear your mark. It's a dream to be yours."

She lets me have that, and something shifts between us.

"I need your help," she eventually says.

"With?"

"People-ing." Her brow crinkles. "This vulnerability shit. I'm not good at it, and… she needs it."

My brow lifts. "Why me? I'm not exactly a relationship guru."

She heaves a huge sigh and leans forward, shoulders slumped, as she wrinkles her fingers in her lap. "For some reason, you seem to have cracked the code on all things Courtney. I feel… things when I'm with you." Her voice falters, so she clears her throat before continuing. "I feel them with her too, but then I open my mouth and just… I keep messing things up. I just… I need you to be the Courtney whisperer because…" She pauses at that, and a beat passes. Then two.

Then several.

"Courtney."

She looks away and stares off into the distance. Rounding the island, I reach for her legs and pull them from underneath her body. She's sporting an amused look as she watches me pull her body to the edge, push her thighs apart, and nestle myself between them.

"You seem to be doing pretty well at this," I tell her.

"I'm not."

"You are. Look at us. We're talking. Freely, I might add."

She sighs. "It's different with you," she tells me, and I feel that in every pore of my body. "I could always tell you things. Even when I was…" she trails off at that.

"Torturing me?" I offer.

She nods. "You weren't just a voice on the other end of the line. I knew you were a living, breathing person. One who felt genuine pain." She pauses at that, blinking away tears that form. "For what it's worth, I'm sorry."

"Seriously, don't be." My fingers work themselves into the soft skin of her nape, and I pull our faces together. Instead of kissing her like I want, I nuzzle into her temple, kissing down her hairline and across her ear. "You're serious about making this official, and that's all I need. That's all CC needs, too. When in doubt, just talk to her, like you're doing with me. Or spank her; she loves that too."

Her throat shifts against my lips. "I don't want to hurt you, Oscar. Not physically. That's why I said what I said last night. I don't want to be your Domme. I want to be your partner. All I was taught is now tied to my Black Widow persona, which I use when working. If I put cuffs on a man, I'm sawing off his wrists. And if I'm sticking a choke pear up a man's ass or down his throat? He won't have a prostate or teeth by the time I'm done with him."

Oh, I don't doubt that. "You do all that with CC, don't you?"

"She's different. She can take it. For the record, I don't hate men. I fuck them just fine, but I never let myself get close enough to one."

"Not even Charlie's dad?"

She pulls away from me and cups my face in her palms. "Not even him."

"You share a kid."

"Don't believe everything you hear, Oscar. Howard and I were never a thing."

"That still doesn't explain—"

Courtney presses a thumb against my lips, shushing me. "I kill scumbags for a living, Oscar. If anything, he's more likely to get a paddle shoved up his ass, and not in a fun way. I won't do that to you. And I don't want to talk about killing my son's father while you're between my legs. It'll taint what we are, and I can't have that.

"Now, I know I did plenty of that to him already… well, to you, and with how we ended, I just… I want a fresh start, okay? I need a fresh start. And he… *you* were someone I couldn't move on from, and now you're here—"

"Move on from me?" I ask slowly, speaking around her thumb and interrupting her tirade.

"Not *'move on,'* move on. Not like that." She squeezes her thighs around mine. "Everybody has unfinished business, and he is that for me. Well, *you* are that for me since you're one and the same. Then there's *her*, the one who supposedly started all of this, if Abby is to be believed. But she's long dead, so I can't exactly—"

I pull her thumb further between my lips and suck on it hard. That gets her to stop talking, albeit momentarily, as full-body tremors move through her.

It's the good kind, I think.

CC wasn't kidding last night. We both haunt her. I, her memories, and Yong, her dreams. She's carried us with her all this time, except…

"Did you get help?" I ask, suspecting I already know the answer to that.

Confusion clouds her features. "Help?"

"Yes, help. Professional help. Isn't that why Dr. Goodman took your Mom's place on the team? To help all of us when we needed it?"

She pushes my digit out of her mouth. "No, Sonya joined to bring Phoenix with her. That was her only condition. Phoenix has always been her main priority, and everything else followed. Besides, what kind of help could she give someone like me? I'm beyond saving, Oscar. I *am* this. I was born to be a killer, and Mom made sure I could never deviate from that path. By the time Sonya came along, the damage had already been done."

It is just as I feared.

Dr. Goodman did what she could with me, but Courtney? I doubt she was helped.

Instead, she spent all these years perfecting the art of deception, of duality. Just like her mother did.

The thing is, I *do* like her. The real her. The parts of her that are raw and genuine. Like this side, the one she's showing me.

It's like a switch has been flipped in her, and I love it.

What a difference twelve hours can make.

"Courtney, what we were put through was pretty fucked up, and everybody got help afterward. Or, at least, that's what your dad said. It's one of many reasons he gave for instituting the gag order."

"That's not what Lorenzo told me, and I didn't deserve to be helped. I threw myself into my studies, and I had Marc. You had, well, everyone else. Seems to me like you turned out okay."

"Do I look okay to you?"

"You look pretty well adjusted, all things considered."

"Because I got help. I'm not saying it was easy for me either. I had a mental breakdown. *Several* mental breakdowns. They got so bad that I had to be committed a few times, and Dr. Goodman helped me. Abby helped me, too. Still, it took me a long time and a lot of hard work to get to this point.

"I don't hate you for it, okay? I don't blame you for what transpired between us back then or afterward. There's more to me than being a genius with a penchant for numbers. You made me discover a lot about who I am, not just physically but also sexually. And Dr. Goodman helped me come to terms with all of it. You know what else she taught me?" She shakes her head, so I continue, "She taught me that it's not about saving; it's about acceptance. I accept what transpired between us because it made me who I am today. And if I had to do it all over again, I wouldn't change a thing."

She smiles at that, then wriggles against my cock. "I'm glad, 'cause I wouldn't either. But I'm not hurting you. Not anytime soon. I'm not saying no, just that it'll take some time and work on my part for me to get there."

It's a big fucking step for her to admit that, and y'know what?

I'll take it.

I'll take her any which way I can get her.

The good, the bad, and the ugly.

Chaos runs in our blood. It's who we are. Besides, we all have ugliness inside of us, so why not embrace it?

"I'm already your perfect fuck toy, so let's enjoy the rewards. If I want to be spanked, I'll ask CC. Deal?"

It's making light of what we went through, but I don't want her beating herself up about it.

She doesn't answer me but yanks my mouth back down to hers. I tug her bottom lip between my teeth, sucking on the soft flesh, and she makes a low choking sound. Next comes her tongue, and an answering shudder wracks through her.

"Let's go wake our girlfriend up," I mutter into her mouth.

She wraps her legs around my ass. "Sounds like a great idea."

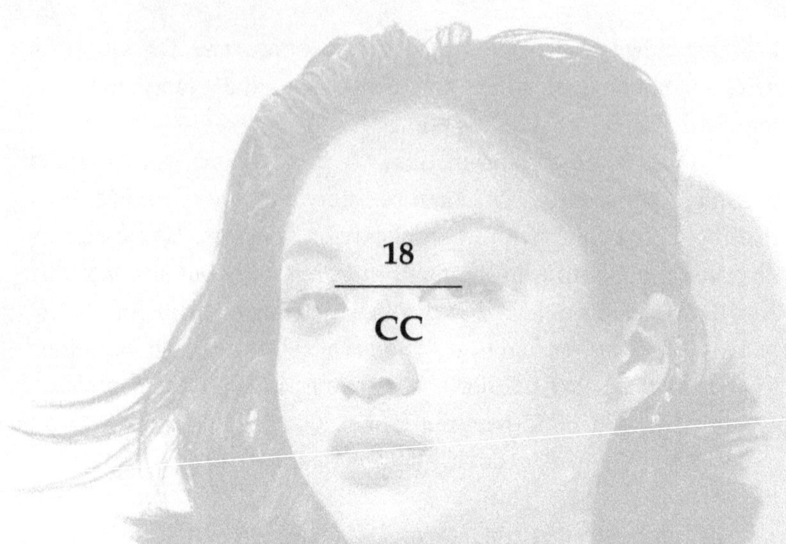

18

CC

The diner across the street from the Rochester Art Center is an unassuming, hole-in-the-wall place with exquisite cuisine. The owners are from Chongqing, China, so Sichuanese cuisine heavily influences the menu. Their dishes bring unique ingredients together that combine for a fabulous flavor harmony on the palate.

I ordered for us both since I arrived first. Abby would've done the same had she gotten here first. We're both foodies, so we like to switch things up and find obscure restaurants for our monthly meetings. Although, this is the sixth time she's picked this diner for our meet-up.

She's spent the last twenty minutes with her eyes glued to her smartphone while simultaneously playing with her Ma Po Tofu. In the meantime, I've scarfed down half of my Dandan Noodles, and I'm considering placing a to-go order.

Or rather, I'm considering taking hers once I'm done with mine since she doesn't seem to be interested in eating anyway.

It's like she reads my mind because she pushes her plate toward me.

I shrug, switch out dishes, and dive right in. She watches me for another ten minutes, not-so-subtly shaking her head.

Whatever.

I need the sustenance, okay?

My man and woman have been keeping me busy every night.

If Abby wants to watch me eat, who am I to deny her?

"Can we stop by the Art Center when we're done here?" I ask once I've cleaned out her dish. "The Bardales Exhibit will only be up for another week, and I need more pictures."

Aptly named, it's an homage to her mother and chronicles their early life in Detroit, Michigan, before her untimely demise. It features thirteen large, simple, yet complex monochrome paintings of their life then. It's how young Courtney saw the woman who taught her everything she knew.

Because of Sarah Bardales' reputation within the Italian Mafia, it's as though Courtney has been on a personal quest in the last nineteen years to portray the woman who gave her life as anything but that. The number thirteen seems to be the magic number, as that's how young she was when her mother died, and her life irrevocably changed.

It's obvious Sarah Bardales is still loved and revered by her children, even to this day. Marc named his law firm after her. She goes by the name Courtney Bardales in the Art world to purposefully distance her Art from the Sotelo Crime family.

This isn't the first exhibit Courtney has been featured in. More like it's the twenty-ninth in the US alone and the fifth in Rochester. She tends to go for the smaller galleries, as she's not doing this for notoriety or fame. She's also not one to toot her own horn and doesn't tell me when one is going up. The thing is, I've been following her career as an artist for sixteen years, and she just keeps getting better and better each year.

Either way, I'm fucking proud of her.

I'm fucking proud of my girlfriend, of the beauty she infuses into the world, despite the fact that her hands are steeped in blood.

And fuck, it feels fantastic to finally be able to call her my girlfriend.

Problem?

Abby can't even let me have that. She just has to go and shit all over it.

"This isn't a date, you know." She's scribbling something into a notebook.

"I never said it was. Just say no if you don't want to go with me."

"No, I'm not going in there with you," she continues, her tone flat. "It could give *some* people the wrong idea about us."

"Some people? Is that why we're here? Are you spying on someone? Meeting another client after this?"

"It's none of your business."

"You brought it up first. You can't do that and then expect me not to ask questions. If there's someone you think I should be avoiding—"

The words die out as she pauses mid-action, and our gazes lock. Something passes through her eyes — pain, I think — and it's gone in a flash.

"Naimo?" I ask of her former fuck buddy slash *not* ex-girlfriend. "I saw her name online as one of this month's visiting artists."

The Art world is small, and Naimo runs in the same circles as Courtney. She's the reason Abby and Naimo met a few years back at the Winter Park Sidewalk Art Festival in Florida. They hit it off too, to everyone's surprise. But, like Courtney and myself were, those two were never big on defining their relationship either, hence the former fuck buddy slash *not* ex-girlfriend label.

"Did you know she moved back to Rochester?" I infuse as much sincerity into my tone as I can muster, even if I'm just being nosy.

"She's originally from here, and I'm not discussing her with you."

"Why not?"

Abby sighs, then rips the page out and hands it to me. "The new code for Oscar's place."

Took her long enough. "I might not need this," I say, even as I fold the sheet and tuck it into my jeans pocket.

Her eyes narrow. "Why not?"

"We've been spending a lot of time at my place."

"Who's *we*?"

"Do you really have to ask?" I signal for the waitress.

"Did she see it?"

"Oscar's ass? Of course she did."

"And you're still here."

It's my turn to sigh. Where did she think I'd go?

"Where's Phoenix?" I ask instead, changing the topic.

"South Korea. Lorenzo gave the green light for her final procedure."

"Why am I not with her?"

"Because. Unlike Dr. Goodman, I don't have the credentials or experience to navigate those. I barely got her back into the clinic you two used two years ago since they still had your information on file. Before you suggest it, no, I refuse to go to fucking Nalina for assistance. That one has a big mouth, and she pissed off the twins."

I sag back in my seat and blow out a resigned breath. "That was unfortunate."

That turn of events had been surprising, to say the least, but it's been a long time coming.

And, as far as everyone is concerned, Phoenix never got a training partner.

Only, that's not true.

She got me instead.

And well… let's just say that's not the sort of thing to advertise to the group.

See, Lorenzo didn't *just* put a gag order on the entire group to keep them from telling Courtney about Oscar's true identity. He kept my identity a secret from all of them.

Why?

Because Deloise Milligan had to die.

Our waitress arrives, and we both place to-go orders and our checks all in one order. She lingers on for a bit, probably eye-fucking my tits like she has the last five times we came here before disappearing in a huff when I ignore her not-so-subtle attempts at flirting again.

I don't have time for that. I haven't, for years now.

There's a difference between *flaunting* the girls every chance I get and outright *flirting*. I don't do the latter, haven't for years, because I'm a taken woman.

"Speaking of," Abby suddenly says, shifting in her seat, "Can we make this quick? I have to get back."

"To?"

"South Korea. Where did you think I just came from?"

I shrug. "You're about to tell me."

"I just got off a fourteen-hour flight, and I only have six hours to get things done before I do it all over again. I also need your passport to get back."

Shrugging, I pull it and the manila envelope from my purse and slide it in her direction. "I found a few more familial matches. Those keep popping up out of the woodwork like fucking mold."

As a silent partner in Brewer Health — emphasis on the word *silent*, since I have a vested interest in flying under the radar — I get certain administrative privileges. I try not to abuse those too much, though.

Once upon a time, Sonya told me that I could use this third chance at life to become anything I wanted and that obsessively chasing Courtney around the world was not a sustainable life goal.

She had a point, I begrudgingly had to admit. I already have the brains and brawns and wasn't using any of it in a meaningful manner. The truth is, I like the twins. I like them as people, and I enjoy working with them. So when I first learned of their intent to establish Brewer Health, I asked that they sign me up, no strings attached. It's not like the money would've done me any good had I died.

Not even our attorney, Marc, knows who I am. Or, if he does, he's pretty tight-lipped about it, as is my agreement with the twins.

I also went into research, as that's as under the radar as one can go. Now, I use my mitochondrial DNA to track down remnants of my relatives in Japan, particularly the relatives of my ex-fiancé Hyouga Yamamoto and his sister. They're both dead, but I can't take any chances. That entire fucking family is as scummy as it gets. I can't have any of them getting a whiff of my existence and coming after me for revenge. I know Abby does a fantastic job of keeping *this* identity clean, so the least I can do is find any potential friends, foes, or threats first. I pass those names on to Abby monthly; she does her magic.

She purses her lips as she peruses the pages. "Half of these are on my radar already, but this one's new. You never told me she had another daughter."

"She didn't. At least, not officially. DNA doesn't lie; that's why I flagged it." I don't care what she does with the names on the list. "Do you need anything else?"

"Like?"

"I could refill Roxane's prescription for Diclegis," I offer.

Her eyes narrow again. "And you care… why?"

"I don't, but you do. Clearly."

"I didn't ask you to fill it the first time."

"No, Courtney did. She also said it was for a friend, but then her name showed up on some labs that Dahlia had sent specifically to the lab."

"What kind of labs?"

"That's proprietary information, and our arrangement doesn't cover that. Unless…"

"No," she bites out. "Count me the fuck out."

"You didn't even hear what I have to say."

"I don't have to. It's about Courtney again."

"Well, yes. But—"

"But nothing," she bites out. "You're playing with fire, Charlena. This obsession you have with Courtney has gone on for too long."

"Obsession? You really don't get it, do you?" It's absurd that I still have to justify my feelings to Abby after all this time.

She leans back in her seat and folds her arms over her chest. "Enlighten me."

A beat passes, and nothing.

Wow. She really did break free of her programming.

"You really have got a lid on it, haven't you? How *did* you manage that?"

She scoffs. "Like I'd tell you."

The waitress chose that moment to bring the check and our to-go orders. When she lingers this time around, Abby waves her off.

"That was nice of you," I tell her, my tone sincere.

She shrugs. "I'd rather wrap this one up quickly. What's your endgame?"

"I don't have one."

"Everybody *has* an endgame, including me. *Especially* Lorenzo, when it comes to her. And thanks to him, she thinks you are dead. She wholeheartedly believes you are dead. That's what drives her to do the things she does. Guilt, remorse, take your fucking pick. What do you think will happen when she finds out that the woman in her bed is the same one who haunts her dreams?"

These are all things I already know.

My lips part to tell Abby this, but something comes out instead. "I'm in love with her."

"No, you're in love with the idea *of* her. That's not the same thing."

"You're one to talk."

"And you underestimate just how deep Lorenzo's hooks into her go." She looks around for a beat, then leans in and grabs both my hands, squeezing them together. Her voice drops an octave. "I take that back. You know exactly what he's doing to her, and you're going along with it. And for what? Honor? Haven't you had enough?"

"You know nothing about me." I move to pull my hands out of hers, but she tightens her hold on me.

"This isn't a fucking game, *Yong*. It's not going to end in a fucking happily ever after. Not for you. So do yourself a favor, no, do everyone a favor and get the fuck out of her life before things get any worse than they already are."

"No can do."

"Don't push me, bitch. You have no idea the lengths to which I'll go to protect my sisters. If I have to, I will gut your fucking—"

The bell over the door chimes, and the last person I'm expecting walks through the doors.

Naimo Blithe, a silver-tongued goddess and the only woman

I've ever known who can and has rendered the great Abigail Sanders speechless.

Even though the look on Abby's face tells me that she had, in fact, been expecting this, seeing Naimo still knocks the wind out of her sails as the words — threats, really — die a swift death on her tongue.

With Abby momentarily distracted, I pull my hands from hers and not-so-subtly rub on my bruised wrists.

Naimo sees us, of course, and she's not one to play the *'it's fucking awkward running into my ex in public, so I'll run off and cower in the corner'* game. She ditches the group she's with and makes a beeline for our booth.

"Charlena," she says, as she sets her purse down next to Abby and effortlessly slides into the space beside me. "Fancy seeing you here," she adds dryly, flipping her neon-green braids over her shoulder and resting both elbows on the table.

Abby doesn't answer her right away. Instead, she shoves my passport and the rest of the papers into her purse and stands. "Not here," she bites out and holds a hand out to Naimo. "Not in front of her."

I watch as Abby practically drags Naimo out of the room and in the direction of the kitchen, and I can't help the answering smile that plays on my lips.

Abby can judge me all she wants, but she's just like me.

She's a slave to her heart, just like I am.

19

COURTNEY

I've been known by many names.
  Angel of Death.
Bringer of Death.
Collector of Souls.
Deadly Weapon.
Enforcer of Death.
Weapon with a choice.

Some of which are straight-up comical, yet all of which I love. These all have a recurring theme, highlighting the one thing I was born to do, trained to become, and an art I have perfected over the years.

I am ruthless. I am merciless.

I am Courtney Sotelo, née Bardales.

The only daughter of the deceased Sarah Bardales, a woman who, arguably, was the most ruthless contract killer for the Sotelos' Midwest chapter. One of many daughters of Lorenzo Sotelo, a man who rules said Midwest chapter with an iron fist.

I never stood a chance.

I was born a psychopath. My brother and I do have that in common. Our psychopathic tendencies are practically ingrained in our DNA. To some, it's a lethal combination. To others, they are the essential building blocks, the makings of the perfect serial killer.

As for me?

I choose to embrace it for what it is. Not only that, but I also choose to embrace it for what it can be, could be, and will always be. The circumstances surrounding my mother's death did push me to the life I choose to lead, and leading this life I choose comes with built-in anonymity, something I never expected but relish every single day.

And yet, because of her, I choked.

For the first time ever, I hesitated.

I showed weakness. I was… interested.

In her.

But the thing is, she isn't like the others.

She started this, all of this. She placed the hit on this trio.

Granted, they had it coming. I have every reason to want two out of three of them dead.

But her?

I can't figure out her end game.

In her eyes is a dead, soulless look as she studies the lifeless corpses of the trio who once were her mother, father, and betrothed. Or is it fiancé?

They call them all sorts of names.

I just killed all three before her, but she didn't blink. Instead, she looks… free. Relieved, almost.

Like me.

And I hate that, so I want to snuff that out.

"Leave no witnesses," I remind Lorenzo.

He loops an arm over my shoulder, reaching for the knife with his free hand. I relinquish the blade without a fight. After all, if I wanted it back, I could just as easily get it from him.

That's the beauty of growing old. Or, in our world, being plagued by this silly little thing called attachment.

"We need to work on curbing your blood lust," he tells me.

To disprove his point, I swipe my hands on my jeans instead of licking them.

Baby steps.

"I have it under control."

The look on his face, though. It's pure magic.

Like he's proud.

I should've expected this. He and I, we're cut from the same cloth.

"As much as I enjoy a good bloodbath, this one's a teensy bit overboard. Look at how well they've mastered theirs," he adds, angling his chin in Abby's and Phoenix's direction. "You taught them well, even though they've been at this much longer than you have."

A scoff bubbles up. "Check your math, Lorenzo. Phoenix is new at this."

"Phoenix has to worry about leaving traces behind."

"Why? She can just burn it all to the ground. That's what I'd do, but fire doesn't love me as much as it does her."

"You sure about that? How about her?"

I turn my attention to the one who started this, who called us here today. "What about her?"

"She hasn't stopped staring at you."

Is he being serious? We're working, and he's playing matchmaker?

"It's called multi-tasking. She's coming with us."

Why? I want to ask, but challenging him publicly won't be good.

People like her are dangerous. It certainly doesn't help that in the span of sixty minutes, I've seen too much of myself in her.

We are the same, after all.

How long would it take before she snaps? How long would it take before her mind fractures?

I would know. It happened to me. When her parents killed my mom right before me. All I've done is repay the favor.

Slowly, with the grace of a gazelle, she glides over to us. I'm drenched in the blood of her family and her fiancé; still, she's gazing at me like I'm the center of her universe. There's something in her hand, something she's clutching like her life depends on it.

From what I can make of it — circular, jagged edges, solid gold

— I'll wager it's a crest. A family crest, I think. Families like hers always have one.

Once she stops before me and holds it out to me, her fingers go slack.

I don't hold out my hand. I'm soiled in their blood. I'm afraid I'll stain it.

It doesn't seem to faze her, though.

Looking deep into my eyes, she thrusts the crest into my hand. Our skin touches briefly, sending tingles down my arm.

Dangerous.

"To die by your hand would be an honor," she whispers.

An honor?

Who the fuck says that?

As always, I'm ejected from that memory.

It's not gentle either. It's violent.

My body bolts upright, drenched in a rather nasty cold sweat. Night terrors, Dr. Goodman called them. I take a few deep breaths, willing my heart rate to return to normal, slowly but surely purging all remnants of heartache that still linger.

This is why I don't dream.

It's been sixteen long, torturous years, but the memories remain.

They haunt me, even though they shouldn't.

She's dead.

Has been for sixteen years now.

Lorenzo told me she'd died shortly afterward.

A drug overdose, he said. *Some people just can't hack it in the Network.*

It's a shame I couldn't bring her the death she desired.

20

COURTNEY

My house is eerily quiet this time of night. The purple glow of the antique but modified alarm clock on my nightstand reads 2:49. An exasperated groan bubbles up. I fall back with my arm draped over my face, my head hitting the pillow with a soft thud.

Going back to sleep is pointless, so I unceremoniously roll out of bed, letting out an appreciative groan when my feet sink into the plush carpet. I grab my phone off its charger and stuff it into my pocket. Since it's just me, I don't bother with the lights as I make my way to Charlie's bedroom. Habit, I suppose.

Contrary to what others may think, I enjoy spending time here. I camp out in Charlie's room on the nights he's home when I can't sleep. Even when he's not, I go in there. He's a reminder of one of the few things I've ever done right in my life.

It takes a minute for my eyes to get used to the darkness. Goosebumps prickle my skin, and only then does it dawn on me that I'm not alone.

"I gave you that code for emergencies only." My voice carries across the dark space to the figure sitting in pitch-black darkness, leaning against Charlie's crib.

I can barely make out the subtle perk in Roxane's ears at the sound of my voice. She turns to face me, the corners of her mouth tipping up into the beginning of a smile.

"This *is* an emergency."

"Just because we're neighbors doesn't mean you can break into my house anytime you see fit."

"It's the only way I could get your attention. You've been avoiding me for weeks, Courtney. You're barely home, ignore my text messages, and won't take my calls. Hard not to take that personally."

"I've been busy."

"Busy avoiding me, you mean?" She shifts, then places her hand over the protrusion before her. That's when I notice… him.

Make that *two* figures huddled in the darkness.

The other is curled beside her, with his head in her lap. She's threading her fingers through his hair; her lips are moving, but no sound comes out. He must be enjoying this, whatever this is. The even rise and fall of his chest reveals he's fast asleep.

He's not panicked like I would've expected. Instead, he looks content.

"If this isn't the weirdest shit I've seen in years," I whisper, flipping the switch on one of Charlie's night lamps before joining them on the floor, sitting directly opposite them.

Pinprickles run down my spine, and an eerie feeling of déjà vu settles over me.

It's brief, gone as swiftly as it appears, clearing up my mental faculties so I can fully absorb just what the fuck this is.

My brother-in-law, Harris — who *technically* isn't my brother-in-law, but he and Marc have been together for over sixteen years, so he might as well be — is in Charlie's room, and of his own volition, it would seem. He's also fast asleep, partially curled up in Roxane's lap, my very pregnant neighbor.

It really is quite the sight.

If only Marc and Delilah were here to witness this.

Those three are fighting over something, and it must have been major since Harris left home as a result of it. I don't think it has to do with his latest blowout — or rather, tantrum — at our last dress fitting for the annual Sotelo Ball either, since it's common knowledge in the group that he detests those things. Then again, Harris has been tight-lipped about the whole thing. Personally, I'm not invested enough in their relationship to pry.

Oh, who am I kidding?

I'm a nosy bitch, but I also love my brother, and by extension, I care about the people he surrounds himself with. I may not be the best mother to Charlie, but I care about my son's well-being. I'm not ashamed to admit that Marc's place is the most stable environment for him, not mine. As such, my interest primarily lies in keeping *that* environment stable at all times… for my son's sake.

Right now, it's anything but.

My guess?

The topic of children came up again.

Marc wants them. Their partner, Delilah, has always wanted them. Harris does not. I don't know what Harris was thinking when he spent all those years actively pursuing her, knowing she wasn't changing her mind about kids. I'm guessing it came up again after his tantrum, and it was bad enough that Harris showed up at my doorstep that night.

I know it was bad enough that I had to wake Ida — Charlie's nanny — up in the dead of night to get him and return him to his uncle's, and he's been there ever since.

Talk about drama.

Don't get me wrong, I love drama — as long as it's other people's. Not so much the kind that involves me. Yet somehow, my son and I are caught in the middle of it, even though neither of us wants to be. Sure, it gave me a few child-free days, but those days have stretched into a few weeks, and there doesn't seem to be an end in sight.

Or maybe there is one on the horizon if this is the sort of thing I get to witness in the middle of the night.

"Why's this weird?" Roxane eventually asks when the silence stretches on for too long.

"You know he's allergic to kids, right?" I angle my chin at Harris, my gaze transfixed by how she rakes her nimble fingers across his scalp, seamlessly weaving them in and out of his hair. He and I are alike in that the texture of our hair is identical, and we're also very selective about who we let near our manes. I'm impressed she talked him into letting her fingers in his.

Then again, she is good at that.

She's good at convincing people to do the things they generally shy away from. She's also good at getting them to act against their self-interests, however selfish those might be.

Still, this isn't the craziest thing I've witnessed in this room, not by a long shot, but it is the weirdest.

Roxane chuckles at that. "There's no such thing."

"Tell that to the man curled up on your lap. Speaking of, how did you manage that?"

"Oh, this?" She keeps her eyes on Harris as she talks. "I found him standing out there, staring at the crib. He didn't seem in the least bit fazed that I'd gotten in."

"Broke in, you mean. I told you that code was to be used for emergencies only, and this is anything but." I give her a look-over. "At least you seem to still be in one piece, save for that. Mind telling me what you two have to talk about?"

"Not much." She gives me a noncommittal shrug. "He wanted to know about all of this. He also said the only other pregnant woman he knows hates his guts. I can't fault the guy for asking questions, and he *is* curious about many things."

"Surely you can't be that naive. He's here, in my house, in my son's room, and Charlie isn't. What does that tell you?"

"That we all have our hang-ups, Courtney. It doesn't mean we aren't capable of working through them."

"By using Charlie's room? I can't say I approve of it."

Another shrug. "In a way, this is some exposure therapy for him."

I shake my head, unable to hide the smirk that forms. "Harris has been around Charlie plenty, so whatever this is, exposure therapy," I put air quotes around the word, "as you so eloquently put it, won't do. He doesn't work that way. He's not like us."

"Us?" she asks, her lips morphing into a mischievous smile. "So, you admit that there is an us?"

"Don't make this weirder than it already is," I reply with a glare in her direction.

She schools her features and, with her gaze downcast, mumbles, "Sorry."

"Don't be," I say softly. "I just don't need people misunderstanding what we are and aren't."

And by people, I mean CC.

Putting myself in her shoes, there's no easy or logical explanation for why my single, drop-dead gorgeous, and heavily pregnant neighbor-slash-friend is in my son's nursery. Or even why she has free access to my house when my girlfriend doesn't.

Then I remind myself that this is what she wanted all those years ago — keeping us a secret. It's been hard, but I've respected her wishes, whether I liked it or not. Marc had this place built for me when I was pregnant with Charlie, so CC doesn't know where I live now either, per *that* arrangement. I don't question or nitpick over who her friends are, but that hasn't stopped her from flying into a jealous fit every chance she gets, particularly about the people I choose to surround myself with.

I suspect that's going to change now, except… I don't know how to do any of this. I don't know how to conduct a relationship like normal people do. I wouldn't even know where to begin with all of that, as my life is complicated enough.

It had been my mother's dream to see Marc and I properly assimilated into the world while simultaneously hiding us from our father. The first part has been a success, all things considered, but that's thanks in part to the second.

I don't know how Mom thought she could've pulled off the second part. One could argue it was the eighties and things were different then. But knowing what I know now — that Lorenzo keeps track of his bastard children like they're some kind of trophies — he had to have known about us the entire time. He didn't have us removed because he genuinely believed we were better off with her.

That, and she was the love of his life.

Until she died, then he dragged us into his criminal enterprise with every intention of turning us into his fucking puppets.

Back then, I wanted to believe that the reason he officially brought us into his family to be raised alongside the rest of his children was because Mom's blood was on his hands, not because he felt the need to do right by her or some other sentimental bullshit.

Marc and I, we don't do sentiment, and we don't do bullshit either.

That's not to say that the damage hadn't already been done. That's what happens when psychopaths raise psychopaths.

I don't have normal friends. I never learned how to forge regular bonds with others. Lorenzo, bless his heart, tried his best in that regard, but he was too busy training us on how to be the perfect mimics — while simultaneously turning me into the perfect killing machine and one of his deadly weapons — that this was never a priority.

I kill people for a living. I do other things too, mostly to appear normal by societal standards. Like having the stereotypical white picket fence, birthing the obligatory child, maintaining a flourishing career as an artist, and keeping up with the ordinary job as an art teacher.

None of that changes who I am, nor the things I've done and will continue to do. I'm not a good person, and I've never pretended otherwise. So even though I know I will regret the next words that come out of my mouth, I say them anyway.

"Can I ask you something? It's about the Chun-ja family crest."

Her hand pauses mid-action. "Do I have to answer?"

I shrug, even though her gaze is trained on Harris's sleeping figure. "That's up to you."

She scrunches her face up in concentration, and several beats pass. "It's gonna cost you," she eventually says, her hand resuming movement.

I don't doubt it. I've been racking my brain for days and still can't come up with a plausible explanation for why Oscar would bear that mark.

Simply put, it's a kiss of death.

According to Lorenzo, the best way to keep it safe and hidden — along with the billions of dollars funneled through their coffers — is to break it apart, but it's a catch-22. Its bearers knew that for the pieces to be put together, the skin had to be carved off their bodies. Whether or not they would survive it…

"It's been years," Roxane says, interrupting my thought. "The Chun-jas have been dead for sixteen years, so why are you asking about their crest now?"

If only it were that simple. "Just because they're all dead doesn't mean they've been forgotten."

"Well, duh. Let me guess, you're still having nightmares about that night. You just had another one, didn't you?"

I don't answer her. Granted, she's not wrong, but I refuse to reward her lack of boundaries.

Except my silence doesn't dissuade her. "Just because you killed them doesn't mean you have to live with their deaths on your conscience. They brought that on themselves. Abby and Phoenix were willing, but they let you have the honors."

Urgh. That word.

She has a point, but that's not what this is about.

It has to do with my two worst nightmares converging upon each other, and I need to make sense of it. Right now, she's the only one capable of giving me unfettered answers. "I know Lorenzo destroyed the original, but not before Mattie had me redesign the crest and modify it for human skin. She also had me split it into three parts. You got one of them. Who got the other two?"

She bites the inside of her mouth.

"What?"

"I didn't get it. After learning what it would entail, Abby had me put mine on her back instead, then covered it with that giant koi fish tattoo. She said it would be her honor to die in my place."

Urgh. That word again. "Why did Mattie allow the switch or the cover-up? Everyone knows she's a stickler for the rules, especially where it involves her precious granddaughter."

"Why else?" She shrugs, her lips morphing into a mischievous smile. "Dr. Goodman intervened, and Olive Hyun sided with her. Considering those two never saw eye to eye on anything, it caused quite the uproar."

"How come I didn't know about any of this?"

"Your dad." Another shrug. "He kept you in the dark on purpose. He kept you across the country on purpose."

"No, he didn't." I'm almost impressed with how easily the lie rolls off my tongue.

Lorenzo lying to me is nothing new. After all, he claims that he *and* Marc were against me taking my mother's place on his super-secret death squad. As I later found out, it was his idea. It's a point of contention between them.

Unfortunately, you can't train a child to kill and then expect her to flick a switch and turn it off.

"If that's what you want to believe, that's your prerogative. He still lies to you, you know? You just want to see what you want to see." Roxane pauses, and it's a heavy sort of pause. "That's not to say I got out of it scot-free. They all agreed that I was to take over those duties since Abby and I were the only two trained tattooists in the group. As Mattie phrased it, putting the crests on everyone else was my punishment."

That makes sense. "Who got the second?"

"Phoenix," she immediately says. "She wanted hers done in invisible ink since her surgeries were still ongoing. Even though Dr. Goodman oversaw those, the fewer questions either had to answer to her surgeons about the tattoos, the better it was for everyone involved."

I press the bridge of my nose between two fingers. All this time, my friends made selfless sacrifices for their prey, and I was... hiding? Playing a part in Lorenzo's twisted fantasy? Both?

"And the third?"

"Olive's son."

That makes no sense. "Why?"

"Why else? He's expendable. We all are. It's the nature of the beast."

"That's beside the point. Unless someone was actively planning for Olive's untimely demise, which they weren't, there's no chance of him ever becoming a weapon. Why did you do that, knowing it was futile?"

"I don't understand the question."

I grit my teeth at that, reminding myself that my anger isn't directed at Roxane but mainly at the training program itself... and the woman who ran it.

"Orders or not, why did you put it on him?"

"You'll have to take that one up with your dad, Courtney. If you ask me, Oscar should never have gotten into the program in the first place. But since an exception was made for Phoenix, the same was made for him. At his *mom*'s insistence."

I'm seeing red at this point.

All this time, I wanted to pretend I didn't know why I felt so protective of him. It had nothing to do with CC. More so that despite outward appearances, I could sense the hurt he carried with him, and just how deep his metaphorical scars ran. As much as I'd like to pretend otherwise, I can't unsee what I saw.

Now I understand why CC was always so cryptic about his body. About him. Never, in a million years, did I imagine he was *mine*. I didn't want to think Olive could do that to her own child. After all, it was *she* who warned me off him years ago.

"I pity him," Roxane suddenly says. "His is in the worst possible location, too." She winces at that, and I have to concur.

"Yeah, I saw it."

"You did, huh? Took you long enough." She tilts her head to the side, letting her gaze roam all over my face as she studies me. Those eyes are unnerving, and I wish I didn't feel so exposed under her scrutiny.

"Whose idea was it to put it on his butt cheeks?"

"His mom's." Another pause. "If you saw it, then... did you two...?"

My cheeks warm, heat spreading through me. "I'm not answering that." Not in front of my brother-in-law, I'm not.

"You don't have to. Your face looks like someone poured flaming hot Cheetos all over it. If you must know, Oscar has always been very protective of his body, so if he willingly showed it to you, it means he trusts you."

Hearing that gives me warm fuzzies. Still, "My sex life isn't up for discussion, Roxane."

"Right." She clears her throat. "What happened between you two was not your fault. There was too much bad blood to begin with, and you were caught in the crosshairs. You were both doomed from the start. With your parents' blessing, Mattie took certain... *creative* liberties with your training. She threw out the rule book, and no one thought to tell you. Lorenzo and Olive signed off on everything done to you both, and then some.

"Back then, Olive made sure that Oscar didn't have a choice, but Lorenzo made sure you did. It's why your pairing was done the way it was. You were never meant to meet, and that was by design. Just as it was intentional, not telling you who got each piece of the crest. After everything he had already been through, I thought you would've stopped it at the first session, not make him go through all nine sessions."

I'm mortified. "Nine sessions?"

I don't have a tattoo, but I didn't think it would've taken that long.

"You designed it, Courtney. And since you've seen it, you know that he got the largest piece. The ass is very sensitive, so I could only do parts of it at a time. The skin took forever to heal between sessions, and Mattie made him sit on it bow-legged after every session. She said it builds character or some bullshit, but she was just looking for an excuse to up the ante.

"Something you said must've pissed Mattie off because she took you guys from water-boarding exercises straight to that, no break in between. What's worse, she turned the whole thing into some twisted sex game, making sure you were in his ear the entire time, coaxing him on. I was there, and I remember thinking how messed up it was that you were both into that sort of torture play, but Phoenix warned me it wasn't my place to judge since neither of you knew what was going on.

"And then you left him. Graduated early, Mattie said. You cut off all contact with him. Then his mom ditched him or supposedly *retired* and moved halfway across the world. It's a miracle Oscar didn't break after all that. It's a fucking miracle that he's still holding it together, considering everything Mattie and Olive are doing to him to this day."

"I didn't cut him off." My voice is hoarser than I intend. "Not completely. I… I didn't know. I just…"

"Don't you think I know that? I'm just telling you as it is since you asked. I don't give a flying fuck about some pointless gag order. Put yourself in his place. It's hard not to take that shit personally when the woman you like keeps in touch with everyone else in the group except you. But he stopped asking me about you years ago, he must've found a way to insert himself into your life.

"As messed up as it sounds, you're the only thing keeping him together, then and now. If you're asking about that stupid crest, it tells me you must've liked him back, not just because you two were manipulated into regularly having phone sex as part of your training."

"That's not—"

"I get it, okay? She did the same with Abby and me and for much longer. Take it from someone who knows. There's still hope for you and Oscar. Just don't push him away again. I'm not sure if he could survive it a third time."

We sit in silence as the weight of everything settles in on me. Of just how much I've wronged him all this time.

What I'm about to propose, it's against the rules. I know this. But Mattie tossed the rule book first, so who's to say I can't do the same? It's not like she has to know.

Even if she does, I don't care.

Or rather, I shouldn't care so much. I really shouldn't.

But if Roxane is right, I've always had a say in this. That my right to exercise *that* say was taken away from me, from us both, irks me to no end.

Still, I say, "Can you re-do his piece on me?"

She barks out a laugh. "That's gonna cost you. Big time."

"Name your price."

21

COURTNEY

I feel her gaze settle on me. "Carte blanche? Bad idea, Courtney."

When I say nothing else, Roxane blows a tired breath and runs a hand over her swollen stomach. A dreamy expression comes over her face, and I feel it, deep down in my bones, that she's about to turn the infamous Lavenworth charm on me.

Then she does.

"I was hoping you would reconsider," she says, keeping her voice even.

Dread takes the place of anger and settles in the pit of my stomach. "My answer hasn't changed."

This isn't even my business. It's Abby's to handle, yet somehow it ended up on my fucking doorstep.

"But she'll be here in a few weeks, and I can't do this alone. I need a logical and organized person to ensure my birthing plan gets followed to a T, and you are that."

Did she miss the part where Marc handled all of mine? I distinctly remember telling her that when she first brought up this preposterous idea.

"Whoever gave you that impression ought to be shot, their entrails carved up and redistributed to their family members. I'd happily oblige, except I'm too busy avoiding you."

She laughs, unfazed by my words. "See, that's where you're wrong. It's not me you're avoiding. It's all of the responsibility that comes with this."

"What's the difference?"

"The difference is, I *know* you, Courtney. I understand you better than most. And if that not-so-subtle threat was supposed to scare me—"

"That wasn't a threat."

"— then you'll just have to try something else, but know that it won't work."

"You sure about that?"

"I am." She nods, holding my gaze. "The thing is, I trust you. Unconditionally. I can't help it. You know it's how she conditioned me to feel about all of you. I don't care if you abuse that trust, as it won't change a damn thing."

"That's what they all say. Until the pain starts. Then they all go running for the hills."

She waves me off. "You can stab me in the back for it if you so choose, or you can strangle me while looking me in the eye, and I'll keep on trusting you with my dying breath."

"You shouldn't trust me, Roxane. You really shouldn't."

"Oh, but I do."

"This isn't you talking. It's the hormones, and it'll pass. It did for me."

"But you had help."

"That I did. Your point being?"

"It's all I'm asking for. Help. Call it foolish or reckless, but the truth remains that you're the only one I can turn to in my time of need."

And here comes the guilt card.

It's hard work holding back the eye roll. She ought to know by now that flattery will get her nowhere fast with me.

"You can skip the theatrics, Roxane. I'm not going to be your birthing partner simply because you bat your eyelashes at me. And I'm not helping you raise this kid just because we're neighbors. That you're willing to trust the well-being of your child to a killer,"

I shake my head, a tsk-tsk noise slipping past my lips, "I can't decide if you're stupid, irresponsible, or both."

Her mouth falls open, and a glossy sheen springs into her eyes. If not for the rays of moonlight catching it at just the right angle, I'd have missed it too.

My words, callous as they seem, hurt her. I know they did. She can't cover the hurt in her expression, even though I know she's trying.

She's just like someone else I know.

"Hurts, doesn't it?" I ask, my tone solemn as I state the obvious.

She looks away, blinking back tears. "You think?"

"That's how Abby felt when you fucking left her. Twice."

She winces, and I almost feel bad for her.

"So this is about payback?"

"No, this is who I am. It's who I've always been. You did say that you know me, and that you understand me better than most, so it should come as no surprise to you, the fact that I'm a vindictive bitch.

"You hurt my friend, Roxane. I know you're hurting too, but it could've been avoided from the start had you been honest with her. Despite all that, she's willing to help you. Say the word, and she'll drop everything and rush to your side in a heartbeat. All you have to do is pick up the phone and fucking call her."

She shifts in her position on the floor. "I can't."

"Can't? Or won't?" I toss back at her.

Her lips straighten into a firm line, and that tells me all I need to know. I'm annoyed that her reluctance to answer the question isn't putting my mind at ease, so I do what I do best — poke and prod even further.

"What about Evan?" I ask, referring to the third person in this weird love triangle they've got going. "You gonna ask him?"

Truth be told, I'm not above hitting below the belt. If it gets her out of my hair *and* my son's nursery, even better.

Her eyes meet mine, tears flowing freely. "I can't ask this of him."

"Why the hell not?"

"He's not even my boyfriend."

"But he wants to be," I counter.

She gives me a sad smile. "It'll only lead to more misunderstandings at the hospital, especially since the baby isn't his."

"What about me? You think people won't misunderstand if I'm there, cutting her fucking umbilical cord and signing off on things I have no business getting involved in?"

"I have you listed as my sister. That should clear up any confusion."

"We look nothing alike!"

"*Adopted* sister. They won't look into it that deeply. No one ever does."

This time I laugh, but it is humorless. "What happens when Lorenzo gets wind of this? Then what?"

"Trust me, he won't."

"I'm his daughter, Roxane. He keeps tabs on me. He keeps tabs on all of his bastard children since we're just things to him, fucking trophies for him to manipulate as he sees fit. If he treats his own blood like that, what do you think he'll do to you?"

"He doesn't care for someone *like* me," she tosses back. "Even if he *does* find out, he has better things to do than get into a pissing contest with her sperm donor."

That's a nice way of referencing the asshole that got her pregnant, something she conveniently refuses to address. She claims not to know who he is, but I'm not heartless enough to dismiss what has been staring me in the fucking face all this time. Something *did* happen to her. Her not wanting Abby involved has nothing to do with boundaries. It only fuels the nagging thought in my mind that it can't be good. Abby has a way of drawing information out of her, so she's keeping her distance. And whatever it is, heads will roll.

I wish they would figure out their shit and leave me out of it.

"Honestly, Roxane. If not Abby, then just pick the path of least resistance and call Evan. He wants you, and he wants her. From what I've heard, he considers her as his own. He wants to adopt her."

She laughs at that, but it's strained. "That's news to me."

"Bullshit. You talk a big game, but when it comes down to it, you're just as scared of relationships and commitment as the rest of us. You can have all the help you want at your disposal, but you're either too proud or too stupid to ask for it. Instead, you come groveling to me, of all people. I know your sense of self-preservation is much stronger than this. Heck, it's much stronger than *her* conditioning. It's also how you were strong enough to walk away from it all, even knowing how much it'd hurt Abby, then and now."

"Or maybe I'm not as strong as you're making me out to be."

"Again, bullshit. Why come to me, knowing full well I'd just tell her? Why move in next door to me, knowing that associating with me in any capacity spells danger for you and your baby? And why ask for my help when you know what I'm capable of?"

"Because if it came down to it, you'd protect me. It's who you are."

I shake my head. "I don't know who you *think* I am, but make no mistake. I will toss you to the wolves if it means protecting my skin. Besides, I have my own problems to worry about. I don't need yours thrown into the mix."

She tilts her head, studying me with tear-filled, unnerving eyes. "You're not going to hurt me, not until after I have this baby," she evenly says. "Courtney Sotelo doesn't harm the innocent, and this baby is that. An innocent."

My shoulders sag against the wall, my lips thinning out.

She has a point.

I hate that she knows this about me.

"Believe it or not, I want to do right by her," she continues, now that she has me where she wants me. "After everything we've been through, I'd rather drag my tits through a bed of hot coals than have her face the same fate I did. And if you can do it, so can I." She continues to rake her fingers through Harris's hair, who, as it so happens, is still asleep. We're not exactly quiet, so how he can sleep through this beats me. "I'm not cut out for relationships, so I'm going to pour everything I've got into this parenting thing instead."

"Best of luck. Lord knows you're going to need it."

Roxane gives me a tight smile. Her tear-stained cheeks look flushed in the nightlight. "I don't need luck. I have you. That's my trade-off."

"No can do. Unlike Lorenzo, my word is not my bond. I can revoke it at any time."

"And I told you this was going to cost you — big time. Consider everything else I told you a freebie. You take me to the hospital, and I'll put Oscar's tattoo on you. Stick around, and I'll show you how to de-program the sex code that Mattie buried in your subconscious. I'll even show you how to remove that pesky little thorn in your side once and for all."

For her sake, she had better not be referring to CC. "You know I could just give Evan a call, right?"

Her eyes narrow. "You wouldn't."

Before I can answer, my phone buzzes in my pocket.

"Would you look at that? Duty calls."

"Right," she drawls sarcastically. "Anything to get out of this."

The resigned undertones in her voice give me pause. "I'm only going to say this once, so listen carefully. Call my brother tomorrow morning and tell him I sent you."

"Why do I need—"

"Because he dealt with my shit two years ago. Whatever this is," I point to her swollen abdomen, "is bigger than I can handle. Whoever the guy is, he needs to be stopped. And since you don't want Abby to handle it, try taking the legal route for a change."

"But he's—"

"A good lawyer," I deadpan. "The best of the best. Do yourself a favor and tell him exactly what you're so scared of. Tell him if it's Lorenzo, Mattie, or even Olive, and he'll handle it. Then I'll reconsider this preposterous idea of yours."

She's looking at me, wide-eyed. "How do I know I can trust him?"

"Because he's the reason I was able to graduate from the program early."

22

COURTNEY

I t's been forty-eight hours since my encounter with Roxane, and her words still weigh heavily on my mind.

I've been going through the motions every day, thoroughly distracted by the things I can't unsee and this new information I can't unlearn. To make matters worse, I still have two weeks' worth of commissioned art to finish up for the Blakeleys, and I can't bring myself to focus on those.

Instead, I've been obsessed with Oscar's ass, no pun intended.

At least Harris has intentionally kept himself scarce all morning since he knows better than to get in my way when I'm working.

I can't brush aside a nagging feeling that there is something else that I'm supposed to be doing today.

The back patio is a mess. I'm covered in pencil lead, several papers were strewn about, and I'm still no closer to recreating Oscar's exact piece.

When in doubt, start from the beginning.

Or freestyle it; that works on occasion.

I sit cross-legged and on my ass, like Oscar showed me he used to after each session. Then I take in a deep, calming breath, and my eyelids drift closed. On autopilot, my mind wanders back to that place, to that day.

The date that haunts me. The day of reckoning for the Chun-ja's.

Pencil and sketch paper in hand, I let the past flicker in front of me. Each memory that surfaces is accompanied by an annoyingly painful jolt. I allow myself to revel in those as each still flicks past in my mind's eye.

My hand starts to move. In the present, it's mapping out a blueprint of that house. Specific images spring to the forefront of my mind as the lines form, taking on a life of its own. Starting with our arrival at their compound and how easy it was to break past their defenses and incapacitate their guards.

It was too easy, now that I'm thinking back on it.

He's the first one to go: the husband, Geon Chun-ja. Eliminate the biggest threat first, and you have everyone else right where you want them. My blade runs deep as it slices across his throat, and the arterial spray covers me instantly. It takes a full minute for the life to drain out of his eyes, and even longer for him to bleed out.

His wife, Hwang Chun-ja, isn't so lucky. Unlike his, her cut is shallow, like she directed her husband to do to Mom. Her eyes dance back and forth between her daughter and me; the former is currently perched on a stool behind me with her legs crossed, watching the scene unfold.

I don't have to look to see the look on Yong's face. I can see it so clearly. Or maybe it's my mind playing tricks on itself, letting me see things I know shouldn't exist in this memory, like the sinister smirk plastered on her face. But I *do* know that as Hwang expels her dying breath, she knows that her death comes at her daughter's hand. Her own flesh and blood.

My hand moves faster now, the rustling of paper a momentary distraction as each one fills up. I'm not worried about perfection; those kinks can be smoothed out later. As long as I commit these images to paper, I can always eliminate the ones I don't need.

I'm good at that. Eliminating things. People too.

And so was Yong.

I remember thinking then that just because she isn't the one wielding the blade doesn't mean she isn't as deadly as the rest of us.

Yong's fiancé is next.

Hyouga Yamamoto.

There's no denying that she saved the best for last. The man gives me the heebie jeebies, and I've only just met him. Meanwhile, she's had to put up with him all her life, so I can't imagine what that's been like. He wasn't supposed to be here that day, but Lorenzo pulled some strings to ensure he would be. He's the perfect patsy, even though he's no innocent. This wasn't a case of *wrong place, wrong time* either. It's more like the *right place, right time, right circumstances*. Their eldest daughter's blood was on his hands, so no one would bat an eyelash at this.

I never understood families like that. The kind that will toss their flesh and blood into the lion's den to save their skin. Someone murders your first child, in cold blood, on her wedding night no less, and your response to that is to… hand over your next and only surviving child to *him*?

I pitied her. And at the same time, I didn't.

This is about payback. This is about taking revenge on the ones who killed my mother. But why does it feel like I'm missing a piece of this puzzle?

Before I can dwell on this any further, she's moving.

Yong is.

Toward me.

She should be running for the hills. I look like a still from the movie Carrie, covered in their blood from head to toe. I'm dressed in black, so aside from my face and arms, one can't tell. But I can feel it. The stickiness of their warm blood against my skin. I like it too.

I'd like it even better with her blood on my skin, too.

But no. Lorenzo disagrees.

He physically stops me, teases me for my insatiable bloodlust, and then takes the switchblade from me.

"Some people are worth more alive than dead," he says.

Everything else fades to the background, but not her. She's still moving toward me with her family crest in hand. Her lips are moving, but I don't grasp the words. I can't because my auditory senses are focused on something else.

The lilt in her voice. It's familiar.

I've heard it before. Recently too.

But *where*?

Our gazes lock, and our skin connects. It's brief, and another jolt hits me. Good tingles, I think. Past and present.

Then she says those blasted words.

"To die by your hand would be an honor."

God, I loathe that word. I hate it with a passion.

Familiar or not, I remind myself that she did die, just not by my hand. Why fight so hard to live, only to die so foolishly and without the honor she craved?

My movements are slowing down now. My body feels like it's coming off the tail-end of a marathon. My erratic breathing slows.

I scoot back and stretch my legs out from underneath my body as I survey my handiwork.

The first thing that comes to mind is, *Did I do all that?*

There have to be over thirty different sketches strewn about, maybe more. How many of these will I keep, and how many of them will *actually* mean something? How much of it is simply white noise my brain needed merely to sort through?

I could give all of this to Roxane and see if she can make sense of it, too. Or see this one through to the end.

A shadow falls over me, and a small hand curls over my shoulder.

Charlie?

No, it can't be. He's at his uncle's place, and I would've gotten advance notice if he or Ida, Charlie's nanny, were planning on bringing him over. Especially with Harris not-so-subtle in his lurking, he's eyeing me like I've officially lost my mind.

Even though I haven't. There's just… a method to my madness.

This isn't a dream, either. There's a very real person touching me.

"Is that Yggdrasil?" Feorie asks in her sweet, childlike voice.

Oh.

Shit.

There's that missing piece of this puzzle. I have a class today with Feorie.

"Kind of," I tell her. "I was having a bit of an epiphany."

It's the best excuse I can come up with since I'm not even prepared for her, and that's a first for me. I've never had to cancel a single class in the two years we've been doing these private art lessons. It didn't matter where in the world I was or what I was doing; I always made it back for this.

In some ways, she reminds me of… well, *me*, when I was her age.

Also, these classes aren't just for me but for David, too. It's a chance for him to spend time with his daughter. More often than not, he's a distraction to her when he tags along, so I just charge him three times as much to make up for it. Feorie doesn't care since she sees him as competition, which is what he wants, so he's happy to pay, too; even though he'd never admit that out loud.

Nor can he legally acknowledge her as his, not when her mother, Rose, put her husband's name on Feorie's birth certificate. Then again, their situation is complicated enough, so I'm just doing what I can to help.

Feorie's hand falls off my shoulder, and she steps closer to my mess. "I didn't think you were into Norse mythology, Courtney."

She hit the nail on the head with that observation. "I could be," I say instead.

"It's all wrong," There's a trace of a smile on her lips as she's surveying everything before us. "Roots are supposed to go down, while branches go up and to the sides. You have everything going everywhere, but… they all seem to converge in that spot over there," she points to a far-off corner, then tilts her head to the side, "at the… is that a crypt? And all of these markings… I didn't think you could understand Japanese?"

Say what now?

"I don't."

I mean, the Chun-jas lived in Japan. That's where we killed them and torched their estate. A lot was happening that day, so it's possible I saw a lot more than I thought but couldn't recall, and now my muddled mind just regurgitated all of that for me.

"So all of this came from your head then. What was this epiphany you had, and can you teach me?"

"I wouldn't know where to begin," I tell her.

Art is my forte, not languages.

I see her point, though. The markings are new, and I have no clue what any of it means.

"… recognize some of the words. That one roughly translates to *'true mother,'* and the other is for—"

I stand and wipe my hands off my shirt. "Which one?"

I'm looking at the same thing she is and not seeing what she's seeing. Not even when she picks out the sheet in question and hands it to me. I remind myself that with how her brain works, she sees patterns where others might not.

That, and I drew this what, fifteen, sixteen years ago? Most, if not all, of this went into the modified version of the information I pulled from that damned crest, but I don't have my notes from that time. Did I just do more work for myself by doing things this way?

I could just ask Mattie for those notes. I know she still has them. Or better yet, I should've just asked Oscar to pose for me; that would've been easier. Faster too.

To her credit, Feorie stays silent as I flitter between the living room and the backyard, setting up the space for her lesson. I cannot, for the life of me, recall what I told her we would be working on this week. Was it more live portraits? I hope that wasn't it because I don't have any new subjects lined up for her. I'm pacing about the backyard, wondering where I'm going to find one on such short notice.

I've been her teacher for almost two years now. I should've done the responsible thing and canceled. I should send her home; it'd be the right thing to do. Except Rose, her mother, will throw a hissy fit about it, and sometimes, these lessons are about getting Feorie away from that woman, albeit for a short time.

That woman just loves to threaten that she would put a stop to these lessons for any reason she can think of, no matter how trivial.

Sometimes, it's because she woke up on the wrong side of the bed. Sometimes, it's because her tool of a husband complains about how much this is costing him — even though they aren't the ones footing the bill for this. David is.

It's not like there's anything sinister afoot. Who my father is was never a secret. As far as anyone is concerned, all we share is DNA, so she can't use that against me. And even though Feorie has her quirks, there's no denying that there's no one better suited to handle those and her.

Plus, Rose knows that if David wanted to, he would push for custody of Feorie. Marc's firm would take it on since he represents him in all personal and professional matters. Not only would she lose, but her perfect house of cards would crumble instantly.

He doesn't want to go that route because the only person this will ultimately hurt is Feorie, and he loves his daughter.

Who now plants herself in my path, a disapproving scowl etched into her features.

In times like this, I can't help but wonder who the adult is in this relationship. It certainly isn't me, not at this moment.

"We don't have to do today's lesson," she tells me, those assessing eyes taking in my appearance. "We can just talk."

I laugh. "Talk?"

She nods, her curls bouncing around her face. "It's okay to cancel if you're having grown-up troubles. David has them too. I think that's why he hasn't been coming around lately."

Wow.

She hit the nail on the head with that observation.

I don't think she knows the real reason why David sponsors her lessons or why he occasionally tags along. But he has been noticeably absent the last few weeks, and I figured she would put two and two together.

Did I mention how intuitive she can be? For a six-year-old, she's quite mature for her age. Still, she shouldn't have to worry about things like this. Or adults not being able to put their emotions in check.

Crouching to the floor, I take both her hands in mine.

"We have to do something, or your mom will throw a fit—"

Her little nose scrunches into an adorable pout. "She will."

"—and when that happens, I'll handle it. Deal?"

"But—"

"But nothing." I give both hands a gentle squeeze. "In this scenario, you're the child, and the rest are the adults. You're not responsible for managing the expectations of the adults in your life."

I say this, knowing that those roles seem to be reversed today. I really should learn to take my own advice sometimes.

She angles her chin at my mess. "Fine, but can we work on that?"

I bark out a strained laugh. "No, that's grown-up stuff." Not that she'd listen. She has an eidetic, echoic, and photographic memory — a rare triple combo she inherited from David — so I wouldn't be surprised if she recreates all of this later on. Her curiosity knows no bounds. "Tell you what. Harris is hiding somewhere inside. We'll do live portraits if you can talk him into being your model for the day."

She lights up at that, then goes off in search of him.

With how Harris is, I don't think she'll succeed in her quest. He locked himself in his room the last two times she was here since my house wasn't big enough to keep them apart. It's not big enough to keep Harris and Charlie apart, and I miss having my son home.

But after what happened two nights ago, I'm somewhat optimistic there is an end in sight. Harris still won't talk to me, but he's not moping about the house as much as he was when he first got here.

That gives me an idea of how to handle Roxane's issue while reminding her of our deal. I pull out my phone and snap a few pictures of my mess, then send it to her.

> Courtney: Some initial renderings of what I remembered from that day. Will send you the rest once it's ready.

She opens it immediately, then leaves me on read. That could only mean one thing.

> Courtney: Did you call Marc?

Three dots appear, then disappear. Then, a single word comes through.

> Roxane: No

It's funny that she thinks she now has a choice in this. I've already decided to get Oscar's tattoo done on me; everything else is inconsequential. It'll be my first and quite possibly my only tattoo. And it'll be too much of a headache to find someone else to do it for me.

It's one thing to handle these things how I usually would, but someone still has to clean up the legal mess it would undoubtedly leave behind.

> Courtney: I wasn't asking. That's my trade-off.

> Courtney: Hire Marc's firm. Let them sort out any potential custody issues with the baby. And with her 'sperm donor' whom you won't talk about.

Hopefully, she listens. And if she doesn't, I'll call him myself.

23

COURTNEY

R ose is an hour late for pick-up, and she doesn't complain that Feorie isn't ready to leave yet either, both of which are firsts for her.

Instead, we're both listening in as Feorie and Harris are engaged in a scintillating discussion about guillotines and the Disney movie Inside Out. I'm expecting Rose to interject since part of that conversation, technically, isn't a child-appropriate conversation. But she doesn't; instead, she waits patiently for them to run out of steam before alerting her daughter to her presence and the time.

She doesn't even complain when Feorie intentionally leaves behind her jacket, forcing them to return fifteen minutes later.

After waving them off a second time, I climb into my car and drive to CC's place.

Not because I miss her, even though I just saw her seventy-two hours ago. It's for Harris's sake since he's all peopled out for the day.

I rationalize this decision throughout the thirty-minute drive as any sane, normal person would. Harris needs his space, so I'm doing him a favor by staying away from the house for the next few hours. I chant that mantra over and over as I weave in and out of traffic, earning myself a few car honks and middle fingers.

I let myself into her place, and the sight that greets me stops me dead in my tracks.

CC, Oscar, and Evan huddled in the middle of her living room… working?

I can't say why this surprises me, only that it does.

I've always known these three frequently worked on special projects together, as evidenced by the several papers strewn around the coffee table. CC always referred to those as Trust Fund projects, so I never gave it much thought. I simply filled it under white noise, information to be processed later.

Now, from their various sitting positions in the room, three pairs of eyes remain trained on me, all watching me with varying degrees of curiosity displayed on their faces. Their unspoken questions ring loud and clear.

Then Abby's voice comes through on speakerphone. *"Pourquoi tout le monde a-t-il soudainement arrêté de parler?"*

[*Hello? Why did everyone suddenly stop talking?*]

That should've been my cue to turn around and leave. Instead, I say, "Pretend I'm not here," too tired to make idle chitchat.

CC leans back and crosses her arms over her chest, giving me a bold once-over. The puffiness around her eyelids is a little troubling and gives away her exhaustion. Oscar mirrors her stance, and a flicker of emotion passes over his face too quickly for me to read.

Evan, on the other hand, just stares at me with a blank look on his face. "Everything okay?" he eventually asks. His voice is soft and easy, which somehow rubs me the wrong way.

"Yeah, why wouldn't it be?" There's a bite to my tone, one that has his eyes widening slightly before he schools his features.

"C'est Courtney? On devrait conclure avant que cette garce de Courtney vienne jouer," Abby adds.

[*Is that Courtney? We should wrap this up before bitchy Courtney comes out to play.*]

It's probably a good thing I don't understand French, so all that might as well be gibberish.

"Pretend I'm not here," I repeat, giving them a tired smile and pointing toward the bedroom. "I'll just hit the shower and head to bed."

It's pointless waiting for a response, so I don't. I just head for my destination.

Five minutes later, a rap comes on the bedroom door as I'm stationed at the bathroom sink, de-tangling my hair.

"I said I'd stay out of your way," I call out, head tilted to the side as I run my fingers through my curls.

The door opens anyway, followed by a click.

"Evan left," Oscar says, shrugging off his shirt, "and CC is wrapping up with Abby..." His words die out as his gaze lands on me.

I won't bother with feigned modesty at this point. After all, I did announce my intentions of hitting the shower to everyone in the living room. He should've expected to find me naked, and I won't do the lame thing and kick him out.

He saw himself in. He can see himself right out if that's what he wants.

Only he doesn't.

If anything, he seems to be having difficulty looking away. The heat in his eyes burns my skin, causing a flush to travel across my breasts and slowly spread all over my skin.

Not that I mind. He's adorable.

Oh, so adorable.

Tall with broad shoulders, Oscar's features are exquisite, like an Adonis carved out of marble. My eyes track his defined biceps, pecs, and a rather delectable six-pack, coupled with those gorgeous obliques tapering off in the perfect V shape and pointing to the treasure trove below his waist, one that hangs thick and long between his thighs, inconveniently tucked away in his charcoal gray sweatpants.

A beautiful man. Truly breathtaking.

One I wouldn't mind staring at all day long.

They don't make 'em like that anymore.

He's a man that I want to take advantage of every minute of the day, except he's always been off-limits to me. And I, to him. Until now.

As though he can read my thoughts, his hungry eyes settle on my breasts, and warmth pools in my core and has my nipples hardening further.

"Oscar," I manage to croak, needing to rein in my traitorous body's reaction to his assessing eyes. Never mind that all I really want to do is crawl right up into him.

His eyes meet mine, half-mast and dark with desire, then skitters over to land on my hair. His gaze lingers on for a moment, and his chest rises and falls hard.

"Oscar," I repeat, infusing some hardness into my tone.

The other side of him, the one he keeps hidden, immediately responds to the unspoken command in my tone. Squaring his shoulders, he sinks to his knees with both hands on his thighs, palms face-up.

Interesting and flattering.

Still…

"You're not mine to control or command," I tell him. My breaths escape in shallow pants as I wrestle with myself, wondering why I'm enjoying this so much, even though I don't want to be.

On the other hand, restraining myself just might make me self-combust.

It's the Sotelo genes in me. It's that irrationally possessive streak my brother and I have, courtesy of my dad. The thing is, you can tell yourself all sorts of things to justify it. Or, in my case, to *not* justify it. It's why I don't own things. It's why I don't possess things or people. It's why I don't want to command him.

Even though I want to own him. It's a feeling that, once it takes root, it's nearly impossible to shake. My life is complicated enough, so I shouldn't want or need the additional complication that is Oscar Hyun as badly as I do. Even though I can't seem to help myself when it comes to him.

Speaking of, he hasn't seemed to move an inch.

I let out an exasperated sigh and hold out a hand to him. "Stand. *Please.*"

He obeys and rises to his feet, even though he keeps his hands clasped together behind him. Circling behind him, I go to unlace his fingers, but he keeps them tightly interwoven.

"Oscar, I'm flattered but this isn't what I'm…" I trail off at that as another thought occurs to me. "Where's CC?"

"Can I wash your hair?" he asks instead, and the question catches me off guard.

"Why?"

"Hm?" He's only half-listening to the question, his eyes fixated on my hair.

"I don't let just anyone near this mane."

He chuckles. "It's not a mane."

"Don't be a smart ass." I move to stand before him. "Why do you want to wash my hair?"

"You seemed stressed earlier, so I want to do something nice for you. And I love the feeling of the soap foam forming under my fingers." He wriggles said digits before him. "Plus, CC said you could use a scalp massage, and I do have nimble fingers, so—"

"CC sent you?" It's less of a question and more of a statement.

That would explain this.

Something flashes in his eyes, and his body goes rigid. A beat passes, and then his shoulders relax slightly. He stares at me a moment longer, his throat working.

"Umm… yeah, s-she did." He clears his throat. "She did."

Huh.

So… a peace offering. That's what he is.

Although there's something about this that just seems… off.

Then his next words catch me off guard. Again.

"Remember when you said you would quite enjoy railing me?" His eyes travel appreciatively down my top, lingering on the swell of my breasts before rising again to meet my eyes, smiling lazily. "CC decided to take matters into her own hands."

My stomach tightens involuntarily, intensifying the pulse between my legs. "How?"

"As you know, we experiment sometimes, but CC's a taker, not a giver. But we're switching things up a little since you said this is what you want." His body tightens up again, and his Adam's apple moves. "I… umm… have a plug in my ass. It's a bigger size than the ones we've used before."

I'm not sure what I expected him to say, and I swear my legs almost give out under me. "Bigger?" It's meant to be sharp. Instead, it sounds suggestive, like an invitation to find out, almost. I bite my lip, fighting the urge to bend him over and see it for myself.

Judging by his amused grin, he can tell the thoughts running through my mind. "I wear them when I'm coding. It helps me focus."

Damn, he really is the perfect fuck toy.

"How long have you had it in?"

"Two hours." He shrugs. "I can go longer; it's just… this one can be remotely controlled, and CC has the remote."

Fuck. Me.

That's how she wants to play this?

I swear, some days I don't know what goes on in her head, even if this is one that I won't be protesting any time soon.

I'm not sure if it's pure unadulterated lust, or just my synapses not firing on all cylinders, but I stare at him slack-jawed.

Like it or not, there has always been a tug of something else between us. Something more than just the headiness of his energy becoming mine.

It's damn near impossible to ignore this thing that sizzles between us.

It has a life of its own, and I can't stop it. I don't want to fight it either.

Instead of turning away and shutting this down, I watch him. I watch the rise and fall of his chest, the taut peaks of his nipples, and the quiet groan that bubbles up from his chest and past his lips, parted and inviting.

My lips part to call out CC's name, and he closes the distance between us and puts his delectable hands firmly around my waist. He half-lifts, half-pulls my body closer to his, and presses the length of our torsos together. One hand moves to my ass and grips tightly, almost painfully.

"Your hair," he murmurs, as his other hand digs into my nape, then into my scalp. "Can I help you wash it?"

I want to answer him, to say anything, but I'm so overwhelmed by lust that I can barely speak. I can feel his hard-on straining against my crotch, and the promise of him entering me is almost more than I can bear. I'm wet, beside myself, and squirming against him like a bitch in heat.

"Can I have you?" he whispers in my ear, his voice heavy with need.

It's almost… desperate. Anguished, even. I have half a mind to put him out of his misery, but something else comes out instead.

"You've always had me," I hear myself say.

He leans back slightly, and our gazes lock. A thousand thoughts flash behind his eyes, but I can't decipher any of them. For someone whose physical expressions have always been like an open book to me, I'm slightly irritated by this turn of events.

"Have I?" he asks, his voice breaking, piercing my heart.

"You do. I didn't just break you, Oscar. You broke me, too. You ruined me for all other men long before you stuck your dick in me."

Oscar's brows crinkle in confusion. "How's that even possible—"

"It is possible because you were always mine. *Mine*, Oscar. You weren't just unfinished business to me; you were always my first boyfriend. *Are* my first boyfriend. My first and only boyfriend. If you don't believe me, ask Abby." I place a hand over his chest, over his erratically beating heart. "You were someone I could never move on from, not that I was even trying to. I'm a possessive bitch, and I don't let go of my toys."

His eyes stay on me, and I watch as he sheds layer after layer, knocking down wall after wall to reveal the depths of his soul to me.

After what seems like an eternity, he finally lowers his mouth onto mine. His lips are firm and possessive on mine as he runs his tongue along my lip, dancing with my tongue. His fingers clench fistfuls of my hair, and his kisses deepen, becoming more urgent.

As our bodies meld together, I can't help the feeling that he's opening up all of me, not just my mouth. Not just my legs either, as those lift up off the ground and wrap around his torso. Something cold presses against my ass — the countertop, I think — just as something else deep within me cracks wide open and drinks him in, all of him. His hands dance across my back and waist, exploring me, owning me, making me want more.

More of this, more of him.

"Oscar," I moan into his mouth, panting and thrusting against him, my need so great that everything else around us fades. I grind my weeping cunt against his crotch, unable to help myself, the friction exquisite. Somewhere in the recesses of my mind, it barely registers that prey or not, I am his to do with as he pleases. I've officially lost all self-control, all because he wants to wash my hair.

Also, because he has a lubed plug in his ass because I said I wanted to rail him. Which I still want to do.

His kisses move outwards to my earlobes, my neck, my collarbone. He nibbles and teases as he runs his teeth and tongue over the ultra-sensitive skin, driving me towards recklessness.

I reach for the waistband of his sweatpants, and that's when I feel it.

Or rather, she turns it back on.

"F-fuck," he groans, his body seizing up as his lips clamp down on the sensitive skin of my nape. Then his teeth sink in as he sucks hard on the flesh, probably hard enough to break the skin.

My orgasm hits me at the same time as his does. We cling to each other as full-body tremors wrack our bodies; shuddering, shaking, and shattering as our entire beings, our very essence, blend into each other.

He keeps on sucking, drawing in several mouthfuls of blood, and I can feel his throat shifting against my shoulder as he drinks me in. I've never experienced anything like it. It's intense and strange, but also, it's… euphoric, and the screams that rip through my throat are inhuman as a second climax hurtles into the next, knocking me off kilter as waves of ecstasy pulse through me for what seems like forever.

Spent, I collapse into him, my breaths escaping in shallow pants as my heart rate slowly returns to normal.

Normal. I almost scoff.

What we just did, that last part was anything but normal.

He wasn't inside me, and I just came harder than I ever have in my life.

Then again, that's just us. And if this is what I have to look forward to for the rest of my life, I can't say that I mind it.

Not one bit.

24

COURTNEY

"I've never done that before," Oscar murmurs as reality sets in for both of us.

I know what he's asking, but still, I ask, "Done what?"

I push away from him and slide to my feet. My legs still shake as I head for the shower and turn it on, adjusting the temperature to how I like it. Once done, I turn back to him, impressed he's still standing. I can hear the low hum coming from the plug in his ass, something he seems indifferent to it.

"Done what, Oscar?" I repeat, taking in the glossy sheen of his sweat-soaked delectable abs.

He's rubbing his thumb over his bottom lip, smearing the crimson all over. "Bitten hard enough to draw blood. Bitten hard enough to drink blood."

"I enjoyed it. In case you couldn't tell," I tease, but he's not amused.

"I hurt you."

"You didn't."

"But your neck—"

"It'll heal. Turn around."

I don't miss the relief on his face as he turns and braces his forearms against the counter. I hook my fingers into the waistband of his sweatpants and push them over his ass, soaking in my masterpiece that's permanently etched into his ass, as he steps out of them and kicks them away without any hesitation.

My eyes shamelessly roam all over his delectable ass, memorizing every inch of skin. I'll work up the courage to ask him to pose for me in the nude someday. For now, I gently work the plug out of his ass. The vibrations kick up several notches once it's out, and he lets out an amused chuckle as I toss it in the bedroom.

"She knew you'd take it out," Oscar says weakly. "That's why she sent me in here."

Now, why does that not surprise me?

I'll deal with CC later. For now, I want more of him.

It's crazy that, for the first time in as long as I can remember, I'm content with just this.

The bathroom is starting to steam up, so I make my way over to the shower, expecting him to follow. When he doesn't, I turn to see he's still bracing himself against the sink, rooted in place.

"Join me."

It's not a request. It's an order.

One he complies with, maybe all too easily.

My gaze dips lower as he walks toward me, and I'm struck mute for a second. My jaw hangs open as I take in his thick arousal, which lies nestled between powerful thighs on a manicured tuft of jet-black hair. It twitches as I stare at it unabashedly.

A slow smile creeps across his gorgeous face. "Like what you see?"

I'm about to say something witty, then decide… eh, fuck it. I'm fucking exhausted, going on two days with little sleep, and he's offering himself up like a delectable treat.

Suffice it to say my self-control is shot, and all logical reasoning has fled the building.

Whatever game he and CC are playing will have to wait.

Right now, I just want to enjoy this.

I curl my fingers at him in a come-hither fashion.

He doesn't seem surprised by this, not one bit. He also comes to me so quickly. So easily. I wonder if he's thought about this too. If he fantasized about this as much as we have.

He reaches out to touch me and I take a step back. At his puzzled look, I add, "I never said you could put your hands on me, Oscar. Except for up here," I point to my hair. "And since you so nicely offered, I won't say no to those nimble fingers.

"Oh. Okay." He blushes slightly and again, and it's adorable.

"Where do you want me?"

"Over there," he points to the bench in the shower.

Shrugging, I do as he says, and he pulls out all of my hair products in the order I use them and sets them next to me. I'm impressed.

I half-turn and lean back so he can easily reach my hair. He pours some shampoo into his palm and starts rubbing it into my hair, section by section, massaging it in with both hands. I keep my eyes shut because I don't want the shampoo to run into them. That, in combination with the movement of Oscar's hands on my scalp, makes me sleepy, so I give in, dozing off and surrendering to his ministrations.

"I'm hoping this isn't a one-time thing," he says, rousing me from my mini-nap as he finishes.

"I never said it's a thing," I tell him.

"I know." He shuts off the water before pulling me to my feet and cupping my face in both hands. "Thank you for trusting me with your mane."

Is he thanking me?

I can't help the smile that forms. Could this man get any more perfect for me?

I can't say who moves first — him or me — just that my brain is slow to register his hands on my body, smashing my breasts against his steel chest and his mouth hard and hot on mine.

It's like every cell in my body is lit by a fuse, instantly reacting to the kiss. It is an overwhelming yet delirious feeling, the possessive manner in which his hands grip my body, the delicious feeling of his lips on mine, and the unmistakable bulge pressing against my thighs as he commands not only my mouth but my entire body, bending and molding it to obey his every command.

Simply put, Oscar wasn't asking. He was taking.

Demanding.

Had I been reading him wrong all this time?

Before my brain can catch up, his tongue swipes against my lips, and they part without hesitation. He thrusts his tongue into my mouth ruthlessly as he sucks my breaths directly into his body. His hands are rough and unyielding as they grab the curve of my ass, hiking me up and setting me on the countertop.

I moan with pleasure, one that bubbles up from deep down in my core, as I wrap my arms around his rock-hard butt and pull him closer.

Then he pulls my tongue into his mouth and sucks on it hard, and I just about fall apart in his hands. An involuntary shiver runs straight through my spine and spreads, and it goes on and on as I cling to him.

"Oscar." His name falls from my lips in a desperate plea, wanting more from him. So much more.

Then, just like that, the kiss stops and his hands fall off my body as he steps back.

"Fuck, Courtney. I'm so, so—"

"Shut up and kiss me again." I reach for him with every intention of fusing his delectable lips back on mine, but he stops me.

"I want to taste you," he says, his eyes continuing to drink me in.

"I'm not a sampling menu, Oscar."

"I know you're not. It's just… your tits, they're so fucking perfect, and I…" he trails off at that and swallows. "I need to taste you, or I'll—"

"Go ahead." I think I'll die if he doesn't do this. If he doesn't give me this as well.

His gaze drops, then he ducks his head and lowers his mouth down over one breast. A low, uncontrollable moan of pleasure rips through my throat as my fingers sink into his hair, clutching fistfuls as I practically smash his face to my chest, holding him against me with no intention of letting go.

A deep groan rumbles through him, vibrating against my skin as his full-on assault on the sensitive skin only made me hang on tighter to him. The touch of his lips and his delectable tongue stroking across my nipple sends another jolt of pure desire through my body, from head to toe, strong enough that I don't know how my body manages to hold it all inside without breaking apart.

"Oscar, please."

Instead of giving me a chance to catch my breath, he shifts his dangerous attention from one breast to the other and resumes his sensuous torture. Every cell in my body hones in on what he's doing to my body, and I arch into his mouth to get closer, pushing even more skin into his mouth.

He releases the areola with a pop, and then his mouth travels up over the small curves of my breasts, across my collarbone, settling in the hollow. His lips find a particularly sensitive spot and close in on it, sucking hard. A second involuntary shiver originates from the spot and runs straight through my spine. It spreads and spreads, going on and on, and I have no other choice but to cling to him yet again.

"What're you doing to me?" I whisper.

He pulls his mouth away from my skin, and his eyes meet mine, burning with desire. "Learning."

Huh?

I lift both hands to his face and press my thumb to his lips. "Why?"

"You know why." He turns his face into my hand, his tongue brushes against the tip of my thumb.

If I'm not careful, I'll lose myself in him. In this.

It's happening already; I can sense it. I can feel myself melting deeper into him, completely losing the thread of where I end and where he begins.

Amazingly, at the same time, I feel like I could stay in this moment forever, sensually suspended in time, with him.

But isn't that what you've wanted?

I shake my head. "I want to hear you say it."

He uses his tongue to circle the pulse point on my wrist, sending my poor heart rate into overdrive.

I want more.

I need more.

Utterly overwhelmed by the waves of ecstasy washing over me, I realize a little too late that I'm already on the verge of climax.

How's that even possible? He's using only his mouth on my wrist, one hand on my hip, his taut muscles pressing along mine.

As my brain processes this information, his eyes meet mine again. "I'd rather show you."

He falls to his knees before me. On the descent, he presses his mouth into my stomach and dips his tongue quickly against my exposed belly button.

Impatiently, I rock my pelvis against him. "Oscar—"

"I told you, I'm learning," he murmurs against my skin.

Leisurely, his mouth moves across my stomach, his lips sucking, his tongue sliding against one hip bone and the other.

I've had enough, so I grab fistfuls of his hair and pull his face and lips away from my body. "Cut it out with the games, Oscar. Either fuck me or get the fuck out."

Something flashes in his eyes, something I never thought I'd see in this lifetime. Something dark and dangerous, and oh so him.

He nods, and a heartbeat later, his mouth is on me, and two fingers slip inside my slick heat.

Throwing my head back, my body relaxes and opens up to him even more as he alternates between this gentle sucking and licking motion, coupled with some rough strokes of his tongue, before firmly sucking on my clit with those lips of his.

I press my hips harder against his mouth, his face too, as I can feel myself tightening and clenching around his fingers, so close to the edge, yet not quite over it. Coherent thought swirls in a jumbled fog of arousal, my brain working much slower than usual.

He moves away suddenly, leaving me breathless and wanting more. An ache pulses through my chest from the emptiness, one he quickly rectifies when he stands and pulls me to him. He leans me back, then his arm encircles my thigh and hooks my legs around him, anchoring my body.

He's inside me in one swift motion, burying himself to the hilt as he fills me completely. Then he fastens his lips to my neck, and his tongue lightly scores over the sensitive flesh.

"I'll be careful," he whispers against my skin.

"Don't be," I grunt, "it's all yours."

His teeth sink in as his thrusts pick up speed and intensity, pounding me so hard I can barely catch my breath. I can feel the intoxicating yet addictive warmth of his skin as my hands roam down his back, then back up and across his broad, muscular shoulders. It still isn't enough.

This total, all-encompassing need for him is something else. It's been a long time coming, and I didn't stand a chance in hell of stopping this.

His body tenses slightly, and the first rope of his thick cum hits me on the inside, sending me over the edge. I completely let go as my body takes over, sparks ignite under my skin, and warmth floods through my veins as I come undone in his arms.

"Did I pass?" he rasps as I'm coming down from my high.

"What?"

"Did I pass muster?" he repeats, and the mischievous glint in his eyes tells me he already knows the answer.

Still, I humor him.

"Take me to bed, and we'll find out."

25

OSCAR

"**D**id you have fun?" CC asks when I wander into the living room hours later.

She's curled up on the couch, reading. Or rather, she appears to be reading, but the book in her hand is upside down.

I spare a glance at the clock and it's nearly midnight. "Why didn't you join us?"

Courtney is in bed, thoroughly satiated, and passed out from the many orgasms I gave her. I watched her for some time while she slept, her lithe body languidly stretched across the bed, unable to look away. She looked incredibly young and impossibly sweet, and not at all the blood-thirsty killer I know she is.

That, and I think I unlocked a new kink for myself. Who knew I had a thing for blood? Not me, that's for sure.

Although I'm not sure what prompted her to come over in the state she was in, I'm glad I could offer her a reprieve from it all, if only for a brief moment.

"You want anything?" I ask as I head to the kitchen. "Bourbon with a side of coffee, perhaps?"

"I'm good," she calls out after me.

Right.

It's not so much her words; it's its underlying tone. One that's masking the hurt. She should've joined us. She dared me to ask Courtney to take the damn plug out, knowing I'd tell her why I had one on in the first place.

This is going to be one long night.

Opening the fridge, I grab two bottles of water and a yogurt cup for her. When I return, CC's staring at me with a loaded gaze, a glossy sheen in her eyes.

"You should've joined us." I hand over her snack.

She reaches for it, and our hands touch. Hers is ice-cold. How long has she been sitting out here?

"You were having a moment and I didn't want to interrupt." Her voice is flat and devoid of emotion, but just beneath her eyes simmers her barely contained anger and hurt.

"Bullshit." I settle into the couch across from hers. "What's going on in that head of yours?"

Her gaze lowers, and she worries her bottom lip.

"I know you've always liked her, and I don't want to get in the way of what you two share. That's the last thing that I want. I just…" her voice trails off, and she blows out a breath. "I'm struggling with this."

"Which part?"

"Does it matter?"

My eyes narrow at her, at the fact that she's dancing around the question.

Then she surprises me.

She rises and walks over to where I'm seated, nudges my thighs apart, and sinks to her knee before me. It's a submission pose, which makes it all the more fucked up. It should be me in that position and not the other way around.

"CC, don't." My tone is harsher than I intend it to be.

Except, a part of me understands her need to do things this way. A reversal of roles, so to speak. Her gaze lifts, and I'm taken aback by what I see in them.

I reach out and brush her hair out of her face before cupping her cheek. Her breath huffs against the inside of my wrist, in time with my pulse. I curl my fingers in and stroke the backs of my knuckles along her temple, and she tilts into my caress.

"Did she tell you what was bothering her?"

"We weren't talking."

"Oh."

"Is that why you kept turning up the vibrator?

She nods as she pulls her lower lip between her teeth again, and she looks so fucking vulnerable right now, and it takes my breath away.

"You know this isn't supposed to be a competition, right?" At the puzzled look in her eyes, I add, "You own me, CC. It's safe to say that the last few years have made it quite clear that I belong to you. In every sense of the word."

She shakes her head. "I'm not... this. All of this. I'm not who you think I am."

"I guess not," I whisper breathlessly. "And I'm not who you think I am, despite all... this. So, I guess that makes us even. In a way."

She laughs, but it's not an amused one. It's pained. "When you look at me, what do you see?"

"Everything," I tell her. "I see everything you are to me, CC. My past, present, and future all rolled into one." I don't know where that came from, but it's the truth. Since I'm on a roll... "I see what she sees. The fact that you're not normal. You were never normal, and that's okay. Because you're extraordinary. You always have been."

With that, I pull her off the floor and onto my lap so she's straddling me, and our cores are flush.

"I can't seem to look away from you, CC," I continue, knowing that she needs to hear the words just as much as I need to say them. "But unlike Courtney, I don't want you to kneel at my feet, ever. I don't want to own you. I want you to ruin me. I want you to fucking shatter me. Always."

"And why would you want that?"

"Simple. I'm the idiot who's hopelessly in love with you."

Fuck.

I don't know where that came from. But again, it is the truth.

"You love me?" she echoes, her voice breaking.

"I've been telling you this for years now, so why does that surprise you—"

She cuts me off by leaning in to press a chaste kiss to my lips. "I know you do. You just took me by surprise, is all."

Then she cups my cheeks. "I wasn't going to ask you to choose between her or me," she says softly. "That would be lame and petty, and I don't do bullshit like that."

Her words say one thing, but I can see the indecision warring in her eyes. God. She looks so conflicted, and knowing that there's nothing I can do about it, nothing I can do to ease the turmoil boiling within her soul just guts me.

"Falling in love was never a choice, at least not for me. The past, present, and future I see include both of you. I choose you both. I can't live without either of you." Her eyes go glossy, but she doesn't say anything. "Do you know why I put up with the Morellis?"

She shakes her head.

"For someone so determined to disregard every facet of my existence and our biological ties, Gerald spends a lot of time sticking his snotty nose into my business. He constantly uses my mother to threaten me. He's trying to force a marriage between Courtney and Reuben to screw with me because he knows that I like her. Once both of those things fall through, who do you think he'll come for next?"

This time, her eyes widen ever so slightly, and she makes a noise in her throat — a cross between desire and pain — but she doesn't say anything.

"Gerald Morelli is a tenacious asshole, and the last thing I want is for him to start looking at you a little too closely. The same goes for the rest of them. They're not family to me. They never were. But I put up with them to protect the family that I do have. I'll deal with their bullshit if it means keeping you. I'll put up with Reuben's lead fists even. I like pain, so it's not exactly a hardship. I'll deal with that jerk because you are home to me, and I'll do whatever it takes to protect my home.

"I don't care how we started, only where we go from here. And this, right here, is what I want."

She gulps. "Y-you sure about that?"

"I've never been more sure of anything in my life. It's what I've always wanted. More than anything in the world. I want to be your last everything. That's why I choose this, all of this. I choose you, every twisted, deranged, obsessed part of you. I might not always understand *it* or the things that go on in that brain of yours, but I won't shy away from it. I never have, and I never will. No matter what you do, I will never fucking let you go. Not even—"

The words barely leave my mouth before she's on me, her lips attacking mine and coaxing them into submission. Then she reaches between us, her hand disappearing into my trunks and wrapping around my dick, already hard and ready for her. It only takes a bit of maneuvering — okay, a *lot* of maneuvering, but we've done this so many times before that it almost seems effortless — and my breath hitches as the head of my cock nudges against the warmth of her wet pussy.

Our gazes lock as she slowly settles her weight, as her weepy cunt swallows my cock until she's fully seated, and we're joined, completely.

This sensation is nothing compared to the closeness and intimacy that comes from all the other times we've done this. It's different this time, the way we cling to each other as she rides my dick, as our hands roam all over each other's bodies, seeking ways to get as much of our skin in contact with each other as possible.

"I love you," I say in a raspy, lust-filled tone.

Her eyes search mine, and she smiles. It's warm and sincere and hits me straight in the heart. "I love you too."

Then I show her how much, staring into the depths of her soul as we lose ourselves to and in each other.

PART III

26

———

COURTNEY

One Month Later

"I love it when packrats make our jobs so much easier," Phoenix says from her position across the room, where she rifles through our latest target's drawers.

"Or harder," I say, giving Louis Pecora a few more kicks to the torso, the satisfying sound of ribs cracking filling the room.

His pathetic whimpering grates on my already buzzed nerves, something he hasn't let up on in almost five minutes. Instead of fighting back like any normal person would when faced with a situation like this, he cowers in the fetal position with both wrists tied behind his back as his entire body shakes uncontrollably.

Not that it would've made the slightest difference. Louis is not the brightest bulb in the box. Or, at the very least, that's how he presents himself to others. Partly due to his age, something he plays up quite a bit when it suits him. As if willful ignorance excuses the things he has done and will continue to do if we leave him alone.

At least he's smart enough to know there's only one way this ends. And if he doesn't, too fucking bad for him.

"Courtney," Phoenix calls out after some time. "Give it a rest, would you? He's had enough for now."

I pause long enough to crouch next to him, then place two fingers on his neck to feel for a pulse. "That's too bad. I was just getting started."

Of our deadly trio, she has always been more in tune with the human body and the limits to which it can be pushed when it comes to pain and torture. She also happens to be the deadliest among us, so I'm not sure what to make of it when she's the first one to put a pause on things.

Then again, this idiot passed out again, and torturing someone who's unconscious isn't nearly as satisfying for either of us.

Louis had a lot more fight in him than either Phoenix or I had been expecting for someone pushing eighty. The old geezer gave us a run for our money. I knew he wouldn't come quietly, but I wasn't expecting a five-mile run through the overgrown forest on the back of this property.

Abby is familiar with those grounds since part of her childhood was spent here, and not the fun parts of it either. She made sure to give us the lay of the land before we got here. She also had the foresight to don her night vision goggles before shooting him with his own homemade tranquilizer mixes. He must have built up a tolerance to it over the years, as he still thrashed about and fought us for a good fifteen minutes before Phoenix put him out of his misery with a good ol' whack to the head.

I still think that was over far too soon. Just as *this* is over far too soon. It's not nearly as satisfying for me. I could've gone for a few more miles. After all, I wore my running shoes today for a reason.

And I haven't even gotten through half of my toys.

Rising, I pull out my pocket knife and flick open the blade. "He's still got some fight left in him." I trace the blade along the edge of my fingertips. "He'll regain consciousness eventually, and then his fight or flight response will kick back in. I could use a few more laps around the block. How are those useless papers coming along?"

"It's mostly breadcrumbs." She pulls out several papers from the open drawers — more useless ones, I deduce — and dumps them on the floor. "I'm afraid all the heavy lifting falls to Abby now."

Save for a few curse words here and there, Abby mostly ignores us. Her eyes remain glued to several screens as she sifts through the firewalls on his computers and electronic devices, occasionally pausing to flick her jet-black hair from one shoulder to the other.

I mean, seriously? How many of those does one person need?

But the man is also a paranoid fucker. It is to be expected of someone in his position. It makes sense why all three of us were assigned this job. It's a shame that Abby won't get to play with him because she's too busy playing with his toys instead.

Not that she minds. Curse words aside, she looks like she's in tech heaven, so who are we to interrupt?

Phoenix places a hand on my shoulder. "This was supposed to be a quick job. We're already behind schedule by an hour, at least."

As if I don't already know that. "You know," I say, turning slightly so I'm looking directly into her eyes. The light gleams, hitting the glossy sheen of her contacts at an odd angle. "This would've gone so much quicker had you mixed one of your—"

"No." Her voice is stern. Unrelenting.

"Things are a lot more efficient when we each do our roles—"

"I said no." She looks away and draws in a shuddering breath. "I really wish you'd stop bringing this up."

And I really wish I *didn't* have to keep bringing this up.

I get her hesitation. I do.

The thing is, I've heard all of this before. Her reluctance. This isn't the first time she's told me no, and I'm confident it won't be the last. It's all she's been saying for almost eight years, and I've just about had enough.

Her concoctions are legendary. With those, death is the secondary intended effect. Pain and suffering is the primary goal.

So yes, people get hurt. Sometimes they die.

It's kind of the point.

She is dubbed Lady Poison for a reason.

Was dubbed Lady Poison. That side of her has supposedly been 'retired' for eight years, much to Abby's and my annoyance. She is a natural at it; there's no denying that. It made no sense that she spent over a decade perfecting her craft only to up and quit because of one bad batch.

While everyone else seems to have accepted this, Abby and I haven't. We keep calling her that since it annoys her to no end; and because it's her name. Poison and fire are her specialties, except Lady Fire doesn't have the same ring to it, and Lady F is far too literal.

Unlike Abby and myself, Phoenix has got this duplicity thing down to a T. She looks like a porcelain doll, with her sickly pale skin tone and sapphire contacts, things one doesn't associate with fire.

"It's been long enough. It's time to come out of retirement."

Her fingers press into my shoulder. "Not gonna happen."

"Try a better argument. Or even a convincing one, since 'not gonna happen' isn't cutting it."

"There are consequences for that shit, and you know this. Irreversible ones."

"Like Delilah?"

Her shoulders go stiff at the mention of her name.

I really should leave this alone, but it *has* been eight fucking years.

And yes, Abby and I know that the bad batch that prompted her retirement was the same one that ended up in Delilah, courtesy of Harris. It all worked out for the three of them anyway, so all's well that ends well.

I take a deep, measured breath before continuing. "You had no way of knowing what Harris planned on doing with it, so don't you think it's time you stopped beating yourself up about that?"

Her breathing shudders. That brings her gaze back to mine, and I can see her expression in the glow of the light inside. It's pained and tortured, not at all what I was expecting.

Her entire body practically vibrates with anger. I've known her long enough to realize that it isn't directed at me per se, but at the fact that I refuse to drop it no matter how many times she's asked.

It has me wondering — and not for the first time — if the reason was the drug or its recipient.

"Umm… if you two are done with the heart-to-heart session," Abby speaks up, not looking up from her screens. She angles her chin in the direction of the floor. "He's waking up."

27

COURTNEY

Phoenix's hand falls off my shoulder, and a detached look effortlessly slides onto her face as she crouches before the slumped body. "What do you think? You going to make us chase you again?"

Still dazed, he grunts out his response before frantically shaking his head.

Not that it would have made the slightest difference. Everyone knows a visit from all three of us — the Sotelo Weapons — spells the end for you. Not only is it guaranteed to be a slow, torturous, and painful death, but it would be a fitting end to someone like him.

Even with his hands tied behind his back, Louis remains cowered in the fetal position, and his entire body shakes uncontrollably.

Pathetic.

"That's too bad." She extracts her pocket knife from her jacket and flips the blade open. "Why don't we make a deal, yes?" His eyes go hopeful. "Make it worth her while, and we just might consider letting you go."

It makes all of *this* worth it, witnessing the moment he loses what little hope he still held on to, watching as it deflates from his eyes. His entire body goes slack as the fight visibly leaves him.

His end is near, and at least he realizes that now.

Had it been someone else — *anyone* else — we would play with them some more. But Louis Pecora is literal scum and deserves to be treated as such.

The sound of his whimpering resumes. It grows louder by the second as his basic survival and self-preservation instincts kick in, except he has no way of getting up or getting out of this.

"Cease your incessant whimpering, or I'll make you," I say by way of warning.

Like a jukebox that runs out of steam, the sound abruptly stops, plunging us into silence.

It's pointless, except he doesn't know that. I intend to make him stop, but sometimes, people like him latch on to that little ray of hope. It does make things easier for me in the long run.

The death they usually see coming but hope to stave off longer.

Like that would work.

Hint — it won't. But we love to let them think that.

Crouching next to him on the other side, I run the sharp tip of my blade along the seams of his ear. He heeds my warning this time. His teeth sink into his bottom lip so hard it draws blood.

My gaze narrows in on the bright crimson liquid as it trickles down his chin. "Tell me something," I say, piercing through the silence as the first drop of his blood hits the floor. "Does this feel as surreal to you as it does to me?"

He takes a moment to consider his response, and I give him all the time he needs. It was a rhetorical question, after all.

Only for him to shake his head.

That was not what I expected, especially from someone who makes his living talking people's ears off. Still, I did tell him to cease his whimpering, and I'd like to think that there's a part of him that realizes I fully intend to follow through on it.

Humans are pathetic like that. They'd say or do anything if they thought they had even the slightest hope that it would save their skin.

Forcing a small smile that doesn't reach my eyes, I say, "You may speak, Louis. Make it good, or else."

"It isn't nice to play with your food," Phoenix interjects.

Truth is, I had momentarily forgotten she was here.

She's good at that, blending into the shadows. She *is* a fucking shadow, always has been.

"Prey," the whimpering bastard says almost immediately. "The expression is prey," he adds when I lift a questioning brow in his direction. "It isn't nice to play with your prey. You shouldn't play with your prey; just put them out of their fucking misery. It's a kindness you owe them."

Anytime I hear the word prey, I think of Oscar and all the shit he's been through. Then, the urge to paint everything crimson threatens to take over. For my sisters, though, I'll keep it in check.

"You think I owe you anything?" This idiot clearly doesn't get what is about to happen.

He huffs out a short laugh. "Isn't that why you're here? To kill me?"

"Oh, good. You're finally catching on." His pathetic but slow realization shouldn't please me as much as it does, but it does anyway.

"All done. Fucking finally!" Abby triumphantly declares as she rises to her feet, then proceeds to make a show of wiping the non-existent sweat off her brow. "Nobody needs that many firewalls unless they have something to hide."

I scoff. "We all have something to hide, Abby."

"Yeah, well, *that* took longer than expected, and I'm annoyed." She walks over to join us. "He certainly had a lot to hide, don't you, old man?"

He grunts out his pained but resigned response.

"Like?" Phoenix prompts when Abby doesn't elaborate.

"There are the usuals — blackmailing, racketeering, drugs — but that wasn't enough for him. Lorenzo was right to suspect his unusually high success rates."

I can't help but feel irritated by this when she stops talking yet again. "Why don't you dumb it down even further, for those of us who don't speak cryptic?"

Abby's hands clench into fists at her sides. "He's been preying on his charges for almost five decades. Not that I'm surprised by it. He tried it with me back then, but Mattie put the brakes on it. It's how he got that nasty scar. I guess he didn't learn his lesson. He just got better at hiding his tracks." She lets out a dry, strained laugh. "Almost better. Guess he didn't count on our paths ever crossing."

I'm still stuck on the part where Mattie, her adoptive grandmother, knew about this. "If she knew he was doing this back then, why the fuck didn't she just take him out? It would have spared a lot of innocent children from being subjected to him." Not that *she's* any better, but still.

"And you're conveniently forgetting that people like him have friends in high places," she counters, then looks away before sighing. "*Had* friends in high places," she corrects. "It's not that I'm not sympathetic to their plight. I am. I know some people whose mission is keeping tabs on and helping those children and others like them, even well into adulthood."

"Still—" Phoenix starts to say, but Abby cuts her off.

"I've also been tracking this asshole's movements for decades." At the expression mirrored on both my and Phoenix's faces, she quickly adds, "Don't look so surprised. This is me we're talking about. Paranoia is my middle name."

"Why didn't you say anything all this time? We could've helped."

"I knew you would've. I just couldn't say anything unless it were a sure thing. If you'd taken a closer look at the jobs we've been working on as a group, you would've realized that we've been cutting off this fucker's limbs for the better part of two decades. Lorenzo is smart, I'll give him that. It shouldn't have taken me this long to realize it was him we were after all this time. But you should know that we've barely scratched the surface."

Phoenix's mouth flattens in annoyance. "How so?"

"She means he wasn't working alone," I add.

"Of course not," Phoenix says dryly. "Where do we find his pals?"

She's already on the warpath. No surprise there.

"Oh, we caught a break on that one," Abby says gleefully.

"Deciphering his lists is what took so long, but that's done. His pals are in or adjacent to the Sotelo family. At least he was quite thorough about keeping tabs on all of them. Mutually assured destruction would be my best guess. There's some crossover with the Milligan list… and Staton list too."

Now, *that's* a name I haven't heard in almost three years.

Winford Staton, Howard's old manager.

What in the actual fuck?

"Is Reuben on that list?" I ask her.

"No, but Gerald is."

Shit. This just keeps getting better and better.

"That explains the marriage he's trying to force between Reuben and me. How does my stepmother fit into all this?"

"She doesn't. Her father does. He's been one of Howard's unofficial backers since the start of his career."

Jesus Christ. This is turning out to be an even bigger mess than I anticipated. "I wouldn't mind getting rid of them, but this one hits a little too close to home."

"No shit, Sherlock. Phoenix and I can handle them. Lorenzo already gave the green light on rooting out the rotten apples from the Network, so there's a big purge coming. If his wife is involved, he wants her gone too. It'll be murder and mayhem, my two favorite things. We'll be busy for at least a year."

Phoenix takes her hand and laces their fingers. "I can't believe you kept this from us."

I shrug. "I do. Some of those rats are from Abby's past, and we don't discuss our pasts. Before this, I mean."

We don't, and we're pretty open with each other about everything else. Our bond is forged in blood. We would kill for each other. We would even die for each other, yet we know nothing about each other from the time before Lorenzo brought us together.

For all I know, there could be a family that loves and misses Abby. She's been a part of the Network since she was five — or was she seven? — thanks to our predecessors' cohort. Even though Mattie is her adopted grandmother on paper, it's also possible Abby was originally stolen from her home under my grandfather's say-so.

As for Phoenix, I wouldn't even know where to begin. We met a little over eighteen years ago, and suffice it to say she's been living as a ghost all this time. She hardly ever talked about her life before this, and she's changed so much of her appearance over the years that I doubt her family would recognize her should their paths cross.

I'd say I'm more of an open book, but that's because Abby can dig up whatever she wants about me. Chances are, she knows more about Phoenix than she's letting on. She's also a vault of information, so what goes in doesn't come out unless absolutely necessary.

"Someone had to take that first step, and I don't mind being it," Abby adds, then takes my hand and laces our fingers together. "Maybe someday you two will get around to trusting me with yours."

As usual, Phoenix grunts out her response, and Abby laughs. "In due time, of course."

"You're enjoying this, aren't you?" Phoenix mumbles, hints of appreciation filtering through her tone.

"Why yes. Yes, I am. As I should."

"How about we skip the mushiness," I say as a reminder to get us back on track.

"You know, I always suspected I wasn't the only one," Abby continues. "People like him don't just stop because they get a lasting physical reminder. Sure, it bruised his ego a little, but he figured out who the more vulnerable ones were and how to ensure they couldn't tell on him.

"And before you ask, I wasn't doing this because Mattie asked me to. She didn't know about it. If anything, she ordered me to stay as far away from him as possible, but we all know I'm not a very good listener." She pauses just long enough to deliver a sharp kick to his torso. "Actually, I wouldn't mind another lap around the block. Let's make this fucker suffer some more before we put him out of his misery. It would be little consolation to his victims, but still."

The not-whimpering bastard hacks up a loogie — rather painfully, I might add — then has the audacity to spit on my running shoes. "I'd rather die than run for either one of you bitches."

"Look at him run that useless tongue of his," Abby says. "He thinks he gets a say in all this."

"I know I don't, so fucking do it already. Put me out of my misery."

Unlacing my hand from Abby's, I crouch down next to him. Setting the knife down next to him, I reach out both arms and cradle his cheek in my palms. "Where you are going, misery doesn't even begin to describe it."

"Whatever. Just know that if I make it out alive," he spits, like *that* would happen, "know this. I'm coming for you. All of you. I'll come for your loved ones first."

"That a fact?" Phoenix counters with a mirthless laugh.

"I might not know who yours are, but I know who hers are." He angles his head in her direction. "Your parents, for one. Rumor has it they've been itching to get their hands on you. I just might lead them right to your doorstep—"

He doesn't get the chance to finish that statement or sentence. Phoenix is on him in a flash, ripping his tongue right out of his mouth.

The gurgling sound that follows is music to our ears.

"You have got to teach me that trick," Abby says the moment the sound dies out. "The human tongue is difficult to rip out with just the bare hand. Speaking of, what's your deal with tongues anyway? You were never this," she snickers, "merciful."

"I don't do nonsense," Phoenix counters.

She also doesn't do parents either, but for the sake of argument, I bite my tongue on that one.

It's that past I was referring to, the one we each don't talk about.

But Phoenix has always been an enigma. Her reaction isn't necessarily an overreaction. I've known her long enough to realize that anyone who brings up her so-called elusive parents — whether in jest or in seriousness — generally doesn't live long enough to follow through on whatever thinly veiled threat they have in mind. I get the sense that it's not talking about her parents that bothers her, it's something else.

Or *someone* else.

Eh, we all have our secrets. We might not know what those are, but they bind our little band of misfits together. That, and the fact that we are all psychopaths.

I spare one last glance at his carcass. "You two can handle clean-up here, right?"

The kill is what I care about. They do too, but they love the clean-up process just as much. Especially Phoenix, since she's concerned about leaving traces behind. If the occasion calls for it, I'll join in, but for group assignments, I don't enjoy it as much as they do. I'm more of an in-and-out kind of girl.

Abby rolls the carcass to his back and begins cutting the clothing off his body. "Sure. Why?"

"I have to run. Places to be. Favors to repay, that sort of thing."

Babies to meet, I want to add.

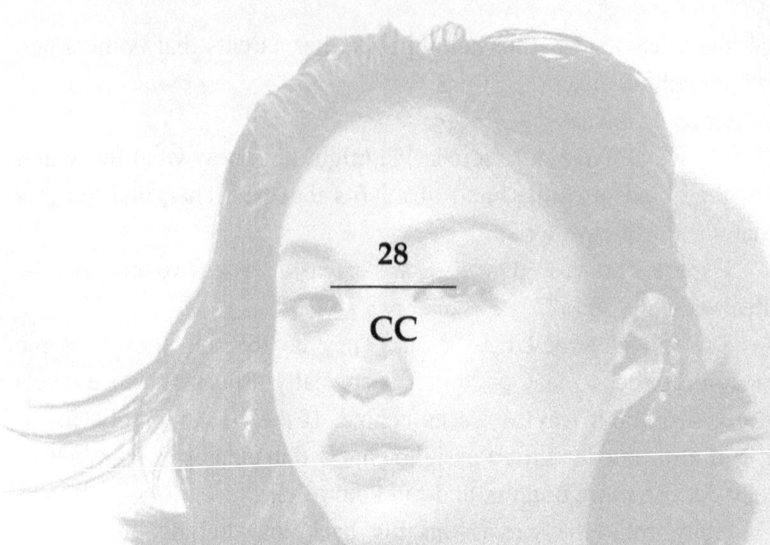

28

CC

Inventory days are my favorite.

It's that nerdy part of my brain that seeks out patterns, structure, and chaos to make sense of it. As a geneticist, it's in my nature to do so. I get that the inventory part is off-brand for me, but I love it. It's easy to lose myself in purchase orders and tally sheets since it comes with the added bonus of being left alone.

This helps the morning breeze by.

I manage these processes for Brewer Health as a whole, and I do the same for Brewer Diagnostics LLC, where I work, as well as Brewer Medical Clinic. They all share a common supplies space, and it's not the supposedly non-existent one in the sub-basement. The twins remain adamant that the room is off-limits.

There has to be a reason for all the secrecy, and as someone who is enshrouded with enough secrets, I know better than to pry. The space doesn't even show up on the blueprints for the Brewer Health building, so that must be a hint to leave it the fuck alone.

Which I do, for the most part.

I'm also a nosy bitch, so I'll find out if they are keeping the secret to Nirvana down there or if it's something a lot simpler. Like it's dead space with a shitty draft or something. Maybe it's a super-secret treasure.

It's better than dwelling on the shit show that is my life.

I've always known that Oscar is sensitive about role-playing, but I didn't expect him to react the way he did that night.

I don't like being coerced into making promises I intend to keep anyway. I don't like being coerced, period. I'd rather be the one doing the coercing.

That's too many uses of the damn word in the same paragraph, but my point remains.

Now that Oscar finally got what he wanted, is it wrong of me to be jealous? I envy the bond they share. I envy how easy it is for her to open up to him. I shouldn't have been eavesdropping on them that morning, or every time it's happened since, but I can't help that I want that with Courtney too.

Not much has changed, except for the part where we're now fucking like rabbits every chance we get. We're always at his place or mine, never hers. I'm not complaining about that, but I want more. She says she does too, but neither of us fully understands what that will entail. Especially her. We're fumbling through this like fucking newbies, and it's only a matter of time before we arrive at yet another stalemate.

Once I wrap up my relevant tasks for the day, I delve right back into my research. Devin the dingbat continues to irritate me throughout the morning, but no more than usual.

A soft rap on the door breaks my concentration. Delilah Brewer, my friend and boss, pops her head in. "Charlena, you ready to go?"

A quick glance at the clock tells me it is a little after one PM. "Is it that time already?"

Forcing a smile, she adds, "If by 'that time' you mean time to shove some food down Dahlia's throat while doling out copious amounts of guilt for not taking care of herself, then yes, it's that time already."

"It's just lunch, right? Not some sort of an intervention." I log out of my computer and retrieve my jacket. The fall weather in the Midwest can be brutal. Don't even get me started on winter.

"That depends on how much eating she does this time."

Dahlia, her identical twin sister, is very heavily pregnant. I get the concern for her well-being, especially since her not consistently eating means her nausea keeps flaring up. Which means I have to keep refiling her prescription for Diclegis.

I don't mind doing it. Not only am I happy to help a friend out, it's not the first one I've written in the last few months.

Grabbing my purse, I join her, and we walk together to Dahlia's office.

"I still think you need to cut her some slack, Delilah. She's got a lot on her plate."

"You say that like you forget whom you are dealing with," she says as we pile into the elevator. "This *is* me cutting Dahlia some slack. It's only one meal a day. And let's face it, you're hungry too."

I laugh. "I won't say no to food, especially some I don't have to make."

She rolls her eyes. "I know. Why do you think I enlisted you for this?"

"And here I thought it was for my charm and wit."

"That too," she adds with a laugh.

Dahlia is typing away on her phone when we enter the conference room. Her brown hair haphazardly hangs over her face, and she occasionally pauses to push errant locks behind her ears.

Delilah gives me a look, and I pull a hairband out of my back pocket and hand it over. She mumbles thanks and walks over to her sister, gathers up her hair, and secures it in a high ponytail.

"Thank you," Dahlia tells her once she's done.

"You're welcome." She hooks both arms under her armpits and nudges her to her feet. "It's lunchtime."

"I'm not hungry."

"I know you're not, but I need you to do this for my favorite nephew."

It is sneaky and underhanded of Delilah to use the baby as a guilt card, but it is effective.

Well, *mostly* effective.

Dahlia's eyes lift to meet mine. She manages a smile, one that doesn't quite reach her eyes. "Help?"

I raise both hands in mock surrender. "I'm with Delilah on this one."

———

Thirty minutes later, we're at a café a few blocks from the office. The twins are familiar with the owner, who personally shows us to one of the more private booths in the back. I order for everyone as usual, since I'm a bit of a foodie. It's also a comfortable tradition we established in medical school each time we ate together. I still don't understand why they've always implicitly trusted me with their dietary needs, but I also learned to stop questioning it a long time ago.

Dahlia mostly plays with her soup, the corners of her lips down-turned as she stares expectantly at her phone.

I drop a pointed gaze at her hand, particularly where she's white-knuckling her phone.

"You break it, you buy it," I say, mimicking Delilah's sing-song tone.

The corner of Dahlia's mouth tips up into the beginnings of a smile, and it's the first real one I've seen from her today. "Send me the bill."

Delilah snickers and then holds out a hand for the phone. "Here, give me that."

Dahlia's pert nose wrinkles as she tucks it into her back pocket.

"He's not going to call," Delilah continues. "And your brooding isn't helping matters any."

He? "You're not back with Curtis, are you?" The thought of that happening is as distasteful as the man himself.

They both scoff.

"I will castrate that tool if he gets anywhere near her," Delilah immediately says.

Noted.

I can't say I disagree with that plan. Even I know better than to question how far Delilah would go to protect her sister. She's also quite handy with a scalpel, like someone else I know.

Curtis's womanizing ways are well-known in this town, but it has gotten worse now that Dahlia is expecting. Personally, I don't see what's so appealing about Curtis, even though a lot of our friends do. And as much as I love sex, I value my relationship with the twins even more.

Thoroughly intrigued by this turn of events, I bring my water glass to my mouth as I ask, "So, who's this mysterious *he*?"

Dahlia's lips thin out, and Delilah gets a mischievous spark in her eyes.

"I'll give you a hint. It rhymes with honey."

Huh.

My hand freezes mid-action, Oscar's words from weeks ago replaying in my mind. This could only mean one thing — *person*, rather. "No way… Clark Holcomb?"

"He prefers David," Dahlia blurts out, and I can't help but laugh.

A satisfied smile curves Delilah's lips. "And she's clearly not in love with him."

Oh.

Oh, dear.

The laughter dies a swift death on my lips.

"I'm not in love with him," Dahlia hotly objects.

"The denial is strong with this one," she declares in a sing-song tone. "It's not a good look on you."

"I really wish you would stop reading into things so much."

"Oh yeah? Give me your phone then."

"Not a chance." She picks up her spoon and noisily slurps on a few mouthfuls. "There, your precious nephew is all fed. Happy now?"

"Ecstatic," Delilah drawls.

I sigh and set my empty glass on the table, glancing around the room. I know better than to get between these two once they start bickering. Hell, I know better than to pick sides. I love them both equally. Not just for who they are as people but for what they do for others. For me. Unlike others, I never had to pretend with them.

Our paths first crossed at a medical conference in Florida

sixteen years ago. Their parents, Jordana and Derrick Brewer, and my then-guardian, Dr. Sonya Goodman, were presenters at that conference. I was a nobody back then, starting over in a new country with no family, no friends, and no place to belong.

It was a unique time in my life and also a time of many, many firsts. First losses, first time falling in love, first heartache, and the first time truly being on my own. The first time with no parents to answer to or dictate the course of my life. Also, it was the first time without a name, as I hadn't even decided what my new name would be.

I was barely a week into the Network when I met the Brewer twins. Lorenzo had handed me over to Sonya earlier that week as part of my assimilation, so I barely knew her. I remember wanting to spend that entire weekend confined to my hotel room, brooding. Once the Brewer twins got wind of it, they invited themselves into my hotel room, made a mess of the place, and then dragged me all over town to their favorite hangout spots.

I have nothing but fond memories of that weekend. It had also been a while since I last felt a sense of camaraderie or belonging with anyone. When I look back on it, it was thanks to Dahlia that all of it happened. I felt a connection with Delilah then, as I could recognize a number of the same emotions cycling through her as the ones I was feeling.

What I didn't expect, however, was to see them again after that, so I gave them my real name. After my first placement fell through, I didn't think anything of it when Sonya immediately recommended that I move to Rochester for a repeat of my senior year in high school. Since I had to change my name again anyway, I put off moving to give my second placement with the Cantor-Dietrichs a fair chance. Months later, I was singing a different tune. They weren't bad, per se, but I'd given up too much of my life to be stuck on ski slopes.

When I eventually took Sonya up on it and moved to Rochester by myself, the Brewers were the first to accept me with open arms. They never questioned why I had a different name, was still the same age, or even the countless surgeries I had in the years that followed. I didn't realize it then, but I sorely needed their unconditional love and support. I wouldn't have assimilated as quickly as I did without their help.

"You could just call him," Delilah is saying. "You're the one that broke things off with him."

"It's not that simple, Dee."

"It could be. There's no shame in feeling regretful for our actions. It's what makes us human." At Dahlia's scowl, she quickly adds, "Yes, that includes you. I get that this was out of character for you, but look at how things turned out. I can't believe I'm saying this, but it wasn't all bad. And as much as I hate to admit it, he's good for you."

As the twins bicker, my phone buzzes, alerting me that one of the sensors inside my house has been tripped. There are two people who would be at my place this time of day, and I'm curious to know which of them it is. Out of habit, I pull up the app and turn on the video feed. I can't help the small frown that forms as I watch the scene unfold.

"Something the matter?" Delilah asks after some time passes.

"I… uh, yeah." I force a smile as my eyes lift to meet hers. "Not really."

"Spill."

I shift in my seat. "It's nothing."

"That didn't look like nothing." She holds out her hand for my phone this time.

"I don't think so." I stuff it into my back pocket.

"You two are so overprotective over inanimate objects," she murmurs, pouting as she leans back in her seat and crosses her hands over her chest.

As tempting as it is to spill all, this is one thing I'll be playing close to the chest.

"Tell you what, Dee. I'll call him," Dahlia leans forward, a mischievous spark adding a twinkle to her tired eyes. It is an odd contrast to the eager expression on her face. "When CC finally comes clean about her mystery girlfriend."

"Why are you bringing me into this?" I can't help but object hotly.

"You're right there, scowling at your phone. It's hard to ignore when you're sitting right there."

The last thing I want is to be dragged into one of their squabbles. Excusing myself from the table, I step outside the café and give Oscar a call. He picks up on the fifth ring.

"Hey, CC, can this wait?" is the first thing he says.

There's a sharpness to his tone that rubs me the wrong way. Frowning, I pull the phone away from my ear and just stare at it.

What is with him today? He can't still be mad about what happened a few days ago. He needs to learn to let shit go.

"CC?" His voice carries, piercing through my irritated thoughts. "Why call if you're not going to say anything?"

"Yeah, I'm still here. For a moment, it sounded like you were about to brush me off."

"I was," he deadpans.

I blink again. So, I wasn't reading into things. "At least you're honest. I've always loved that about you."

He blows out a breath. "Can you make this quick? I have a prior engagement I'm late for."

"How long will it take?"

"As long as it takes. It's one of… those."

Oh.

My spine straightens. "Is that wise?"

"Probably not, but it's necessary," he says, letting out a weary sigh. "You didn't call to ask about my day, and making small talk isn't your style. What's this really a—" He pauses like he's catching himself. "Is she okay?"

"No. She's camped out on… well, you know."

There's a rustling sound on the other end, like he's running a hand through his thick hair. "I probably won't make it tonight."

"I figured as much." Am I annoyed that he's not taking this seriously? A little. But since I get her to myself, I'm not complaining.

"CC?"

"Yeah?"

"You should consider telling her the truth about yourself. Don't let her find out from someone else."

"Where's this coming from?"

"A place of love and concern. Also, your accent is slipping."

I'd be lying if I said I wasn't concerned about that. But as far as Courtney knows, Yong Chun-ja is dead. And so is Deloise Milligan, the identity that can be tied directly to her.

As Charlena, I've been good. For sixteen years, I've kept a low profile. I do as I'm told, even to this day, with no complaints. Even though Courtney is my reward for my stellar track record, Lorenzo forbade me from telling her who I truly am. Phoenix and Abby know, but their hands are as tied as mine.

"I can't tell her, Oscar. You know this."

A weary sigh comes through. "Don't do what I did. Delaying the inevitable will only hurt you both."

"I know. I choose to look at the big picture."

"You mean the one Lorenzo put into perspective for you? Because he's never wrong."

"I never said that. Do I think his word is the be-all and end-all? I don't. But we all get what we want as long as I don't outlive my usefulness."

I imagine him shaking his head. "There's no changing your mind on this today, right?"

"Nope."

"Fine. Keep me posted?"

I end the call and resume watching the live feed from my house. There's so much I wish I could tell her. So much of what they all currently do, Oscar included, is built upon the premise of a death that never happened. Lorenzo is shamelessly exploiting that as a means to an end, to keep Courtney in line and compliant. And I've been an unwilling participant in it.

My heels click against the concrete sidewalk as I make my way around the block, replaying what just happened. A part of me hopes Courtney will figure it out eventually, but I'm scared of how she would react. She could very well kill me, as deception isn't something she handles well. But at the same time, it wouldn't be fair of me to expect that of her when I can't do the same in return.

Still, it is odd that she's back from her trip early, so when she starts cleaning, I text her to make sure everything is okay.

CC: Rough day?

She doesn't answer, as she's busy sterilizing my bathroom. I decide to call it an early day, so I also shoot Delilah a text. It'll only fuel more questions from them, but I can handle those another day.

29

COURTNEY

R e-acquainting myself with the toilet bowl and cold marble of the bathroom floor was not how I intended to spend my evening, yet here I am.

This rarely happens to me after a job. I pride myself on keeping it together. On not losing control, whether before, at, or after a job. It wasn't always this way.

Yet here I am, twenty-four hours later, dealing with this shit.

It was a lot worse when I first started out, but as the years went by, I've gotten so much better at compartmentalizing. It's a necessary skill to have, keeping that part of my life separate and isolated from everything else — the things I hold near and dear to me — but this time the job hit a little too close to home.

Or *not* home.

I can't go home now because my home is currently occupied by my brother-in-law, Harris. Possibly by Roxane, too. She knows not to ask questions, but he doesn't. I know that if he sees me in this state, it will only spark more questions, most of which I have no intention of answering. Or he'll sic Marc on me, and... I'd rather not.

It's a case of self-preservation, mostly.

A girl is entitled to have and keep certain things to herself, and *this* is not a conversation I intend to have with my brother, now or ever. Marc is a bit of a control freak, something I've become quite adept at maneuvering around in order to indulge myself in my extracurricular activities. He knows enough about what I *really* do for the Sotelo family, but as far as he's concerned, I'm the only active weapon. As such, I can't have him breathing down my neck or bringing his attention to my other two compadres' identities.

Nor can I clue him in that, like Mom, I lose a little of myself with each kill. And also that one of my greatest fears is that Charlie *will* turn out like me — or worse, that I'll be the one to make him that way, like Mom did with me. It's probably not going to happen, not with the arrangement Marc and I have, but a mother worries she would ultimately become her child's worst nightmare.

When one thinks of monsters, one thinks of fangs, talons, and glowing orange eyes, not those who are meant to keep you safe, to love and protect you unconditionally because they chose to bring you into this world. Even the boogeyman gets a bad rep for no reason other than he makes for a much more believable target. People will rush to blame the imaginary monster hiding under your bed, not the one who crawls into bed with you to chase said monsters away.

To me, Sarah Bardales was that monster. She kept me safe from those monsters. She also taught me how to slay them without remorse. And while it's easy to claim there was no undoing the damage she'd done after she died, I chose to pick up the mantle. I chose to avenge her death. I chose to keep on killing. I could quit at any time, but I don't because I enjoy the thrill it gives me, having that much power over a person's last breaths.

My soul is doomed; I know this. There's no hope for redemption for someone like me, so why stop now? Why not go all the way? With my luck, my demons will catch up to me sooner rather than later and dole out whatever gruesome punishment they see fit. Or I'll die a pathetic death like Mom did, all in the name of love.

Like many others, Marc still sees me as an innocent, someone who's meant to be shielded and protected from harm. And if he wants to hold on to that delusion, who am I to take that away from him?

So CC's house it is.

Or rather, CC's bathroom. She's not home yet, so I get unfettered access to her bathroom. I plan on cleaning up after I'm done so she won't know. Or she *will* know, but she won't care.

Mostly won't care.

The thought has another bout of bile hurtling up my gut. My head spins, and I once again retch up the non-existent contents of my stomach. I linger on for a few extra minutes, hoping this recent bout of nausea will pass, preferably sooner rather than later.

That takes five long, excruciating minutes, during which I sit on the cold marble floor and count backward from three hundred to zero. That mostly settles my stomach, so I crawl to the cabinets under the sink and unpack the cleaning supplies.

The smell of hydrochloric acid soothes me, so I remain seated and take my time, occasionally crawling or scooting over to the spots I still need to get at. An hour later, the whole room is as clean as it will get, the smell stronger than ever. I find that I am unable to stand after all of that. My entire body shakes from pain and exhaustion, so I curl up in the fetal position where I end up — next to the clawfoot tub, cleaning supplies next to me — and close my eyes.

Just as I drift off to sleep, too easily given my insomnia, it occurs to me that perhaps this is not the brightest idea on my part. Should CC step into her bedroom, she'll get a strong whiff of this. The smell does travel, after all. And finding me in here will only prompt her to start asking questions. She does that sometimes, and my non-answers occasionally seem to placate her.

Although compared to Harris, I'd rather she did the asking. She doesn't always ask questions. Not about what I do, anyway. I now know that she's been getting those answers from Oscar. Every so often, she'll ask about us — what we are, how secure her place in my life is, and about Oscar — all questions I don't plan on answering.

From the start, she set the terms of this... whatever we have, and I'd be lying if I said I hadn't grown somewhat complacent. Ours was never a conventional relationship to begin with. Fuckbuddies with benefits isn't the proper term for it, either. I had no intention of muddying up the waters further by demanding that she define what we were then. Despite having Oscar's hot, decadent self immersed in every aspect of our non-relationship, I didn't ask for more, and she didn't either, and for the longest time that worked just fine for me.

But after four years, I could tell she wanted more. The odds must be in our favor because I do, too. I want more out of this life. So I asked, and they both said yes. It's a foreign feeling, seeing eye to eye on something major like this. It'll change the dynamics of everything, and I can't wait to delve in.

Plus, I get to keep him too.

But the million-dollar question is, does he want to keep me?

30

OSCAR

I have never been any good at waiting.

Patience is just not a virtue I possess. It was never in my nature. Not only does my impatience precede me, but it's also what earned me the not-always-flattering reputation as a shrewd businessman and a hardass. The second name I like, since my ass *is* hard. The first, not so much.

Yet here I am, being forced to wait even longer.

On a blind date, no less. One I have no business being on.

One that will undoubtedly earn me a blistered bottom, thus leaving me unable to sit for days. I'd welcome it too, relish it, and probably beg for more simply because it came from her.

My true soulmate.

Who, at the moment, is having some sort of existential crisis again, and instead of going to her, I'm stuck here doing this.

I swallow thickly, rechecking my watch. It's now five minutes past the agreed-upon time, which tells me this outing is shaping up to be a waste of my time.

Good to fucking know.

I don't have time for this. I'm busy enough as it is. After dipping my toes into cryptocurrency eight years ago, Hyun Industries, my latest and greatest venture, took off and has grown steadily in the last five years. Financially, I've been in a secure place for longer than that, but that will never be enough. These days, I've prioritized re-investing in start-ups and smaller companies, most of which pan out and I make back double and triple what I put in. I'm also very selective in whom I partner with, and for every stack of new contracts I sign off on, another, even bigger pile takes its place.

But I digress.

The point I'm trying to make is, these blind dates are pointless — pun intended. The only reason why I do them is to appease Mom. Her overbearing nature has no bounds. She's been setting these up for me for over a decade, once every month.

At first, she said it was because she had my best interest at heart. All she wanted was for me to find my so-called elusive soulmate, the supposed one who would turn my life upside down in more ways than one. When that reasoning didn't pan out, she switched tactics, claiming she only needed to live long enough to see me settled down and cranking out the grandchildren.

The idea was laughable, to say the least. But like the dutiful son I am, I humored her and went on those dates. Only to quickly discover a pattern emerging from these. I would get a napkin at the end of each date with a bunch of numbers scribbled onto it. There was no rhyme or reason to it. Sometimes it was a single phone number; sometimes it was several. There have been sequential and non-sequential numbers, IP addresses, and local and foreign bank account numbers. One time, I got coordinates for the fucking Bermuda Triangle.

If my 'date' shows up, she hands it to me at the end. If she no-shows, a waiter brings it to me with the check. I've relocated a few of these dates, sometimes at the last minute, and the hand-off process remained the same.

I pass them on to Mom, obviously. I'm not stupid, and I don't have a death wish. I've always known Mom was into some shady stuff — as evidenced by who my sperm donor is — but I refuse to get mixed up in any of it. That doesn't mean I'm not taking active steps to protect myself should shit hit the fan. I've been passing those notes on to Abby as well, just for good measure, and thus far, she assures me they are harmless. I take her word for it, and I trust her wholeheartedly.

Mom, not so much. Not when she's using me to play with other people's money. But as long as Abby tells me it's harmless — which is code for *it's other bad guys' money* — I'm staying out of it. Likewise, as long as Mom keeps her nose out of my business, we're square.

I don't trust Gerald either. Whatever fool's errand Mom currently has me on must be interfering with his business since he keeps summoning me to his house to play happy family. Or to lure her back into the country. If only he knew, she's not taking the bait for two reasons — she either doesn't know or is letting him do her dirty work.

My phone chimes with an incoming text message.

> CC: I hope your blind date is going better than my evening.

If only.

> Oscar: This one's a no-show.

> CC: Come home then.

> Oscar: I can't. Not done here.

> CC: <Bathroom selfie>

> Oscar: You're killing me.

> Oscar: I love you both.

> Oscar: Be sure to delete that. She won't like it.

A glance at my watch tells me it's been thirty minutes, and there is no sign of... Penelope? I think that's what Mom said my date's name was.

As long as I stay put for another thirty minutes, I'll get what I came here for.

It's just as well. I'd rather deal with a waitress who understands the value of hard work than with another spoiled, privileged, and posh princess who thinks the world revolves around her and her Louboutins. Mom knows how to pick 'em, and the thought of sitting through yet another one of these blind dates…

I can't help but shudder at the thought.

Been there, done that, not looking forward to doing it again. I'd rather feed the beast inside of me, that which constantly yearns for the darkness.

After tonight, I'll tell Mom this is the last time. And when Gerald calls, like I know he will, I'll tell him to stick it where the sun doesn't shine.

At the hour mark, I signal for the waitress. As she walks over, I don't even have to look to see the apologetic gaze in the waitress's eyes to know I've been stood up. Again. That much is obvious. Besides, I'm more interested in what she has for me.

She discreetly hands over the obligatory napkin tucked in with the check. I'm off on my merry way, hopefully for the last time.

I give Mom a call as I exit the upscale restaurant, but only after putting one in to my driver for a pick-up.

She picks up on the third ring, almost breathless. "You lasted a whole hour this time."

Y'know… I refuse to imagine what she's doing at the moment. One would think the fact that we're in different time zones would affect our communication, but no. The fourteen-hour time difference between us never mattered to her. Anytime I called, she answered. And vice versa.

Does that make me a momma's boy?

Maybe. Maybe not.

I won't deny that there have been times when I shamelessly played up how close Mom and I are — even though we really aren't — since it's a huge turn-off for some women and a source of amusement for me.

At the thought, a smile tugs at the corners of my lips. "Yes, I did. It was lovely."

"You mean she was lovely."

"This one didn't show." I bite down on the urge to toss in a snide remark. "Dinner by myself is such a wonderful and fulfilling experience, Mom. You should try it sometime."

There's a sharp intake of air on the other end, like she's stifling a moan. "Did you get it?"

"What part of *'she didn't show'* didn't you understand?" Per her instructions, I have to call her after every one of these dates. However, the last thing I want is to listen to my mother having sex. There is such a thing as voicemail; hers works just fine.

"Oscar, when will you grow up and start taking this seriously?"

"I am taking this seriously. I indulge you in this, do I not?"

Poor choice of words on my part, as she then launches into a long tirade that's enough to make any sane person's head spin. I rub my free hand over my face and press my fingers to my temple, giving her as long as she needs to get it all out. Then, she officially loses me when she switches over to Hanguk Mal, something she does when she gets really frustrated with me.

Truth is, I don't understand a lick of what she's saying. I never learned Korean. I never wanted to learn either, something we agreed to disagree on. I'm already fluent in four languages, all of which serve me well from a business perspective. As it so happens, Korean isn't one of them.

Likewise, I don't do business there. I have no interest in garnering favors from Mom.

"Do I need to keep an eye on things myself?" she's saying, having switched back to English.

"Keep an eye on what, exactly?" It's a silly question, but I have to ask. "You live halfway across the world."

"I'm not above moving back there," she threatens, as if that would ever happen.

Mom and I are close, but it's a different sort of close. We never had a typical parent-child-loving relationship. It's more like an obligation. The kind you are forced to make when you find yourself in a foreign country, pregnant with a child you never wanted, and abandoned by a man you thought you had a future with.

So the story gets told — ad nauseam.

I have to nip this in the bud. We do better when we are as far apart as possible.

There's rustling in the background. I hope that means they're done.

"Why don't we do this again next month?" I tell her, instantly regretting the words but wanting to be done with this conversation already.

"Will you take it seriously next month?" she counters.

I don't bother dignifying that with a response. She already knows she has me right where she wants me. And since I have to humor my mother with these once a month, so be it. But it doesn't mean that I'll be helping the process along.

A sigh moves through her. "For what it's worth, Sylvie is a nice girl."

Ah. Sylvie.

So that was her name.

"And I'm not getting any younger," she adds.

… here comes the guilt card.

Christ, could she be any more predictable? This one must be important since she's laying it on thick.

Is it wrong that I'd rather she goes back to what she was doing before?

"You have many years left on you," I remind her since flattery will get me everywhere with her. She eats that shit right up. "And Sylvie will find someone else worth her time."

"I'm sure she will," Mom drawls sarcastically. "And when that happens, I'll have her mom send you an invitation to the wedding. Which you will attend on my behalf, like the dutiful son that you are."

I wonder if Sylvie's parents' money is what she's after. It must be a lot, and it must be filthy, because when she says things like that, I have no choice but to yield. Nothing brings me greater joy than throwing away my hard-earned money at all these lovey-dovey couples around me who keep shacking up.

Barf.

"Seriously, Mom. I got it. You can stop with the guilt trip."

She falls silent for a beat, then, "I'll send you the dossier for the next one."

She hangs up with that.

With my luck, it will be in my inbox within the week. Mom is predictable like that. Where she keeps finding all these women remains a mystery.

Not that I care. It will end the same way.

31

COURTNEY

At some point, I wake up in a cold sweat. The floor is cold, hard, and unrelenting. Uncomfortable as fuck too. My whole body shakes and trembles uncontrollably, and I really do hate how weak I am now.

It takes me a minute for my brain and body to register the warmth of CC's body curled up behind me, except we are both still on the bathroom floor. And while the sentiment barely registers — I'd like to think that it would for someone normal, and I'm anything but — this is inefficient.

Dangerous too.

I should be surprised that she's here, but I'm not. I don't know what she's thinking, putting herself in harm's way like this. She knows better than to try and wake me up in the middle of a night terror, something she usually avoids doing unless absolutely necessary. She also knows better than to be curled up next to me when I'm in this state.

I attacked her once in the middle of a nightmare — something I genuinely have no recollection of — but we discussed it afterward and agreed it was best that she kept her distance should she find me passed out on the bathroom floor again.

She seems to have conveniently forgotten this. And what is she thinking, lying on the floor in a thong and flimsy tank top? I do it all the time so my body is used to it, but she's not and the last thing I need is her coming down with pneumonia. She's not a very good patient, and I'm not a very nurturing person either.

This time, she barely stirs as I lift her lithe body and carry her to her bedroom. After getting her settled under her extravagant, fluffy but gaudy quilt blankets — several layers of them since she gets cold so easily — I turn to leave, but she reaches for my arm and tugs on it.

"You need your rest too," she whispers hoarsely.

I could argue that I don't need it anymore and that my floor nap was enough for me, but I don't. After all, she is right. I'm exhausted. Drained, more like. With sore spots all over my body. Who knows how long I had been passed out on the floor?

She pushes the blanket to the side, and I crawl in and curl up behind her. I still don't trust myself not to hurt her. But she doesn't seem to care as she repeats the position we were in on the bathroom floor, with me being a small spoon instead of the other way around, which she prefers.

She kisses my bare shoulder, and a shudder runs through me.

It's the good kind, I think.

"I'm fine now." My voice comes out as a dry rasp.

"I'm not," is all she says. A beat passes, then, "We don't have to talk about it now."

This can't be good. "Bad day?"

She mumbles something incoherent, which is CC's code for yes.

"What happened?" I ask again. That's the appropriate question to ask, I think. It's better than saying something snarky or insensitive, which is pretty much a given in my case.

A slow sigh moves through her, and she tightens her arm around my waist.

Well, then. I did my duty. I asked. If she doesn't want to answer, I can't exactly make her. It'll take time for us to get to the point where offloading our emotional baggage on each other is the norm. Even though Oscar has a point, with him it comes so easily.

"They're getting worse," CC whispers against my nape before adding, "Your nightmares."

Or not?

It's not like she doesn't already know about my nightmares. I just haven't told her why I get them.

It's funny. My insomnia makes it hard for me to get a decent night's sleep, so I deal with that by filling my waking hours with all sorts of extracurricular activities, hoping to pass out from the sheer exhaustion of it all.

Sometimes it works. Sometimes it doesn't.

When it does work, and I do sleep, I don't have dreams like ordinary people do. I have fucking nightmares.

I offer her a nonchalant shrug. "One day, I won't have them anymore."

We both know that's wishful thinking on my part. Still, she indulges me by agreeing with me.

"I know." She kisses my shoulder again. "Until that day comes, I'll be at your side." Another kiss. "Always. And if that day never comes, I'll still be at your side."

I draw in a quick breath, and it's painful on exhale. "Why?"

"You serious?" Her warm breath feathers my ear lobe.

I nod as words escape me.

At her core, CC has a warm and generous heart — so nothing like me.

Sure, she has her quirks. Who doesn't? Our dynamic must be confusing to Oscar, but there's a degree of trust in there that has been cultivating for years. Although there are times I wonder how and why she and I are together when we are such polar opposites.

Where she's warm, I'm cold and calculating. While she's generous, I'm incredibly selfish. Add psychopath to the list, and that right there makes for an unlikely pair. Yet this inexplicable pull I've always felt toward her baffles me. Like the pull I've always felt toward Oscar.

In his case, it makes sense now. It doesn't in her case because CC is not *her*.

The thing is, I don't spend too long dwelling on it. Like my mother, I'm selfish. Like my brother, I'm irrationally possessive. And in many ways, I'm more like my father than I care to admit. I'm not sure what that says about me.

While I'm lost in thought, she uses this to her full advantage. Before I can comprehend things, I'm on my back, and she's on top of me, her thighs straddling my hips on either side, our cores flush as thin layers of cotton and lace separate us.

I'm impressed. It's a defensive maneuver that I taught her years ago, one I know she kept fucking up on purpose so she'd end up under me. While I'm thrilled she's been practicing, I'm not sure if this was the intended purpose.

Seemingly proud of herself, she leans in, flattened palms on either side of my face.

I am proud of her, too.

I show her this by grinning shamelessly. "What now?"

Her lips morph into a small smile. "What do you mean *'what now?'*"

I lift a curious brow. "Are you looking for a 'good girl'?" Her whole body shudders at that, so I say it again. And again.

After the fifth time, she's rocking against me. "Stop, please," she pleads, her breathing shallowed. "I'm trying to have a serious conversation."

"But I'm having so much fun with this."

"Courtney…"

"You've been practicing, and good girls deserve to be rewarded."

"Please…" Her dark brown eyes go soft and serious. "You don't get it, do you?"

I give her my best fuck-me eyes as my fingers dig into the waistband of her thong and push it down slightly. "Get what?"

She makes a low sound in her throat, a half-smothered groan of desire and frustration.

Our gazes lock for a few seconds, and her eyes search mine with a hint of vulnerability I haven't seen from her in a long time.

"You and I, we don't talk about this," I say instead because it's the truth.

We just don't.

It is new territory for us, so it goes without saying that I should tread lightly. As much as I'd like to deny it, a small part of my brain comprehends her meaning — the thing I'm supposed to 'get' — but I don't want to have this conversation right now. I'd rather not talk at all. Especially while she's straddling me like she's doing right now.

"We could try," she offers.

"Like this?"

She nods. "What if we…" she trails off at that, and her expression goes wistful.

Or better yet, I'll just fuck her until she passes out from the sheer bliss brought on by multiple orgasms. And vice versa, either option works just fine. I also never imagined there would be anything stronger than the urge to kill — I *am* the daughter of two killers, after all — until I tasted her.

Suffice it to say, I'm hooked on her. On this.

On this between us. On this thing we share, one that has taken on a life of its own.

And I like how things are between us. We're official now, so there's no need to muddy the waters with all this talk about our feelings and emotions. Defining things — what we are and what we're not — is too long and too deep a conversation to have right now, and I don't have the mental wherewithal to process it at the moment.

What I am, is starving.

And my feast between her legs awaits.

"What happened today?" I eventually whisper, not wanting to dwell on the wistful look in her eyes and what that means.

Her gaze falls to my lips, and her eyes morph into an even darker shade. "You happened."

"Me—"

The words barely leave my lips before her lips are pressed against mine, claiming every inch of my mouth as her fingers snake around the back of my neck and pull me closer.

I melt into her touch, taking freely what she so generously offers me. It's a cleansing of sorts. My lips part, and her tongue sweeps into my mouth, seeking and coaxing. Then she pulls my tongue into her mouth and sucks on it. Hard. I involuntarily shiver underneath her as a deep-seated desire within me flares to life.

I suppose one could call me a tongue junkie. Who would've thought that was one of my erogenous zones?

"CC," I groan, fingers digging into the soft skin on her thighs.

She smiles against my lips in a 'gotcha' moment.

As she should.

For all the craziness that goes on in my life, CC has always been my one constant. Anchor. Tether. Whatever else you want to call it. I don't delude myself into thinking that what we have is just sex because it's not.

I'd just rather not think past that. When I do, I come to the same conclusion each time.

What it is, what we are, is complicated.

Then again, so is she. And so am I.

If that's how she wants to do this… well, two can play that game.

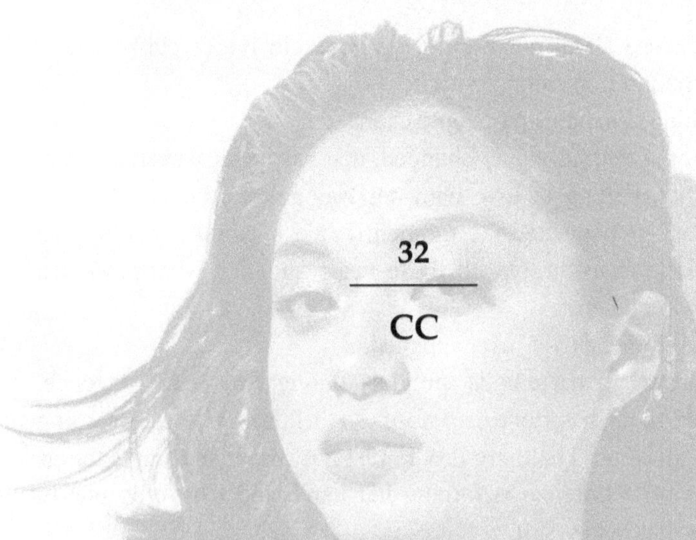

32

CC

I can tell the exact moment when the sadist in Courtney wins out over the curious-on-occasion and mostly detached side of her. But if she thinks I'll be tabling this discussion anytime soon, she's got another think coming.

"Just so you know," Courtney says as she switches up our positioning in one swift movement and pushes my thighs apart, "I wasn't expecting anything when I came over."

"I know you weren't, I just—" Words escape me, so I leave it at that.

What I am, is tired.

Horny as hell, but also emotionally exhausted.

I'm tired of dancing around this subject for years. Tired of not knowing where I stood with her, of my place in her life outside of these four walls. I'm tired of this stalemate we're in.

But more importantly, I'm tired of having to justify myself to Abby, and by extension, the rest of them.

There, I said it.

I fucking love her, goddamn it. I love Oscar, too, so why can't that be enough?

How we got to this point is mostly my fault. I should've come clean years ago, but I panicked. I shouldn't have made up that bullshit excuse about not wanting to be exclusive or public, and I wish she hadn't gone along with it.

But things change, and people change.

One thing that has never changed, that has never wavered, is my love for her. Falling in love with her was never a choice. Not for me, at least. It happened the moment I laid eyes on her. It's what drew me to that bathroom all those years ago. It's what propelled me to stay with her.

Everything else… it just happened.

I know what that entails, publicly dating two people at once. Neither of them has done it before, so it'll be quite the learning curve for all of us. The thing is, I'm just not sure if she wants things to change or if Lorenzo is forcing her hand, and I have no one to blame for that but myself.

Courtney drags two slender fingers between my folds and presses them against my clit. "Such a good girl," she whispers, a satisfied twinkle in her eyes as she teases me with light brushes of her hand. "So swollen and so ready."

I get even wetter at her words. "Only for you."

For now, I'll settle for indulging ourselves in what we do best. Fucking.

Two fingers tentatively slip in and out of me, teasing and stroking my slit in a gentleness that's… not like her. Except my body has a mind of its own, and I jut out my hips into her hand, moaning.

"Safe word?"

My lips curl up into a smile. "Not tonight." The last thing I want is to set her off accidentally.

"Thank God," she immediately adds, not bothering to utter it under her breath.

"Just… no toys tonight, okay? I just want to feel you."

"I do too." Leaning in, she pulls my bottom lip into her mouth and sucks on it before releasing it with a pop. "I'm going to do that to your clit, and I want you to coat my face with your juices. Deal?"

"Deal," I say in a naughty voice. "I'm your clit slut for a reason."

"You got that right."

Despite the tough airs she puts on, I know she can be tender and gentle both in and out of bed. Still, it's no secret that she enjoys dominating me.

Then again, I enjoy that too.

The no-toys request is more for me. Courtney gets very creative with them; her middle name might as well be unconventional. Not so much with Oscar, but we'll get there eventually. I've had all sorts of things stuffed into my pussy. Her knife and her fist are my two favorites to date.

She always strives to make me feel good, and I do the same for her in return. But when she says things like this, nothing brings me greater pleasure than a total and complete surrender to her. When that happens, she goes completely, utterly feral.

Her nimble fingers snake down the waistband of my thong, then snap the flimsy material in one swift motion. I can't help the soft gasp that escapes.

"I'll replace it," she promises as her wandering fingers make their way between my thighs.

"I don't care."

It's not the first time she's said this to me, and it won't be the last. I have always wanted the best of both worlds, but it's safe to say I hit the jackpot with her.

Or rather, we hit the jackpot with each other. And if there's one thing I can always count on when it comes to her, she always follows through on her promises. In bed, that is.

Leaning in, she kisses me slowly, sensually. Her hand pushes inwards, slipping two fingers inside me... and God, I'm so wet.

Then she adds a third, and I buck into her hand.

"More," I gasp into her mouth, spreading my legs wider for her.

If I didn't want her hot lips on my clit that badly, I might consider taking back the no-toys. I could use a fist in me.

"You're so fucking wet right now," she says, working her fingers in and out of me, "and I'm starving. I want to feast on your pussy and make you come so hard, you'll remember it for days."

I whimper, not bothering to hide my need.

Before her, this was something I'd always been self-conscious about. My leaky pussy. It was a turn-off for some of the lovers I had in the past. Yet she never made me feel that way. Not once. She says it's one of her favorite things about me. It didn't take me long to realize that she didn't mean that figuratively. She could feast on me all day long — for breakfast, lunch, dinner, even fucking dessert — and still won't get her fill.

Courtney's fingers slide out of my pussy, and with the fullness gone so suddenly, an involuntary shiver runs through me. I feel so empty, and at the same time, so aroused that it probably wouldn't take much to get me off. She trails kisses down the length of my body, then pushes my thighs apart and hooks both of my legs over her shoulders, giving her better access.

"She's so fucking gorgeous," she says of my pussy, in a seductive, dreamy voice.

She says that every time. That she's a sight to behold. I would've never imagined that having someone's gaze fixated on my pussy, having someone feast on my juices as much as she does, would be a turn-on. I can feel the slickness working its way down from my pussy and onto my asshole and the sheets underneath us.

Maybe it's just… this.

Her. Us.

A combination of both.

For us, intimacy has always been its own delicious monster — a living, breathing thing that consumes and defines just about everything we are, leaving little to no room for anything else. Sexually, we feed off of each other. We know what the other likes because we pay attention to each other's likes and dislikes. And while parts of that have seeped into other aspects of our lives, I also realize that we don't have much in common outside of the physical, so sustaining this insane chemistry between us outside of sex would be a challenge. That doesn't mean I'm not opposed to trying.

Leaning in, Courtney feathers warm kisses against my hardened clit. My back arches, and I cry out her name. Her hand comes to rest on my stomach, holding me down as she fastens hot lips over the sensitive bundle of nerves.

My eyes drift shut as all rational thought flees my brain. A string of words slips past my lips, and she chuckles, the humming sending vibrations through me.

"Oh, I plan on it," she murmurs with her mouth flush to my body. I feel her lip curl, and she adds, "You know how much I like hearing you beg. So indulge me, please."

Fuck.

That should not make me even wetter, but it does.

As promised, she takes her time with me, licking and savoring like she has all the time in the world. My mind goes hazy as she alternates between suckling on the swollen nub and dipping her tongue inside me to lap the wetness constantly pooling there.

She keeps this leisurely but steady pace going, and it's not long before I'm squirming and wriggling underneath her, desperately begging for a release that tethers on the edge.

No one sucks clit as well as she does. Amongst other things.

Using my juices, she lubricates her middle finger thoroughly and presses into my tight pucker. My body twitches again as she seeks out my sensitive spot. She finds it and presses down on it, and my whole body convulses.

"C-Court, I—*oh, f-fuck!*"

It's like watching someone go through electroshock therapy in real life, except it's like having an out-of-body experience. I moan and thrash and twitch and buck against her fingers and tongue, and she still doesn't ease up on me until the last of my orgasm ebbs and flows through me. Only when my body goes completely slack does she slow down her movements.

"So fucking beautiful," I hear her say.

The backs of my thighs meet the coolness of the sheet, not that it makes a difference. My whole body is on fire, from the inside out.

Next to me, the bed dips as she props herself up on her elbows. My eyelids part to find her hovering over me, our faces and lips just inches apart. Her stormy-gray eyes meet mine, moisture glistening on her lips, running down her chin. She runs a thumb over her lip as her eyes fixate on my lower lip.

"Your turn," I weakly mumble, my bottom lip trembling as the residuals of my toe-curling orgasm ebb through me.

Not sure what I'm thinking. I'm barely able to keep my eyelids open.

She looks like she's actively fighting the urge to lean in and capture my lower lip between her teeth. I wouldn't mind it, though. It drives me wild when she nibbles on it, sometimes hard enough to draw blood. I know it drives her crazy, too.

Instead, she says, "I'm not done with you just yet."

As if it wasn't bad enough, my heart rate shifts gears, hurtling right into overdrive. It's right there, on the tip of my tongue, the words I so desperately want to say to her. They remain stuck in my throat, terrified of her response. Of how she would or wouldn't receive it.

And of the ultimate unraveling that's sure to follow when she rejects me.

Why does it always have to be a worst-case scenario with me?

"Courtney?"

As if in a trance, she visibly snaps back to awareness, and her gaze slowly drifts back upwards until our gazes lock. Her lips twist into a smile. "Yeah?"

I drag in a pained breath, the words hovering at the tip of my lips.

I love you.

Cupping her face in both hands, I stare directly into her eyes. "I'm yours," I say in a breath, my heart beating faster.

She beams, cheeks flushed and coated with my juices. By God, she's beautiful. "I know." She studies me for several more moments, until a shrewd gleam slides into her eyes. "You didn't say his name."

Yeah, about those fantasies... "I-I was thinking it."

Her lip curls. "Liar." Her tongue darts out to lick her lips. "You get another chance, so fucking scream it this time, okay?"

33

COURTNEY

After several hours, CC is thoroughly exhausted and satiated. I hope she's forgotten all about what was bothering her earlier on. If she hasn't, she's not talking because I made sure all of her words and energy are spent. Once I'm done with her, it doesn't take long for her breathing to even out and her arms around me to go slack.

Sleep, the elusive bastard, still escapes me. I'm plagued by yet another bout of insomnia, which is par for the course these days.

If I were home, I'd be doing other things to pass the time — like hanging out in Charlie's nursery and watching him sleep. I'm his mother, so it's not creepy. Or maybe it is, I wouldn't know. I didn't exactly have a good role model in that department. It's no wonder Charlie does so much better with his uncle and the nannies he employs for him.

A long time passes before I untangle her arm from around my waist and scoot away from her. I grab my phone from the bedside table and make my way into the bathroom again. Once there, I settle in, back on the floor, then stare at the screen expectantly, willing it to ring so I can get on with this assignment.

I wasn't lying when I told Abby and Phoenix I had somewhere

to be and favors to repay. Damn my sense of chivalry. Roxane drives a hard bargain. She's the reason I came to CC's place first, to decompress before I went off and did that. I need to be at my best for it, and she would expect that from me.

When it comes to CC, try as hard as I might, I can't keep myself away. Not just from her physical space but also from her.

For all the horrors I've seen — some of which I've had a personal hand in — she's become some sort of a grounding anchor for me. Everything I do, have done, and will continue to do seems inconsequential when I'm with her. She has the power to make me forget who I am, a feat I never thought possible for someone like me — a trained killer with an affinity for violence etched into the fabric of my DNA.

Re-propositioning Oscar was a no-brainer. Our shared history aside, I know how important their relationship is, and I won't be the one to jeopardize that with my selfishness. They're both important to me, so making this thing we have official means bringing both of them into my world full-time.

That, in and of itself, will present its own set of challenges. It's something I'm willing to —

The toe-curling screech of my emergency ringtone goes off. I take a look at the caller ID and smile.

Her words tumble out in a rush. "Hey Courtney, I'm sorry to bother you so late—"

"You're not a bother, Roxane," I cut her off immediately as I absentmindedly run my fingers through my thick black curls.

"Yes, but—"

"But nothing." It doesn't surprise me that she rushes to apologize, and I can't help the chuckle that bubbles up. Had I known she would be this compliant, I would've said yes to this months ago. It's a refreshing change of pace from the hounding of the last few weeks.

All I hear are the sounds of heavy breathing on the other end, which is not an uncommon occurrence these days, given her condition. Then comes her exasperated sigh.

That can't be a good sign. "What's wrong?"

"Everything?"

Was that a question or a statement? "Are you having weird pregnancy dreams again?"

Another sigh. "Is this normal?"

"Is *what* normal?"

"I thought the mental sluggishness was as bad as it gets. Now some creepy older woman is invading my dreams. That's all they are, right? Just dreams?"

"Beats me."

"Or is it my subconscious playing tricks on me?" An image of her worrying her bottom lip pops into my mind. "You've been through this before. Tell me, when do the dreams stop?"

"I don't dream." The words fall from my lips before my brain can filter them out.

"What does that mean?"

Granted, it is a strange thing to say without providing any context, so I take a deep, fortifying breath to recalibrate my thoughts, then I try again with, "I didn't have pregnancy dreams, Roxane. Not like yours."

A beat passes, and a soft laugh comes through. "What's your secret?"

"How much time do you have?"

"All the time in the world, apparently," she says dryly. "This kid won't get out, and I'm over it *and* her. So tell me your secret. Maybe that will be the thing that gets this moving along. Since nightmares clearly aren't doing the trick."

Yeah, well.

If only she knew.

I don't dream because there's nothing *to* dream of. Nothing but a never-ending sea of death and destruction, some of which I have a personal hand in. Why bother cultivating hopes and dreams when they could and will all come crashing down at a moment's notice?

I crack the bathroom door and spare a glance at CC's sleeping figure still in the bed. The steady rise and fall of her chest looks forced. It could only mean one thing: she's listening to my conversation.

So much for being thoroughly exhausted.

While I've always known she has needy tendencies, she doesn't snoop. Most of the time, anyway. But this, *this* is strange and out of character, even for her.

"Courtney, you there?"

"Yeah, I'm still here." I rise to my feet and make my way back into the bedroom. If CC wants to snoop, she might as well do it properly. I fall back in the bed, and the back of my head hits the pillow with a low thud. Just enough to let her know that I am onto her. "You were saying?"

"What did you mean by 'I don't dream'?"

This, again? "I just don't."

"Everybody dreams."

"Not me."

"Bullshit."

I sigh. "Roxane, is there a point to this call?"

Another sigh. Then, "My water broke."

"When?" It could be another false alarm, and not the first one.

"When the creepy lady was invading my dreams."

That's all it takes for me to sit up. I won't even dwell on the fact that we just wasted precious time on nonsensical things. "What about contractions? How far apart are they?"

"I… don't have any."

"Call an ambulance, Roxane."

"Why bother? You're taking me to the hospital."

I grit my teeth. "Call a fucking ambulance and I'll meet you there."

"You're trying to get out of this again, aren't you?"

"Of course not."

"Then I'm not going alone. I'll clean up this sticky mess while I wait for you."

Or I could strangle her and be done with it.

Patience, Courtney. It's just the hormones talking.

I take a deep, measured breath, releasing it slowly. "Fine. I'll send one over, and if you turn them away I'll call Abby *and* Evan and wash my hands of you."

She falls silent at that, then huffs out a sigh.

"As long as there are no objections, I'll meet you there in…" I spare a quick glance at the clock, "…thirty minutes."

34

COURTNEY

After hanging up with 911, I stare at the back of CC's head.

"So you're doing it." As expected, there's a tinge of annoyance in her voice; this time, it's laced with something else. Pain, maybe? Resignation?

I run a hand over my face. "I am."

She releases a sigh. "Why?"

"She's a friend."

A responsibility, more like. But I don't dare point that out because it will only lead to more questions from her and non-answers from me.

"Can't you get someone else to do it?"

"It doesn't work that way."

She makes a disbelieving sound and rolls to her back. A moment later, the flick of the lamp switch reverberates throughout the room, and the soft glow of the orange mood lighting fills the room.

"Call Abby *and* Evan. Let them deal with it."

"Last I checked, I don't need your permission to help out a friend."

Spying my discarded jeans, I climb out of bed and make a beeline for them. As I tug my jeans on, she sits up and straightens the sheets on and around her.

She's doing this on purpose. Fighting turns her on like nothing else does. She's trying to hide this with the crumpled-up sheets, but I can still smell her arousal from across the room. It's potent and long-lasting, and also my favorite thing about her. What I'm addicted to the most when it comes to her.

But then she levels her gaze with mine before asking, "What am I to you, Courtney?"

The question makes me laugh, which is probably not the brightest move on my part.

Her eyes narrow to slits. "You think this is funny?"

It's not funny. It's ridiculous and bordering on absurd. It's absurd that she thinks we could be anything more than we currently are.

To me, she's a crutch. A tether to what normalcy is or should be. I know it's selfish of me to use her that way, so I'm giving her what she wants. We're official. What more does she want from me?

I go about retrieving the rest of my clothing from its various discarded places. I take my time, knowing her eyes are trained on my body. She could be pissed off about anything, but she can't stop looking at me. She can't help it, so I'm going to milk every second of her attention before leaving.

"Did you hear me, Court?"

I'm in the process of pulling my T-shirt over my head. "Yes."

I didn't.

But that's not what captured my attention. It's her tone.

It's not her fight tone; it's her needy tone. Or whatever else she's on this evening. She has these moments from time to time, and I'm used to it by now.

"So is Sunday a good time?" she asks.

My brow scrunches. "A good time for *what*?" I should've been paying closer attention, but CC talks a lot. Outside of sex, most of it is white noise. Five recurring topics keep coming up, so those are the ones I latch on to.

Oscar, obviously.

Her job.

Her trust fund.

The charities her bottomless coffers help.

Then there's her *other* best friend and quasi-business partner, Evan.

Roxane's Evan.

I'm not sure what this business is, exactly, but I've always known these three — CC, Oscar, and Evan — frequently work on special projects together. CC refers to those as their Trust Fund projects, so I never gave it much thought. I filed it under the five topics and white noise information to be processed later.

The thing is, I know a lot about CC and Oscar, but nothing about Evan. Nada. Zilch. That irks me to no end. The man exists, something I can confirm with my own eyes. I've walked in on them a few times, huddled in her living room with several papers strewn around her coffee table. But I can't find a single social media profile for him, not even something he was tagged in for publicity reasons. The man co-owns a successful public relations firm with two of his sisters, and while *that* is all over the internet, its three owners aren't. That tells me they are either, A, paying someone a lot of money to constantly scrub their internet presence, or B, they're hiding from something. Abby says they are good people, so—

CC lets out a tired sigh, interrupting my thoughts again. "You weren't listening, were you?" There's the tone again, with a hint of irritation.

I turn to face her. "No, I wasn't listening."

She huffs out a breath and grins. "I would like to meet Charlie. Preferably at your place, since he will be most comfortable in his own domain. Is Sunday a good time?"

Huh.

Now that I know this is what she was hinting at earlier, my first thought is that her timing sucks.

"Harris is staying with me, so Charlie isn't at home," I deadpan.

She knows how Harris is about kids. Everyone and their grandmother knows how Harris is about kids, so it's not hard to put two and two together.

As expected, her smile deflates a little. "When were you planning on telling me this?"

"Never, Charlena. As I told you both, Charlie isn't your concern."

Her dark brown eyes narrow at my usage of her full name. Still, she says, "He could be."

Fuck.

Are we really doing this? Right now?

I have to go, and she knows this, so she's just starting shit for the sake of it.

Not wanting to drag this out further, I cut to the chase. "What's really bothering you, Charlena? And stop using my son as a shield."

Another belabored sigh. "I'm tired of sneaking around, Courtney. And I'm tired of tiptoeing around this, of being your dirty little secret."

I snort. "Isn't it the other way around?"

Her face falls, and that's a cue that I have taken things too far. It's just... catering to her fragile feelings right now was not on my to-do list.

"Why do you do that? Why do you hurt me like that?"

"This isn't about you. It's about Charlie and what's best for him, and I'm not it. Neither are you."

"Is that why you iced me out of his life?"

Is she for real? "Whenever I'm not working, gallivanting around the world doing who knows what for my family, I spend it with you. Not him, you. I spend more time here than I do in my own house. Ever wonder why that is?"

She doesn't answer. I'm not sure she understands the question, or what I'm hinting at here. If I'm being honest, I'm not sure I do either.

Coming to terms with my own shortcomings as a mother brings with it that all too familiar deep pain in my chest. He deserves so much more, I know this.

Let's face it, so do she and Oscar.

If I had my way, I'd keep those parts of my life — relationships and parenthood — separate. All in the interest of feigning normalcy, if there even is such a thing. Clearly, I suck at this whole compartmentalization thing. I'm just too selfish to let either one of them go.

I want my cake, and I want to eat it, too. Since only one of them is here, I'll use these last precious seconds to convey that as best I can.

Closing the distance between us in a few strides, I put one knee on the bed and reach out to brush CC's dark hair out of her face. Her cheeks are flushed with her arousal, and her eyes roam my face, hungry and uncertain, as she bites her bottom lip.

How does she do this? How is it that even though she looks so adorably annoyed with me, all I want to do is push her body into the mattress and fuck her senseless again? She'd let me, too. If I wanted, I could re-enact every single filthy fantasy I've ever had on her lithe body, and she'd let me because it buys her more time with me, which is what she wants.

Just as long as I'm not with another woman, 'cause that's the crux of her issue here.

I bury my hand into her hair, fingers encircling her neck. Her lips part in response, and her warm breath feathers my lips. "You're important to me too, CC. I'm yours."

I lean in, desperate to kiss her, but she presses her hand against my chest. "I know what you're doing, and it won't work, not this time."

"Then you know," my gaze falls to her slightly parted lips, plump and kissable, "why I can't do this right now."

"There never is a right time with you. Avoiding and/or running from this conversation is what you do best."

My hand falls off her neck, and I push off the bed, taking a few necessary steps away from her. "Your timing sucks," I tell her, not bothering to hide my irritation. "You and I both know you were listening to my call, so you know why time is of the essence." At the now-blank look on her face, I add, slowly, like one would to a petulant child, "Roxane's water broke, and since I'm her birthing partner, I really do have to go."

She pushes the blanket off her and moves to climb out of bed. "I'll come with you."

"No." The bite in my tone isn't intentional, but it comes off that way. "She needs me at a hundred percent, and that's exactly what I'll give her."

She plops back onto the bed. "Fine. Go. Play fucking knight in shining armor to poor helpless Roxane."

There's the tone again.

So bitchy Courtney comes out to play.

"Charlie is off-limits, always has been. Anything to do with him means you'll have Marc to contend with. You know how he is, and that hasn't changed. It's only gotten worse."

"So?"

"So unless you are prepared to handle everything that comes after, you can forget about that dream." I'm practically vibrating with anger, but I don't care. She asked for it.

"I can handle—" she starts to say, but I hold a hand up to silence her.

"To answer your question, no. You will not be meeting Charlie. It'll only confuse him."

"He's two years old, for Pete's sake!" she screeches. "How's that confusing?"

"It just is. How the fuck am I supposed to explain who you are?"

"I don't know," she grits. "Maybe you can start by telling him we're friends. That's as close to the truth as you can get."

"Truth?" I counter. "We're not friends, CC. Try again."

"Oh, that's right. We are fuck buddies. Isn't that what you were going to say?"

Blowing out a tired breath, I run my hands through my hair. "I don't know what the point of this is, but maybe you should start by being truthful with yourself."

"And maybe you shouldn't go about spouting nonsense, demanding things of people when you have no intention of holding up your end of the bargain."

"What's that supposed to mean?"

"If you want a relationship with us, you need to start acting like it."

I'm so confused. "Where's this coming from?"

"This," she says and waves a hand between us. "Oscar and I, we're not ornaments for you to parade around as you see fit, then shove into a box whenever it's inconvenient for you."

"Jesus, CC. What aspect of my personality gave you that impression?"

"Oh, I'm not sure. Are you planning on introducing us to your family anytime soon? Or is fucking all we're ever going to do? 'Cause if that's your idea of 'official', it fucking sucks."

"You're one to talk."

Confusion clouds her gaze. "Meaning?"

"These head games you love to play. I know you get off on it, so I let you because it makes you happy. But guess what? There's more to life than sex, and there's more to *me* than what you see outside of these four walls. If I want to help out a friend, I will, and I'm not gonna ask your permission before doing so because not everything is about you. Maybe you should try, I don't know, getting the fuck over yourself. The whole world doesn't fucking revolve around you. Mine certainly doesn't."

She visibly freezes at that.

Even I have to cringe at my own poor choice of words. If I had been paying close enough attention, I would have seen the subtle changes in her demeanor before her brain and the rest of her shut down.

I am now.

I see it now.

In hindsight, I should've been nicer about it. But when you have places to be, it is best to rip the band-aid right off.

She lifts her chin with fake bravado. "You made your point, so we're done here."

My stomach tightens. Now *that*, I wasn't expecting.

Granted, I've said worse things to her in the heat of the moment, but even I know this is the cruelest thing that has come out of my mouth.

"For now, or forever?" I ask cautiously, a lump forming in my throat. This is the first time she's specifically used the words *done* and *we* in the same sentence. I might as well get clarification on what the fuck that's supposed to mean and adjust accordingly.

She crosses her arms over her chest, a slight pout on her lips. "What do you think?"

I think she's full of it, but I'll bite my tongue on that one, especially since this image and the words coming out of her mouth are in direct conflict with each other.

But leaving her? That's never going to happen.

I'll give her space, sure, but we're not done.

Not by a long shot.

35

COURTNEY

I 'm back in that wretched place again, relishing the night of my greatest failure. Rehashing the moment when, faced with the ultimate challenge, I froze. I choked.

Me.

This doesn't happen to me.

Ever.

Because I am who people think I am — the privileged, sheltered, illegitimate daughter of one of the deadliest Mafia families in the Midwest — I still have to play that part in this twisted-up charade called life, irrespective of whether I like it.

Only when I am in my element, doing what I was born to do, do I truly feel free. When I hold the power of life or death over another, my body and soul come alive, buzzing with an awareness like no other. It is the closest I have come to being and feeling alive. It's an addictive high I chase every chance I get.

Yet, for the first time, I choked.

It was her eyes.

She haunts me. Or rather, her eyes haunt me.

And until it happened, I never knew I was capable of it.

Of hesitating. Of showing empathy. Of caring.

Of feeling emotion other than a general disinterest and overall disregard for human life.

She makes me feel the feelings, and I truly hate that.

"I still say we toss her in as a freebie," I tell Lorenzo. Again. "Leave no witnesses, you always say."

But as the words pass my lips, there's a teeny part of me — the human, emotional part, I think — that wouldn't be capable of seeing this through.

Of seeing her death through.

I couldn't because... her eyes told a different story. They pierce through me with a sharpness that pins me in place.

Ever so observant, Lorenzo sees this. Then he does the unexpected.

He laughs.

It's a deep, hearty laugh.

"Some people are worth more alive than dead," he says once the laughter subsides.

I usually don't question him, but in this case...

"Is she going into the Network? It's her money you want, isn't it?"

She has plenty of it. And as the sole survivor, she stands to inherit all of it.

Except...

"I don't care about the money," she speaks up for the first time.

Yong.

That's her name.

Yong Chun-ja.

It means perpetual and brave one.

But there's something else in between.

It's in the way she carries herself. Her body language is that of a young woman — practically a child — forced to grow up too soon. It speaks of someone who's seen too much of the world and its ugliness and has embraced it in her own way, the darkness inside of her.

Like I have.

That's how I know that darkness she possesses; it is a thing of beauty.

Like she is.

Right then and there, I knew it would be a shame to deprive the world of this. Of her.

Not of what she has to offer the world, but of what the world has to offer her.

Everything.

PART IV

36

OSCAR

After spending the last hour poring over the latest financial statements for Hyun Industries, I'm satisfied with the numbers I see. It's a nice break from today's back-to-back stuffy boardroom meetings, most of which could have been resolved in an email or two.

But alas, as CEO and founder of Hyun Industries, I am obligated to show my face at headquarters once a month. If I had my way, I would opt for anonymity. After all, it is by design that I don't have a board of directors to answer to. Because I already offer rather generous employment packages, I prefer that my employees spend their time and considerable skills doing their actual jobs, not kissing up to me. I have a knack for spotting bullshitters and freeloaders a mile away, so getting rid of deadweight is never an issue.

It was a hard pill for some to swallow at first, especially when I was just getting this latest venture off the ground. While it had a rough start, Hyun Industries has been making good progress over the last decade, with business steadily rising over the last five years and at a rate I am comfortable with. Everything is trending in the direction I expect to see, with no glaringly obvious red flags.

Then again, it is possible that's what my accountants want me to see. And since it isn't in my nature to blindly take people's word for it, I intend on having Abby take a second look at this. I'm good with numbers, courtesy of genetics and Mom's *special* brand of training, but just because I know what to look for, it doesn't mean I'll always catch everything. Since Abby is like me, it doesn't hurt to have a second set of eyes on things. Not only is she efficient, but she also thrives on discretion.

My accountants also have no idea I've had her double-checking all of their work for decades, and I intend to keep things that way.

As it so happens, she is someone whom I wholeheartedly trust. Not just with my money, but also with my life. Plus, having her with me frees up my time to pursue other things. Hyun Industries isn't my only source of income, it's more like my fifth.

Or is it the tenth?

I stopped counting after that. That's what I have Abby for.

Like Mom would always say, diversifying my income portfolio is just as crucial to growing and expanding upon what I already have. We might not see eye to eye on certain things, but that's not to say her advice is invalid. People in my position do not get the kind of money, power, and prestige I have by putting all of their eggs in one basket.

Likewise, as far as business is concerned, on principle, I do not mix business and family. Ever. Given my family background, it would be the fastest way for me to destroy everything I've worked so hard to build. As long as Mom gets her notes, she keeps her nose out of my business. And if the Morellis come sniffing around, Abby will take care of it. She's offered to, on more than one occasion, and her way of 'handling things' translates into a permanent ejection from this life.

Have I entertained the idea?

Of course.

But why do someone else's dirty work for them? Not only has Gerald pissed off more than his fair share of people in his day, Reuben seems to be heading down that path. I'm not sure what they're thinking, blackmailing Lorenzo into handing Courtney over to them. I don't care either. I only hope that Hallie doesn't get caught up in the crossfire since she's innocent in all this.

Plus, she wants out. It's an achievable goal, if only she would stop dragging her fucking feet about it.

As I take another sip of the whiskey that I've been nursing for the last hour, a chime on my computer draws my attention. It's a Skype alert from Evan Whittmore, one of my best friends and another quasi-business partner. His texting me at this time of the day is usually not a good sign. As I ponder whether or not to take it, he switches to video calling, so I have to answer it.

"We have an SOS," is the first thing he says when his face fills the screen.

I lift a curious brow at his overly dramatic attitude. "Who's calling for one, you or CC?"

Like Evan, CC is another quasi-business partner. Except our 'quasi-business' isn't the revenue-generating kind, it's more like the 'making up for the sins of our fathers' kind.

"Not me." He lifts both hands in mock surrender. "She needs some work to distract her, so let's do that."

His propensity for theatrics isn't new. This SOS-calling business is a little suspicious to me, even more so with Evan doing the asking.

"Work, huh? Did she say that?"

He shrugs. "She didn't have to, Oscar. It was implied."

"When? How?"

"Since when do you get hung up on the details of who needs what and when?" he asks, sarcasm with a hint of concern tinging his voice. "And what's with this game of twenty questions? Just..." he heaves a sigh before adding, "Our *friend* needs our help, so call her, please. You'll see."

I retain the eye roll as I shoot her a quick message. She responds immediately, much to my surprise, so I invite her into the chat.

The moment she joins, I do a double-take.

"What's so urgent?" she asks in between sniffles.

Holy shit.

I draw in a sharp breath, exhaling slowly as I take this in — take her in — absorbing and cataloging this for later. Without a doubt, CC is one of the most charming, vivacious, self-assured, albeit overtly sexual women I know — the other one being the one who most likely put her in this disheveled state.

Truth be told, I can count on one hand the number of times I've seen her like this. No, post-orgasmic glows don't count.

At least Evan's SOS has merit.

"Who died?" he counters with a question of his own.

His twisted sense of humor is infamous with this group. Then again, it's disheartening to see a woman who always looks so calm and collected looking like crap, for lack of a better word, so his question is valid.

"No one." Her tone is almost too defensive. "What's so urgent?"

"It can wait," I tell her as I take in her haggard appearance. "What's going on with you? Why didn't you call me?"

"I didn't call anyone." She wipes her eyes with the back of her hand, smearing the tears and mascara more than wiping them away. "Did Evan call for an SOS?"

"No," he says at the same time I say "Yes."

She laughs, a bright, sharp sound, not at all like her usual warm chuckle. "At least you're honest, Oscar. You just…" Her voice fades for a moment. "You caught me at a bad time."

Evan only digs in further. "Define a bad time."

I bite back the retort that threatens to spill out since CC can speak for herself.

"Let it go, will you?" There's an edge to her voice that we both recognize, in addition to the stubborn light in her dark brown eyes.

We all know that a 'bad time' is a gross oversimplification of whatever this is. Just as we all know there's only one person who can get her looking like this.

"What was so urgent?" CC asks again.

Evan ignores her question, posing one of his own. "Do you need us to come over?"

"No."

"You sure?"

"Positive."

"Because if you need—"

"I'm terrible company right now, so no."

Through it all, I say nothing. There's no point in getting in the middle of these two once they start going at it. There's nothing to be said when she's this way. CC has always been a force to be reckoned with, that's for sure. Stubbornness, pride, willfulness — call it what you will, but if she says she isn't up for company, I know better than to push it.

It takes Evan sixty seconds to see the light. "Okay," he reluctantly concedes.

I don't believe for one second that he'll stop pushing the issue. Maybe for now, but not forever.

As for me? I have other ways of getting her to talk.

"Now, somebody, please distract me with work," she says with a rueful smile.

It only takes Evan all of five seconds to launch into the whole reason why he called this SOS in the first place. "You would love this. I finalized things with the project manager regarding the multi-campus project. The final numbers are in. Permits are all lined up. We will be ready to break ground as soon as two weeks from now."

"You mean we all have to be there in two weeks," I interject.

He waves me off. "Sure, if you want to get all technical about it."

"I do. You know lining up international flights to Nicaragua at such short notice will be a logistical nightmare, right? I'm a miracle worker, but I'm not that good."

I could be *that* good — I own the majority shares in several lucrative private jet companies — but I don't have the right kind of favors to call in to get us the proper entry visas at such short notice. I also prefer to keep things legit and above board. It's how we've managed to operate under the radar with what we've been doing.

Maybe we could go in as tourists, but that probably won't fly for very long with immigration and customs, or even the authorities, for that matter.

It's not even a pride thing, more like a principles thing.

For a man like me, sticking to the right side of the law as far as business dealings go has always been the best course of action. I go out of my way to keep my dad's name and our association as far out of my business dealings as possible since one slip-up will ultimately lead to the next, and the next. It's not a chance I'm willing to take, and I don't hesitate to cut out anyone in my life who even suggests that I do.

When it comes to Hyun Industries, it's already bad enough that my rigidity and unwillingness to compromise my ethics have gathered a healthy amount of enemies. It's what has made me weather the storm each time the sharks came swimming too close and my competitors crumbled.

It's no secret that I enjoy having money and all the comforts it brings. I also enjoy having the power and prestige that wealth affords. Having grown up in a single-parent middle-class household, there were times when money was tight.

Gerald never wanted to acknowledge my existence then, but he wasn't above hiring the woman he scorned to clean up his blood money for him. She didn't mind playing games with it either, since his money, by definition, is blood money.

Those billions that she gave my half-siblings? I have some of those. She said it was the child support she was owed at the time. Fifteen years ago, it was a modest amount and has more than quadrupled in value since, and then some.

Just as Gerald can't touch it, she can't touch mine either.

It's the Olive Hyun effect, and not even she is exempt from it.

37

OSCAR

I never intended to touch that money either, but what better way to get back at the man?

That's how I got into this quasi-business with these two. We all have some sort of blood money to get rid of, one way or the other. We were either born into it or inherited it from our parents. With such money comes responsibility, and our collective philosophy has always been that it should go towards worthy causes, except we take a more personal approach to it.

For starters, we all have our legitimate money.

CC is a silent partner in Brewer Health, something she would rather keep on the hush-hush as she'd rather the spotlight stay off her for obvious reasons. There's also the matter of her biological family, the Chun-jas, being chaebols in South Korea, and they pay a lot of money to keep her ties to them hidden. In addition to their successful public relations firm, the Whittmores inherited billions from their great-grandmother, textile heiress Elfriede Shafer. As for me, my money comes from multiple income streams and several investment companies I own, as well as the Hyun family. Olive Hyun never wanted her family's money, so she passed it on to me, whatever that's about.

Then there's the blood money, and we're all drowning in it.

CC has the most out of the three of us, courtesy of her biological ties to the Yakuza clan and the Yamamotos', her deceased fiancé's family. There's a very long and complicated history there. The same goes for the Whittmore siblings, who are very distant relations of James Phillip "Doc" Dearborn of Kansas City's Black Mafia.

Then there's me. The reject child.

Mine is the *supposed* child support money that Mom took from Gerald Morelli.

There's only one common denominator amongst all of this blood money. And yes, she wrapped those billions around our respective necks like suffocating nooses we could never be free of. She's been doing this to Mafia brats for decades.

Some of those Mafia brats have gotten wind of what we're doing with it — including those who went into the Network — and have passed those funds onto our quasi-business. Just because they can't get rid of it doesn't mean it can't be spent in other ways, which is precisely what Evan, CC, and I are doing.

The best part?

It's a built-in loophole that Mom didn't think I'd eventually find. But hey, working for her, albeit part-time, does have its perks.

"Do we all have to be there?" CC suddenly asks.

My brow lifts in surprise. If I could see my face, it would be touching my hairline.

"Is that supposed to be a trick question?" Evan answers her question with yet another one of his own.

"If Oscar says two weeks isn't enough time to get us all there, then I see no sense in delaying the groundbreaking ceremony so that we can stroke our egos."

Huh.

She's making some valid arguments, but something about this seems... off.

"Aren't you the one who insisted on a hands-on approach to all this?" Evan asks, not bothering to disguise his surprise. "We're putting up a lot of money for this, CC."

It's not like we're talking chump change. Each of us has

upwards of twenty million dollars to get rid of. Not to mention, our respective skill sets towards getting rid of said money vary, too.

It's also what strengthens our little band of misfits.

CC is all about the ideas. Legit ones, of course. She comes up with some of the most innovative ideas, and that's because she's actually lived through the various clogs in this flawed system that we're feeding the money back into.

When it comes to the actual execution of said ideas, Evan is a whiz with logistics. He's more of a twenty-steps ahead kind of guy. He's exceptionally good with all of the finer details that go into our projects.

Depending on how you look at it, I'm the executioner and money guy in all of this. Or the penny-pincher, as Evan likes to call it.

"It's really not that much money," I point out. The money aspect isn't what has me concerned. It's her sudden need to take a step back that has me worried. "You sure everything's all right with you?"

"Or, if you have to, you could push this thing back another month," CC continues, ignoring my question. "Or even two months. But if we don't all have to be there so this thing can get underway, even better."

Suffice it to say that we both stare at her as though she has suddenly grown two heads or something.

Granted, this project is on a smaller scale compared to others we've done. But being physically present at the groundbreaking ceremony is something she's always insisted on. She loves it all — the travel, meeting new people, and securing some of those much-needed contacts for current, past, and also future projects.

She can charm the pants off of anyone. It's her superpower. So, for her to suggest we don't go is unheard of.

"We're coming over," Evan immediately says. "Clearly, you're not okay."

She shakes her head. "No, you're not. You need to be at the hospital, and you," she angles her chin in my direction, "you have another one of your 'blind dates' in an hour."

That was yesterday.

My lips part, but she cuts me off. "Please tell me you weren't planning on saying something foolish like you'd cancel. You better go, or your mom will start blowing up my phone. Again. I can't have that on my conscience."

"You're deflecting, CC. It's not a good look."

She shrugs and turns to Evan. "Isn't your girl having the baby today?"

His mood instantly sours. "Why do you do that? You know she's not my girl yet."

"But her water did break, did it not?"

He sighs. "Not that I'm aware of. What are you getting at?"

"Well, it did. It's why Courtney hightailed it out of here a few hours ago. I thought you were going to nip that in the bud weeks ago?"

Ah.

So that's what this is about.

"And I told you, it's not that simple," Evan objects hotly.

"Maybe. Maybe not. All I'm saying is, she should've called you instead of calling *my* woman."

And therein lies the rub.

Oh, I can't wait to watch this one play out. As enticing as it is to want to stay out of this one, I already know I won't be watching from the sidelines. It's how these things usually go. I tend to end up right in the thick of it whether or not I want to.

Because Courtney Sotelo is… complicated, for lack of a better word. The simple version is that she is a literal physical embodiment of the things we are trying to get away from.

But also, it's never that simple.

I would know.

Also, CC is being selfish. She gets very one-dimensional in her thinking when Courtney is involved. Possessive too. Irrationally possessive, even though neither woman wanted to define what they were for years until a few weeks ago.

But the thing is, this possessive streak of hers, I get it. I am too, but I just hide it better. I think.

"…unreasonable about this," Evan is saying.

"I don't want any of you showing up at my doorstep. I swear I'll leave you out there looking like a fool." She now seems more agitated than sad, which is an improvement.

"That's absurd," he counters. "You wouldn't."

"Wanna test that theory?" When he doesn't answer, she adds, "That's what I thought. If that's it, I'm gonna go do something I'll probably regret in the morning, and I don't need either of you talking me out of it. So… good night."

CC hangs up before either one of us can say anything.

Evan and I stare at each other for a moment, processing what just happened.

"What do you think that's about?" I ask, hoping he has some more insight into this than I do. Mostly, I want to know what he said to her to agitate her even more, because it could be anything with him.

He bites back his smile.

"What?"

"Nothing."

"That didn't look like nothing. It didn't sound like nothing, either. What did you say to her?"

"Nothing she doesn't already know." I can tell he wants to say more but is purposefully holding back.

"Meaning?" I prompt when he's silent for some time.

He heaves a heavy shoulder. "It takes a village, and I didn't make the cut."

"Evan, I don't know what that means. I don't speak cryptic."

The barely concealed grin morphs into a full-blown smile. "I know you don't. That's why I said it."

With a sigh, I run a finger around the edge of my whiskey glass. "Did you really not know?"

He shakes his head. "No, I didn't. I also won't be interjecting myself into a situation where I'm not wanted. That's a surefire way to get labeled a stalker."

"I don't think it'll come to that. Your soulbond is much stronger than that." I'm not being in the least bit sarcastic when I say that.

He believes in all that mystic bullshit, and I don't. Still, he's made it his mission to wear me down on the subject, and I just might let him win.

Evan leans back in his seat, leisurely crossing his hands before him. "I thought you didn't believe in those?"

I could think of a thousand ways to answer his question, none of which are pleasant or appropriate for the situation.

"Are you really that dense?" he eventually asks.

Here we go again.

"That's between them. I'm not interjecting myself in their lover's squabble."

His eyes soften momentarily. "Interjecting, huh?"

All I can do is shake my head. "Stop projecting. It's not a good look."

"I'm not projecting. Just making an observation."

"Yeah, well. I'm not in the mood to play twenty questions either, so if you have something to say, just fucking spit it out."

He knows I'm in love with CC and that our relationship has been sexual for years. He probably suspects the not-so-secret torch I have for Courtney as well. I wasn't exactly being subtle about that either.

He doesn't know that we've taken things to the next level. He won't know for a while; no one will. Not when this is all still so new to the three of us. Well, mostly to me. They both have experience sharing partners, just not with each other. In a manner of speaking, I suppose this is new to them, too.

I wonder if that's what they were fighting about. CC wants our *grand* introduction to happen at the Sotelo Ball, which takes place in about two weeks. That could be why she's pushing so hard for us *not* to go on this trip. Logistics for that aside, I'm okay with waiting longer.

I'm hers. Theirs. Finally. It's still a relatively new emotion to me — this sense of belonging somewhere, to someone — *two* someones. I want to stay in that for a little longer before the world shits all over it.

And they will.

Evan peers at me for a beat, his eyes unusually hard. Hostile, even. "How's this for direct: how long will you let that go on for?"

I don't get it — his hostility, that is — but at the same time, I can understand why he would ask me that question.

"I'm not *letting* anything go on. Same as you aren't at the hospital right now. Ever hear the saying about people and glass houses?"

"Yeah, they should throw bigger stones."

"Okay, Wednesday Addams."

His brow crinkles in confusion. "I don't know what that means."

"There's a shocker."

"You don't need to be an ass about it."

"And you really need to learn how to read the room, and when not to interject your opinions into things that don't concern you." I shouldn't be mean to my best friend, but sometimes I can't help myself.

"Jesus Christ, man. What crawled up your ass tonight?"

"You know, for someone who does a lot of talking for a living, you're taking a really long time to get to the fucking point."

He sighs. "Never you mind. Go get ready for your *date*." He says the word so distastefully, like sand mixed into oatmeal. "May this one be as vapid, materialistic, clueless, and just your type."

"That was so yesterday, dude." It's his roundabout way of cursing me — a fuck you, so to speak — but not coming out and saying those words because, as he says, his momma raised a gentleman. Then he hangs up, leaving me staring at the ominous blue screen.

It's going to be a long night.

With a groan of exasperation, I toss back the rest of my whiskey. I let it slide down my throat, savoring the burn and the ensuing warmth it leaves in its wake.

I spend the rest of my night doing the one thing I promised Roxane I wouldn't do: retracing her digital footprint from ten months ago.

38

COURTNEY

I have met many stubborn women in my lifetime — heck, I work with two of those on a somewhat regular basis — but Roxane Lavenworth just might take the cake.

I understand her desire to want to fully experience the miracle of childbirth or some other bullshit like that, but there's a place and time for that. Now is not the time. Not when this kid, whom she has been demanding get the fuck out of her body for the last week, has decided to take the scenic route through bumpy terrain for the past twelve hours.

In hindsight, I should've known what I was getting myself into with her with this.

She's exhausted; that much is obvious. And when it boils down to the logistics of this, as in making sure Roxane's basic needs are met and her birthing plan is followed to a T, I'm on top of it. Including making sure she got that epidural she subsequently caved and asked for thirty minutes ago.

As for the fluffy shit?

Count me the fuck out.

Seriously.

I don't do warm and fluffy. I don't even have a soothing voice. Mine is a logical and sometimes menacing voice, something I have no desire to change. I don't hold people's hands and sing kumbayah, or tell them it will all be okay. I'm more likely to be slitting their throats and bringing them to their untimely deaths.

Knowing oneself and owning one's demons. That's what it's all about.

That's what my mother taught me.

And now, I signed up to help another woman bring new life into this world.

A birthing partner.

The thought is laughable, yet here we are.

Me, who regularly eliminates life from this world. Worthless and meaningless lives, but still. It makes me wonder what this kid will turn out to be like. Since we're neighbors — Roxane and I — our kids are destined to be friends, probably best friends. They can reminisce about what it's like to be raised by mothers like us.

That is if the kid ever comes.

I keep hearing the words *'Stalled Labor'* and *'High-Risk Pregnancy'* being thrown around by her nurses, mostly in hushed tones. None of which make any sense to me. While I understand their desire not to scare her, I wish they would keep it real with her.

Or I could hit one of her pressure points and she'll be knocked out cold.

I'm bad at this. It shouldn't come as a surprise to anyone. Marc handled all of this for me two years ago. I wasn't in a good place back then, so his take-charge attitude was much appreciated.

Maybe I should've just called him for this part. I know she called him, finally, and whatever is going on with that is pretty major.

Major, as in, not only are we in a restricted area of this hospital's maternity wing, but I've also seen a few of Marc's men lurking about. He called to give me a heads-up when I first got here, and for the most part, they're staying out of everyone's way. I hope this doesn't turn into a fucking bloodbath.

I don't have the mental wherewithal to dwell on that, not when I'm preoccupied with all the work that goes into this. As expected, there are parts of it that I'm good at and parts I suck at. I don't beat myself up about it because this is so far out of my comfort zone that it isn't comical. All of that is making me a tad murderous at the moment.

For the sake of everyone involved, I'm taking a page out of Marc's security team's playbook and staying out of the nurses' way while they do their thing. I do everything I can to fight the annoyance that builds when they talk to her in their nauseatingly soothing reassuring nurse voices.

Not long after she finally dozes off, I excuse myself from the room to begin the obligatory series of phone calls. The first call is to Abby, except she doesn't answer and I don't do voicemails. The second to Harris, to confirm he's still holed up at my place and to let him know I won't be home for at least another day. Then I shoot Rose a quick text to cancel Feorie's art lesson. It's not for another forty-eight hours, but there's no guarantee I'll be home and prepared for it.

The third call is to Marc, my brother, who picks up on the second ring.

"This is a strange turn of events, you calling me first," is the first thing he says. "Everything okay with you?"

"Everything's peachy. Same as it was when we spoke four hours ago."

"Are my men giving you any trouble?"

"Nope, they've made themselves scarce. Do you mind telling me what this is about?"

"You'll tell me if anyone gives you trouble, right?" he asks instead, ignoring my question.

"You forget that I can hold my own, Marc."

"Oh, I know. Refrain from killing the nurses and you'll be set. Remember, they're just doing their jobs."

I roll my eyes, even though I know he can't see me. "How's Charlie doing?"

"He's fine."

"Just fine?"

"He's asleep."

That sets off alarm bells. "Why? Is something wrong?"

"It's nap time, Court."

Oh.

"It's the same time every day," he adds.

"Right." I sink to the floor and run my hand through my hair. "I knew that."

Our arrangement with regard to Charlie is unconventional, but it works for us. It's also what's best for Charlie, so I don't think too hard about it, especially on a day like this. I just wish I could make CC understand that. Oscar, too.

Marc's laughter comes through the speakers. "You know that it's okay to miss him, right? He's your son."

Even though he says this, I can sense my brother's impatience and sarcasm bleeding through the phone. As much as I empathize with it, I haven't seen my son in weeks, and I'm starting to get antsy about it. It has nothing to do with CC or Oscar. It's because Harris is currently staying with me, and since my place isn't nearly as big as my brother's, there's no way to keep them apart.

Oh, the things we do for family.

But then, there was that display with him and Roxane in Charlie's nursery. Even though he was asleep for all of it, he now knows I saw them like that. Or he put two and two together. He did wake up in his bed the following day, and there was no way she would've carried him to it in her condition. Funny that he hasn't mentioned it since.

"How are you doing?" I ask because this has to be the longest those two have spent apart.

"Fine," is his curt response.

"When will you be collecting your man from my house?"

Extended silence is the response I get.

It's fitting because even though this is a maternity ward, the hospital hallways are quiet this time of day. Or maybe it's lunchtime?

Leaning against the wall, I stretch my legs out before me from my position on the floor. I'd checked on Roxane between phone calls and she was fast asleep, the epidural finally having done its job and knocked her right out. I'm nowhere near her room since she doesn't need to hear me breaking down and losing my shit with my brother. And since I'm not someone who loses my shit with anyone, not just with my brother, I'll have to take matters into my own hands. Everything's getting flipped over on its axis, and I'm not sure I care too much about this.

"How's H doing?" Marc eventually asks.

Given the circumstances, I could lie to my brother or tell him the truth.

Option two wins out.

"Not good, Marc."

A belabored sigh comes through. "So this time apart is pointless, then?"

"I didn't say that."

"What *are* you saying, then?"

"Look, I don't know what happened, but he's hurting. He won't talk about it with me. Or anyone, really. Maybe he's worried that I'll take sides, I don't know. I don't push it and mostly stay out of his way because he needs this time apart just as much as you and Delilah do. And I'm honored that he trusts me enough to take this time out at my place."

"Thank you for that. I really do appreciate it."

"Yeah, well. I need to know, when does it end?"

"When do you want it to end?"

"Again, that's not what I'm saying."

"What's with the cryptic bullshit, Court? If you have something to say, fucking spit it out."

I press the bridge of my nose between two fingers before adding, "Just… I know what I said, but could you three please sort out whatever issues you're having? I need your man out of my house."

"You could always kick him out."

"I tried that already, and it didn't work."

"I meant physically kick him out, not play these mental mind games with him. H will see right through it."

I bite the inside of my cheek. "I could bring up the safety blanket thing."

He chuckles. "I'd rather you didn't."

"Why not? If it'll get him home faster—"

"That's the opposite of what you told me to do. Whatever happened to practicing what you preach?"

I hate it when he calls me out on my bullshit. There's an annoying heat lurking behind my eyes, and it doesn't matter how fast or how many times I blink; it doesn't go away. "I miss my son, Marc. I'm not a fucking mind reader. I just wish people would just stick to the stuff they say and quit asking me for shit they know I can't deliver on. Or without even thinking it through. Not to mention all this wishy-washy business. I just can't, okay? My brain can't handle that, and I just—"

I clamp a hand over my mouth. I hadn't meant to offload all that on him. It just popped out.

A beat passes before he responds, and it's more than enough time for me to recollect my thoughts.

"Are you okay?" he asks, concern laced in his tone.

I run my hands through my hair. "Not at the moment," I admit unhappily, because that part is true. "I'm not okay. I'm so far from being okay, it's comical. But I will be."

A pause, then, "Where are you?"

"Still at the hospital."

I envision his brow furrowing. "You need me to send someone over?"

He's referring to my elusive bodyguard. The one assigned to protect me at all times, yet I'm not supposed to know who they are. Jokes on him because I've known who *she* is all along. It was fucking obvious, and I figured it out long before Abby told me.

Only a killer can serve as a bodyguard to another killer.

That, and she and I have an arrangement that works for us just fine. I don't care if she takes his money, she's worth every penny. The things she does for us, the lengths she goes to protect our cohort. It's more than just a job to her. It's a calling.

It's also how I can do favors for her, like this one. Technically, I'm counting this as a favor since I haven't broken Roxane's trust yet.

"I'm with a friend, and we have all the protection we need. Thanks for the offer, though."

He hums his response but doesn't say anything else. The silence stretches between us, heavy and smothering.

Once it turns suffocating, I blurt out, "What's really going on here, Marc?"

39

COURTNEY

Marc remains quiet, and it's making me antsy.

Antsy Courtney is adjacent to bitchy Courtney. I don't like either version of myself.

To me, antsy feels like wet vines crawling up and around my skin, leaving behind this wet and uncomfortable feeling that makes me want to crawl out of my skin. There's only one surefire way to purge that from my body, and that won't go over well with, I don't know, the fucking morality police.

"Is my friend in danger?" I ask again, hoping and praying that he doesn't have it in him to lie to me. Not right now, or I really might go on a murderous rampage.

"She doesn't know the details yet," he mumbles, his tone unusually soft, "and I'd like to keep it that way for as long as possible."

"That's a non-answer, Marc. Just say yes or no."

"Not yet. She's not in danger at the moment, and as long as she puts 'Father Unknown' on her baby's birth records, she should be fine for a bit."

"So there *is* a father." It's not a question. It's a statement.

"That we know of, yes."

"She said she doesn't know who he is."

"That's what happens when you're doused with scopolamine."

That doesn't make sense. "She and I went through the same poison control training, and scopolamine was on the menu."

"It doesn't last forever," he counters. "Yours faded in the ten months you were pregnant with Charlie. It's been over seven years for her."

"I know that. Still, she's always had protection."

"Experience has taught me that if someone wants to get to you, they will. She remembers intimate details from her night with Evan but not from the night before. She's positive that the baby isn't his, and so is he. So I went digging—"

"You mean David went digging."

"Fine, David went digging and he found him. He tells me someone paid a lot of money to have that tool's digital footprints from that night erased. But that's not all. They were both dosed with it, so what does that tell you?"

"Someone has to pay?"

Why hasn't this crossed our radar yet? This is the kind of shit Lorenzo dispatches his weapons to deal with.

Does Abby know this? I can't imagine she does. They might not be together, but she's fiercely protective of Roxane. Sanctioned or not, heads will roll for this. Hell, I'll join. We all will. It's what we do.

"Hold your horses, sis. We're still gathering all the facts, and I would hate for innocents to get swept up in your murderous rampage." It's uncanny how well he can read my mind. Or maybe it's the murderous vibes rolling off of me. "As I said, she doesn't know the details yet, and I don't want her to know, not unless it's a sure thing. I can tell you this, she's mixed up in something she shouldn't be, and moving in next door to you was the best thing she could've done for her baby. It sent a clear message, and it goes without saying that she's now under my protection. Officially. Evan, too. And his siblings. I'll let you give all of them the good news. Or not."

"Sure, I'll do that." Once I find more about the guy, 'cause the Whittmores are a fucking enigma!

I know *of* his two sisters. I didn't know there were *more* of them. How many more brothers and/or sisters does he have? Does it fucking matter?

Still, my heart aches for Roxane. All this time she never said a word. But she came to me, and I chastised her for it, clueless about what she'd been through.

"Is Evan there?"

"She doesn't want me to call him." That's all Marc needs to know. It's too bad he doesn't get the memo.

"Call him anyway. They'll both regret it if he misses this."

"How can you be so sure?"

"Because I know what a man looks like when he's head over heels in love with a woman he *thinks* he cannot have." A beat passes, then he adds, "And I know what a woman *sounds* like when she's in love *and* in denial about her feelings, especially when that woman *is* my sister."

Leave it to Marc to turn the tables on me like that.

"Remember when Charlie was born," he continues, "and you didn't think you could love him? Because of who his dad is?"

I release a nervous laugh because it's true. "Don't remind me."

"Someone should."

He was unplanned and unexpected, the epitome of an occupational hazard. His dad, Howard, might be a tool, and there's no love lost between us, but he is a means to an end. The only reason he's still alive is because we — Abby, Phoenix, and myself — were there that day for his business manager, Winford Staton, and not him. What happened between us was part of the job, and having Charlie just means I have him by the balls, figuratively.

But yes, I have grown to love the little booger. Even if he's a responsibility, he doesn't deserve to suffer for the sins of his parents.

"You have a big heart, Courtney, and don't you ever let anyone tell you otherwise. I know this isn't easy on you either, doing for Roxane what I did for you two years ago. But that's just who you are, deep down. I'm not just saying this because you're my sister. I'm saying this because there's so much more to you than the weapon Mom and Dad turned you into. You are more than capable of love. Unconditional love. Like H and D and I have. It's not a myth, so don't deprive yourself of happiness, not when you have so much of it to give and receive."

My throat tightens as he speaks, clogged with emotion. A tear slips past my eyelids, and I let it fall. "I've been seeing someone," I tell him, pausing to swallow around the lump that forms. "It's been four years."

A hearty chuckle comes through. "No shit," he teases, and I want to deck him through the phone. "Is it a certain dark-haired raven you insist on keeping private?"

"It is." I nod, even though he can't see me. "As for the other, well, he's more recent." Oscar's name is on the tip of my tongue, but I don't say it out loud. I gave him another hint since he knew about the training program; ergo, he knew what Oscar meant to me. "I've actually known him for longer. And I... it's... well, it's complicated."

He's quiet for a long moment, silently digesting this new information. The silence stretches for too long, and antsy Courtney rears her claws again.

"Say something."

"Something," he deadpans, then chuckles. "Will we ever get to meet them?"

"That depends."

"On?"

"I already know you wouldn't approve if you knew who he was." There's an edge to my tone that I wish I could take back, but it's the truth.

I'm not sure what we are right now, and I hate the uncertainty.

God, why am I like this?

"Why is that?" Marc asks, his voice breaking through my reverie.

Pushing out a breath, I press my back into the solid wall. "Because it's... *him*."

"Him?" I hear the humor in Marc's voice as he prompts.

Why does my brother have to be such a smart-ass? He knows whom I'm referring to, yet he wants me to spell it out for him.

"He is… *was*, my prey." I swallow thickly, and my eyelids drift closed. "In a way, he still is. He found me first, like he promised. Years ago, actually. I should've known it was him. But I just… I made things difficult for him when I pushed him away."

His next question comes quickly. "Do you love him?"

"I never stopped," I admit, speaking the words into existence for the first time in fifteen years. "I don't know how to do this, Marc. I don't know if I can be this happy without constantly worrying about when the other shoe will drop. My life is fucked up as it is, and a part of me wonders if I'm doing this for the right reasons. Or the wrong ones."

"I know the feeling. What does your heart tell you?"

"To be selfish again." As the words slip past my lips, I ignore the twinge of guilt that runs through me, settling in the pit of my stomach. "I love her, and I love him. I love Charlie too. I'm just not sure how to put those three things together."

Four things, actually.

Because there's *her*.

Yong Chun-ja, the woman who still haunts my dreams.

"Let me get this straight. You were seeing each other before Charlie was born."

I nod. "We were."

"And you were still seeing each other when Charlie came into the picture."

"That too."

"How *did* you manage that?"

I bark out a strangled laugh. "We didn't. She hasn't met him."

"You iced her out of his life? That's cold, Courtney."

"Why do you have to say it like that?"

"Like what?"

"Like… you know what I mean." I can't tell which part bothers me more. That he's right, or that he's siding with CC on this.

"I'd say I'm sorry, but I'm not," he laughs. "Complicated doesn't even begin to cover it. A word to the wise: don't let this go on for longer than it already has. I take it they both know he exists, right?"

"They do. Neither wants children."

"Fact or assumption?"

"What's the difference? He's indifferent to the idea. She brought it up and we fought. The end. Charlie's better off with you anyway."

"Jesus, Courtney. That's not—"

"Not what? You wanna hand him back to me full-time? Fine. You do that, and one or both of us will die as a result. I hope it's me this time around since—"

"Courtney, stop. It's been two years. You're not in that place anymore. I know it might not seem like it, but Charlie misses you. The last few weeks have been rough on him, so stop by when you can, okay?"

Before I can answer, a familiar face rounds the corner and starts walking in the opposite direction, away from me.

"I have to go," I say, rising to my feet. "We'll talk later, okay?"

He mumbles something incoherent, something along the lines of 'This isn't over,' but I hang up on him and take a few steps toward her.

"Dahlia," I call out.

She pauses mid-step, and so too does the group she's with. Someone hands her the clipboard, and the group leaves her behind.

When she turns to face me, I do a double-take.

For someone who has always looked so put together each time our paths crossed, this is a new look for her. From what I can see, she isn't doing so well, like someone else I know.

I take a step toward her to hug her — a default reaction on my part — and she flinches slightly at it.

"Right," I mutter, stepping back and lowering my arms. "No touching."

Her lips stretch into a tight smile.

My gaze falls to her stomach. She's also massively pregnant, out to here, so I can't help but ask, "How's the baby doing?"

It's a reflex, I swear. I'm surrounded by babies and pregnant women left and right, and these things just pop out.

"He's fine." Her words strike me as more of an afterthought.

"How are you holding up?"

That question, in itself, is the understatement of the century.

Something flashes in her golden-brown eyes. She bites the inside of her cheek and looks away. "Work keeps me busy."

Of course, I know how she's doing. It's a sentiment I share. It's also a sentiment I can understand since she's doing what I'd do if I were in her position.

Never mind that, she's doing exactly what I'm currently doing: thrusting myself into work to keep busy so I don't have the time or energy to dwell on my own heartache. Except that's all I seem to be doing lately.

David seems to be holding up somewhat okay. I know that he's not doing any better than she is. For someone who never really cared for others — or pretended not to, most of the time — this change in him is refreshing, one I hope to see more of in the future.

But knowing him, I'm sure he's also up to something, and I'm not sure I have the mental capacity to process it right now.

Christ, I need some sleep.

"I'm here with a friend," I rush to say. From her perspective, I can see how my being here is odd. "She's having a baby, and I'm her birthing partner slash cheerleader. I was… kind of volunteered for it at first, but then she asked me to. She doesn't have anyone else."

"That's good. No one should have to go through that alone."

I get the sense she's talking more about herself. From what little I've gathered — which isn't much because Delilah is being very tight-lipped about it, no matter how many times I ask — she's planning on handing this baby over to her not-exactly-in-laws.

Even I know that the McWhorters aren't good people, despite outward appearances. I believe she was fully justified in leaving her fiancé at the altar.

What has me tripped up is that she plans on handing over her child to them. But who am I to judge how she chooses to go about this? Some women aren't cut out to be parents, which is okay as long as they're being honest and upfront about it and thinking of the child's wellbeing.

Hell, my brother is more of a parent to my own child than I am.

She shifts on her feet, her floral dress slightly swaying underneath her lab coat. "I… umm… have to go change into scrubs."

I nod. "Please, don't let me keep you. You have patients to see, and I should return to Roxane anyway."

She pauses, and her brow instantly furrows. "Roxane?"

I nod. "My friend," I say. "She's who I'm here with."

She stares down at her clipboard for a long moment. "Roxane Zainab Lavenworth," she mutters under her breath. "Well, what do you know?"

No way. "You're her doctor?"

She chuckles. "Looks like I'll be seeing you in a bit. She's the first on my rotation, so I'll check in right after I get changed."

I chance a nervous laugh. "Small world, huh?"

"You have no idea." She looks me up and down. "See that one of the nurses gets you some scrubs, since you'll most likely be in the OR with her."

"Will do."

We say our goodbyes, and as I head back to Roxane, I can't help but throw in this one thing. "Dahlia?"

She half-turns. "Yeah?"

"For what it's worth, he misses you."

She gives me a sad smile, and her hand moves unconsciously to her stomach. "He misses what we had, is all."

"You don't believe that, do you?"

She shrugs but doesn't say anything else. She just waves and turns. I watch as she walks away, slightly swaying her gait. I continue to watch long after she disappears from sight, and all that runs through my mind is how full of it I am.

God, I'm such a hypocrite.

I pull out my phone and stare at it.

Not a single missed call or text message from her.

This time, I should be the bigger person and reach out first. The things I said were uncalled for. I knew that even as I said them. But all I was thinking about was the next task ahead of me and how to get out of a conversation that seemed to be heading toward yet another heart-to-heart.

Because even if I don't do those, I can't lose her.

I just can't.

40

CC

When your girlfriend's brother calls you, you take his call, then you fucking go wherever the fuck he tells you to. Especially if he's Marc Sotelo, a man with all the power to make or break my relationships.

Yes, that's plural. Relationships. As in Courtney *and* Oscar.

I'm not stupid. I know I lucked out with both of them, and I'm in awe of how well we all fit together. If I can't keep Courtney, there's no guarantee I can keep him too. Because if it comes down to it, he'll pick her over me.

I can't have that, not after everything I've done to make her mine. Dr. Goodman once called it a form of Stockholm syndrome, but I don't care. Not after everything I've risked just to be in her life. Our ties might be ill-fated, but those bonds run deep. Trauma bonds tend to be that way, and that's not something that can, or will be, severed anytime soon.

That's why when Marc said jump, I asked how high. Then I did it. Knowing full well it would piss her off.

From my position on the front porch, I watch Courtney climb out of her car, slamming the door a little too hard. She stalks over to where I'm seated and stops a few feet away. Her hands are tucked into her pockets, and the barely concealed rage rolls off her in waves.

"What are you doing here?"

There's something about the way she says this that's… different. Or maybe it's the darkness in her eyes — that flat, blank look — at my showing up like this, unannounced, that has me seeing things that aren't there.

If there's one thing I'm familiar with, it's what Courtney looks like when she's been pushed to her limit. This time I fear I took things too far. Again.

"Marc called," I say with a nonchalant shrug. On the inside, I am anything but.

Her features instantly soften, and it's like night and day. "He shouldn't have done that."

"I'm glad he did. I'm not here to fight you. I brought a peace offering."

She lifts a curious brow, so I point.

As if on cue, Oscar chooses that moment to step out of my car.

"Jesus Christ, CC. Why the fuck is he here?" She's going for hard and disapproving with her tone, but the slight hitch in her voice gives her away. As does the flush crawling up her chest.

"Why wouldn't he be? Last I checked, he's *our* boyfriend."

Oscar's mouth tugs upward at one corner, and a light flickers behind his brown eyes. "I'm supposed to be a peace offering. Or Switzerland, depending on how this goes."

"He insisted on coming," I quickly add. "He wanted to visit Roxane and the baby but couldn't get into the hospital for some reason."

"Evan got in fine, but I got turned away," Oscar says. Whines, more like. "She's my friend too."

"Oh, please. They're doing fine. Evan sent us lots of pictures. They'll both be home tomorrow, and you can visit them then since they'll be right next door. Speaking of," I turn to Courtney, "everything all right with her?"

Courtney's jaw clenches. "What do you think?"

I don't want my mind to go where it's taking me, but I can't pretend or play the ignorance card. I also talked to Dahlia last night — or rather, she called me — and she had *very* specific questions about how well I knew Courtney's neighbor. Technically I don't, so I told her as much. Especially since she was asking as a friend, not a medical professional. It doesn't take a genius to figure out that putting an entire hospital wing on lockdown for one baby is absurd, and I have to agree. Then I saw her full name and things didn't seem *that* far-fetched.

"I'm sorry for being a bitch the other day," I tell her because, like it or not, I owe her an apology. I knew she wasn't in any state to have a heart-to-heart conversation, yet I pushed her anyway.

She doesn't answer me right away. Instead, she pinches the bridge of her nose between two fingers. I watch her lips silently move as she does the mental math in her head, counting backward and forward, over and over again. Oscar does it when he's stressed or pissed off, and I'm reminded again of how deep their ties run.

"Courtney?" The uncertainty in Oscar's tone tugs at my heartstrings.

She draws in a ragged breath. "Do you realize what you've done? Showing up here like this means no going back from this." There's regret in her voice. "For both of you."

"That's kinda the point," I tease, rubbing both palms together. "Is this the part where we move in and take over your life?"

She doesn't laugh at my poor attempt at a joke. "You don't get what you've done, but you will. Soon."

"I look forward to it. *We* look forward to it. Right, Oscar?"

Not that she needs to spell this out to me. I knew what I was doing when I came over. Just as I knew she would hate it. I knew this would irreparably change things between us, and I'd be lying if I said I wasn't enjoying this.

"If you're going to punish me, then punish me. Spank me, gag me, do your worst. I can take it. But we do need to talk. All three of us."

"Oh, we will. Get your asses inside."

"We can't. Not yet, anyway."

Her lips part on a silent O. "No one's home? Where's Harris?"

"He wasn't here when I arrived thirty minutes ago. Oscar is lucky I was already here when his driver dropped him off, or he would've been delicious bait for all those mosquitoes flying around."

She grins at the prospect of that. I do too. "You could've called."

"We wanted to surprise you. We could've waited inside, but I don't have a key. Obviously."

She gives me an incredulous look. "It's a keypad, CC."

"I know. I still don't have a code."

"It's your birthday," she tells me like it's the most obvious thing in the world.

Only it's not.

It really isn't.

I let my eyes fall closed and draw a shaky breath. "My birthday?"

I don't celebrate my birthdays. Plural, since I've had three.

I don't bring it up either, because when you're juggling that many dates, chances of slipping up exponentially increase. That, and I've been reborn twice, and neither date holds any special meaning. Only one does.

June ninth.

My actual birthday.

It's funny that the day I was born is also the day I should've died. Not only was it the same day my family died, but it was also the day my only sister died twelve years prior.

It's the date we first met as Yong and Courtney.

It's the date I first fell in love and never fell out.

The problem is, as far as Courtney is concerned, Yong Chun-ja is dead.

Deloise Milligan, my first rebirth and the only identity that can be directly tied to Yong, is also dead. Technically, I *did* die. I was declared legally dead for two minutes. The Milligans were pieces of shit, feral wolves in sheep's clothing, and my 'death' unearthed the first of many flaws in the Network.

Lorenzo decided then that for him to send a clear message to everyone involved, Deloise had to die. I only know this because Dr.

Goodman showed me the video of their execution and that I needed closure. Then she suggested I move to Rochester anyway, much to Lorenzo's chagrin.

That's how Charlena Cantor-Dietrich came to be.

Oscar knows this because I promised him I would never lie to him. Abby knows this too, since she's responsible for keeping this identity squeaky clean. And as long as I'm alive, three people get to keep their skin intact, not get skewered for access to some stupid vault.

At least, that's what Lorenzo claims.

But I digress.

My point is, there's too much pain and anguish and grief and joy and heartache tied to one fucking day. But if I had to do it again, I wouldn't change a thing.

Of the people in my life — the ones I truly care about — only three know this date.

Make that *four* people.

She mistakes my response and subsequent silence for disbelief. "Try it for yourself if you don't believe me."

I shake my head. "It's not that I don't. I just… how long?"

"How long what?"

"That code. *Date*. How long have you known—"

"You told me four years ago." Her face softens, her eyes too, as she bites her lip. "You told me the night we first made love."

Warmth floods through my veins at the memory of that night. Tears unexpectedly prickle my eyes, and for once, I don't laugh them off or blink them back.

"I did, huh?"

She swallows before whispering, "You're important to me, CC. And belonging, it goes both ways."

My heart rate kicks up a notch, and a familiar ache pulses through my chest and pools between my legs. I rise to my feet and close the distance between us. My breathing comes in pants as her soft hands wrap around my neck, pulling me down until our lips are a hair's breadth apart.

"You've always been important to me," I whisper against her lips. The warmth of her breath on my face is intoxicating.

She fuses our mouths together, her tongue demanding entrance as she licks against the seam of my lips. My body responds, melting into her warmth as I lose myself in the kiss and in her.

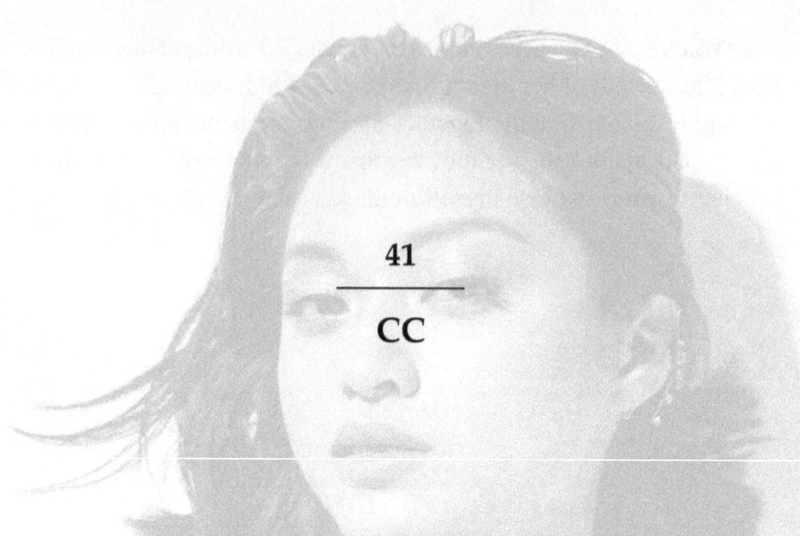

41

CC

I'm not sure what I'd been expecting of Courtney's place, but I didn't expect it to be so… homey. I'm standing in the middle of the living room, looking around with what can only be described as a deer-in-the-headlights look on my face. It certainly feels like it.

Oscar, on the other hand, settles into her couch like he belongs there.

In a manner of speaking, he does.

So many times, I've envisioned what her domain would look like, what she's like in that space. Him, too, if I'm being honest.

This is nothing like I expected. I bet she was thinking of him, of *us*, as she decorated the place.

There are little touches of *us* in every crevice.

The throw blankets draped over the arms of both couches? They're identical to those I have at home.

The couch Oscar is currently perched on? It's similar to that at his place, complete with all that lumbar support bullshit he's so into.

Don't get me started on the artwork. Courtney's art leans towards the macabre, which has a certain timeless beauty to it and is on par with what she does for a living. I never thought a painting of my own decapitation would turn me on, but it's something I mentioned in passing years ago, and here it is.

I've often wondered how she got into art in the first place. Her process isn't something she talks about much, she just does it.

"It's so… normal," I say in awe.

It's mostly just an ordinary house, save for the assortment of guns and knives on the dining room table.

She chuckles, and those sultry eyes slide back to mine. "What were you expecting? A lair?"

"Do you have one? Can I see? I bet it'll fit in here."

"It fits. There are two more floors underneath us."

My eyes widen slightly. "That's not legal, is it?"

"Probably not. But then, half the things I do aren't, so…" She trails off at that, then shrugs. "This house was custom-built for me, and it is by design that on the outside, it looks like every other house on the block. I don't spend a lot of time here, as you know. I spend more time with you two than I do here. Unless Charlie is home or I have art class with Feorie or commissions to work on."

Oscar and I look at each other, and then around the room.

"I suppose that explains all the artwork," he says, waving a finger around the space. "Anything in particular you're working on?"

"Ah, those?" She glances around. "Those aren't commissions. They're mine. No Picassos here, obviously." She brushes aside her talent like it's no big deal, then turns and heads for the kitchen. "Does anybody want anything to drink? Juice? Water?"

Oscar and I don't want anything, so she returns empty-handed.

"Can you sit, please?" She gestures to the couch. "Next to Oscar, preferably. I just… I know we need to address the elephant in the room, and I… it has to be now, and I need to be looking at you both, or else I'll lose my nerve."

The words fall out of her in a rush, jumbled and incoherent. I'd rather play with the knives, but I'll humor her. Also, Oscar pats the space next to him, and a not-so-subtle smile dances at the corners of his lips. I join him, and he takes my hand in his, lacing our fingers together.

Courtney paces the room, wearing a hole into the carpet. "Instead of asking you both this, point blank, I made assumptions based on what was or wasn't mentioned in passing years ago. I shouldn't have done that, and I'm sorry. So I'll ask now. Let's assume Charlie isn't in the picture. Do either of you want children?"

I turn to face Oscar, and the look on his face directly reflects how I'm feeling on the inside.

Confused. Panicked. Scared.

I'm reminded, once again, that we've been doing all of this backward. We skipped the four big-ticket items — money, politics, religion, and kids — and went straight for the commitment. It didn't matter that none of us wanted to explicitly define this thing we have until recently. In my mind and heart, I've been pretty much committed to both of them for years.

Money? Between us three, there's a shit-ton of it to go around. Our views on politics and religion align: those can shove off and stuff it up theirs. And as for kids?

Well, there's Charlie.

It's been two years, and per Courtney's request — or demand — we've either been pretending he doesn't exist or carrying on like he's a foreign entity. Was that the correct choice? I don't know. I'm not his mother, even though I would love nothing more.

"It's not a trick question," Courtney quickly adds, "and if it helps, I'll go first. No, I don't want them. I never wanted any. Charlie was an accident."

Oscar turns to face her, tightening his hold on me. "I do. With you and with CC. But only if you both want that. Which you don't, and that's fine with me. As long as I have you."

They both turn to me.

"I'm indifferent to having biological children but not opposed to parenthood. It matters who I do this with, and that's with both of you. Like Oscar, I'll only do it if you both want that."

"I see." She smiles at that, but it's a sad, resigned smile that doesn't quite meet her eyes, and my stomach twists at her expression.

"Can we *please* stop talking in the abstract?" Oscar rushes to say, equal parts irritation and impatience lacing his tone. "Between us, we have Charlie. You can't say we're equals, and then completely freeze us from his life. That's not how relationships are supposed to work. When you think about it, we're not being careful either. We've been going at it like fucking bunnies, with nothing between us. I know CC isn't on birth control, and unless you are—"

"I'm not," she immediately says. "I never had reason to be."

"Then… then you could… fuck," he curses, brushing his hands through his hair.

Yep.

Backwards.

Then again, we're a special brand of fucked up.

"For what it's worth, I'm not sure if I *can* get pregnant," I eventually say, keeping my voice even. "If it were possible, it would've happened already. I'm not having sex with anyone else besides you two. It's been four years with you, five with Oscar."

"Same," he acquiesces. "On the *me* part, I mean."

Courtney's mouth falls open, startled by our combined revelations. "I thought…"

"You thought what, we were gonna cut and run? Mark my words. That is never, ever gonna happen."

"Oscar—" she starts to protest, but he cuts her off.

"Forget it, Courtney. You're stuck with us forever." His voice hardens, leaving no room for doubt. "Look at us. We're not normal. We were never meant to *be* normal. I'm already all kinds of fucked up. My body craves you twenty-four-fucking-seven, this stupid heart muscle," he pats his chest on the space above his heart, "doesn't know how to quit you. CC is the only one who understands you *and* me, and what we are, and she still wants me. She still wants us. Where do you think we're ever gonna find that? Where will we ever find someone like her?"

Courtney doesn't answer him. I don't either. I'm too busy staring at him, stunned by the words and praise coming from him. Oscar isn't typically this assertive with Courtney. It's usually the other way around.

But he's so not done. "You tried to leave CC two years ago. How *did* that work out for you?"

"It didn't. But there was Charlie to consider, and—"

"And that's another thing. You talk in absolutes, saying things like *'Charlie isn't your concern,'* but you won't tell us what that means. I get that he's your son, Courtney, but he could've been *our* son. Fuck it, he's *ours*. I'd like to meet him. *We* would like to meet him. Officially. We're ready."

"I'm not," she bites out.

"Will you ever be? You never gave us a choice that day. Instead, you told us you were pregnant and then dropped us like hot lava. But then you went back to CC, and all you did was tie her hands. It's been two years, and you're still doing it. Do you not trust us?"

"It's not that I don't trust you, Oscar. I don't trust myself."

His brow furrows. "That doesn't make sense."

"I love Charlie, obviously," she lets out an exasperated sigh as her shoulders sag, "but it didn't start out that way. He's my son, but he's also a job. An occupational hazard. I know it hurts you when I say that, given your contentious relationship with your mother, but we both know I'm not one to sugarcoat things. Not with you. And Charlie, he's not here because I'm a danger to him."

"You—" Oscar starts to say, but I squeeze his hand.

"Let her talk, Oscar."

I swear, we will be talking around in circles if these two keep this up.

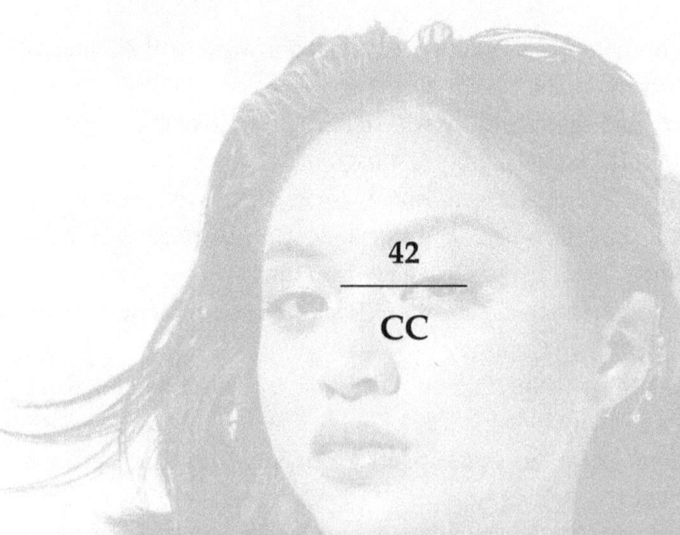

42

CC

Courtney is… complicated, but that's something I already knew.

So is Oscar, and so am I.

If we could turn back the clock to our dinner weeks ago, I don't think we would've done things differently. I know I wouldn't have. Whether it's a few weeks or sixteen fucking years, the outcome remains the same.

These two? They're mine.

"I'm not who you think I am," Courtney begins. "I'm not a good person. I'm not even a decent person, and I will never be. Everything I do, this life I lead, it's all a cover."

"That doesn't make a—" Oscar protests, but I squeeze his hand again.

"Just let her talk, please," I force out between clenched teeth.

His lips form a small pout, but he says nothing else.

She gives me a tight smile, then settles on the couch directly opposite Oscar and me. "I'm an enforcer for my family, and I… you know who my mother was, don't you? *What* she was?"

Oscar and I both nod.

She leans forward, resting both elbows on her thighs as she watches us. "What I'm about to tell you must never leave this room.

I will not hesitate to kill you if you breathe a word of it outside of these four walls. Understood?"

We both nod again because what choice do we have?

Parts of this I know already, but most of it I don't.

"The only reason Howard and I crossed paths is because we were sent to kill his sleaze bag manager. He just happened to be there, and he… well, he was just a penis to fuck."

"Why do you keep saying that?" I immediately interject. "You know that's not true, Courtney."

I know I'm not being fair, but I can't have her entertaining these absurd thoughts any longer.

This time, Oscar laces our fingers together. "Whatever happened to 'let her talk'?"

Courtney doesn't say anything at first; just observes the gesture.

And… why does the look on her face tell me she would rather sit over on this side with us?

"Come join us," I tell her because I can't help it. I want her with us.

She shakes her head. "I can't." She forces her eyes to meet ours. "As tempting as it is, I can't put this off any longer."

"Then don't do it, at least not tonight. We can do this tomorrow."

Another head shake, then the dam unlocks.

"For decades, the Sotelo family has overseen a program called the Network. It's a bit derivative, but think of it as Witness Protection, but done Mafia style. It's for people who want to disappear. Good and bad. Some people just want to disappear for a few months or a few years, others permanently. Some wish to hide their children, too. All requests go through Lorenzo, and then the Network makes that happen for a select few only, in exchange for… well, a lot, then they're monitored constantly. As long as everyone abides by the rules, they do just fine. That includes those who wish to remain hidden and those who help make that happen. If they don't… that's where I come in, as an enforcer.

"The Sotelo family's Weapons, AKA Lorenzo's super-secret kill squad, are in charge of monitoring this program, amongst many others. Although we each have our areas of expertise, I am sort of the de facto leader of the current cohort because of my body count. My mom, too, was the last cohort's de facto leader; part of her job was figuring out people's weaknesses and using them to leverage their compliance or cooperation. Thanks to her research, we have many more havens for clients.

"But no system is infallible. Anyone who goes in has a vested interest in staying invisible, so they're less likely to raise a stink if their placement is a bad one. This means there will always be scumbags who weasel their way into it, posing as havens but intent on taking advantage, knowing full well the clients won't complain.

"Winford Staton was one of those sleazebags. He was a real piece of work, infamous in certain circles. He started as a foot soldier for several of my family's distribution channels and worked up to mid-level management. Because he was disturbingly good at peddling to the stars and made a lot of money, someone saw fit to plant him in the entertainment industry for 'easier access' to his target demographic. The whole story about him clawing his way out of poverty and a life of drugs and violence was a publicity stunt, which worked. I was told that Mom first noticed his ruthless ambition and figured it and his connections would work in our favor. His supposedly making it 'big' as a talent manager was thanks to her vouching for him, and as part of his cover, Winford was promoted to one of many liaison roles to be the go-betweens for the Network's clients. Due to the nature of his job, he was constantly on the road, making it easier for him to keep tabs on them.

"That's how Howard's and my paths crossed. Winford was his manager. He wasn't one of ours, but he was a drug addict and the perfect target. We didn't know Winford had since pivoted to peddling drugs to the Network's clients and used the fact that Mom personally vouched for him to fly under Lorenzo's radar. It took five of his charges ODing in two months for him to get on our radar. Come to find out that not only had this been going on for years, but he had been paying off various coroners across the country to report these as natural causes. We only found out because one of his coroner buddies in California had retired abruptly, and he didn't get the chance to grease up the new one before she filed their death certificates. That many deaths in one place tipped us off, and even worse, the drugs had been the least of his offenses. He wasn't the only one doing it. Winford was part of a group exploiting clients for years, mainly the ones who wouldn't come forward.

"Lorenzo was pissed, and understandably so. There had been another incident sixteen years prior, where a high-profile client ODed barely a few months into the program. That's when Lorenzo instituted a zero-tolerance policy, then he sent us to execute the couple she had been placed with as a warning to the others. This group knew better and had been covering for each other. But with this slip-up, we were sent to take out Winford and get the names of his pals, and Howard just happened to be there that day."

Dear Lord, she's talking about me.

So, is this what Lorenzo meant when he said Deloise Milligan had to die?

"I think Winford planned for Howard to be there," Courtney continues. "He knew he had fucked up, majorly, so he planned to use his most high-profile client as a shield. We arrived just as he was shooting Howard up with some of his tainted drugs. The bastard got his hands on one of Phoenix's older special K recipes, added scopolamine and Rohypnol to it as she would've, and gave that to Howard. He planned to dump that mess on our laps and bolt, but we weren't about to give the bastard yet another pass so he could fuck up someone else. We did our fucking job and killed him, but then there was Howard to deal with. We couldn't let him die, or the drugs in his system would've led back to us directly. So we took him with us. We had to, at least until he was completely detoxed.

"The problem is, when you pump someone full of date-rape drugs, the fastest way to get it out of their system is… well, for them to orgasm, preferably multiple times. Howard was so out of it that he would've fucked anything with a pulse. And he did try, but it's hard to do that when you're tied to a fucking bedpost with no control over your body. Now, before you go feeling sorry for him, Howard was not innocent. That shit that Winford shot him up with?

It's the same shit Winford used on the Network's clients before he assaulted them. It's the same shit Howard used on his unsuspecting fans and groupies.

"Here's the thing. What *had* to happen happened since he's still alive. Of the three of us, I was the only one who *could've* fucked Howard that day. And I…" She pauses, and our gazes lock as she says this next part. "I took one for the team. I chose to have sex with Howard."

That part, her admission, hurts more than I care to admit. All this time, I had my suspicions that this had been the case, but I'd always been too scared to come out and ask her. We weren't exclusive then, so it wasn't my place to demand answers from her. But the fact that she didn't harbor any resentment towards Howard, and still doesn't, to this day, always bothered me.

And now I know.

The sex between her and Howard wasn't consensual.

Courtney claims not to have a conscience. She claims not to have a fucking soul, but if all of this isn't proof that she does, in fact, possess both things, I don't know what is.

"It doesn't matter," I hear myself say, keeping my eyes on her as the words fall freely from my lips.

I don't miss Oscar's sharp intake of air, and I *certainly* feel his eyes boring holes into the side of my face. "That's the first lie you've ever told me," he says, his tone strained. Pained, even.

I want to tell him he's wrong, but the words escape me. And because he knows this, so too does she. Because I didn't just lie to him, I lied to her too.

Our sex life, Courtney's and mine, has always been different. Unconventional, if you will. But everything we do to, for, and with each other has always been consensual. That has always been her number one rule from the beginning. I knew she still felt guilty over what happened with her and Oscar in the past, which was part of why she didn't *do* relationships. Or let herself get attached.

Even now, she's different with Oscar than she is with me. She's rough and abrasive with me but gentle with him. She'll gag, spank, and choke me all day, but she handles him with kid gloves. Every time we make love, she's constantly checking in with him through verbal and visual cues, making sure that he's okay with all of it. While it makes me love her all the more for it, I'm equally sad and angry for her, for everything she's been through that's giving her some seriously warped perceptions about what sex with men is supposed to be like. And I'm pissed that a scumbag like Howard Beals is why she's second-guessing everything we share with Oscar, this beautiful soul whom we both love.

But at the same time, I get it.

I fucking get it.

It's true that she helped him and that her actions saved his life. But if we call it what it is, she raped him. And I refuse to use that word to describe it. I fucking refuse to fucking label it as rape because it doesn't fucking matter.

"It shouldn't matter," I repeat. This time, I'm addressing her directly.

"It does to me, CC," she tells me. "You know it does." A myriad of emotions is cycling through those stormy gray eyes of hers, half of which takes me a bit to place. Pain, mostly. Touches of regret and sadness, too. But there's another emotion wrestling for center stage.

Guilt.

But why?

Winford had it coming. The bastard got what he deserved. So too, did Howard. She has nothing to feel guilty about. If I were in her shoes, I would've let him die and probably pinned Winford's death on him. Then Howard wouldn't be our problem, since every murderer needs a patsy to pin shit on.

But then we wouldn't have our son.

"So when you say Charlie isn't our concern, what does that mean, exactly?" Oscar asks.

And you know what? That's one question I really do need the answer to.

"You still don't get it?" she asks, her expression fighting between pained and guilty. "I chose to fuck Howard, but I did not choose to have Charlie. Yes, he's my son, but he's also a product of rape. *Howard*'s rape. That's what happened. He wasn't in a position to consent, so I don't blame the guy for wanting nothing to do with him."

Why is she still saying that? "It doesn't change that he's Charlie's father."

"Yeah, well. He's never met him, and he never will. The official story is that Howard stays away from us because being associated with the Italian Mafia is bad for his image and entire brand. Or I'm a jilted lover; take your pick. Unofficially, Charlie is a bargaining chip. He's a noose around Howard's neck, a leash Marc put on him. I'm not making excuses for my part in it, but you both know what my brother is like. Marc would do anything to protect me, and that's precisely what he did. He dug into Howard's life and found over a dozen other Charlies, all born to women that Howard raped using the same fucking drugs that Winford used on him.

"Howard doesn't want any of that to see the light of day. He might be a victim in this isolated case but not in the rest. And those two go hand in hand. He can't come after me because I didn't give him those drugs, Winford did. Winford might be dead, but his reputation for being the peddler to the stars isn't. Not to mention, all of his victims will come forward, and it will be a clusterfuck that no one wants to deal with, least of all him. So the bastard took the easy way out. He's shelling out millions to make it all go away.

"Every month, he pays Marc a fortune in child support, which is then redistributed to all of his children's mothers, myself included. The only reason Marc didn't have him sign away his parental rights to Charlie is because Howard is easier to control as long as his legal ties to Charlie exist. So not only does he pay another fortune in exchange for keeping his *true* ties to Charlie — and, by extension, our family — a secret, but Howard knows that he'll be done if one more baby turns up.

"And me? I got away with it. I got away with rape. What does that make me? That everyone in my life is willing to bend over backward just so I don't have to take accountability for my actions."

You know what? I've heard enough of this guilt trip she's on. "Why's *that* the part you feel guilty about?"

"CC, that's not—" Oscar starts to protest again, but I cut him off.

"No, I'm done tiptoeing around this. We're not good people, any of us. Chaos runs in our blood. It's who we are, so let's just accept that once and for all and move the fuck on. Especially you, Courtney. You kill people for a living, and you're concerned about rape? Give me a fucking break. Since when does rape surpass murder on the fucking morality scale? You did what you could to save Howard's life, even though he didn't deserve your mercy. And while we're on the subject, he didn't deserve your pussy either. I don't give a rat's ass who shot who up with what. You should've left him to fucking die. Instead, he got a taste of that magical pussy of yours, and you gave him a kid too, and the best he can do is whine about his fucking reputation? No, fuck that."

Courtney's lips part as she pushes out an exhale. Her head tilts, and she's looking at me as if she's seeing me for the first time.

In a way, I am too.

My actions mirror hers.

It's eerie how in sync we are and have always been. Words pass between us. Though unspoken, they ring loud and clear.

Then her eyes briefly dart to Oscar, and a little ball of dread forms in the pit of my stomach.

"Did you tell him?"

At the unexpected question, my heart plummets to my stomach.

I know what she's asking me. I just didn't think she would bring it up now. Or even why she would think I'd betray her trust like that.

"Tell me what?" Oscar asks, oblivious to the subtly rising tension in the room.

I grit my teeth, reminding myself it *is* just an innocent question. But Oscar, bless his heart, really needs to learn how to read the fucking room.

"He *thinks* I came back to you," she continues, her eyes glued to mine. "He *thinks* I took you back but left him in the lurch. Now, why *does* he think that, CC?"

I could pretend I don't know what she's asking or feign

ignorance. But I can tell she's also studying his reaction from the corner of her eye. I know this because I'm doing the same thing.

She knows I'm doing it. Just as she knows his eyes are trained on me. She fucking knows that if I lie, he *will* call me out on it.

"Because it's the truth," I admit.

"Bullshit," he breathes.

Urgh.

Fine.

"It's a partial truth, but still a truth. And it's better than the alternative."

"What alternative?" He's getting impatient now.

"I was six months pregnant at the time," Courtney continues, answering his question while simultaneously driving a dagger into my heart. "I wasn't in a good place, mentally, with the pregnancy and everything to come. That night was one of my lowest points. I didn't go to CC's place because I wanted a reconciliation. I went there to say goodbye."

I'm watching him as her words sink in, and the look on Oscar's face… it's not confusion, it's… I don't know what to call it.

Even though he voices an "I don't understand," his body language says otherwise.

"I think you do." It's my turn to be impatient now. "Scratch that; I know you do."

He swallows thickly as my words sink in.

I told him about the night Deloise Milligan died. He told me about his mental breakdowns, including the one that put him on suicide watch for a week.

He *knows* what the words 'say goodbye' mean.

Sure, I embellished the details a little, but I did what I had to in order to keep her with us.

"I'm still alive because CC refuses to let me go," she adds, seemingly oblivious to his confusion. "That night, she did… what she always does. And it helped, for a bit. Until it didn't."

Even though she's saying these things, even as she lays bare that which she wishes to remain hidden, I can see that something is shifting in her.

Just as a similar something shifts in him. Pain, I think.

It's potent. It's an all-consuming pain, and we all feel it.

For me, it's a harsh reminder that I almost lost the only woman who's ever owned my heart.

For Courtney, it's because just talking about that day means she's forcing herself to relieve those moments and the many more that followed.

And for Oscar, it's because he's learning this for the first time. I hear his heart breaking for her, just as mine did. This is why I didn't want him to know any of this. I wanted to spare him a world of hurt, so I gave him a partial truth.

Did it help?

Maybe. Maybe not.

Probably not, but he's like me. Neither of us can stand to let her go.

"It only got worse after he was born," Courtney continues, her voice breaking. "Marc tried his best. He thought… that if Charlie and I had a chance to bond, things would improve. They didn't. And when Marc found me asleep in the hot tub, with a three-week-old Charlie asleep on my chest, we both knew then that something had to give."

That I did not know.

I *do* know that she disappeared for almost six months after Charlie was born. Then she returned, and we fell back into our old patterns. She made it clear that she wasn't interested in discussing Charlie in any capacity. I was terrified I'd lose her again, so I kept my mouth shut. An alive Courtney with secrets was better than a dead one, and I picked the former because I don't know how to live without her.

I just… I wish I could've known, then I would've done more for her.

"So that's why you disappeared." It's a statement, not a question.

She nods anyway. "Perinatal depression, it's a real bitch. Marc got me the help I needed and kept it under wraps. But as I said, there had to be a trade-off. Charlie *is* the trade-off. Unofficially,

Marc is Charlie's guardian, and I get visitation. He makes all the decisions, and if need be, I sign off on it. Happily. Because Marc gives Charlie three things I could never give him: stability, unconditional love, and keeping him out of Lorenzo's grubby paws." She turns to face Oscar now. "You wanted to know why Charlie isn't with me twenty-four-seven. Well, now you know."

43

COURTNEY

B eing vulnerable is hard.

I suspect this is how normal relationships are supposed to work. People share pieces of themselves, and not just bodily fluids. It's all about the give and take, opening oneself up, and being vulnerable with each other.

I hate it.

I fucking hate it.

It's fucking hard, and I hate doing it.

Still, of all the people in the world, I can't think of anyone else I'd want to do this with besides these two because I love them.

Holy shit, I love them.

My lips part to voice this, but no sound comes out. So I snap them closed. All in due time.

I feel drained. I've talked enough. I've shared enough. It feels like I've run a fucking marathon, but we've barely scratched the surface.

I lean back in my seat, and the shift in Oscar's Adam's apple is the last thing I see, just before my eyelids drift closed.

"I… I didn't know."

I'm laughing now, but it feels more like crying. "That's okay. Not even Delilah and Harris know why this arrangement exists, and we would prefer to keep it that way. Not for my sake, but for Charlie's sake. He's innocent in all this. He deserves so much more than I can give him. He deserves better parents. He deserves a better mother, period. Unfortunately, I can't change that. Nor can I change what's going to happen to him. Being born of me is a punishable offense, and not even I can change his fate. But Marc can."

These two have developed stealthy ninja skills because I don't hear them move, or fucking breathe. All I know is, as I'm talking, the couch dips next to me on both sides, then two sets of arms envelop my body, which is meant to be a comforting gesture. I think it's what people are supposed to do when a loved one is in distress. I think. Or I read that somewhere in a book. *Normalcy 101 for Dummies*, probably.

My point is that I was never wired to *be* normal, and thus my brain doesn't process things that way. Instead, it sees it as an attack, and my fight response kicks in. Next thing I know, I've got one of them flat on their back and pinned to the floor, with my switchblade slightly pressed into the throbbing pulse in the base of their neck.

Oscar's neck.

"I probably should've seen that coming," he says in a dark, sexy tone.

My fingers go lax and the blade falls, hitting the carpet with a low thud. "Are you nuts? I could've killed you."

I probably would, even though my whole body is covering his, my hardened nipples are pressing into his clothed chest, and my thighs are straddling either side of his muscular ones.

"Not like this, you're not," he responds with a light chuckle, then thrusts upward, grinding his unmistakable bulge against my core.

There's a part of me that's still fucking human because I can't help the heat that spreads across my cheeks.

"I wasn't being fair to you, and I'm sorry."

I want to protest, but the look in his eyes stops me.

He's always worn his emotions on his face, but this is different. He's different, and I can see it in his eyes. Something has changed. Something is different about him.

"Charlie is one lucky boy for having a mom like you. Your willingness to put his well-being above yours speaks volumes about who you are. And I… I don't know what to say other than thank you. Thank you for holding on. Thank you for coming back to us. And also, you're not alone. You'll never be alone. Let us help you, Courtney. And let's give Charlie six parents who will all love him."

It's been a long time since I've had such tender words directed at me. I don't know how to handle it. I don't know how to process it either. All that heat, all that warmth, it's spreading fast throughout my insides. Its warmth blooms in my chest, making my heart soar.

If I were fucking normal, I'd say something expected and boring. But I'm not, so all I can do is stare at him, while hot tears fall freely from my eyes and drip all over him.

A shiver radiates down my spine as CC's body envelops my back as she presses herself to me. With her lips next to my ear, she whispers, "What are you waiting for, Oscar? Flip her."

She steps back and he complies swiftly, like a good fuck toy. I've never been a fan of being manhandled — I've stabbed people for less — but I find that I don't mind it as much if it's Oscar doing the handling.

He braces on both elbows, keeping most of his body weight off me. I loop my arms around his neck and pull his mouth down to mine, but he stops me.

"Oscar…" I whisper against his lips, squirming underneath him.

His lips graze mine softly, then he pulls away slightly. "There's something else I need to tell you."

"Now?"

He heaves both shoulders, an impressive feat given how much of his weight they support. "No time like the present."

"Your timing sucks." I squirm underneath him again, hoping to get him to hurry up. And it works. Sort of.

He groans. "I know, just one more thing." He lowers himself on one arm, then cradles my cheek in one palm. "I love you," he whispers softly, then his mouth is hard and hot on mine.

Every cell in my body is lit by a fuse, instantly reacting to the kiss. It's an overwhelming yet delirious feeling, him molding our bodies together, and his words barely register as his tongue invades my mouth.

It's even better when he pulls my whole fucking tongue into his mouth and sucks on it. Hard.

Fuck, he's always been a fast learner.

Is it possible to come just from getting your tongue sucked? Maybe.

I'm a total tongue junkie.

One of his hands slides between my thighs, and I spread them wider as he thrusts a finger inside me. Hard, punishing, as he hits my sweet spot over and over.

"So wet," he whispers against my ear, and another shiver radiates down my spine.

"You make me this way," I tell him because it's the truth. "You both do."

Oscar's lips stretch against my neck, no doubt forming a smile. His thumb finds my clit, and as he strokes the swollen nub, a second digit slides into me. Then, a third.

Holy fuck! I gasp at the tightness but desperately need more.

Like a thief in the middle of the night, my orgasm sneaks up on me. The sound that rips from my throat is inhuman as I ride out my orgasm on his fingers.

My eyelids part, and I look over his shoulders to see CC kneeling beside us, biting her lip. Her heavy-lidded gaze is fixated on us, the heat in her eyes potent. I want more of it. I want more of her.

"Make love to me." The words stumble out of me in a rush, but it feels so natural. "I want to feel you both inside me."

He pushes off me and stands, keeping his gaze on me as he sucks my juices off his fingers. Then he pulls me up like I weigh nothing, setting me on my feet. When I'm steady, CC hurls her body at me, knocking us back onto the couch as she fastens her lips on mine. She melts into my touch as our tongues tangle, but there's no mistaking who's in charge here.

It's not me. It's certainly not Oscar either.

It's her. It's always been her. She's the glue that holds us together.

We stumble into the bedroom in a tangle of legs, arms, and clothes. Well, not so much the last one, as we somehow manage to shed enough clothing along the way. There isn't much foreplay to be had here, as we're all desperate to be inside each other.

It doesn't matter that this is the first time both have been inside this space. Our bodies are so in sync that we find where we need to go just fine, and at least my bed is big enough to hold us all.

CC pushes Oscar onto his back in the middle of the bed, then grabs one of my scarves to tie him up. I don't know where she found that, but I stop her anyway.

"I want to touch him," I tell her, "and I want him to touch me."

Confusion clouds her face. "What about…"

"I have something else planned for you." I climb off the bed and head for the closet, reappearing a moment later with the contraption. "I want you to use this on me while I ride him."

I hear her breath catch, and her mouth falls open. "You had this made…" her voice is shaky, and her eyes lift to meet mine, a glossy sheen in them, "for me?"

"It's not going to fit me, obviously," I say with a slight shrug.

I didn't think it would elicit such strong emotions from her. It's an inanimate object. It's a black leather harness, custom-made to fit her. This one was a head-scratcher for Harris when he realized the specs I gave him were *not* my measurements.

It's the attached dildo that does her in.

Had I known she would react like this, I would've given it to her long ago.

It's an exact replica of Oscar's magical dick, which she constantly rants and raves about. This one, though, she's seen it before, several times. I had a few dozen custom-made back when I thought I couldn't have him. This was something she and I shared with each other. A piece of him, so to speak. I've used *it* on her several times, but I want her to use *it* on me this time.

It means something. She knows this.

It's a role reversal, and it's not role-playing.

In the past, when I submitted to her, it was because she *made* me by employing those head games she loves to play.

My faculties are intact, and I'm handing the reins to her. After all, with great power comes great responsibility. Or in her case, the ability to make or break me.

Her eyes dart back and forth between the contraption and me. She pulls her bottom lip between her teeth, her eyes wide with emotion. "Will you… put it on me?"

I nod, excitement setting in. We're going to do this, finally.

Again, Oscar props himself up on his elbows as he takes in the exchange. "That's so fucking hot," he tells us, but I hear the nervousness creeping into his voice.

I can only hope he's far enough away that he doesn't see the slight tremble in my hands as I fasten the leather harness around CC's hips. But she does, and once I'm done, her lips are on mine in yet another intoxicating kiss that threatens to swallow me whole.

I'm not ready to let her go when she pulls away from our kiss. A yelp escapes me as she palms my ass cheek and squeezes harshly. "Mount him, but just the tip."

How the fuck am I supposed to manage that?

With a lot of patience and an incredible amount of willpower, that's how.

Underneath me, Oscar's stomach hollows out, and his fingers dig into my thighs in a punishing grip as my tight channel spasms around the tip of his bulbous cock. CC takes her time to generously lube up my ass, fingers stretching out the tight pucker. It's different, and my thighs shake with strain and need, anticipation too, as I envision being double-teamed by Oscar times two.

CC's fingers curl inside me in a come-hither fashion, and Oscar grunts something garbled and throws his head back. We've got enough pillows propping us up that I'm not worried about him slipping out. Then again, I'm too busy studying the myriad of emotions dancing over his face to register what she's doing.

But he is. And… I do too.

She's… teasing the tip of his cock, inside me, through the skin. It's fucking erotic as hell but also pure savage, and I love it.

Someone's got to remind him that he's our little fuck toy, and I'm glad she's doing that because I certainly forgot.

But then, I did almost stab him, so there's that.

"CC, you're fucking killing me," he grunts again, and I have to agree with him there.

She leans in, and the vibrations from her hearty chuckle pass through me. "Ready?" she whispers into my ear.

I nod, then she reaches over to grab the base of Oscar's shaft and guide him inside me, all the way. She places her hand on the small of my back and pushes me forward so Oscar's chest is flush with mine. Our heartbeats pulse against each other, and he's looking at her over my shoulder.

I wish I could see the expression on her face, too. Whatever it is, it has Oscar in a seemingly trance-like state.

"I can't feel anything, but you both can," she says, pushing into me, inch by inch, until she's fully seated, her hips pressing against my ass. My eyelids flutter, then close, as my body adjusts to the sensation of feeling so impossibly full that I can barely breathe.

"How does that feel?" she asks.

I can't tell if the question is directed at him or me.

"Fucking amazing." His words seem to come from deep down in his chest in a resounding growl, and it passes through me. It's a good thing Oscar's speech is still intact. "Like I'm fucking myself, but with you both. It's... complicated."

Yeah... complicated doesn't even begin to describe what this is.

That warmth spreads again, covering every inch of my body, coating my pores from the inside out. It's crazy that, for the first time in as long as I can remember, I'm content with just this. It makes sense. We make sense.

They start moving slowly at first, as they each find a steady rhythm. As if choreographed, she picks up the pace, and he follows her lead. I'm in a euphoric daze as my body completely surrenders to their ministrations. I think she senses this. It's the only way I can explain her ferocity commandeering my body.

Moving like it's hers.

And it is.

Why did I wait so long to do this?

I can't pinpoint when it happened — the exact moment when I fell in love with her. I think it was on that day when I went to say goodbye to her but ended up sticking around for the long haul instead. Or is it the first night we met four years ago? Or is it further than that?

Definitely further.

But where? When?

There's something about her that has always called out to me. It's been a slow but torturous journey into what we are.

I'm not expecting my orgasm to slam into me with the force it does. My eyes roll back, and I see stars. Or is it fuzzies? Emotions and memories collide and crash against each other, and I see *her* as I feel CC's touch on me. I feel her lips against my shoulder, peppering little kisses on my skin, whispering sweet nothings into my ear like she did that night.

For once, I don't shy away from it. I embrace it because I know that I'm safe. I'm here, alive, and I'm still breathing.

It's all too much. It's all just enough.

It's just right.

And it goes on. And on.

I swear, you'd think these two have been taking notes on how to fuck Courtney senseless. But the joke's on them, because there are only so many orgasms you can tease out of a person before it hits you in return. Full-body shudders wrack CC's body as she comes, and Oscar's right there with her. His moans match hers as he shoots thick ropes of his cum inside me, his thrusts remaining steady as he pushes all of it in.

Once again, we are a sweaty tangle of arms and legs, and it takes a while to come down from this high. There are so many things I want to say to them both. Like this permanence I suggested for us weeks ago.

But how does one go about making that a reality? Do I ask nicely? Or do I pull a Marc and just… move them in with me? Sure, there'll be logistics to figure out with all that, but people do this shit all the time, right? I don't want to hide from them anymore. I want them to have all of me, just as I want all of them.

And if anyone has a problem with that, fuck them.

Fuck them, ten ways to Sunday, and then back.

"Courtney, you okay?" I don't want to hear panic from Oscar, not right now.

Not when I feel this good.

I shake my head. "It's just… this. Keep fucking me, please."

"We will," he mumbles, his breathing coming in pants, his thrusts shallowing. Hers do too. Lazy strokes, mostly, but they were still going? "Just tell us, are those happy or sad tears?"

Say what now?

Am I crying? Again?

CC hooks a finger under my chin and turns my face to hers. "Courtney, eyes on me."

My eyes fly open, and the next thing I know, I'm drowning. Her dark brown gaze traps me, holding me, pulling me in so deep I can barely breathe. Every bit of air I'm breathing is hers. It's ours.

I don't want this to end.

Now, or ever.

"What's wrong—" she starts to say, but I cut her off.

"I love you."

Something passes through her eyes, she beams, and my heart seizes at the sight. "I've been waiting for you to catch up," she says instead, her arm tightening around my torso. "You're mine, both of you."

Smartass. I turn to Oscar. "I heard you earlier. And I love you too. I did back then too, and I just… I never stopped."

The look on his face mirrors hers, and I feel like I'm on cloud nine. "I'm yours," he says instead.

"I know." I fucking know it. "Now, can you please get back to fucking me?"

44

COURTNEY

"What happens now?" Oscar asks hours later as he draws lazy circles in the middle of my back.

I'm lying on my stomach with my head propped on his lap, my gaze honed in on the erratic rise and fall of CC's chest. His other hand is tucked between her legs, I think. Her moans tell me she's enjoying whatever he's doing to her.

"What do you think happens now?" she counters with a question of her own, a hint of amusement in her voice.

She's sprawled out on her back with an arm draped over her face, the other buried in my hair as she runs her nimble fingers through it.

We've been this way for a while — it's been hours, I think — mostly breathing in the silence as we caress and explore each other. Her fingers clench into fists every so often as a shudder runs through her body. I know he can keep this going for hours, teasing out subtle orgasms from her body. I also know she won't be protesting any time soon. Her body is so fucking needy and responsive, and I fucking love it.

Holy shit, I love her.

I want this every day for the rest of my life — however long or short that may be.

"Move in with me." The words pop out with no filter. It's directed at her mainly. But at him too.

She pauses mid-action, her fingers steeling in my hair. "You asking or telling?"

I take a moment to mull over the question. "Does it matter? It's not like you're attached to your place."

A hearty chuckle bubbles up from Oscar. "She's not. She's been waiting for you to ask her to move in."

"It extends to you too," I remind him.

A beat passes, and he gives me his answer. "Okay."

"Really?" Why do I sound surprised?

"Yes, really. There isn't much of a choice to be had, is there? You own me, Courtney. I wear your mark and your collar. Where you go, I go. I don't care where we live as long as we're together."

"Good," I say breathlessly, "'cause I'm never letting you go."

The bed moves, and I feel his lips against my temple, then my hair, before he goes back to drawing circles on my back.

CC's fingers resume movement, but she doesn't say anything. When the silence stretches on too long, I get antsy. Reaching over, I pull her arm off her face. Her eyes are open but wet with tears, and her expression alternates between pained and ecstatic.

"I want you here too," I tell her.

A single tear slides down her cheek. "Do you mean that, or are you only saying it because you know I want to hear it?"

My breath hitches. "I *need* you here," I amend. "I need you, CC."

Instead of answering, she's looking at me as if seeing me for the first time. Her eyes pierce through me, and my stomach clenches with an irrational, unfamiliar fear.

I reach out and cup her cheek. Her breath puffs against the inside of my wrist, in time with my pulse. I curl my fingers in and stroke the backs of my knuckles along her temple.

"I'm not who you think I am."

"I don't care," I whisper breathlessly. "I'm not who you think I am, so that makes us even. In a way."

She laughs, but it's not an amused one. It's pained. "When you look at me, what do you see?"

"I see the woman I love," I tell her, feeling weightlessness washing over me as the words flow freely. "I see the woman who's been a constant in my life, even when I couldn't see this for myself. I see the woman who's brought me back from the brink of death more times than I can count. I see the woman who, quite frankly, I don't think I can live without."

Her mouth falls open as she stares at me, then relief floods her features as she tilts her head into my caress. "I can't live without you either. My heart is yours. It's been yours since the day we met."

Something about how she phrases that last sentence has a flicker of doubt nagging at the back of my mind, but I push it down as I drag her lips to mine and kiss her hard.

"So, yes?" I mutter into our kiss.

"Hell, yes. No take-backs, no matter what happens."

Is she kidding? "Why would I—"

I don't finish my question because she's on me again, molding our bodies together as she kisses me senseless.

As for Oscar?

Well, I don't think he's capable of shutting down that genius brain of his. Even as his hands are on me and her, I hear his brain firing with unspoken questions. Maybe I'll start calling him the worrywart of our trio. He worries enough for the three of us combined. I guess he just can't help it.

"As long as I can fit my man cave somewhere in your illegal basement, I'm good."

"I'm sure it'll fit just fine," CC tells him, and when she's satisfied my brain is thoroughly scrambled, she turns to Oscar with a mischievous glint in her eye. "Who's going to give Olive the good news?"

Oscar groans and flops to his back. "Way to kill the mood, CC."

She laughs as she pushes off me, settling into an upright position. Pulling my shoulders onto her lap, she returns to playing with my hair. Seriously, she's obsessed with my hair. I don't get it, but it makes her happy, so I leave it be.

"You can avoid it all you want, but she'll find out eventually. They all will once we're all moved in together."

Another groan comes from him, though it's weaker this time. "My sex life is none of her business."

"Oh, but it is. Remember how she flipped her gasket when we first started sleeping together?"

"Urgh, don't remind me."

"Someone has to, don't you think? In case you forgot, she and Mattie never wanted you two to end up together, and Sonya isn't here to play referee anymore."

I can see that CC is having too much fun with this. As much as I'd love to settle in and offer Oscar some sort of reprieve, I want to hear this.

But he shuts it down as quickly as it began.

"So what? As long as I do as I'm told, she stays out of it."

At his words, it dawns on me how little he talks about his mom. I don't speak much about mine, but that's because she's dead, so at least I can use that as an excuse. His, on the other hand, isn't.

I glance over at him, my curiosity spilling over. "What does '*do as I'm told*' entail, exactly?"

He chuckles at the question. "And what, exactly, do you do for a living, Courtney?"

"What is it that you *think* I do, Oscar?" I counter.

CC sighs. "Are we really doing this again?" An undercurrent of steel in her voice is the only sign of her displeasure. She should know by now, ignoring her disapproval at our bickering is Oscar's and my favorite pastime.

"The usual stuff," he says. "Art teacher. Art forger. Apparently, you have a thing for the A's."

I shake my head, and a hint of a smile pulls at the corners of my lips. "You're cute, Oscar, but no. Try again."

"Mafia princess?" he adds with an answering smile.

I have to laugh at that last one. "Do I look like a princess to you? I kill people for a living, and I enjoy doing it. Apparently I'm wired this way."

"And I clean up the Italian Mafia's blood money as a side job, and I *don't* enjoy it," he immediately answers. "But I can't help it. Like you, I'm wired this way. It's my mother's twisted way of making me earn a life I wasn't supposed to have in the first place."

"What does that mean?"

"It means not all mothers are like you, Courtney. Mine keeps me around because of what I can do for her, but she won't hesitate to throw me to the wolves to save her skin. She uses me however she sees fit, and as long as I do as she says, she keeps her nose out of my business. It's a good thing we live on different continents. It's harder to control someone when you don't have immediate physical access to them."

His voice sounds wistful and sad, and I can't help but think of my mother.

In a way, I can relate to the plethora of emotions running through him. At the same time, it's a foreign feeling since I know that his mother and mine are as different as night and day. Literally. Mom was Black, and Olive is Asian.

Yet, in other ways, they were cut from the same cloth. Figuratively speaking, of course. The Sotelo family brought them together — Sarah, Olive, Mattie, and later Sonya — but their blood lust bound them.

They are all weapons. Members of the previous cohort, to be exact.

The thing is, I don't know much about Olive Hyun as a mother, but I do know a lot more about Sarah Bardales, the woman who brought me into this world. The woman who molded me in her own image. The woman who turned me into the unfeeling killing machine I am today.

I think of her, of the times we spent bonding as mother and daughter. Where some mothers took their daughters shopping or to get their hair done, mine took me to her jobs. When my friends were learning how to be children, I admittedly had a different type of childhood.

By age seven, I was proficient with a scalpel. I knew how to dismember a body by the time I was nine. I learned how to skin a person alive when I was ten. She always said it was for my own good as she stood over me and supervised. She would say it was for my protection, as she took my hand and showed me by example. Things like what parts of the body can be easily dislocated. Or how to remove chunks of skin without nicking an artery.

She succeeded, too. She had to, as it was the only reason she had me. To replace her. To be far more ruthless, far more deadly than she ever was.

I can only hope that Charlie turns out so much better than I did.

As if he can read my thoughts, Oscar asks, "What are we going to do about Charlie?"

I can't help the sigh that escapes. "I've given this a lot of thought, and I... it's complicated. Children are sponges, and even though he doesn't understand it now, someday he will. He'll question why this arrangement exists. I won't know what to tell him, not without doing to him what my mother did for me. I don't want that for him. I see so much ugliness in the world, some of which I've had a hand in bringing about. He doesn't need me for a mother on top of all that. He shouldn't have my legacy hanging over his head like a cloud or to be forced to live up to expectations that just..."

I trail off at that.

CC's lips part, then come together as she swallows. "What if we did it together?"

"Did *what* together?"

"This parenting thing. What if we did it together?"

"Why would you want that?" I ask them, my eyes darting back and forth between CC and Oscar. "I barely rise to the occasion."

"You're not alone, Courtney," CC says, her voice a barely audible whisper. "We're a family, and that's what families do for each other."

"I wish it were that simple."

"It could be. I want to try. At the very least, I'd like to be given the chance to be a mom."

"Me too," Oscar adds. "I'd like a chance to be a dad. I promise I'll be everything you'd want me to be for your son. Our son. I will be the dad you'd be proud to see him with. I'm going to take care of him for you. With you."

Isn't that what any of us want? Isn't that what I've always wanted for him? He'll have all three of us looking out for him. Make that six if you count Marc, Harris, and Delilah.

So why am I still dragging this one out?

It's simple.

Charlie's *supposed* crime isn't that he exists; it's the fact that I'm the one who brought him into this world. His punishment? He's destined for the same fate I was, simply because he was born of me. It's a vicious cycle, one I wouldn't wish on my worst enemy.

"Charlie's fate has been decided, and I don't have the power to stop it. Just as my life isn't mine, Charlie's isn't his to live. They'll turn him into another me. I'm supposed to train him to become my replacement, just like Mom did with me. I don't want that for him. I will never, ever want that for him."

They both look adorably confused, and I don't blame them.

Oscar speaks up first. "But I thought—"

"You thought only women could become weapons?" I finish with a bitter laugh. "Yeah, I thought so too. Until I… According to Abby, it's my fault that this all started."

His brow scrunches. "What is? Us?"

I shake my head. "No, not us. Before that. I… umm… did something sixteen years ago, something I shouldn't have. I knew it was a test, but I was being selfish. And I liked her. I think she liked me too, or else we wouldn't have… Gosh, this is weird."

CC chuckles. "What is? Talking about your ex?"

"She wasn't my ex. She was the high-profile client who ODed sixteen years ago."

"Oh."

Yeah. "After we handled the family she'd been placed with, I told Lorenzo I was done. That I only wanted to focus on my art. He said okay on the second part, but he'd have to think about the first part. I got into Harvard a month later, then moved to Massachusetts three months after that. The training program started halfway through my first semester, and he and Mattie set everything up. I couldn't back out since I didn't want to disappoint Abby and Phoenix. I couldn't move back either, so I had to be remote.

"But things were different. The whole cohort too. So when it came time for, well, training, the fucking rule book got thrown out the window with us. I think it started with Sonya, and when she brought Phoenix in, things snowballed from there."

"What do you mean?" Oscar asks.

"Weapons come in threes. Always. It's been that way for decades. If one dies, they don't get replaced. But when the previous cohort lost a member, they replaced her. It consisted of Sarah, Mattie, and Olive. Later, Sonya took my mom's place when she died. They're well-versed in the high-level workings of the Network, and it's their job to mentor the current cohort of weapons — me, Abby, and Phoenix — and when the time comes, they pass on the torch and retire. Mattie and Olive have been ready to retire for years, but not Sonya. I guess, in a way, she is now since they haven't replaced her.

"Even though each weapon starts as a foot soldier, we're also responsible for finding our successors. The hand-off process can only happen if the next generation of weapons is in the works. Marc didn't know this when he told Lorenzo I was pregnant. He thought he could use it to get me out of being a weapon, but that backfired. If Lorenzo had his way, he would've chained me to a bed the entire time I was pregnant. If not him, Mattie and Olive would have. They don't care about gender anymore. They know they're not getting any kids out of Abby and Phoenix, so Charlie is their best chance at retirement. I think they'll take it at this point. In his backhanded way, Lorenzo keeps asking why I haven't named Charlie as my successor yet. Say I have another child, and it's a girl; it's fucking game over for her. If it's another boy, it's the same thing. They could do the same with Roxane's baby if they choose.

"Then there's the matter of only women could become weapons or prey. They didn't tell us you guys were our prey at first. They called you 'training partners.' Phoenix never wanted one, so she didn't get one. Abby probably picked Roxane because she didn't know what would happen afterward. And Oscar, your mom probably offered you up because I'm not merciful. They knew you guys weren't meant to survive training, but they didn't tell us. They also didn't tell us that weapons were supposed to kill their prey to graduate from the program. It was the ultimate test."

We both turn to face Oscar.

And he seems… surprisingly calm and not shocked by this revelation.

"You don't seem too bothered by this," CC points out.

He gives her a nonchalant shrug. "Am I surprised that my mom signed me up for death training? Not really. She never does anything without a plan and a contingency in place. She had me as a means to an end, but that didn't work out the way she'd hoped. She's been trying to get rid of me for decades but won't do it herself. Finding others to do her dirty work for her is what Olive Hyun does best. I think she hoped I'd come out of it broken enough that I'd do it myself, and I probably would've if Sonya hadn't intervened.

"Then again, Sonya always did have a soft spot for broken kids. I think that's what made her such a damn good therapist, but it was her ultimate downfall. There's something she used to say, which I found odd then. She used to say Lorenzo's word was his bond, and thanks to a pact he made with a fifteen-year-old, three people survived who otherwise would have been dead."

I know she was referring to Marc's deal with Lorenzo, but I don't see what that has to do with… oh.

Marc never wanted us to be bound by the same rules the rest of Lorenzo's kids were. At least as it pertained to our personal lives. As for Lorenzo? He knew what I was like, and he would've done just about anything to get his hands on me, and he was willing to agree to anything Marc proposed. As much as he wanted Marc to succeed him, I'm far more valuable to him. I think Mom made sure of it, too. I suspect she meant to use *me* as her bargaining chip to get out of this life, only that backfired on her.

Is that what Marc was going for?

To think… no, that's crazy.

"I told Marc about you," I tell Oscar. "I wasn't about to kill the first boy I ever loved because of some stupid test. Maybe that's why they put that crest on you. They'd have to kill you to get at it and put the pieces together. You, Abby, and Phoenix. Now, that's just dumb. Also, the branding part was new, and it wasn't in the fucking rules. They just wanted to change shit, so they've been using us as an excuse. I still don't know what they want with the Chun-ja family's crest, that they're going to great lengths to hide it. It's not like the damn thing will unlock the gates to fucking Narnia."

"Oh, you'd be surprised," CC mumbles.

"In any case, I didn't start all of this changing business. I wasn't the one who brought Phoenix on board. Sonya did."

Oscar is smiling at that, and I'm not sure why.

"I'm guessing no one ever told you just how much your word is worth, right? I will. CC is the type of woman who turns heads wherever she goes, but you make them roll. Mine included. As for this crest? It's because of you that they're holding on to it. Thanks to you, they're going to great lengths to hide it, too. Whoever is gatekeeping the damn thing," his gaze slides to CC's briefly before returning to me, "won't release it without your say-so. I can't speak to what happened with my situation, but I do know that Phoenix became a weapon because of you. Sonya also said you gave the okay when she brought her to your house eighteen years ago."

I'm shaking my head. "Lorenzo asked me if I wanted a new friend, and I said okay."

His grin turns infectious. "Phoenix said the same thing."

"I didn't think they planned on turning her into a killing machine, though."

"The way I heard it, you saved her life. Not only that, but you were a damn good teacher. She'll never admit it, but she looks up to you. Abby, too. Hell, even Roxane. You have something that neither Mattie nor my mom has. You're a natural-born leader, just like your mom was. You have this uncanny ability to you, one in which people flock to you. All it takes is one look, one word, one touch even, and they can't help but fall in love with you. I'm not immune to it. Neither is CC, in case you didn't notice."

My eyes mist up.

What's with all the mushiness today?

After everything I revealed to them today, they're still unfazed by all this.

PART V

45

COURTNEY

Sometime around noon the next day, Abby barges into my house.

Unannounced, for the record.

"Did I just see who I think I saw leaving Roxane's place?" she demands, slamming the door behind her.

Under different circumstances, I would be irritated by her antics, but I cut her some slack since she's running on little sleep and tons of Red Bull.

"How was your flight?" I ask instead.

In the last three months, Lorenzo has had her traveling back and forth between Minnesota, Seoul, and Tokyo. I'm not always appraised on what she's doing since some degree of compartmentalization is healthy for the group. I know she needed to get Phoenix into South Korea for her procedure, back for the Pecora job, and off to Tokyo for another job Olive assigned her.

I'm surprised Mattie didn't step in and put a stop to it. After all, Abby is her precious granddaughter. Not to mention, how *is* she managing to pull off all that international travel? I know she uses some pretty creative back-channel means to move Phoenix within the US and around the world, seeing as she's been living as a fucking ghost for the last eighteen years. But Abby's pretty tight-lipped on how she moves herself around.

After I called her two days ago, she hopped on yet *another* fourteen-hour-long international flight to rush to Roxane's side without hesitation. Now, she's in my living room and looking a little worse for wear, instead of next door where we would both rather she be.

"Good. Long. Thanks for calling me." She recites the obligatory words of appreciation like she were a drone.

"Anytime," I say with a chuckle, running a finger over one of my blades.

"Now that we got that out of the way, did I just see who I think I saw leaving Roxane's place?" she repeats.

"How am I supposed to know who you saw? I've been inside all morning."

I was hoping for some time alone to put away all this dangerous non-child-friendly shit and maybe ask Ida to bring Charlie over later today. I finally got Harris to go home, albeit through some unsavory means, but it was about damn time.

Even better, I played the safety blanket card Marc specifically told me not to, and it worked like a charm.

She waltzes over to me and slams both hands on the table. "The only way she was there is if she came from here."

Hmm. The hostility in her eyes is new. "You talking about CC?"

"Who else?" As if on cue, her phone goes off. It's one of those classical tunes that bug the shit out of me. She pulls it out of her pocket and scowls at it. "Why was *she* there?"

"Because Oscar and Roxane are friends, and she was with him. What's with the third degree?"

Nothing about today's events warrants this.

For all intents and purposes, the morning started out just fine. We didn't get much sleep because there wasn't much to be had. Since CC is the early riser, she woke up first and made breakfast. It was nice. It felt strange, yet domestic.

Nothing amiss, for the most part.

Then they saw Evan's car pulling into Roxane's driveway, and they both went next door. Again, nothing out of character. Oscar and Roxane are friends, and CC needs more time with her. If anything, to realize that Roxane isn't a threat to her.

"Abby, what's with the third degree?" I ask again when her eyes don't leave her phone.

She waves the screen at me. "Lorenzo wants to see you."

"Since when do you play intermediary between my dad and me? He has my number. He can fucking call me himself. What's this about?"

"Your *girlfriend*," she says with an annoyed scoff. "You know who she is, don't you?"

"You're about to tell me. You know we've been seeing each other for years, so why are you acting like her staying over is so strange?"

She doesn't know the intimate details of what transpires between CC and me, or why I've kept CC out of Charlie's life all these years. Besides Marc, Oscar, and CC, no one does. As far as Abby's concerned, CC doesn't come over because I prefer going to her place.

Yeah, let's go with that.

Except Abby's watching me through narrowed eyes. "Because she's never spent the night *here*. What changed?"

Everything, I want to scream. Instead, I say, "You knew who Oscar was all this time, and you never told me. I'm angry and frustrated, but I get it. I fucking get it."

"Do you?" She lifts a brow. "*Je t'ai dit de laisser tomber celui-ci, n'est-ce pas? Que si vous continuez à tirer sur ce fil, vous n'aimerez pas ce que vous avez trouvé à l'autre bout.*"

[*I told you to let this one go, didn't I? That if you kept tugging on that thread, you won't like what you find at the other end.*]

Oh boy.

"Abigail Sanders. In English. Please."

She switches back so effortlessly. "I warned you, Courtney. You keep tugging on that thread, and you won't like what you find at the other end of it."

"And I told you, I get it. I'm not holding this one against you. Oscar is your friend, and you were just protecting him. From me."

"Not from you."

Okay, now I'm confused. "From who?"

"Let it go."

But she brought it up. She barged in here, all hot and bothered, and now she wants me to let it go?

No. Fucking. Way.

"From CC, then. What's your problem with her?"

"My problem? For starters, she's not who you think she is."

"And you're about to tell me she's the queen of fucking England, right?"

"No, but if that's what it'll take to get her out of your life, I'll fucking do it. It's not too late. You have him now; you two can ride off into the fucking sunset and live happily ever after. You don't need her anymore, and we're all tired of tiptoeing around the fucking elephant in the room."

"Is that what you think? And who's this *we* you speak of?"

"Let. This. One. Go."

"No can do, boss."

She's like me. She hates that moniker just as much as I do. "I'm not your boss."

"Could've fooled me," I drawl sarcastically. "Look, my personal life isn't isn't up for discussion. It never was. But if you must know, I love her. I'm in love with her. Him too. Whatever your problem is with her, either get the fuck over it or keep it to yourself." I pause, then retrace my words. "You know what? Before you do that, answer this first. Consider it the second of many favors I intend to cash in on. What has CC ever done to you?"

"It's not about what she's done. It's…" she groans, then lets out a strangled laugh. "Honestly, Courtney. You're smart. You're fucking smart, and I refuse to believe Little Miss Perfect managed to weasel her way into your life a second time and you let it happen. Her pussy can't be that magical—"

I suck in a sharp breath. "Watch it."

"—and after all these years, I thought you would've figured it out yourself."

"Figured *what* out?" There's a hardness infused in my tone, one that has her planting her pretty little tush into the seat across from me.

She knows that talking around in circles doesn't do it for me. And since I've already asked several times and gotten several non-answers from her, she knows I won't ask again.

And so the damn unlocks.

I always thought happiness was overrated.

Until I got a taste of it myself.

Now, I can't get enough of it, so I'm doing the irrational thing and barging into Brewer Diagnostics LLC, not caring if I set off darn near all of the alarms in this section of the building. Except it isn't for grand gestures of love or professing my undying love and devotion to the woman whose soul has always called out to mine.

Lucky for me, Dahlia spots me first. There must be something on my face, in my body language, that tells her I don't care if I set off yet another… whatever this is.

Her small yet unsteady frame darts before mine, pressing her ID badge to the doors as I push in the door handle.

No cringing sounds. No blaring noise.

Crisis averted.

For now.

Except her hand now connects to my shoulder, halting my movements. Though irrelevant to anyone passing by, the gesture is a big deal. Knowing what she's like, my natural instinct would have been to take a step back, to shrink from her touch, yet a small part of me recognizes how monumental this is for her. That's what keeps me in place. It grounds me, roots me to the spot.

"Whatever you're thinking, don't."

How would she know what I'm thinking? She always keeps

such a tight lid on her own emotions. Plus, there's this other pesky little matter.

Dahlia Brewer doesn't touch people.

Correction — she does it because she has to, not because she wants to. There are only two people — make that *three* people — whose touch she tolerates, welcomes even, and I'm not one of them.

So why would she care? Why would she—

"How would you know—"

"I know what a woman looks like when she's been betrayed by the one she loves."

Betrayed?

I can't say that's the emotion I'm feeling right now. Stunned is more like it. Stunned that she's touching me.

"I don't—"

"Lying to yourself about it, or about your feelings, doesn't make the sting of betrayal hurt any less. I would know. You know that I know."

My lips part to voice the next part of my rebuttal, but no words come out. So I slam them shut because she's still touching me.

The shock wears off long enough that I now register her hands seeking out my skin, fingers splaying across my shoulder, then trailing down the length of my arm. Then something presses into my palm.

"The Executive suites. It's booked for the next four hours. Go. I'll send her up."

I turn and head for the elevators without a backward glance.

I don't ask why she needed those booked for four hours or why she so freely gave them to me. Or how David will feel about this since I'm sure it was for his benefit that she had those reserved in the first place. He and I are a lot like that.

I know all this, yet my feet pivot of their own account and head upstairs.

46

COURTNEY

I don't know how long I've been in here. It could've been minutes or hours, but it all fades away as I pace a hole in the floor, literally and figuratively.

This pesky sting I never expected burns my skin from the inside out, inciting a nefarious series of emotions that I have no idea how to handle, much less curb.

All this time, I truly believed I'd found my person. It never occurred to me to stop and think that she could be a threat to me.

That she could be dangerous to someone like me.

While I came here in a fit of anger, the pieces of the puzzle slowly but surely fell into place. She talks freely about her adoptive parents, Alonzo and Bettina. They don't live together, they barely did, yet I never got the impression that she's estranged from them. She never talks about her biological parents or why she was adopted at eighteen. She never spent time in the foster care system, an even stranger feat for someone adopted after they turned eighteen.

I asked her about it once, a long time ago. It was the anniversary of my mother's death, and like the dutiful daughter that I am, I do something to uphold her memory every year. CC comes with me every year, even though I never ask.

Even though it was outside of our then relationship's defined parameters, I never questioned it. The one time I asked about her mother, the one she referred to as dead, CC went quiet. Deathly silent as something unreadable passed over her face. Her eyes had turned cold and stagnant, the brown flecks transforming into a liquid blackness that sent chills down my spine.

A darkness I was intimately familiar with — a darkness very much like my own.

Sore subject, I assumed.

One she confirmed with, "She got what she deserved. They all did."

And that was the end of that.

I recall that a heavy silence washed over me at her words. One I couldn't explain at the time, especially since it felt a lot like it did when I saw my mom's lifeless corpse being lowered into the ground for the last time. I had been there when she drew her last breath, and I was there when they stuck her six feet under, a finality to her not-long-enough lifespan.

Feeling an onslaught of those emotions at her words made no sense then, but now they do.

I was the one to deliver her biological parents to their fate, just as her parents had delivered my mother to hers.

And here we are, offspring of that unfortunate fate, doing yet another unpleasant dance around each other.

I don't notice it when the door opens or when she slips in quietly, as quiet as a mouse. But I do know that her eyes light up as she sees me. I know it as surely as I know I need to take my next breath.

The air buzzes. It sizzles in that electric way that could only come from her. It's the same one I felt all those years ago.

I never questioned it when she and I first met, on what was the worst day of her life. I did question it briefly when I first met this version of her, then I promptly brushed the thought aside because I knew, in my mind, it wasn't possible.

The girl who once made me feel that way, and the woman before me, were not the same person. Physically, mentally, or emotionally. Lorenzo told me that girl was dead, and I had no reason to question him.

For the longest time, I thought of our relationship as one that wasn't built on lies or distorted truths for the sake of sparing one's feelings. It never was, and I hope to God it never will be.

I thought he did what he thought was best for the greater good.

Or was it just me? Am I the only one who valued that part of our relationship, our shared desire to place the bigger picture above all else?

Is that what will be my downfall?

He still lies to you, you know? Roxane's words about Lorenzo ring loud and clear. *You just want to see what you want to see.*

Or am I yet to master the art of duplicity, the one my mother spent quite a long time teaching me to master and perfect in myself, saying it will serve me well in the future? Have I failed her one and only crucial lesson?

Because Sarah Bardales failed hers, and it was because of me. And look where that got her.

Those eyes remain trained on me as she steps directly into my periphery. "Well," she breathes, her eyes turning molten. "This is different. You came straight from work."

Work? I almost scoff.

She knows what I do. She's known all this time.

Granted, I never lied to her about it. I just surrounded myself with enough normal shit that she would see me as someone normal who holds a great deal of evil in her. Who also has a personal hand in purging evil from this world on a somewhat regular basis.

"Hello, Yong."

She goes still momentarily, then lets out a sigh of exasperation. "Abby told you."

I don't answer.

What's the point? What does it matter who told me when?

She never intended to tell me. Not even after I bared all to her.

"I've always dreaded this day," she continues. "But now that it's here, it's not dread I feel. It's liberation."

Is she for real?

She takes in the look on my face. Her gaze rakes over me, from head to toe and back. "I couldn't have this hanging over my head for the rest of my life, and I was getting real tired of Lorenzo using it as some sort of twisted leverage to get me to leave you alone."

Leverage. Lorenzo.

My nostrils flare. So he has known about this all this while. What was the point of asking — no, daring — me to officially introduce her to the family? Was it intended to be some sort of test? To see if I would follow through with it? Or if she would follow through with it?

Had he planned this from the beginning?

The girls who go underground typically stay underground. We don't necessarily know who they are in the interest of keeping their new identities a secret, but we know where they are stationed. It is our job — the deadly trio, that is — to make sure that they stay underground. It is also our job to ensure those tasked with keeping them safe do precisely that. Until they don't, and they find out just how dangerous of a man Lorenzo Sotelo is and how much of a bad idea it is to get on his shit side.

"What happened to the Milligans, your first foster family?" It's a silly question, but I have to ask it.

"Why ask a question you already know the answer to?" she snaps, annoyance laced in her tone.

"I killed them, Yong. For you."

"I know. I saw the video."

Yong's first placement was a good one. The family wasn't well-off, but they were decent people. Decent-*ish* family. Until she died two months later. Drug overdose, Lorenzo said. Then he sent us to take care of them. So we did. All three of us did, and we left no witnesses.

After all, they were running drugs out of their home. Who would blame a mentally unstable teenager, one still suffering from PTSD, for getting into their stash in the hopes of chasing off that relief, however brief?

Except, it wasn't brief.

And it wasn't *just* about the drugs.

That family deserved what they had coming. They broke Lorenzo's rules and then lied to him about it. But the reason *why* they died technically doesn't exist because here she is, in one piece — looking very much alive and making me doubt everything.

Why we do what we do.

"Why are they dead when you're still alive?"

Her head tilts, and she purses her lips. "Because Deloise Milligan had to die."

"Why?"

"I don't have all the answers, Courtney. Ask Lorenzo. It was his decision to turn her into a martyr."

I plan on it.

But only when I get some straight answers out of her.

"This thing we have, was it ever real?"

"Courtney—"

"With Deloise dead, you had your out. Why didn't you take it and run? You could've returned to your life as Yong."

She scoffs. "What is it about my personality that makes you think I would want any part of *that* life?"

"You thrive on chaos." My voice vibrates with a barely concealed fury.

"So do you, Courtney. It runs in our blood. It's who we are. But here's the thing," she says as she closes the distance between us, crowding me but not quite touching me, "Yong Chun-ja is dead. She died that night in Japan, along with the rest of her family. She's been dead for sixteen fucking years!"

At her words, physical pain shreds through me. It hurts in a way I can never explain, in a way that I'd give anything to forget.

But this tenuous history of ours is rooted in the present. The least we can do is see it through.

"Fine. Let's say she is. Our history is tainted by the blood of our parents. Why not leave things at that? Why build a life here, in Rochester? Why insert yourself into my life? Why make me fall in love with you when you know there's no chance of a happy ending for us? Or was that your intention all along? Was it for revenge? Payback? All of the above?"

"Is that what you think this is?" She sighs, and her eyes search mine. "On the night we first met as Yong and Courtney, I saw something in you. I felt it too, in here," she says, pressing a hand over her heart. "I know you did too. Otherwise, my death wouldn't haunt you so much."

"This had better not be about that honor bullshit again." I can't help the anger laced in my tone.

I can't help it, either, that it pools in the pit of my stomach, and it's only a matter of time before it spreads.

Before me, she shrugs. "It's always been about that. When we first made love," her cheeks pinken at the words, "you asked me about the track marks on my arms. The ones covered by my tattoos at the time." Her hands wrap around her arms, fingers feathering over the invisible ink. "As it turns out, that was one of the few things Sonya didn't want my doctors to touch. She wanted me to use it as a reminder to appreciate this new chance at life and everything it has to offer. A chance to meet you again. To..." Her voice trails off at that, then she swallows thickly. "I was in pain then. Still am. Except then, it would've been unfair for me to die without doing this. And if I was going to die, it had to be at your hand, no one else's."

The fucking anger spreads, but it wrestles with pain too.

It doesn't matter anyway because now that I've heard enough, I finally put my hands on her. First, in the way I know she likes. I grab at the sides of her head, caging her between my palms as my fingers tangle into the hair at the base of her neck. "So what you're saying is, you did all this for me?"

"Why ask a question you already know the answer to?" she repeats.

My forehead drops against hers, and my eyes close as her breath fans across my face. "I *don't* know the answer to that. That's why I asked. I'm no good at this cryptic shit, so fucking spell it out for me."

Another warm breath fans my face. "I've been trying to tell you — no, show you this, for the last four years. I guess I haven't been doing that good of a job at it, seeing as you still don't believe me.

So I'll spell it out for you then. I'm in love with you, Courtney. I always have been, and I always will be."

The thing is, I don't know what to think.

She sounds sincere enough, and I believe her.

And I *do* love her — but what version of her?

Yong? Deloise?

CC?

Does it even matter?

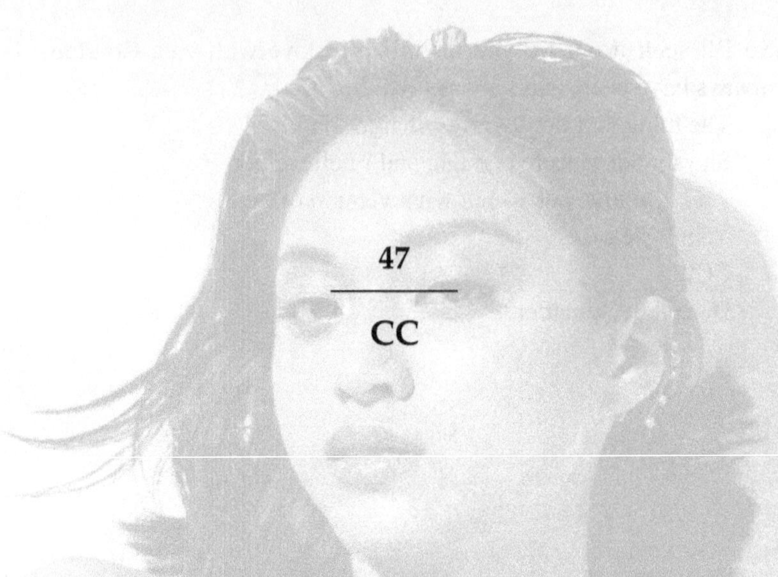

47

CC

I have no regrets.

None whatsoever.

I meant what I told Courtney on the night we met sixteen years ago — to die by her hand would be an honor.

"Do you know what the name Charlie means?" she asks, her voice tight.

Against hers, my forehead rolls from side to side.

Oh, who am I kidding? I know what it fucking means. I know how to Google shit. What I do not know, however, is why she's bringing him up right now.

"Cantor-Dietrich. Those are German names, correct?"

My forehead rolls up and down, but I'm thoroughly confused.

"The name Charlie is derived from the German word karal, which translates to 'free man.' That's the life I'd love for him to have. Not the life that Yong lived, certainly not the one which Courtney lives. It has other variations, like Charlotte, Charley, and Charlene. Do you understand what I'm saying?"

My chest tightens as her meaning slowly sinks in. My heart is beating so hard I think it wants to fly out of my chest and somehow fuse with hers.

Still, I don't answer her because what's the point?

Her eyes are molten lava, and she's looking at me like she can't decide if she wants to devour me or punish me. Frankly, I welcome either option.

She pulls away from me, our gazes still locked, and smiles a hollow, soulless smile. Her hand moves from my cheeks to the nape of my neck.

"I named my son after you, Charlena. That's how deeply engrained you are in every aspect of my being." We're moving, with me going backward, until my back connects with the cold wall. "And for what? Lies?"

A shiver runs down my spine, and heat pools between my legs. "I never lied to you."

Her body crowds mine while her hand holds my throat. "Bullshit."

I swallow around the lump in my throat, and her fingers press in. "I wasn't given much of a choice—"

My words cut off when her grip around my throat tightens, and my body trembles in anticipation. Then she forces my thighs apart and thrusts her fingers inside me, soaked panties and all.

"Pathetic," she sneers.

She pushes away from me, and I'm floating through the air. Within seconds I'm flat on the floor with her straddling my body. One hand is back on my neck, and her fingers wrap around my throat.

A sharp sound pierces through the air, then the sharp tip of her knife slides along my thigh, starting from my knee and traveling upward. Another whimper escapes, a heady mix of pleasure and pain, as the unmistakable sounds of cloth tearing fill the air.

"Death. That's what this is about, isn't it?"

I don't miss the slight hitch in her tone. Or the wetness between her legs soaking up my thigh.

I keep my eyes open, pinning hers to mine. "You think I care what you do to me?"

"I know you do," she tosses back. "Beg."

"Excuse me?"

"Beg for your life," she demands.

I'll die at her hand anyway. I might as well go all the way out.

Isn't that the point of this?

"Kill me or keep me, it doesn't fucking matter," I breathe, my chest heaving. "I live for you. I exist for you. I fucking breathe for you. I will never, ever leave you alone. Not even in death."

Her face goes blank, and her grip turns punishing. "As you wish."

The air leaves my lungs, a slow, torturous, yet pleasurable process. Instead of panic, relief floods my pores. I hold on for as long as I can, drowning in her sharp, soulless eyes as they pin me down, grounding me. As I suck down as much air as possible, she presses harder on my windpipe, cutting off that supply.

On pure survival instinct, two words slip past my lips as all the air and sound in the room is sucked away.

Enlighten me.

The last thing I see is a glossy sheen coating Courtney's soulless orbs. The last thing I feel is the softness of her lips against my exposed neck.

48

COURTNEY

My feet are heavy as I walk out of the room, trudge through the hallways, ride down the elevator, and walk through the lobby. So heavy as I step outside and close the front doors behind me with a gentleness that still feels so foreign.

I have done this before, but this time the click of the door just echoes the premature finality of this.

Of us.

For added measure, I lean against the door — which feels like closing one huge and seemingly important chapter of my life — and let out a relieved breath.

Several breaths, actually. They all move through me in slow, laborious waves.

My mind is numb as I pull out of the parking lot and into traffic. I head to my next destination on autopilot, having made the drive a thousand times before.

You've been through this before, I remind myself.

I have, too.

This isn't the first time CC and I have gotten into it, and I'm confident it won't be the last.

Despite what *I* said, we are nowhere near done.

Insanity is what this is — doing the same thing over and over, expecting a different outcome.

But nothing ever changes.

She might say one thing, but her priorities have remained the same. And so do mine. It's the price we have to pay for being who we are.

It doesn't make it hurt any less though.

That's what this is. This feeling in my chest. This weariness in my body. This heaviness in my soul.

This pain.

This never-ending pain.

I thought I was done with it. Evidently, I'm not.

49

COURTNEY

By the time I pull into the Sotelo compound, I'm seeing red. Or it could be that I have the spoiled or pissed-off princess act down to a T, because no one gets in my way as I march through the house and straight into Lorenzo's office.

I hear voices as I throw open the door, all of which go silent once I step in.

I spot the target of my rage and make a beeline for him. "Did you know?"

Someone clears their throat. I turn to see Gerald *fucking* Morelli settled in the gaudiest leather armchair this room has, casually sipping a whiskey while his squirrelly son leans against the wall, arms crossed, with a sinister smirk on his face.

The bastard is *smirking*. At me.

Now, there comes a time in every woman's life when she has to make a choice. In my case, maintain this nauseating façade or show these assholes my true colors.

Option two wins out. Easily.

After all, Gerald is a marked man.

And so is Reuben, for touching my things.

I reach into my back pocket, and my fist curls around the pocket knife. Lorenzo's hand wraps around my arm, halting my movements. My head lifts, and he gives me a slight shake of his head.

"Anything else, gentlemen?" His eyes are on Gerald, his voice tight.

Oh boy.

What *did* I walk into this time?

"That, right there, is my point," Gerald says, his gravelly voice rubbing on my already frayed nerves. "It's not too late to salvage things, Lorenzo. This marriage is necessary, seeing as you can barely control her. First the out-of-wedlock kid, now this? How long will you let this go on? I hear she's shacking up with my bastard son. Certainly, you don't want that stain on your legacy."

My body tenses. All I hear, out of all that vitriol, is *bastard son.*

There's only one man I'm sleeping with, and he's got inauspicious ties to these two. "*Dad,*" I infuse the word with a saccharine sweetness that makes my stomach churn. "Who's this bastard son they speak of?"

Lorenzo gives me another head shake. "My answer remains the same," he says harshly. "I've humored you long enough for the sake of our friendship. That's done now. The next time this comes up, one or both of you will end up in a body bag, and that's a promise."

I'd be happy to hasten things along, but Lorenzo's grip on my arm tightens.

Reuben pushes off the wall, huffs, and stalks out of the room. But not before his sinister eyes run all over my body, the look on his face giving off 'this isn't over' stalkerish vibes. Gerald's eyes are calculating, and he hones in on Lorenzo's arm. He makes a tsk-tsk noise and walks out.

We stay that way for a minute, then Lorenzo breathes a sigh of relief and releases my arm.

"Oscar Hyun," he says, too casually for my liking. "You asked who the bastard son was."

And just like that, I'm reminded of why I barged in here in the first place.

"Did you know?" I ask again.

"Which part? That he's Gerald's son, that you're sleeping with him, or that you should've killed him years ago?" he says, rounding his desk and settling in. "Of course, I knew. I told you, I make it my business to keep tabs on my children."

"Then you know that I wasn't talking about Oscar."

"Any new developments on the Pecora job?" Lorenzo asks, conveniently side-stepping my question with one of his own.

I grit my teeth. "That was days ago." Shoulders slumped, I lean over and slam both fists on his desk, disturbing a patch of dust. I hold back the inevitable sneeze that follows, my blood still running hot. "Did you fucking know?"

He leans back in his seat, studying me. "You have blood on your collar. Did you kill her?"

My spine straightens. "I did."

He smirks. "Now, why would you do something so stupid, knowing what she's worth?"

"I don't have time for your cryptic bullshit, Dad. Did you plant her in my life?"

"I didn't have to. Yong has always been a royal pain in my ass, but the girl is in love with you. That part was never in question. It was the same then."

"So you lied to me?"

He quirks a curious brow. "I didn't lie to you. Deloise *did* die. She was reborn as someone else."

"Then you stuck her in my life."

"Again, I didn't have to. It was bound to happen one way or another. Sonya's job was keeping her away from you, but she realized the best way to do that was to have her close to you. That was the fix she needed. It made her easier to control."

"Excuse me?"

He reaches over and pulls out one of his files. "The night we left Japan with her, we all saw what we saw. You and she huddled on the bathroom floor of the jet. Tell me, what kind of person comforts the one who just killed her parents?"

Yes, that did happen. "How did you—"

"We knew all about your routine, Courtney. Yong was the only one brave enough or stupid enough to go in there. She got through to you. She tapped into a side of you that only Marc ever could. The caring side. Did we use her? Absolutely. I told you, some people are worth more alive. There's no denying how much her money funds the Network's activities. It's easier to access those funds with her alive.

"She does other things, too. For the last sixteen years, she's been indirectly helping us root out her parents' and ex-fiancé's old contacts. Our allies have more than quadrupled, thanks to her. Our foes have been eliminated. Phoenix got her procedures done and then some. Look at the big picture, and it's a win-win for everyone involved. So, for Oscar's sake, I hope you didn't kill her. Because then I'll have to kill him, Abigail, and Phoenix, and I'd rather not."

I don't answer him.

Instead, I let his words sink in. I don't know what I was thinking. He wasn't going to give me answers, not about this. And since I let my emotions get the better of me, I'll never get them.

"This marriage business has gone on long enough," he continues. "I do not want to see Gerald or that doofus in my office ever again, so here's what we're going to do. Tamara will host a fundraiser for the Mayo Eugenio Litta Children's Hospital this Christmas Eve. That's in three months, so you have plenty of time to prepare."

My brow furrows. "Prepare for?"

"Your official coming out event."

"*What* official coming out event?"

"The one where I publicly announce that you, Courtney Bardales Sotelo, are my only weapon," he deadpans.

Excuse me?

Is he being serious?

Whatever happened to the term *super*-secret death squad? Or did I miss something?

"Or it could be a different sort of coming out," he adds. "If I don't see Charlena Cantor-Dietrich *and* Oscar Hyun draped on either side of those bloody paws," he points to my arms braced against his desk, "I'll round up the rest of the crew. Abigail, Phoenix, *and* Oscar. And you, dear daughter, will carve that crest off their skin, right after you drain the blood from their carcasses."

"And if I refuse?"

He smirks. "Charlie takes your place."

I feel the blood drain from my face as I stare at him, slack-jawed, as his meaning sinks in. "You wouldn't."

"Try me. There are no more loopholes on this one; your brother cashed in that one in exchange for his precious Delilah. I'm sure he'll get creative, but I doubt another opportunity will present itself in three months. Which is how long you have to call the Grim Reaper and sort this mess out. And before you ask, I'm being generous by giving you three months. You already get a pass for the Sotelo Ball since that one's in less than two weeks, and I am a man of my word."

I'm reminded, once again, that not only does my life not belong to me, but I'm also anything but normal.

I am the product of two sociopaths.

I am the Devil's daughter.

And this is Graduation Day.

Or rather, Graduation Day 2.0.

The day the world will see the feral beast that lives in me.

To them, I'm still a clueless, sheltered, illegitimate mafia princess with a tomboy reputation. A rather nauseating persona, I might add. So once I pick up my mother's mantle like I was born to do, I'll become the most ruthless contract killer for the Sotelo Crime Family's Midwest chapter.

I can't say I'm too upset by that, as it would be a refreshing change of pace.

Lorenzo clears his throat and flips open his folder. "Now, back to the Pecora job." His tone is all serious now. "The way I hear it, there were issues with the clean-up."

It's uncanny how easy it is for him to switch back to business mode. But that I take offense to, so my jaw snaps shut. "What issues?"

Without missing a beat, he pulls a different sheet from his messy desk and holds it to me. "What's wrong with this picture?"

I spare a quick glance at it. It's a picture of the Pecora estate. "What's wrong with it?"

"It's supposed to be ashes."

I grit my teeth.

This is why I hate coming here. Lorenzo sure has a lot to nitpick about every time all three of us go on a job together.

"You wanted him gone. He's gone. Without a trace. That's how this works."

The thing is, I know I don't have to tell him how to run his damn organization. I also know that a man like him didn't get to where he is without a certain degree of superior intelligence.

"I wanted him and his property gone. Getting half the job done isn't—"

"You can't just torch an estate of that size. Not without consequences. That's not the kind of mess Marc can sweep under the rug. Not even you can afford to have the authorities come sniffing."

"They've been sniffing around for decades, long before my time. There's nothing to find as long as you three do your jobs."

"They made the call not to torch the place, and I agree with it. It's times like this—"

"Hold up, *they* made the call? Where were you?"

"Busy."

"Courtney, where were you?"

I shrug a heavy shoulder. "I was there for most of it."

"That wasn't the deal."

"I was dealing with something else, Lorenzo. Something that took precedence over Pecora."

"Again, not our deal."

He can say that all he wants, stress it until he's blue in the face, but he knows he can't enforce that rule. Not with me, anyway.

I lean back and fold my arms across my chest. "You know what I love about our little chats?"

"Enlighten me."

My spine stiffens at that, even though my lower half seizes up in reaction to those words. I stand up straighter, and my hands fall to my sides. "Don't do that," I bite out.

"Do what?"

The fact that he's feigning innocence further grates on my already frayed nerves.

"Mattie trained me, so don't pretend you don't know what that does to me."

"What? En—"

I slam his hand over his mouth, muting the words. "I mean it, *Dad*. Unless you're prepared for things to get real awkward real fast, you should think twice before repeating those two words *to me*."

As if on cue, my phone picks that moment to chime, so I pull it out and tap away, ignoring the scowl that forms on his face.

As usual, it's Marc checking up on me. It's almost as if he has some sort of telepathy, that one.

Marc: You home?

This, again?

Courtney: No. Why?

Marc: There's a situation at your place that needs to be handled.

Courtney: Another one?

Marc: Duh.

Courtney: What situation?

Marc: The kind that needs to be handled in person.

Lorenzo yanks the phone out of my hand.

The other palm charged with muffling his words falls off his face. "You must really have a death wish."

He eyes the screen and laughs. "That's it?"

"What, you thought we were plotting your downfall?"

"It's a safe assumption. I did just threaten to kill your friends and your boyfriend. That, and your brother texts you a lot whenever you're here." He hands it back to me. "It's irritating being ignored like that."

"I agree, so let's wrap this up. I don't control the actions of Abby and Phoenix. Just as they don't control mine. That's our deal. Mutually assured destruction, or some other shit like that. Or did you guys change the rules on us at some point and then forget to tell us? Like you've been doing since the beginning?"

By *them*, I'm referring to Lorenzo, Mattie, Olive, and Sonya — the four who brought our murderous trio together. Technically five, if you count Sarah.

"Speaking ill of the dead?" he says of Sonya. "That's not your style."

"So is issuing veiled threats."

He chuckles. "That wasn't a veiled threat."

"No? So it's open season on loved ones. Hmm, let's see. You have so many to choose from." I purse my lips. "How about Lucas, Tamera's baby brother? He's a senior at the Carlson School of Management, right? It'd be a real shame if Bedlam Hall went up in flames, say, right before Thanksgiving break."

He leans back, and a deep, hearty laugh bubbles up. "Well played," he says once the laughter subsides. "But why stop at just one? Why not think bigger? Throw in Olympus and/or Spartan Hall into the mix. Better yet—"

Another chime, so I hold up a finger to him and tap away. It's a picture this time.

The kind that has my blood running hot and cold at the same time.

"We're going to have to pick this up another time," I say as I stand and head for the door.

I don't bother sticking around for his response. He can just summon me here again if he wants.

This, on the other hand, can't wait.

50

COURTNEY

U p until twenty-four hours ago, there were certain things I never thought I would see.

CC and Oscar, in my space — when I'm not home — waltzing around like they own the place. Technically, they do since I asked them to move in with me.

But then, there's Charlie, sitting in the middle of the living room floor and stacking up mega blocks, sorting them out by color before stacking them up high. He's doing toddler-y things.

I look around for any signs of my brother or Charlie's nanny, Ida, and I see none. There's a part of me that doesn't want to conceive of the notion that Marc would simply release his precious nephew to these two.

Or at least, that's what I think until Oscar speaks up.

"Ah, good. You're home." He wipes both hands on his apron as he steps into the room. "Marc said we could pick him up three hours early, that you wouldn't mind."

I don't hear the rest of his sentence, my mind still frozen on the words *'three hours.'*

Three hours.

That's how long Charlie has been home.

Admittedly, it's the longest he's spent in his own home in the last few weeks, without me being present. I might be a psychopath, but at least I feel something for this child of mine. That includes this irrational feeling of over-protectiveness that bubbles up within me.

But why?

It's not like they would harm him. They both dote on him. They both want to jump in, head-first, to this parenting thing, while I'm standing here, frozen, wondering if my son recognizes me.

It has been six weeks, after all.

"Court…" CC whispers tentatively, and I can't bring myself to turn around and face her. I can't look at *them*, knowing I put them there. Her hands slide around my waist from behind, settling on my stomach. "I'm okay."

She rests her forehead against my spine, and I'm melting into her touch, even though I don't want to. She has a pull over me, one that I can't ignore.

I exist for you.

I don't deserve this. I don't deserve to feel her arms around me, even though it comforts me. It shouldn't.

Then I feel it. There's a little tug on my leg. I look down to see Charlie holding his hands up to me. He's giving me a toothy grin as he whispers my favorite word in the world.

"Mama."

Stepping away from CC, I bend and lift him into my arms, cradling his tiny body into mine. I take a moment to bask in his soft, childlike innocence. This goodness is the one true and innocent light in my life. I created that.

I'm not completely screwed up.

This, I can do right.

So I do just that. With Charlie in my arms, I head for my bedroom and shut the door behind me. And I lock it.

———

Sometime later, incessant knocking rousts me from sleep. "Courtney, open up."

I stir, then roll over to find I am on a hard surface. Pulling myself upright, I look around for Charlie, knowing I came here with him. Once I spot his sleeping figure on my bed, I breathe a sigh of relief.

There's more pounding on the door. "Courtney, please. Open up," CC pleads.

An eerie sense of déjà vu washes over me. I'm scooting over until my back hits the door, leaning against it. "Would you keep it down? Charlie is asleep."

"We know. It's after nine PM." That's Oscar. "We gave you time. We gave you space. But we're done letting you push us away, Courtney."

I cross my hands over my chest. "I didn't push you away. I want you gone. Both of you."

CC makes a tsk-tsk sound. "The only way that will happen is if you kill us both. That should be easy enough for you, right?"

My fingers twitch, tucked in at my sides. I want to wrap them around her slender throat, to watch as the light fades from her eyes. Just as I wanted to all those years ago.

"Watch your mouth," I grit out between clenched teeth.

"Why? Because of Charlie?" she taunts.

"No, because I just might do it. And I'll enjoy it, too. Don't think for one second that I won't."

"I know you will. You did that earlier today, and guess what? I fucking loved it."

Huh?

That has me scrambling to my feet and throwing the door wide open. "What are you—"

The words die a swift death on my tongue.

It's hard to argue when the proof stares me right in the face. Or, in this case, the bruising around her throat and all over her collarbone, all the size of my hand.

Today wasn't a dream. I didn't kill her. I know this because she touched me earlier, and I was comforted... and turned on. I think I still am.

CC watches me for a moment, her eyes glistening with unshed

tears. Her face has them, too. She takes a step toward me, and I take an answering one back.

Her brow furrows in confusion, and she repeats her words from earlier. "I will never, ever leave you alone."

Her words and body language are a contradiction.

"In case you didn't realize this, there are cameras in those suites," she offers when the silence stretches. "Not my idea, I should add. It's a liability thing for the twins. Plus, David is really into the whole voyeur thing, so." She heaves a casual shoulder. "My point is, if you really wanted to kill me, you should've gone all the fucking way."

"Are you fucking kidding me? You—"

"You hesitated," she bites out, cutting me off. There's a steely glare in her eyes. "Just like you did that night. You talk a big game, but when it comes down to it, I don't think you have it in you to kill me."

"I still could," I force out.

Seriously, they should've left when I gave them the chance. The window of opportunity is fast shrinking.

"Yeah?" she steps toward me, reaches for my hands, then lifts and places them on her collarbone. "Do it."

My fingers curl around the nape of her neck, and then she's gone from underneath my hands in a flash. There's a tug on my arm, and my feet start to move as Oscar drags CC and me into the living room and shoves us onto the couch, right next to each other.

"What's the matter with you two?" His voice is low, his body vibrating with his barely concealed anger. "You want Charlie to see his Mom strangling his Mom?"

"She wasn't going to—"

"Shut up," he bites. "Intent or not, this has gone on long enough. Either talk like the two grown-ass women you are, or I'll put you in fucking time-out like a pair of naughty children."

He half-turns to leave, and something in me snaps.

I stand and reach for his arm, halting his movements. My hands move on autopilot to his waist. It takes fifteen seconds for me to get the belt off him and loop it around my wrist. I turn my attention to

CC, to find she's naked, her body half-folded over the edge of the couch, and her ass in the air.

"What the…" He reaches for her and jerks her back by her hair, pulling her upright to her feet. "What the fuck are you doing?"

She shrugs him off. "Taking my punishment like a big girl. What are you doing?"

His eyes flash. "Stopping you from doing something stupid. Can't you see she's in no state to be doling out punishment?"

"No one's making you stay," she tosses back as she resumes the position. "Either keep your mouth shut or get out." Her gaze meets mine. "Do it."

I stalk over to her and get into position. "How many can you handle?"

"However many you see fit."

Carte blanche?

Alright then.

My arm lifts, belt and all, but Oscar's hand stops me.

"Don't do this," he pleads.

If I cared, the look of pity and uncertainty on his face would bother me.

"Begging *me* won't help. It'll only make things worse for *her*," I tell him. "I'll spank my toys anytime I want, anyhow I want to. Strip or get the fuck out."

He studies me for a moment, then his hand falls to his side. I shut him out of my mind and return my full attention to her. Whether he stays for this part or not, that's his fucking prerogative.

"You have a safe word," I hear myself say. "Use it anytime, and this stops."

"Not a fucking chance," she bites.

Okay then.

Since she likes the number so much, sixty-nine lashes it is.

She shrieks when the first lash hits her bottom and lifts on her tiptoes. "F-f-fuck, that—" she cries out, but I cut her off.

"Not one word from you, not unless you want to safe-out. Understood?" When she doesn't answer, the three next fall in rapid succession, each one harder than the previous. "Do you understand? Nod once for no, two for yes."

She worries her bottom lip, then nods twice, tears streaming down her cheeks. She bites down on it, probably hard enough to draw blood. This is the part where I either offer her a muffler or free that bloody lip of hers. Option two is much more appealing, but I tamp down on the urge to give in and suck it into my mouth.

This is supposed to be punishment. It's not meant to be pleasurable for her.

Or me.

Or Oscar either, wherever the fuck he is.

She's docile and compliant as I dole out the remainder of her punishment, sixty-five lashes more. The only sound in the room is her sobs. Once done, I run my fingers over her welted bottom, and she whimpers needily into my fist.

So I give her one hard smack to an area I know is extra sensitive. "You want more?"

She frantically nods, her moans a heady, melodic tune that soothes my blackened soul.

I flip her onto her back, then straddle and push a finger inside her. As expected, she's fucking dripping. I find her G-spot and press into it in a few slow passes. She pushes her hips up and bucks into my wriggling finger.

"You like that, huh? You greedy little slut." I have no clue where that came from, but she grows even wetter at the words.

I lift up slightly, then push her thighs apart and around my torso. A second finger easily disappears into her weepy cunt, then a third. I'm in awe as my fingers move in and out of her with barely any friction. This is all her. It's all her natural juices, and I'm coated in it.

With each thrust, she moans and further digs her heels into the plush carpet, her thighs quivering on either side of my torso. It's hard to ignore my body's response to her or the heat that pools at my core. She's toxic, potent even.

This wasn't supposed to be pleasurable for her.

Instead, I hear myself ask, "Fist?" as I rub my thumb over her sensitive nub.

Another nod from her, and my pinkie goes in.

Usually, this is the part where we stop and get some lube, as it helps with the stretch. But since this is meant to be punishment, I'd like to see how far I can take this.

Just how much of me she can take without using lube.

My thumb slips in, and she lifts her hips, shifting slightly as she bucks into my fist.

Then my knuckles disappear into her as well.

My breath hitches as I close my hand, very carefully, into a hard fist inside her. I relish in the delirious sensations running through me as her inner muscles clamp down on my fist hard.

Her thighs snap shut, tightening around me, and the scream that rips from her throat is divine. Full-body shudders wrack her as she thrashes in place. I give in and lean forward, pulling her delectable lip into my mouth. Once that first hit of copper assaults my senses, I'm lost to her. I latch on, sucking down on it, like my life depends on it, and she urges me on.

With her pussy cinched around my wrist and her inner muscles contracting on my fist, I almost miss it — the answering warm liquid that slips past my own folds, soaking my panties and gushing from between my thighs too.

It's a heady feeling like no other, being fully in possession of her body, heart, and soul. I'm humbled by how much trust she puts into me, turning her body over to me like this. I could hurt or even break her, yet I've never felt so powerful or tender, so completely and utterly in love with her.

How did I think I could rid the world of this?

In what universe did I think I could rid myself of her?

Once the last of it ebbs from her body, I slowly ease my hand, one finger at a time, from her cunt before rolling her onto her side. I bring my coated fist to my mouth as I turn to see Oscar seated across from us. The expression on his face has long changed from pity and uncertainty to pure animal lust. He's naked as ordered, his fist wrapped around his cock. His sultry brown eyes are trained on us, on me, as he works his magical appendage like his life depends on it.

I'd much rather *it* be in me, so I strip down in record time, get down on all fours, and press my cheek against the floor, wriggling my ass in the air much like CC did earlier. He takes the fucking hint and scrambles over without my having to ask. He thrusts deep inside me in one swift movement, and then he's pounding me so hard I can barely catch my breath. It's not long before my orgasm hurtles through me, its intensity nearly ripping me open from the inside as a scream tears from my throat.

His climax hits him hard, a strangled groan slipping past his throat as he empties himself inside me completely. His cock and balls continue to twitch and pulse and slap my sensitive nub over and over, my walls clamping down on him as my pussy milks him dry.

I crumble to the floor like a rag doll, still shaking when he pulls out of me. He rolls onto his side and pulls my shivering body against his, curling our bodies into the fetal position. A few feet from us, CC is still sobbing, the sounds quieting until we're plunged into a punishing silence.

51

COURTNEY

We all lie on the floor, silent, as we catch our collective breaths.

I'm utterly spent. The kind of spent one feels after running a marathon. I don't know about these two, but I'll happily spend the night on this floor.

After some time Oscar managed to stand, then leaves the room. I remain in place, eyes closed, because I'm not sure I have it in me to face her.

There's movement, lots and lots of it. The sounds of something being dragged. A gentle whoosh in the air, like linens flapping in the wind. Oscar's strong arms wrap around my body as he lifts me off the carpet, and deposits me onto something soft and plush. Moments later, I feel the warmth of CC's body against my back, and he drapes her arm around my torso.

Her soft lips press into my nape, and a shiver runs through me, my body melting into her touch.

I sense the heat of Oscar's body as he lays next to us, but not quite touching us. He wants us to have this moment, and I just... I appreciate the heck out of him for it.

"I love you both so, so much," I hear Oscar say, his voice breaking. "But, I... umm... what the fuck was that?"

A brief silence passes, then, "That was Courtney at her worst." That's CC.

"O-okay, duly noted." He has to say in response to that. "Remind me to piss you both off more often."

"I'm not sorry about today," she quickly adds.

"Neither am I," I toss back.

We sit in silence for a bit.

"I was Phoenix's training partner," CC eventually says.

That gives me pause.

Then Oscar and I both spring upright and to a sitting position.

"When?" Oscar asks; while at the same time, I blurt out, "How?"

One eyelid opens, then a second. Our eyes meet, and then she smiles. "You're looking at it."

I'm confused. "What am I looking at?"

Slowly, like a gazelle, she stretches out. Legs, arms, everything she is. A beat passes, then she folds her arms over her torso and rolls onto her stomach.

As much as I love a good striptease — if you can even call it that — I'm still so confused. "What am I *supposed* to be looking at, CC?"

It clicks for Oscar. "The surgeries," he whispers.

The... *what*?

"This body," she sighs, then rolls onto her back. "You said it yourself, Courtney. Just as Mattie got creative with you two, Sonya got creative with Phoenix and me. I'm not the same person I was sixteen years ago. Sonya saw to that. This body has been twelve years in the making, and it was custom-designed for Phoenix.

"For every cosmetic procedure she got done, I got one done too. It's easy to forge the records for certain medical procedures when an actual procedure is performed. It works if you can find the right doctors, and there is no shortage of those outside the US. Sonya's resources were pretty vast. We went to Seoul quite a bit, too. If you know where to look, you'll find the right doctors who'll take twice the payment for a twofer but register it as one procedure. Although, some procedures were... admittedly, harder. But I put up with all of it because you are my reward at the end of the day. You both are, so it's a win-win-win."

I nod, the information sinking in. "So that's what Lorenzo meant."

She goes stiff.

"You spoke with your Dad?" Oscar's voice comes out in pained bursts.

"I did. That's where I came from."

"That explains the murderous rampage," CC mutters under her breath.

"Lorenzo gave me an ultimatum," I add.

"What kind of ultimatum?" Oscar asks.

"That I make this official, or else."

"Make *what* official," CC asks, her voice tight.

"This. Us. Our official coming out party will be at Tamera's fucking fundraiser on Christmas Eve, or else."

I watch as her body visibly relaxes, albeit slightly.

"Or else *what*?" Oscar prompts me when I leave things like that.

"Or else he'll publicly announce that I'm his only weapon, right after he forces me to kill and fillet all three of you."

I'm not expecting them both to burst into laughter, but it happens anyway. My own answering smile tugs at the corners of my lips.

"The crest is useless," she says in between laughter.

"I know."

"The vault in question is not a treasure chest; it's a crypt. It's where my sister Yang is buried. Well, she's actually my mom, as you both know."

"Yeah, I know. Abby finished decrypting its markings a few months ago. Did you tell Lorenzo it was treasure?"

She scoffs. "No, I didn't have to. Back then, Hyouga bragged about it all the time. He said it was his reward, or dowry, or some bullshit. I probably should've told him that the only thing he was getting out of there was several bags of bones. If I had known what Lorenzo wanted with the crest, I would've told him."

"For what it's worth, I don't think it would've made a difference."

"To whom?"

"To any of them."

The whole point of the tattoos was to up the ante on the torture. Sure, I designed and modified the original design on Mattie's say-so — the artist in me couldn't resist — but human skin doesn't work that way. Skin is elastic, and it's been fifteen years. The skin would've stretched by now. The ink would've faded.

Even if you could put it back together, like pieces of a puzzle, two of the three were done in invisible ink, rendering the whole thing as useless as a gun without ammo. Phoenix and Abby specifically asked that theirs be done in invisible ink since they knew.

I'm still going to get Oscar's done on me, just for funsies.

"I'm still not sorry about today," CC continues.

I draw in a sharp breath. "How many *more* times do I need to—"

"Do your worst. I can take it," she says, cutting me off. "I don't think you have it in you to kill me. And that's okay because I don't think I have it in me to stop loving you, either. Just so you know, I wasn't completely out of it. I could still feel you, touch you, hear you. I thought I was imagining all of that, and then I watched the video footage.

"You cried when you thought I was dead. And you made love to me once you realized I was still alive. If you claim to hate me so much, why do all of that?"

"I never said I hated you. I was giving you what you wanted, all three versions of you."

"And if all three versions of me wanted you to do it again, would you? Because she would. She'd very much like that. It's who we are. We are all bound in death, by death, and for death. Fighting it is pointless. Resisting the pull between us is futile. Ignoring it is just darn near impossible. Not to mention irresponsible."

"And you?" I turn to Oscar. "What's your excuse?"

"Ditto what CC said," he says evenly. "I belong to you. I belong to you both, in life and in death, and if that's the price to pay for loving you, then so be it. It's a small price to pay for this damaged heart of mine. The heart that can't bring itself to hate you, no matter how hard you try to make it not."

I tilt my face to the ceiling as both hands disappear into my hair, clenching the strands at the roots.

"For years, I wanted to tell you."

My lips thin out. I don't think I want to hear this part.

"About that night on the jet," CC says. "I think a part of me knew it was a test. I knew Lorenzo wasn't just testing you; he was testing me too. But the thing is, I didn't care because earlier that day, I saw something in you. I saw…" she trails off at that. I can only hope she's pausing to choose her next words carefully. "I saw darkness in you. Much like my own."

"Of course you did. I was there to kill all of you. Like you hired us to."

She shakes her head. "That's not what I mean. When you have darkness inside you, it helps you recognize darkness in others. It's the kind we're all born with. We all have it — you, me, and Oscar. And sometimes, when you find that…" she pauses, then blows out a breath. "There's this Japanese legend about fate and destiny."

"This had better not—"

"It's not about honor. I know how much you hate that word." She barks out a dry laugh. "Anyway. It's all steeped in myth and/or superstition, so take this how you will. According to legend, everyone has an invisible red string tied to their little finger, an invisible thread of fate that links those destined to be together, regardless of time, place, or circumstances. Or, if you want to be all mushy like Evan, it binds soulmates together.

"Growing up, my mother kept trying to force one between Hyouga and me, but it could never stick. Not just because he killed Yang, or even because he gave me the creeps. If it were just that, I would've felt something with someone else. *Anyone* else. But I didn't. I just… I'd never felt that strong of a bond with anyone until I laid eyes on you that day. Certain things made sense, but it wasn't until I ODed that they clicked into place.

"I know Lorenzo was watching me that day like a hawk. I suspect he always intended to renege on our deal, but when he saw me watching you, he... I don't know, saw it as a chance to..." she heaves both shoulders. "It wasn't my call to turn Deloise into a Martyr. It was his. He had always known about the issues within the Network and saw the perfect opportunity to kill two birds with one stone. Or several birds with three deadly blades. That was fun."

Fun.

That's not the word I'd use to describe it.

"Let's say that was true. You had your out; why didn't you take it?"

"Where was I to go? Japan? South Korea? I don't belong in either of those places. I've always been a woman with no home. With no place to belong."

"CC..." Oscar starts to say, but she cuts him off.

"Yong Chun-ja has no home. The Yakuzas could never accept Yong because of who her father was. The Yamamotos never planned on embracing her either because they knew what Hyouga and his sister were doing wasn't sanctioned, and they didn't want to deal with the blowback from it. My chaebol family, the Chun-jas, would rather I remain dead. Deloise Milligan had no future.

"Yong wanted an honorable death, but Lorenzo couldn't even give her that. Deloise wanted to fade into the abyss, but the threads of fate that bind us brought me back. And now, as Charlena, I want to live. When I told Sonya all this, she suggested I move to Rochester. I guess I did. I'm not the same person I was before. I'm not boggled down by my past anymore. Every aspect of my physical appearance has been altered. I've forged my own path in life and made a life for myself here. And when it came time, I... umm... slowly began to insert myself into your life.

"I told Oscar this already, but at first, I planned on simply using him to get to you. But then that damned red thread appeared again. On his pinkie and mine. Yours too." She holds out the digit in question and wriggles it in the air. "Obviously, I can't see it, but I can sense it. All this time, and that feeling has never wavered. We're all linked, whether we like it or not. That was the beginning of… I mean, I knew then that I could trust him completely, with all of the sides of me. And vice versa. Just as I knew then," she reaches out and cups his cheek, "that once we made love, there was no going back. That's why I didn't jump your bones when we met; I waited years before taking the plunge.

"Why do you think your Mom flipped when she found out about us? I know she's not superstitious. Hell, I can't say that I am. Still, she knows enough about the red string myth to disavow herself of its effects. So when I say that I'll never, ever leave you alone, that's what I mean. I can't. I'm not capable of it."

Wow.

That is a lot to take in.

It certainly fills in a lot of the gaps about her.

"I hate you both," I say on an exhale, the admission slicing my throat on its way out. "I hate how entrenched you both are in here." I rub a hand over the empty chest cavity. "I hate that I can't bring myself to hate you both properly, the way it would be expected of me."

"And we would deserve it," Oscar says. "But we're all you've got. Just as you're all we've got. So, like it or not, you're stuck with us for the rest of your life."

The rest of my life.

I like the sound of that.

It's a long way from where I started.

My mother was a mercenary who trained me to kill from birth, teaching me what it entails to lead a double life. The white picket fence. The two-point-five kids. The mundane activities like making small talk with neighbors, finding a lover or two, and carrying on romantic relations with them. All the things ordinary people do.

All the things that would disabuse anyone of the notion that I know of at least a dozen ways to skin a person alive and not feel a thing while I do it. Yet anyone who seemingly knows me, knows me as this clueless tomboy who knows nothing of how the world works, an illegitimate yet spoiled mafia princess who is sheltered and privileged.

The bindings of a duality of life.

And as tempting as it is, I do not want to lead him down this path.

I do not want to take any of them down this path.

And yet, here they both are — our paths eternally forged, our destinies interwoven.

I wouldn't have it any other way.

52

OSCAR

3 weeks later

There's something to be said about lazy days.

A perk of a long weekend is that we don't have to go anywhere.

Where CC is an early riser, Courtney and I prefer sleeping in. More than once, I've woken up to find her gone, and Courtney snuggled up to me.

Today is no exception.

When I roll over in bed, I'm surprised to find both Courtney and CC still in bed with me, snuggled up on my other side.

Something clenches in my gut at the sight.

There's something to be said about finding that missing piece, one you never knew you *were* missing. If I were a hopeless romantic like Evan and Roxane, I might even believe in the mystery of soulmates.

I take the opportunity to study them.

Seeing Courtney as the small spoon is… not what I expected. She's closest to me, lying on her shoulder with her face turned toward me. CC is behind her, arm draped over her slender waist, hand nestled underneath the waistband of her pajama bottoms.

Given how much of a dominant Courtney is, I would have expected their positions to be reversed, with CC being the one snuggled into her embrace. Although it's painfully evident from the way she holds her body — jaw clenched even in sleep, shoulders tight — that CC's hand between her legs, stroking her slick folds, just might have been the thing to get her to fall asleep, and perhaps the thing that keeps the nightmares at bay.

My initial apprehension about this has disappeared over the last few weeks.

It's almost eerie how well we fit together.

How much I'm looking forward to what the future holds for us.

To come home to them.

One eye pops open, and Courtney's face lights up when she sees me staring at her.

"Don't be a creeper," she says with a laugh.

"I don't know what that means," I deadpan.

She holds out her arm to me. "Come here."

My phone chooses that inopportune moment to ring. I pull it out to see it's my half-sister, Hallie, calling.

It's a little annoying — okay, a lot annoying — that they only seem keen on acknowledging my existence when they want something from me.

Like the whereabouts of my supposed runaway brother.

Or maybe I'm annoyed that I stuck my neck out for her with Abby, and she pooped all over it. She wanted out, I was helping her get the out she wanted, and then she changed her mind.

Scowling, I answer with great reluctance. "No, I haven't seen him either. I wish you all would stop calling me each time that dipshit decides to take a hike to who-knows-where for who-knows-what. The last time I checked, I'm not my brother's keeper. Or any of you, for that matter. Seeing as I'm the reject child."

Am I bitter about the whole thing? Not really.

Okay, so maybe I am. But only a little bit.

I had no control over how I came to be, yet the fact that their lot chooses to ostracize me for it speaks volumes about their character. Fuck this whole mafia business. Last I checked, the family doesn't turn their back on their own. Even Yong's parents, as messed up as they were, clothed and fed her. Even as they shipped her off to various boarding schools all over Europe.

Then again, she had them killed, so maybe I should take a page out of her book.

I'm met with sniffling on the other end. "That's not why I called, but okay."

An unfamiliar voice. I hold my phone out, blinking once, then twice, just to confirm the caller ID.

Yep, it's still the same.

It's Hallie's number.

I press the speaker button, then the record button, before saying, "Who is this?"

A sigh comes through. "That's really cold, Oscar."

The stepmother.

No love lost there.

It seems like Gerald is grasping at straws, seeing as he's having his wife call me on my personal, confidential cell phone. For the record, I gave it to Hallie for emergencies only.

"Why do you have Hallie's phone?"

"She's not as cold and heartless as you are," she counters.

Closing my eyes, I take a deep breath, trying to calm down. She's perfected the art of getting under my skin; she deserves a fucking Oscar.

No pun intended.

"What do you want?"

A slow breath echoes on the other line. "I need a favor."

"The last time I checked, we don't have the sort of relationship to grant each other favors."

"Your brother was last seen at the ball," she continues, ignoring me.

"Sorry, I wasn't there. I was out of the country."

"I know that, but your girlfriend was."

My blood runs cold at this. "What does she have to do with this?"

"It's her family, so ask her to look into it."

My answer comes swiftly. "No can do. Anything else?"

"Oscar, please."

"That wasn't a rhetorical question. That's the life a Morelli leads. Last time I checked, I'm not one."

"Oscar!"

"While you're at it, lose my fucking number."

I hang up and see both CC and Courtney are now wide awake and expectantly watching me. I'd rather crawl under the covers with them and go back to sleep. Or have wild morning sex — that always boosts up our collective moods.

Then I glance at my non-existent morning wood and sigh. "Reuben is missing, and they're calling me."

CC reaches for my hand, pulling it into her lap. "Why?"

"Beats me."

It's not like this is the first time he's gone MIA. Reuben is prone to that. He likes the attention. And I'm not about to deplete my resources, or call in favors, to find a tool like him.

The bed dips behind me, then Courtney wraps her arms around my torso. "What did she want?"

"It's none of my business what happens to him."

She sucks in a sharp breath. "Oscar."

My eyelids drift closed. "She asked for a favor."

"And you told her to shove it?" CC's tone is gleeful. "I'm proud of you!"

Courtney releases me, and I feel the loss of her heat instantly. That is, until they both push me onto my back, and one of them straddles me.

It's CC. Definitely.

I know this because I feel Courtney's palm against my cheek next.

"So proud of you." She runs a gentle thumb over my lips, then her warm breath feathers my face. "Next time, send her my way. Assholes like that need to be taught a lesson," she orders before kissing me, surprising me with more sensuality than aggressiveness.

I know what's coming next, even before CC says the words.

"Our fuck toy should be rewarded," CC says as her nimble fingers wrap around my half-mast cock, guiding it into her wet heat. "On his face, Courtney. Don't half-ass it, and sit."

She does exactly that.

It's the best morning ever.

53

COURTNEY

After Oscar called Abby, she convened one of her impromptu meetings. CC and Oscar insisted on coming since the meet location was at one of those rare hole-in-the-wall diner-type places that Abby has a knack for finding. It's too bad she and CC aren't getting along since they're both foodies.

Also, they've both been relegated to the corner, a mini-date for them both while I work.

"Can we make this quick?" Phoenix asks the moment she sits. She's got her tray of two purple slushies, nothing else.

"Why? You have something more pressing going on?" Abby teases, waving a French fry at her.

"As a matter of fact, I do." She shrugs off her jacket and loops it over her seat. "I need another place."

Abby's face goes blank. "That's the third place this year."

She shrugs. "Yeah, well." She shoots me a pointed gaze. "Someone's poking around. Again."

"I see." I can guess who that is, and only one name comes to mind, and it rhymes with honey. "I hear I have you to thank for my canceled nuptials."

The look in her eyes turns lethal. "Please. Don't tell me you shed actual tears over that tool?"

"Of course not," I scoff. "Why did you do it? Why would you jump the gun like that?"

"Reuben was spouting nonsense," Phoenix counters. "I don't do nonsense."

She also doesn't do parents either, but for the sake of argument, I bite my tongue on that one.

It's that past I was referring to, the one we each don't talk about.

Phoenix has always been an enigma. Her reaction isn't necessarily an overreaction. I've known her long enough to realize that anyone who brings up her so-called elusive parents — whether in jest or in seriousness — generally doesn't live long enough to follow through on whatever thinly veiled threat they have in mind. I get the sense that it's not talking about her parents that bothers her, so it has to be something else.

Or someone else.

Something strong enough to throw her off her game. Something she still hasn't quite recovered from.

Aside from what happened with Delilah and Howard, there was the thing a few months back where she got wasted over something. I've never seen her like that before, and she won't discuss it.

Then again, we all have our secrets.

"Reuben spouts nonsense all the time," Abby muses. "We were supposed to handle his dad, not him. Is that why you need another place? I'm almost out of safe houses for you. Unless…" she turns to me. "When's your girlfriend moving in?"

"That's up to her. Soon, I think. Why?"

She purses her lips. "What if we put Phoenix in her place? At least until I can find her something more stable."

I'm shaking my head. "Feel free to ask CC yourself, but know it's a bad idea."

"Why? It's the perfect place. No one will think to look."

"You sure about that?" I meet Phoenix's gaze. "It was stupid of you to put yourself on Marc's radar like that."

"He and his posse have my things, and I want them back."

"Yeah, well. Good luck with that. You know David works for

him. That's probably who's been poking around. His skills rival Abby's."

"Rival? He's a baby compared to me," Abby counters.

I stifle a laugh. "Fine. You're better than him. I'm no hacker, but don't you all have a thing about signatures and such?"

"That's an oversimplification of it, but yes. Your point is?"

"I was thinking." Leaning forward, I take both of Phoenix's hands in mine. "It's been long enough. Why don't you come out of retirement—"

"Not gonna happen," she grits.

As always, I don't leave it alone. "It's been years, Phoenix. A lot has changed, and you're no longer the same person. You're different. Stronger. More cunning."

And a complete psycho, I want to add.

"Leave it alone," she warns, keeping her gaze downcast.

"I'm just saying. It would make Abby's life a whole lot easier if she didn't have to—"

"Hey!" Abby objects hotly. "Why am I in the middle of this?"

"Because. If you want to stash her at CC's place, fine. But you seem to have forgotten whom she's been best friends with for over sixteen years."

As I suspected, Phoenix's shoulders go stiff. Again.

It's my cue to leave this alone, but I never learn. That's my fucking problem, especially when it comes to Phoenix.

She really is a psycho, and that's saying something coming from me.

Unlike me, her moral compass has always been skewed to the point that even I can't make heads or tails of it sometimes.

I take a deep, measured breath before continuing. "What if we brought you back? As who you were… before."

Her breathing shudders, and she meets my eyes. What I see in them is pained and tortured, and I'm expecting it this time.

I don't know who she was before we came together, but I've had my suspicions. Now that I better understand the relationship between Yong, Phoenix, and Dr. Goodman, there's a lot about those surgeries that makes sense.

"What did Reuben say?" I tentatively ask.

She blinks once, then her eyes go blank. "Why do you keep pushing for me to come out of retirement?" she changes the subject, then delves into another one. "Is this about Charlie?"

Yeah, well.

I should have left well enough alone.

"What about him?"

"Are you being serious right now?" She runs a hand through her blonde locks. "The only reason he exists is because of me."

"I choose to have sex with Howard that day. In no way is that on you."

"You and I both know that that's a gross oversimplification of what happened that day."

"Well, you didn't hold a gun to my head and demand that I fuck him."

"You don't think I know that? We were all there, yet you were the only one who could have."

That, I also know.

Abby doesn't fuck men, ever — it's a non-negotiable limit and a very hard line for her. Phoenix was in between dilators at the time, so she couldn't have.

It was my choice, no one made me. We could've let him die. As CC says, we should've let him die. Howard was just as big a piece of shit as our intended target at the time — AKA his even bigger piece of shit manager. The thing is, no one thought I'd end up pregnant as a result. I just chalked it up to a side effect of the job. Not an unfortunate one, just unexpected.

Perinatal depression aside, it hasn't been all bad.

And as it just so happens, Charlie is the leverage we never knew we needed.

"So? It turned out better than we'd hoped for."

"Nothing is that cut and dry. It's not always rainbows and roses either. I know what you went through to have him. I saw what it did to you and CC—"

"Don't," I whisper.

An exasperated sigh moves through her, and her fingers dig into my palm. It's not meant to be punitive, and I don't think she's aware she's doing it. But she does get inside her head sometimes, and it comes out this way.

Except now it's like looking in a mirror, and I'm not sure I like this too much.

"I also know you didn't have to do it," she continues. "You didn't have to do any of this, yet you did. I intentionally released a shitty recipe, and you covered for me."

"If the roles were reversed, you'd do the same for me."

"You don't know that, Courtney. Not like this."

"But I *do* know that. How long have we known each other? Sixteen years?"

"Nineteen," she mutters.

"Damn. Has it been that long already?" I can't help but smile at that. She keeps track of those obscure details — the ones that we all know and care about — but she takes it to a whole other level. I bet if I asked her the exact date and time when we first shook hands, she'd rattle it off without a second thought. Dates and numbers are kinda her thing.

Come to think of it, a lot of things are her thing, but she's always been tight-lipped on both *how* she retains this information and *why* she cares so much about it.

But that's what makes her *her*, and we all love her for it.

"I know what you're doing, and it won't work." At least she loosens her grip on my hands.

I chance a noncommittal shrug. "It was worth a shot. I've screwed up plenty of times, Abby too, and you've covered for us."

"But not like this," she insists. "My screw-up came at a hefty price, one you didn't have to pay."

It doesn't escape my attention that that's where her hang-up is — the fact that there's a child involved.

"Even you must admit that this one turned out better than we'd hoped."

"Courtney…"

"What? It's true. Look at us, and tell me the pros don't outweigh the cons." I lift a brow. "Go on. I'm listening."

She looks at me oddly but doesn't say anything.

That's because she knows I'm right. The proof is irrefutable.

With Charlie in the picture, that keeps the mighty Howard Beals on his toes. While the idiot is an absentee father at best, his shitty side has been tamed. Howard knows that any more slip-ups from him mean we will be coming for him next.

Is it wrong that this is the one kill I'm looking forward to?

"It's easy to be detached from it all," I continue when she says nothing else. "Once that shit hits too close to home, everything gets thrown off-kilter. But we deal, right? And we'll get through this. Together. Like we always do. But this is a huge part of you, Phoenix. Mad Scientist. You can't shut that part of you off forever, and I feel like that's what you're trying to do here. It just... it just doesn't work that way. You need a happy medium."

It's not my place to be doling out life advice like some two-bit guru, but somehow, I've been relegated to that role. Not that I mind. In no way am I wise or a guru, but if I can pull *this* off...

"So..." Abby drums her fingers on the table, "Oscar tells me you three are getting married."

Both sets of eyes turn on me, expectant.

I bite the inside of my cheek. "We are."

I still don't know how we will manage that in Minnesota, but we'll make it happen.

Phoenix blinks. "And you know about..."

"About her past? Yes. Abby told me. How come you didn't tell me?"

"I figured it wasn't my story to tell." She pulls her hands from mine. "Doing things like this will give your fiancée the wrong idea about us."

"That ship sailed a long time ago," I say with a laugh. "Besides, it's all working out for the best. I'm getting Oscar's tattoo put on me."

"The fuck you are," Abby grunts. "You know what it means, don't you?"

"Yep. We'll all match." I nod, smiling. "Roxane's going to do it.

It's only fitting, and Lorenzo can't kill us all. Too much of a headache for him."

"Roxane swore she would never pick up another tattoo gun," Phoenix quickly points out. "How did you manage that?"

"I have my ways." At her perplexed look, I add, "You know we're neighbors, right? We can be normal boring soccer moms together. It's only a matter of time before Evan moves in." At Abby's growl, I continue, "One of the homes on my block is for sale. If Abby buys it and moves in, we'll form our four-sided love triangle. Or is it six? Maybe eight? The damn number keeps on multiplying!"

Abby doesn't find that amusing, as is to be expected. But Phoenix does.

Is it wrong of me to use my kid like that?

Probably.

I don't mind having the little bugger around. He helps me maintain some sort of illusion of normalcy. But, most importantly, having Charlie *did* bring the three of us closer together. Physically, it has been the catalyst for a homecoming of sorts.

After talking about it for years, Abby finally relocated to Rochester a few months ago. Unfortunately, she hasn't been spending much time *here* because Lorenzo and Olive still have her gallivanting the world doing who-knows-what. I suspect Roxane partially influenced that decision — moving to Rochester, I mean — but I also know it's because Naimo, her former fuck buddy slash ex-girlfriend, moved back here earlier this year. I know Naimo from the Art world. Creative types like us with a penchant for the macabre tend to stick together. That's how I know those two were never big on defining their relationship, much like CC and I were at first. And who knows? I might talk Naimo into buying that place on my block, just for kicks.

As for Phoenix… I've always known she's from here, but she's spent the last nineteen years running away from something. She's not wrong, though. She witnessed me go through this long and arduous pregnancy and come out of it mostly in one piece. I'd like to think she's finally ready to face whatever demons she's been running away from for… who knows how long. She won't talk about what those were, but neither do Abby and I, even though we all have our baggage that we carry around with us. She's putting down roots. Since Sonya died, she doesn't jet-set around the world like she used to.

Charlie just turned two a few months ago, and we've been there every step of the way, as much of it as we can manage. We all feel responsible for him in our own way. We all have a vested interest in his growth and development.

I incorrectly assumed we had all come to terms with the circumstances surrounding his conception and made peace with this. Evidently, we all still have a long way to go with it. And that's okay since we have nothing but time on our side. Lots and lots of it.

Because as much as Mattie, Olive, and Lorenzo would love to see Charlie succeed me, I don't want that for him. Abby and Phoenix agree with me. There's a possibility they might add Roxane's daughter to the roster of possible candidates, and I can't imagine a world where Abby or I let that happen.

I can't imagine a world where Phoenix lets that happen either. I've only scratched at the surface of my demons, but something tells me she has a long way to go with hers. But that's okay, because if anyone deserves to be happy, it's Phoenix. She deserves the kind of happiness that CC, Oscar, and myself have.

And boy, does it feel so, so good to say that out loud.

Someone like me, who was never meant to be happy. Who never even learned what it meant to love and be loved.

Yet, somehow, it found me.

Or rather, they found me.

My soulmates.

Never mind that I wasn't even looking, but they fucking found me. They crept up on me, and if I had to do it all over again, I wouldn't change a fucking thing because my story isn't conventional by any means.

Neither is CC's, and neither is Oscar's story.

Our road to happiness has been a bumpy road through some rather rough terrain, filled with broken pieces, terrible choices, ugly truths, and several brushes with the Grim Reaper himself. It's also filled with four rebirths, searing heartache, acceptance, and copious amounts of sex.

While our story is far from perfect, it's ours and it's filled with a shit ton of happiness and love.

So, so much of it.

EPILOGUE

SIMONE

Eighteen Years Ago

"You sure this is okay?" I ask Dr. Goodman as we make our way through the grounds of the Sotelo estate and past the main house.

"It is," she tells me.

Our fingers are laced together as she pulls me along with her.

Or rather, drags me with her.

She has to since we're heading for the detached cottage on the opposite end of the property.

My feet are unnecessarily heavy. Even though I've never been here before, I don't dare to look since houses like those tend to blend together after a while.

In this one's case, I'm sure it's just another towering mansion that feels much like the prison I barely broke free of.

"What if they find me? My parents?"

"They won't."

"How can you be so sure?"

She pauses mid-step, then turns to face me. "I just am."

I shift on my feet. "But Dr. Goo—"

She shakes her head, silencing me. "It's Sonya to you now. I'm not your therapist any longer."

Yeah… that's one habit that will take a long time to break.

"Lorenzo is a friend," she continues, "and this is the last place anyone will think to look."

"But my face is plastered all over the news," I remind her, "and unless they're all living under rocks—"

"What better way to hide than in plain sight? You'd be right under their noses, which is kinda the point."

"What about this?" I gesture at myself.

"This will be fine too. This is who you are now."

Then she's back to dragging me with her.

A few moments later, the cottage comes into view, and it is nothing like what I expected.

It's a cabin.

It's a brick cabin, and it is *not* tiny.

It stands two stories tall, with a wrap-around porch on the bottom floor. That's as much as I can tell, and from the outside, it looks homey.

She turns my body towards her and rests both hands on my shoulders. "This is it."

Home sweet home.

For the next… who knows how long?

"The only way this happens," she continues, "is with her say-so. This has to work. She has to like you. She *needs* to like you."

My brow lifts. "*She*?"

"The daughter. Courtney." Something passes in her eyes, and then it's gone as quickly as it appeared.

"What's so special about her?"

"She's his Achilles heel. Everybody has one. You are mine. The twins are yours."

The mention of them has my heart seizing up. "I'm not—"

"I'm afraid you don't have much of a choice. I know you have it in you, so turn on the charm the minute you walk through those doors. Dial that fucker up a thousand notches, if that's what it takes.

Or this fails. And we cannot afford to fail. This is illegal, what we're doing. I could lose my license, my practice, everything. You will lose your life."

"Why didn't you let me die?"

"Stop, okay? Call me selfish, but I cannot stand to lose you." Her gaze darts to the front door and her hands fall to her sides. "I'll give you a moment."

With that, she disappears inside, leaving me out here by myself.

I lower my body to the ground and stretch both legs out before me. Then, with my back flat on the grass, I smooth out my dress and extend both arms as far as they can reach.

In the cover of the night, no one would think this is weird.

Drawing several deep, calming breaths, I look up at the sky that seems to go on forever.

Three months, ten days, and seventeen hours.

That's how long I was last out in public.

The thing is, I shouldn't ruin this moment with my sentimental bullshit, but I just can't help how my brain works.

It works like hers does.

An organized chaos that could only be ours.

This, though, is different.

With my legs and arms spread out, I continue to take in the night sky. For the first time in what feels like forever, I loosen the reins and allow my soul to detach itself from my body.

I hold onto that as another heady emotion washes over me.

It's a foreign feeling, this weightlessness that flows all over me. As the night breeze brushes over my face, I find I can't recall being this relaxed, this in tune with nature.

This could be it. This could be the beginning, a taste of freedom.

It's not the version of it I envisioned, though. Because, like it or not, they're both still tied to this wretched fate. This cursed bond of ours is one I set us all on just for being conceived. They will never be free of it as long as I'm around.

I'd love nothing more.

My eyelids flutter, then close, shutting out the mesmerizing night sky. Calming breaths move through me in slow, laborious waves.

I smooth both hands over the dress. It's also the first time I've been in a dress outside my usual places — Dr. Goodman's office and the Brewer house. This feels so foreign. Mainly because this isn't my dress.

It's a replacement.

A rather shoddy replacement.

It's just a dress, and it's not my dress.

This is the price of freedom, Jordana's voice pierces through the chatter in my brain.

Three months, three days, twelve hours, and thirty-nine seconds.

That's the last time I laid eyes on her.

And I miss her.

I miss them both.

To be continued in

In Plain Sight
(Sin and Sinuosity #4)

Some feelings never fade with time.
They only grow stronger. Brighter. Deadlier.

When faced with an impossible choice, Simone McWhorter made the decision to walk away from it all — her friends, her family, and the love of her life.

To the world, it was a tragic tale of love and loss. Except it was all a lie — an intricate tale of lies, deception, and treachery woven into the fabric of her existence.

Of their existence.

Soulmates or not, walking away was the lesser of two evils and a tragic means to an inevitable bitter end.

Life in the shadows was a tolerable alternative and a means of

exacting her revenge on the lecherous monsters who tainted her
very existence in the first place.

But fate had other plans for her. And so too did the love of her life.
The one she left behind.

Which begs the question: love may be eternal, but can the same be
said for them?

Coming February 20th, 2024
Available for Pre-order:
https://elicenange.com/inplainsight/

THANK YOU!

Thank you for reading SIX FEET UNDER, and I hope you enjoyed
Charlena, Courtney, and Oscar's story.
This book is a labor of love, and I'd appreciate it if you left a review
on as many platforms as possible.

Want more on this trio?
Visit my website for Bonus Content and Deleted Scenes:
https://elicenange.com/bonuscontent/

For more on Charlena and Courtney's origin story, consider reading
their origin story in SIX FEET DARK.

If you want to stay up to date on news about new releases and sneak
peaks of new books, sign up for my newsletter:
https://elicenange.com/newsletter/

PROMISE ME FOREVER

Absence doesn't make the heart grow fonder
It only fills it with resentment and regret.

Nineteen years ago, Delilah Brewer lost the love of her life for four reasons.
Power. Control. Money. Love.
As such, she spent almost two decades shielding her defective heart from heartbreak while amassing an abundance of the first three. Not the fourth, since time doesn't heal all wounds and love is for fools — two things she's far too cynical for.
What she is, is defective and proud, and living her life on her own terms. Until an unconventional proposition presents itself at an inopportune moment.
Turning it down was the hardest thing she ever had to do, but she did so anyway — for her.
For the woman her defective heart still beats for.
And the tsunami that shreds everything in its path, including her barely stitched-together heart.

Note: This is a prequel to In Plain Sight, Book 4 in the *Sin and Sinuosity* series. The story ends on a cliffhanger, and the story concludes in In Plain Sight.

Coming December 2023
Available for Pre-order:
https://elicenange.com/promisemeforever/

ACKNOWLEDGMENTS

It takes a village. Truly.

1. My family, Mr. Nange and ~~Baby~~ Toddler Nange. Thank you for all your love and support as I delve into this publishing journey.
2. Amanda Walker, my PA. You have an uncanny knack for taking my jumbled-up ideas and giving me pretty things. And for indulging my random self at odd times. For giving me this gorgeous book cover — abs galore! For doing all of the graphics for this book. For connecting me with so many, many book people. For… need I go on?
3. My critique partner, Stephanie Quinn. Even though you only say 1% of this book, your feedback was invaluable.
4. My beta readers, Nichole Demello and Malaina Yawn. Thank you for jumping right into this at such short notice. Your comments really made me cackle the entire time I was reading them; and helped pivot certain things for this trio.
5. Leanne Rabesa, my editor. For that encyclopedia brain of yours, amongst other things. Your insightful comments often crack me up, as well as your ability to understand these darn characters even better than I do! I'm sorry I gave you a huge muck of a book. I straightened it all out… mostly… I think.
6. Deborah Peach, my proofreader. Your willingness to jump right into this one (at the last minute) means the

world to me! So much back and forth, so many sleepless nights…

7. My inspirations. Since all three of you are still choosing to remain anonymous, I'm acknowledging you anyway. Anonymously.

8. Last but not least – to you, lovely reader, who's reading this. Thank you for coming on this wild journey with me. Hope you stick around. There's more where this came from!

BOOKS BY ELICE NANGE

Sin and Sinuosity series

Taste Of Hell

Touch Of Heaven

Six Feet Under

In Plain Sight - *February 2024*

Sin and Sinuosity - Novellas

Twist Our Hearts - *Spring 2024*

Six Feet Dark - *Spring 2024*

Promise Me Forever - *December 2023*

ABOUT THE AUTHOR

Elice Nange is a Contemporary and Dark Romance author. She writes from the heart, and her stories often address sensitive subjects like racism, sexual orientation, discrimination, etc.

Outside of writing, she enjoys spending time with her family and copious amounts of reading. She is also obsessed with Maya Angelou, ice cream, and the color purple ~ not necessarily in that order.

www.elicenange.com

 facebook.com/elicenange

 twitter.com/elicenange

 instagram.com/elicenange

AFTERWORD

Musings of a delicatesoul88

It still feels so surreal that this is the third installment of this series. In keeping with the previous two books, let's call this one The Making of **Six Feet Under** as well.

Since you've made it through to the end of this damn book and are here, you know that this is the part where I get to say all sorts of mumbled-up, unedited, and un-prettified things. And since you are still reading this obviously unedited and very choppy sentence, I'm assuming you are just as interested in reading this as I am writing this, and that you really want my ramblings in all of its unedited glory — so who am I to deny you that?

The previous two books (**Taste Of Hell** and **Touch Of Heaven**) had some really, *really* long intros so I'm trimming it down some. In case you haven't picked up on this yet, I tend to get really long-winded and rambly. My editors help me trim the rambly-ness from the book itself, but this is the un-prettified version of my musings, so you get it all.

So let's dive in!

I've read a lot of Mafia romances over the years, but I haven't come across a Mafia Boss like Lorenzo Sotelo. So, I wrote one. He has his regular hierarchy, but he also has his *super-secret death squad*. Yes, he actually calls them that. As a 'joke', mostly; because that group operates in the shadows, completely independent of his existing hierarchy. Yes, I could come up with a better name for that but… umm… I don't want to.

My inspiration for his super-secret death squad is actually the TV show Charlie's Angels [yes, I have a thing for crime shows. And also no, Courtney's son isn't named after Charlie Townsend; he really is named after CC]. The OG Charlie's Angels TV show was considered 'ahead' for its time, so I watched it. I liked how seamlessly the angels blended in each time they went undercover. But since I deal in morally gray characters, I obviously applied this accordingly. The weapons are based on the angels, and the prey/training partners are based on John Bosley. In order to bring this into a 21st-century context, they needed to be of different ethnicities and sexual orientations (at least how I pictured it).

As for his love life, well… clearly, he has a type. A very specific type. He is a cis-White male, obviously. But Sarah Bardales was a Black woman, and he was hopelessly in love with her (but I can't say the same was true for Sarah, which is something I will be exploring in **In Plain Sight** since half that story is told from Marc's POV). But she was the love of Lorenzo's life and still is, even though she's dead. Yes, she's very, *very* dead; has been for 19 years as of the time of this story. As tempting as it is to spin a tale of *'she's been in the Network as a client all this time,'* it would negate the impact her death had on… well, everyone else, especially on Marc, Courtney, and Lorenzo. And later, being the obsessive bastard he is but with very singular sexual tastes, always goes for women who share similar physical characteristics to his lover. He did this even when Sarah was still alive because he couldn't truly 'have' her, not in the way he really wanted. He married Tamera because she looked like his lover. Tamera Sotelo and Sarah Bardales could very well pass for sisters, that part is intentional. ALL of Lorenzo's lovers are some variation of his dead lover and the one true love of his life. It's kind of creepy, to be honest

It's also why neither Marc nor Courtney get along with Tamera (and vice versa) — being moved into your father's house after your mom dies, then having to call a woman who's a dead ringer for your dead mom Mom.

Then again, the Bardales Sotelo siblings have always been a conundrum to me, because of how distinct their character voices are. If you read **Touch Of Heaven**, then you know that Marc has always had a clear and distinct character voice — even though his story is mostly told through Harris & Delilah's POVs. He also gave me a run for my money, and I'm not even done with him.

Courtney, on the other hand, is intended to be the direct opposite of her brother. In her case, I really wanted to explore the dichotomies of nature versus nurture (much like I did with the Brewer twins), but from a place where they each exist and operate on such different sides of the law. They were raised by the same mother (Sarah Bardales), in the same household, yet their experiences with her were so different.

Marc always knew what his mother was turning his sister into, and felt so powerless to stop it. And after her death and their obvious shuttling into their father's criminal empire, he felt the need to protect his sister even more. It's why he made that deal with his father in the first place. It's what prompted him to get into Law. Quite frankly, it's why he even stomachs acting as the Sotelo family's attorney. He's good at it, that's for sure. Good at finding loopholes too, but his sister is his main driving force.

And Courtney, for the most part, makes this 'easy' for her brother. She has her thing, her art. She has her other art. She works for her father, in his super-secret squad, with a posse/friends and a whole bunch of other people. And she enjoys it. Very, very much.

As for her love life… how things turned out surprised me more than anything. For the longest time, Howard Beals had been her end-all-be-all, her happily-ever-after [in my head, that is]. But when I sat down to actually map out his character traits, I couldn't find any. Except for that he's kind of a douche… well, not just *kind of*. He's a big douche, and they had actually nothing in common, besides Charlie. And she is a strong, independent woman who really doesn't need a man who walks all over her the way that he does.

Plus, look at her profession. Look at what she does for the people around her. A woman like that does not need to be saddled with a wuss like that.

So I pivoted, big time.

For someone who keeps such a tight rein on her characters as she writes (screw the whole wielding the pen schpiel), Courtney is the one who changed my mind about all of that. That's how loud and insistent her character's voice was. My initial notes for this story went into maybe 20% of the final version of this book. 50% was me 'free-styling it', which is a lot harder than it looks, but also

When a sinister idea occurred to me, I took it and ran with it, turning Howard into the bad guy (I can't have her secretly pining over him, it ruins everything!). Then hints of her possessive side began to peek out, and I thought… why the heck not?

Courtney has never been in the closet, let's just get that part out of the way. She has always been openly bisexual (there's a reason she's such good friends with David!), and she always saw herself ending up with a woman. Hell, I always saw her ending up with a woman. I always knew she had a thing with CC [we met her briefly in both **Taste Of Hell** and **Touch Of Heaven**].

Oscar kind of came out of left field, to be honest. And as his story began to form… I got goosebumps, and the damn story just kind of snowballed from there. Could you tell I was winging it? No? Yeah, me either. I found out that I am a bit of a discovery writer, so there's that.

If, as you were reading this, all you got out of Courtney were "I hate men" vibes, then I'm sorry, that was not my intention. Now, if Courtney seemed a little inconsistent to you, then know that this part is intentional.

In many ways, she is stunted. Emotionally stunted, that is. There's a certain degree of emotional maturity that she lacks, and my goal was to take you through that journey through her eyes. It's why 60% percent of the story is told through her POV.

Remember that they were all groomed — everyone in the current cohort: weapons and prey/training partners, all six of them. Take from that what you will, but know that this is a ***dark mafia***

romance (my version of it, anyway). I can't tell you who got the brunt of it (since that would ruin the surprise for future books), but they were all affected in different ways. For the purposes of this let's focus on just Oscar and Courtney (and CC), since those three's fates are intricately linked. Oscar went on that journey of healing already, and it was hard and rough. So too did CC (her journey will be covered in **Six Feet Dark**).

Courtney, on the other hand, did not. She just kept at it, burying herself in 'work' and her art, while ignoring the pain. It all had to come to a head at some point. A third act break-up just didn't seem appropriate in this case, so I didn't do one. I don't think I'll do one for the next book either since it wouldn't fit. You never know though!

Also, I did a thing. If you read the Afterword for Taste Of Hell, then you know I said Curtis was not meant to be redeemable. Not to worry, I haven't changed my mind on that. Yes, shitty things happened to him. Yes, shitty things were done to him. But that doesn't mean I plan on negating any of the other shitty things he's done to others in return; and the shitty things he continues to do to others, even to this day. There's a difference between compliance and complacency.

Who knows, if I'm inspired enough I just might write a redemption ARC for him. Just not anytime soon.

But his sister, the prodigal daughter is coming back! I can't tell you how excited I am to dive into Simone's book, **In Plain Sight**. I mean, I didn't put her in Books 1 & 2 & 3 for the heck of it. She closed out all three books, and I always planned on her coming back. If you missed it (mind you, I wasn't being subtle about it either), she was all over this book. If you read the first two books, you know. Hers has a release date of February 2024. If I run into a block, it might take forever to write, who knows?

Alright, that's enough rambling from me, so I'm signing off now.

In the meantime, stay overly ambitious.

Elice Nange